Praise for *Prairie Fever*

"What a terrific book this is, wonderful and strange . . . A whole family acting out what can and can't be forgotten, against the backdrops of prairie and range—characters so magnificently and sometimes comically stubborn I really couldn't put the book down. And what other novel has a character writing letters to a dead horse? I was completely taken by this book."

—Joan Silber, author of *Improvement*

"The novel is timeless and riveting in its strangeness, as it traces [two sisters'] decades-long rift stemming from a devastating accident and, well, love. Parker's gift for language transcends its 1900s setting [and] finds its peak expression in the sisters' letters, as incisive and deadpan as Charles Portis' *True Grit.*"

—Vogue.com

"Let me just say that *Prairie Fever*—concerning the lives of the Stewart sisters of Lone Wolf, Oklahoma, in the early years of the twentieth century—is the most beautiful novel I have read in quite some time. Taking a cue from the irrepressibly inventive younger sister, Elise, I soon began reading it aloud to someone I love, and the novel more than rewards such a shared experience. The language is that graceful and original, the events and characters (horses included) that spellbinding and funny and moving; and always the melancholy beauty and mysterious power of the open prairie shine through. To borrow a phrase from Mr. McQueen—first encountered as a young teacher in a one-room schoolhouse—one comes away from the novel with a keener sense of 'how one ought to go about living one's life.' "

—Tom Drury, author of *Pacific*

"Full of humor as well as anguish, suggesting that some bonds are strong enough to surpass even the most painful betrayal." —*Manhattan Book Review*

"Parker's chimerical slipstream of a novel asks, Is it better to hew to that which is, or to see the world as you wish? Readers will surely be pulled deep into the strange and wild river of Elise's fanciful peregrinations." —*Booklist*, starred review

"That a love story of this strangeness and rightness can come out of the event of a girl nearly dead in a storm is a testament to the wonder that is Michael Parker's talent. Not least, he's invented a language, a formal way of speaking that is perfectly suited to his people and to this dreamy novel."

—Jane Hamilton, author of *The Excellent Lombards*

"In *Prairie Fever*, there is humor as well as danger, love as well as longing, and reconciliation as well as lingering spite. It's splendid reading."

—*Lone Star Literary Life*

"In the tradition of Katherine Anne Porter, Parker's exceptional tale explores the power and strength of kinship on the harsh American frontier."

—*Publishers Weekly*

"A frontier tale of sibling rivalry . . . Parker's novel isn't as much about sisterhood as love, as the two struggle to reckon with their estrangement head-on; some of the novel's most powerful sections are Elise's letters to Lorena, addressed not directly to sis but to the horse she rode during the blizzard." —*Kirkus Reviews*

"Michael Parker has captured a time, place, and sisterhood so perfectly it hurts to turn the last page. *Prairie Fever* is a riveting, atmospheric dream of a novel."

—Dominic Smith, author of *The Last Painting of Sara de Vos*

"*Prairie Fever* is an exceptionally charming novel about the wonders and troubles of love, land, and language. Witty and poignant, the novel is as elegantly constructed as a poem, and it features the best dialogue this side—or any side—of the Natchez Trace. Yet another wonderful book from Michael Parker."

—Chris Bachelder, author of *The Throwback Special*

"Memorable . . . [Parker's] lovely, detailed prose brings his setting vividly to life . . . He leavens his story of a harsh life in a remote place with dry humor, quirky imagination and delightful flights of fancy . . . [A] compelling, wholly original story, one that's a joy to read . . . This is a story about strong wills and overcoming hardships. It's a story about how people decide what matters to them, and what is real, and about how emotions can shape choices with far-reaching consequences. It is also a story about love and family. And it's a story about communication—about how we obscure the truth, or outright lie, and how difficult it can be to tell our true stories, the ones that come from the heart . . . [Parker's] prose is often poetic, even magical at times. The intriguing characters and compelling stories make you want to keep reading to see what happens, even as you savor the language and the images it creates." —*News & Record* (Greensboro, NC)

PRAIRIE FEVER

ALSO BY MICHAEL PARKER

Hello Down There

The Geographical Cure

Towns Without Rivers

Virginia Lovers

If You Want Me to Stay

Don't Make Me Stop Now

The Watery Part of the World

All I Have in This World

Everything, Then and Since

Prairie Fever

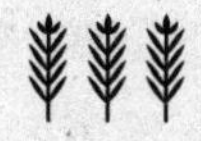

a novel by

MICHAEL PARKER

ALGONQUIN BOOKS
OF CHAPEL HILL
2020

Published by
Algonquin Books of Chapel Hill
Post Office Box 2225
Chapel Hill, North Carolina 27515-2225

a division of
Workman Publishing
225 Varick Street
New York, New York 10014

First paperback edition, Algonquin Books of Chapel Hill, April 2020.
Originally published in hardcover by
Algonquin Books of Chapel Hill in May 2019.
Printed in the United States of America.
Published simultaneously in Canada by Thomas Allen & Son Limited.
Design by Steve Godwin.

LIBRARY OF CONGRESS CATALOGING-IN-PUBLICATION DATA

Names: Parker, Michael, [date]–author.
Title: Prairie fever : a novel / by Michael Parker.
Description: First edition. | Chapel Hill, N.C. :
Algonquin Books of Chapel Hill, 2019.
Identifiers: LCCN 2018029369 | ISBN 9781616208530 (hardcover : alk. paper)
Subjects: LCSH: Domestic fiction. | GSAFD: Love stories.
Classification: LCC PS3566.A683 P73 2019 | DDC 813/.54—dc23
LC record available at https://lccn.loc.gov/2018029369

ISBN 978-1-64375-045-3 (PB)

10 9 8 7 6 5 4 3 2 1
First Paperback Edition

For my sisters:
Edith Ann Parker
Hallie Stewart Parker

Today the grass sings when I speak of love.

—Herta Müller, *The Land of Green Plums*

PART ONE

I

ELISE STEWART

Lone Wolf, Oklahoma, January 1917

Winter mornings their mother kissed them both on the forehead, pinned the blanket around the two of them, and slapped the horse's croup. Lorena held the reins. Elise wrapped her arms around her older sister's waist and both girls shut their eyes against the icy wind of the prairie.

On the way to school they recited items memorized from the pages of the *Kiowa County News*, with accompanying commentary.

Elise: Alfred Vontungien left Lone Wolf to attend O.U. Norman. He is one of our most brightest and most promising young men. Good luck to you, Alfred, in your studies.

Lorena: Good luck, Alfred, outrunning the cow that licks your hair up to five times a day.

Elise: Burr Wells, who owns one of the best farms that ever a crow flew over, says he has a set of farmers this year who are farmers in fact. He can't hardly get through praising his farmers.

Lorena: It is a fact that farmers come in sets.

Inside the blanket, they warmed themselves with words. The horse knew the way to the schoolhouse through the blinding snow. The teacher would be looking out for them. He would struggle into his coat and gloves and hat and come outside to unpin them. Off would fall the blanket, coated with ice crystals. Out would fall the words memorized from the newspaper. The teacher would shake the blanket, and the words from the newspaper would fall to the ground. The other words, not written, their words, along with their giggles, would float off into the snow.

Lorena: While moving a cultivator plow last week near Gotebo, Eli Roberts was struck by the tongue of the machine, cutting an ugly gash under his chin and hurting him severely. The wound was dressed and he is getting along nicely. Roberts now has it in for everything with a long tongue.

Elise: Edith Gotswegon of Lone Wolf has been placed at the top of the list of long-tongued things he has it out for.

Lorena: *In* for, not *out* for.

Elise: In or out for.

Lorena: Chapman Huff had business in Oklahoma City.

Elise: I bet he did, did Chapman Huff.

Lorena laughed. Through the blanket, Elise saw her laughter leak out and lessen the menace of the wind. When the teacher, who was new that year, unpinned the blanket, Elise saw the comma separating the *did*s disappear in a puff of snow. "I bet he did did," she whispered to Lorena, and the new schoolteacher whose name was Mr. McQueen, shook his head and said, "You two!" as he helped first Lorena and then Elise off the horse.

On the first day they arrived by blanket, Mr. McQueen asked

what their horse was called. They had been riding him to school every day for months, but now that Mr. McQueen had to unpin them he wanted to greet the horse by name.

"His name is Sandy," said Elise.

Mr. McQueen looked distressed. Elise assumed it was because Sandy was the color of tar.

"He would like to live by the sea. He *does* live by the sea, I mean. He gallops through the tidal pools."

"I see," said Mr. McQueen, who seemed to have recovered. He introduced himself properly to Sandy and asked if he might accompany him to the shore. He had come from somewhere back east and Elise assumed he knew the ocean, but when asked during geography, he said he knew only rivers. He described crossing the Mississippi by train on his way west. He crossed at Vicksburg, where boys stood by the river in knickers stiff with mud. For a nickel, these boys would tie ropes around their waists and wade into the river and stick their hands into holes in the bank and pull out catfish. He told the story of a man named Charlie Carter who sat beside him for three states snoring drunk. Finally, in Arkansas, he woke up calling for his Beulah girl. All the boys and most of the girls thought this was hilarious, but Elise found it tragic. His Beulah girl having married another. Charlie Carter having drunk himself into a three-state slumber, so sick was he over the events that had befallen him. Oh Beulah girl, cried Charlie Carter.

Elise sat in the middle of the classroom, studying Mr. McQueen. With her most woeful expression she implored him to understand Charlie Carter's predicament. Have you nothing in your body but funny bone? Mr. McQueen caught her staring. He returned her stare as he talked of the Natchez Trace, which he claimed to be a path of prehistoric animals before Indians found it and then white men. He talked on a bit and then he called on her.

"Reverend Womack closed the meeting at Bethel Sunday early due to heavy rains," said Elise, quoting the *Kiowa County News.*

Elise felt her sister's tickling giggle, as if they were still tented atop Sandy. She looked outside. The wind had blown open the door to the storm cellar. Edith Gotswegon stuck out her too-long tongue. Eli Roberts had it in for her and out for her. Oh he did, did he?

"Beg pardon?" said Mr. McQueen.

The class was silent. They knew her to sometimes answer questions with quotes from the newspaper. She did it to them and to the teachers and to her piano instructor. Her classmates stared at their teacher. They were blind to commas adrift among the ice crystals, and their stony hearts were immune to Charlie Carter's loss of his Beulah girl.

She looked outside again, but the snow was too thick to see the storm cellar. Sandy galloped along the edge of the surf. Waves lapped at his hooves. He smiled, tickled. She smiled, tickled. A pelican lit on Sandy, the very spot where Elise had sat clutching her sister the four frigid miles to school.

"Among the interesting relics owned by Captain James Lowery, of Missouri, currently visiting his son in Lone Wolf, is a stout old-fashioned hickory walking cane," said Elise. "The stick was cut and used for some time by Henry Clay, coming from the Clay home in Kentucky."

"Elise," whispered Lorena.

"That is a long way for a cane to travel. It must be very stout," said Mr. McQueen, who did not call on her again that day.

Mr. McQueen was better at unpinning a blanket than pinning it. The way home was colder as the blanket flapped loose in the wind. Sky appeared in the gaps. Elise did not want to see the sky.

Once during recess, she had sneaked into the teacherage, really just a room built onto the back of the schoolhouse with another stove and a bed and a desk. The walls were lined with the *Kiowa County News*. Insulation from wind that came from three states away, as far as Charlie Carter slept on his train ride west. Elise approved of the papered walls of the teacherage. She knew that the news insulated you. She knew that it was no good to you unless you learned it and said it over and over and then talked back to it, making it not news. It wasn't something bad that happened anymore and it was not boring people going to visit other boring people if you cut it up and said it aloud and then talked back to it.

"The band boys left in three automobiles headed by S. P. Barnes to boost the Lone Wolf picnic. The autos were decorated and attracted attention," Elise said into Lorena's back.

When Lorena said nothing, Elise turned her attention to fair Sandy. And, just then, kissed by the surf, the horse's coat turned the color of sand kicked up by his hooves as the pelican rode him into the sun.

"At dusk, is it true that the sun disappears into the ocean and drowns?" Elise asked. They collapsed into each other, tired out, really just a single bag of bones and giggles.

"How should I know?"

"The earth may not really be *all that* curved."

"Heavens to Betsy, not this again," said Lorena.

"Will you play with me when we get home?"

"In the barn and freeze?"

Lorena spent hours in her parents' bedroom brushing her hair with her mother's pearl-handled brush, counting the strokes as she pursed her lips in front of her mother's pearl-handled mirror. Heavens to Betsy, not this again, for she did it every day. She never tired of pursing and counting and handling pearl. Lorena was seventeen; Elise, fifteen. Mostly the two years separating them did not matter enough to count, but lately the gap would sometimes rip the pins from the blanket and let in all the elements.

In the warm months, Elise ran barefoot in the fields with the Bulgarian boys from the neighboring farm.

"They speak gibberish, you speak gibberish, why don't you marry them?" said Lorena. "You could get yourself in the paper once and for all."

The four Bulgarian children and their parents had lived in a one-room sod house, but now they had a real house with two rooms aboveground. They stored potatoes and onions and sometimes bales of hay in the sod house. Elise liked to huddle there out of the wind with the newspaper. She would read to the three boys—Andon, Andrey, and Damyan. There was also a girl named Blaguna, but she had married and moved to Gotebo. She was a year older than Lorena, and for some reason, Lorena admired her, though Elise found her haughty. Her breath smelled of paprika.

"Is paprika a first cousin once removed to pepper?" Elise asked her sister once.

"*Of* pepper, not *to* it." Lorena was particular about her prepositions.

Maybe Elise preferred the company of the Bulgarian boys because her own brothers, Elton and Albert, had died from prairie fever.

Lorena blamed their father for their brothers' deaths. She said he stored water in tanks and allowed the cows to drink from it and then dipped Mother's pitchers in the tank and set them out on the dinner table.

Elise said that their father did not know that prairie fever had gotten into the tank, and Lorena chose not to tell her that prairie fever was a euphemism for typhoid. Elise was led, by omission, to believe that her brothers had died from an allergic reaction to the prairie itself. She did not understand what in their constitutions made them susceptible to such an allergy when she and Lorena, who drank the same water, as did her mother and father, survived. Maybe certain people are supposed to keep out of the wind was all she could figure. But the wind blew also in Axtell, Kansas, which is where they had been before they came to Lone Wolf. Maybe Axtell was not considered prairie? Her memories of it were dim as she was five when they moved. She remembered only the house they lived in, which Lorena called nothing but a shack. The walls were also lined with newspapers, and a ditch ran behind the house where men did their business in daylight.

Her mother had gone for two years to Knox College in Illinois. There she learned to play the organ. Every night before her boys died, she had combed their hair. Mother of Pearl, Elise called her, though she had no daughter named Pearl. That was just Elise's name for her, or one of them.

Where her parents met, or how, was not a story told to Elise. She knew that her father came to Axtell to work on the railroad, and that he was born in Pennsylvania, and that he had many ideas. He called himself an "idea man." Other idea men would stop by to talk to him. Elise's mother would watch them from the kitchen window, the one above the sink, as if keeping an eye on small children.

One of the men, Wilbur Shilling's father, Bud, was big. Elise and Lorena called him Big Idea.

Apparently one of their father's ideas had led them to Oklahoma. First to nearby Hobart, the county seat, along with thirteen thousand other people. Their father had read in the Marysville, Kansas, newspaper about a land lottery in Hobart. They lived for a month in a tent. Elise did not mind the smell of moldy canvas, which reminded her of bread, Madame Curie, and bugles. At dusk she and Lorena took their baby brothers in strollers to the edge of the camp called Ragtown to see the Kiowa. They came every night to stare. People described them as "proud," but they appeared to Elise very curious. Elise had never seen Indians. If they had them in Axtell, Kansas, they kept them locked up somewhere or made them take back alleys.

On the day of the lottery, their father's number was called. He threw his hat in the air, which made Elton, who was four years old then, whoop and clap. Eleven thousand people were turned away that day. He had won, "free and clear," he said, 160 acres in Lone Wolf.

"This is the happiest I have ever seen Father," said Lorena.

"Yes," said their mother. They waited for more, but she tended to the baby, Albert, who would die because of their father's happiness. Their father was happy over winning the right to work acres of matted sod that proved so resistant to the dull plow he bought off a German that he had to straightaway use all the money they had saved for a windmill to hire a team of men with a special steel plow to break it up. A windmill to draw clean water from the ground would have saved her boys. This was what their mother meant by yes.

"Where is Joe McNutt? I heard someone inquiring about him," Elise quoted from the *Kiowa County News*. They were almost home. They could tell they were almost home by Sandy's breathing. He breathed differently when he was close to being put up and allowed his fill of hay.

"It's an interesting question," said Lorena.

"Do you happen to know Joe McNutt?"

"I have probably made his acquaintance," said Lorena. She reached up to mess with her hair, getting it ready to pearl-handle. Probably she was pursing her lips. Elise wanted to pinch her. It wasn't too cold to play in the barn. Sandy *lived* in the barn. Her father had only twenty head of cattle left because of an outbreak of something, who knew what, but the cows *lived* in the snowy fields. Sometimes they had icicles hanging from their noses.

"Blaguna probably has an icicle hanging from her nose," said Elise.

"Blaguna is well married," said Lorena.

"What do you mean by that?"

"I mean that she married well."

"What are the degrees of marriage I would like to know?"

"*Well* would top anyone's list, obviously."

"Did Mother marry well?"

"Why don't you ask her?"

"Why do you like to do the same thing every day?"

"Are you referring to washing beneath my armpits?"

"Mother of Pearl," said Elise. Lorena did not know that this was one of Elise's names for their mother. She thought Elise was referring to the handles of the comb and mirror and she wasted no time informing Elise that mother-of-pearl was not pearl but a cheap imitation of.

"I think that is insulting to mothers everywhere."

"I didn't name it."

"I named Sandy."

"Not everyone calls him that, you know," said Lorena.

"But when I call him, he responds."

"He is responding to your voice. He does not speak English."

"He speaks island."

"What is island?"

"Just never mind," said Elise. Explaining gave her a mild headache and made her sleepy at once. The Kiowa were a proud people and a curious tribe at once. Pride and curiosity somehow did not seem to go together in Elise's mind. Maybe because her mother did not like gossip and if you asked a question about someone—for instance, if you were to march right in the house, because they had reached the house, because Elise heard the screen door slam shut by the wind, which meant her mother was struggling across the yard to unpin them—and asked her where was Joe McNutt, she would say it was none of their business, even if told that someone was inquiring about it in the newspaper, therefore making it more of a public notice than idle gossip.

Her mother's pride did not permit curiosity. It only permitted her to say yes when she meant, What has your father gone and done now?

In the barn, combing the snow from Sandy, wiping him down with the blankets her father had bought from the Kiowa, Elise wondered if she would do well to marry one of the Bulgarian brothers. She tried to think which one. Andon was closest to her in age and he did not have a thing wrong with his nose, or his entire face, for that matter, but Damyan, whom the boys at school called Damn when the teacher was not around, paid closest attention when they met in the old sod house and she read aloud to them from the newspaper. He liked hearing who visited whom, the part Lorena and Damyan's brothers and sometimes even Elise liked the least. The others were bored by it, but the section made Elise sad, for no one ever came to visit her family from Hobart of a Sunday, much less some famous relative who carried in his possession at all times a stout old-fashioned walking stick previously owned by a statesman. Only Big Idea and the other idea men came by their place, but their visits did not make it into the paper.

The Bulgarians worked in the fields in fair weather, which meant that winter was the only time Elise got to play with them. If it was particularly cold, like it was out today, her mother would tell her not to go, but Elise was able to change her mind.

"I will take Sandy," she said, for it was a little over a mile across the fields to the Bulgarian's farm, and if the snow blew up, it was easy to get lost. But Sandy knew the way.

Her mother wrapped her in her grandfather's greatcoat, or perhaps it was her great-grandfather's coat? It was huge and itchy and Sandy did not care for it. "Leave before the sun drops behind the trees," her mother would say, but she must have been thinking about Kansas, because in Lone Wolf there were no trees to speak of. To the east, south, and north was the ocean of prairie and just to the west ran the worn but noble Wichita Mountains, rising from miles of flatness as if discarded, like the detritus cast off by wagon trains of old. The Kiowa thought the mountains sacred, but Elise found them depressing and would prefer nature to speed up its course and wear them down to pebbles, so her view would be unencumbered by lumps of rock and dark brown dirt.

"Sometimes when we arrive at Oklahoma we burn cow dung," said Damyan one day in the abandoned sod house. His brothers shushed him. He was often caught staring out the window by Professor Smythe, who preceded Mr. McQueen. Elise would stare at him staring. His eyes, like hers, could see beyond the playing field, the stable, the outhouse. He was the only person she had ever heard say that barbed wire was a bad idea. She thought to ask her father about it, but if it wasn't his idea, he wasn't that interested.

But Damyan did not like Mr. McQueen.

"He is not much," said Damyan that day in the sod house.

"Not much what?"

He shrugged and grabbed the paper, as if he could read it. She snatched it back.

"I do not have time to teach you English, by the way."

"I speak English good."

"Perfect," said Elise. "But back to Mr. McQueen. He is not much what?"

"Something is in his belfry," said Anton.

"Well, I should hope so," said Elise. "I would think they made sure of that before they hired him."

She learned from the Bulgarian brothers that none of the boys at school cared for Mr. McQueen. But none could say why. If only they had said *why*.

That night, as always, she whispered to her sister in the dark. They had always slept in the same room with their brothers, and she and Lorena had shared a bed. After her brothers died, they got separate cots. Her mother insisted upon it. Elise was aware that her brothers had died of prairie fever so that she could whisper across the narrow space between the cots to her sister in the night. Their room was in the attic and mostly slanting, shadowy eave. They were so close that her sister heard her whispering and said, *What?* But it was so cold up there, with only thin board and shingle separating them from icy, snow-belching clouds, that her words froze sometimes before they bridged the gap. Having turned to ice, her sentence shattered into letters, and each letter tinkled like chimes onto the floorboard.

"It has come to my attention that the boy half of the schoolhouse is not enamored of Mr. McQueen," said Elise.

"Which of your Bulgarians told you so?"

"Damyan," she said and then added, "also Anton."

"What else did they tell you?"

"That when they first came to Lone Wolf they burned cow pies to stay warm."

"I am not, as you know, enamored of your Bulgarians, but you may have noticed that we burn coal? That is because there are so few trees in this place."

"Father might get the idea to plant some."

"You will need to plant the idea in his head."

It was a curious phrase, "plant an idea." It suggested that ideas grew in the manner of, say, cotton. Her father's ideas did not seem to reach maturity before he harvested them.

"You are making fun of me," said Elise.

"I am making fun of Father," said Lorena.

"Do you care much for Mr. McQueen?"

Lorena was silent for some seconds. Elise could hear the wind of her thoughts.

"I feel that, like all of us, he has his limitations."

"Which are?"

"The point of life is to know your limitations," said Lorena.

Elise thought about this. Her first thought was that Lorena's recent tendency to state the point of life was irritating. Her second and subsequent thoughts concerned her own limitations. She was not attentive to the world around her if and when the world around her turned to dirty dishwater that her mother asked her to dump in the side yard. If the world sent her on an errand and the errand was as dull as dishwater, she came hard up against her limitations.

My own limitations, A list. By Elise Stewart.

1. My mind, I never feel it and it is like a fly not satisfied with any surface upon which it lights, and abuzz always.
2. Mother-of-pearl will never be to me what they say it is, which is a lie.
3. I would marry a Bulgarian, why not if I took a notion, and I would not care if the marriage qualified as "well" on Lorena's grand scale.

But she realized that her limitations were many and it would be daylight if she kept up the list. She attempted to sleep, but she shivered. Lorena felt her shivering and came and got into the cot with her. They were pinned inside, the blanket blocking out the wind and snow. She relaxed into her sister's back. Sandy's hooves in the surf. Now she could whisper. Her words would not ice up and break into chiming letters crashing against each other and then to the floor.

"I don't think I put much stock in pride," said Elise.

"Well, that is certainly a limitation."

"When people speak of it, it seems they mean very different things."

"The same could be said for the word 'Sandy,'" Lorena said.

"Sandy is a name, not a word."

"My point has been proven. Rather perfectly, by you."

Sometimes Lorena was a bully. Elise stayed awake as her sister slept like Charlie Carter, across three states. She stayed awake to mourn the loss of her own Beulah girl, only she did not know what her own Beulah girl was. Just that she had one.

On those frigid nights when they slept crammed into a single saggy cot, Lorena's bossy sleep-breath attempted to corral her. It tried to plant ideas in her mind.

What if, Elise wondered in the night, she passed her sister on the street one day and her sister did not even see her?

"You've not said why it is that the boys dislike Mr. McQueen."

"Why don't you ask them?" said Lorena, which is what she always said when Elise asked a question she could only ask Lorena about someone else.

The next morning the pump was frozen. Where was Father to start the fire in the stove? Her mother had to do it. Her mother often moved around the house with one arm crooked as if she were carrying her baby boy. Almost every woman in Lone Wolf, Oklahoma, and likely also Axtell, Kansas, had lost a child, but her mother seemed to take it the hardest. Elise wondered if she did not have a touch of prairie fever herself. Would this not explain why she always told Elise to leave for home when the sun began to slip behind the trees?

Prairie fever, I burn with it. It is the opposite for me of what it was for my poor dead brothers and my addled mother who carries around still her two baby boys in her arms. It is not death but life. I love the wind and the way it makes everything slap and creak and whistle. In the prairie dog villages, I know each hole and who lives there. I deliver their mail. I love the mounds where the Kiowa buried their dead. I can take you there, but you mustn't climb them or the spirits of fierce warriors will follow you always from afar. You will always feel a shadow. Turn and look behind you all you want. You will not see them, they are too quick.

"Hold still, Elise," said her mother as she pinned the blanket in the barn. "If you don't hold still, I will stick a pin in your sister."

"Please hold still," said Lorena.

Sandy set off in a trot. Lorena claimed to be the rider and Elise the passenger, but Sandy knew the way. In blinding snow and sideways wind, Sandy could feel the way.

"Wade Vineyard and Carnie Bickerstaff were at Hobart," said Elise.

"They deserve each other."

"Should they marry, she would be Carnie Vineyard."

"An ever-so-slight improvement."

"Will you ever not be able to see me on the street?" she whispered to Lorena, but the heavy blanket muffled her words, and Lorena said, "Stop grunting, please."

"For rent: two-room house, second door west of schoolhouse."

"One room for me and one for you," said Lorena.

"Mother can come," said Elise. She decided her sister disliked all men. She put her to the test.

"When Charlie Carter woke and cried out for his Beulah girl, did you think that was funny or sad?"

"I wasn't even there. And neither were you."

All the proof she needed.

"Elise," said Lorena.

Elise was all ears and only ears.

"Please try to answer the questions put forth to you by others," said Lorena. "Not everyone cares about what is in the newspaper."

"But *you* do."

"The Sunday school at Bethel purchased an organ through Professor R. C. Adams."

Elise smiled. Her smile warmed her sister's back. It was a kiss on her neck. Sandy felt it and air escaped through his nostrils, a snort of delight.

"But, Elise?" said Lorena.

"Mr. McQueen never said the name of *his* horse," said Elise. She waited for her sister to say, Why don't you ask him? But Lorena did not. Straightaway, as soon as Mr. McQueen emerged in his fur-lined cap to unpin the blanket, his East Coast face flushed by the icy wind of the prairie, snow in his eyebrows, revealing what he might look like when old and gray, Elise said, "Why, Mr. McQueen, good morning!"

Her sister did not have to groan. Their bodies had been touching all night and then the four miles to school.

"Why, good morning yourself, Elise. What news is there from that fine instrument of journalism you favor?"

Mr. McQueen took the paper too. Without it, he would freeze in his teacherage, his eyebrows white with snow. But he was indulging her and she knew it.

She remembered Lorena's plea.

"There is not much," she said, as Damyan said about Mr. McQueen.

"That's a pity. We should make something happen to get ourselves in the paper. What do you say about that, Lorena?"

But Lorena had wrapped her scarf around her nose, exposing

only her eyes, and ran inside the schoolhouse, leaving Elise in the stable with Mr. McQueen and Sandy.

"She got up on the wrong side of the bed," said Elise.

"Some days, Elise, there is no right side." The words seemed to slide out of his mouth and then he heard them. In his eyes was a desperate wish for the words to please come back.

"Actually, I didn't mean that. There is always a right side."

Elise could tell he was lying. One day soon she would say to Mr. McQueen, You need not lie. Perhaps this is why the boys didn't like him, but she doubted it. Boys were fine with lies.

"I shall stable Sandy. He can give me the times of low and high tide. Are they not called tide tables? It would please me if they were. You run along and warm yourself by the fire."

Inside, Lorena was talking to Edith Gotswegon. She'd never seen Lorena speak to Edith Gotswegon on purpose. What was this world?

As Mr. McQueen went about the business of education, she observed him closely. He did not pick on the boys or favor the girls when he asked questions, and the boys immediately stuck their hand up before the question mark arrived, as if they knew everything. Damyan probably knew the answer, but he was busy thinking that barbed wire was not a good thing.

Mr. McQueen did not make them wash the chalkboard as had Professor Smythe.

He did not make anyone stand in the corner.

He did not make a soul feel foolish or sorry for not getting their lessons up.

"Any questions?"

Elise raised her hand lazily as if she were trying to reach something on the top shelf of the pantry, standing on tiptoes. He called her name. Lorena looked across the room at her and then down at her desk.

"What is the name of your horse, Mr. McQueen?"

He had written the multiplication tables on the board and was pointing to them from a distance of however long the pointer was. She had never seen him use a pointer. It was the only thing she noticed about his teaching style that might strike one as objectionable.

"This is math, Elise," said Edith Gotswegon.

"That's okay," said Mr. McQueen. "Sometimes these subjects bleed into one another."

This might have been Elise's favorite thing out of Mr. McQueen's mouth, up to that point, and she wanted some time to think about it, but Edith Gotswegon said, "The name of your horse *bleeds* into twelve times twenty?" She said "bleeds" as if she herself were bleeding.

Mr. McQueen told Edith Gotswegon he was glad she was there. He said he counted upon her. This caused her tongue to roll up and disappear down her throat. Perhaps she would choke on it. She knew she had been slighted but not how.

But Lorena! Lorena was beaming at Mr. McQueen.

"The Beatitudes," said Mr. McQueen.

"Have we now bled into Sunday school?" said Edith Gotswegon.

Mr. McQueen laughed. "Truly, Edith. Such a unique and special pleasure it is to have you here."

Joseph Womack, whose father, the Reverend Womack, closed the meeting at Bethel early owing to heavy rains, began to recite the Beatitudes. But he mumbled in such a register, so low and rote and without feeling, it became clear that he was asleep. He was dreaming that he'd been ordered to recite the Beatitudes. His lip bubbled slightly with spit.

Mr. McQueen allowed it and waited patiently as if these sleep-talk Beatitudes were a flock of sheep crossing the road. God, how many were there? So far, Elise knew only one, the famous one about the meek, which she had never understood, since the whole point of being meek is so you don't have to run things. This might be a question she could ask Mr. McQueen during science: What would the meek *do* with the earth, anyway?

"Thank you, Joseph," said Mr. McQueen when Joseph was done and the road was clear of sheep. Then he told how he had wanted to ride his horse from North Carolina to Lone Wolf, but he had read accounts of the Trail of Tears and understood the journey to be long and arduous.

"Less so for me, of course. No one was forcing me out of my native land."

He paused to stare out the window at the driving snow, which unlike most snowstorms did not vary in intensity, did not light up and allow you to see the outhouse or the stable or the storm door being blown open by the wind, and muffled also every noise save the sound of the wind, which was not muffle-able on the prairie, and thank goodness for that, for the slap and creak and whistle, the orchestra of prairie conducted by the wind. He seemed to be trying to decide whether or not it was true that no one had forced him out of his native land. Elise had heard it said that Mr. McQueen was eighteen years of age. Who had told her this? Maybe she read it in the paper, as there was a significant write-up when he arrived, and it bothered her that she had forgotten a word of it.

She studied him, easily done as he stood in front of the class like an artist's model. He did not appear to shave, but it was difficult to tell on a fair-skinned man. The blue shadow darkening her black-haired father's face was absent on Mr. McQueen, whose hair was the blond they call dirty, though it appeared clean. He was freckled. His hair parted cleanly and stayed parted, even when he took off his cap. Elise preferred things that did not stay put, so she placed Mr. McQueen's hair in the "maybe" column in her assessment of his looks.

Perhaps it was a limitation. Lorena had gotten her thinking about everyone's limitations. She looked over at Lorena who was giving Mr. McQueen her attention. But Elise knew it was divided. Lorena's attention could only always be divided. Her thoughts might not always mirror Elise's, but forever would they intersect.

"You will remember that I arrived by train."

"My Beulah girl!" cried Rickie Stoelenburg, as if this was the only thing he'd learned all year. The other boys, who thought Mr. McQueen not much (which was quite different, Elise knew, than not thinking much of him, though she still did not know what it meant, coming as it did from the Bulgarians), laughed in a way that made Elise panic. Maybe Mr. McQueen was going to inherit the earth while he was still on it but lose control of the class. Their laughter brought to mind her father, holding forth out by the barn with his idea men, including Big. What the connection was she did not care to investigate, out of fear of what she'd find.

"I was not long off the train when I realized I would need a mount. There are so many different sights to see in this area. I wanted to visit them all. The Wichita Mountains, the Red River, all the neighboring villages."

"You mean the prairie dog villages?" said Arthur Leak.

"Why yes," said Mr. McQueen to Arthur Leak. "That is one thing I mean. You will not interrupt me again, Arthur, as I was asked a question and I am answering it. If anyone else cares to interrupt, it would be best to hold your tongue."

Quickly the vision in Elise's mind—of Big Idea listening to her father hold forth by the barn—faded.

"I inquired around about horse traders in the vicinity and was told about a man of Kiowa blood. I went to visit him. He is a noble man and the grandson of the man for whom this town was named."

"Everyone knows Quickly Speaking Wolf," said Edith

Gotswegon, as if she were exempt from Mr. McQueen's warning. He did not tell her how lovely it was to be in her company. He did not look at her at all, which is all she wanted. The only way to shut her up was to ignore her.

"Now let me tell you all something you might find hard to believe. It was not that many years ago that I was sitting where you sit." (Elise did not find this hard to believe. He barely shaved, did Mr. McQueen.) "Though in a different school, of course. My school was also small and I walked to and fro. I did not own a horse. It was six miles round-trip. Where I come from there is a streak of redness in the earth that is violently beautiful. But it is tough going in rainy weather. The same qualities that give the soil its beauty—I am talking about the color of the clay—make it the devil to get off of your shoes.

"At the home of the Kiowa horse trader, whom Edith claims is well known to you all, I saw a horse the color of the red mud, which was the bane of my existence when I was your age. Had I brought west with me the old pair of mud-caked boots I wore to and from school and mounted this horse, my shoes would have been indistinguishable from her flank. The horse appeared to have lain down in the road I knew so well. She reminded me of certain struggles I faced.

"It is good," said Mr. McQueen, "to be reminded of your struggles.

"I can't say that the owner of the horse, who you all know by name, did not warn me that her nature was recalcitrant. Do you all know what 'recalcitrant' means? Because now that I have used it, I am not so sure I do. In fact, I often get it mixed up with 'intransigent.' Let's just say she's stubborn. I have a few skills and one of them is memorization. I can quote song lyrics and passages from Latin and also the one hundred counties of North Carolina. (As an aside, I plan to commit to memory the counties of this fair state, but I thought I would wait awhile as someone recently told me they are not done making new ones.) Anyway, and I am ashamed to say it, Joseph, I know very little of the Bible—to quote, I mean—but I do know the Beatitudes. I attempted to settle the horse by singing to her, but this only riled her, so I started in with quotations and only the Beatitudes turned her downright docile.

"She has limitations, as do we all, but her name is not one of them."

Ella Holman, who was seven and was not expected to follow all the rules, said that she had never met a horse or a dog not named after a person. Elise loved little Ella Holman and she loved that she said "met," as if she had made the acquaintance of many dogs and horses, whereas most people would have said, I have never *heard of* a dog or horse not named after a person.

"I hope this brief digression has been enjoyable to you all," said Mr. McQueen, but he was looking only at Elise.

That afternoon in the stable before Mr. McQueen pinned the blanket over them badly, Elise studied his horse. She might not have appreciated her beauty before she knew about the violently beautiful clay that clung to the shoes of Mr. McQueen and was in many ways the bane of his existence. The Beatitudes might have appeared to her an ancient and broken nag. One thing she did not appear to be was fleet. And yet she reminded Mr. McQueen of his home and of his struggles.

One of his current struggles was pinning the blanket tightly around the Stewart sisters. Today the cracks were wide enough for the muted white sky to appear at the top of the blanket. Inside the blanket had always been their own world, so why not have their own sky within it? The blanket was meant to protect them from the elements. The sky was more than an element. It was the source of elements. The snow that fell from it was its words and the wind its song.

And yet a snowy sky was as violently beautiful as the streak of red in the earth in Mr. McQueen's home place. *Violently beautiful* was Elise's favorite new phrase. That night at the supper table, she would apply it to a stew of rabbit and carrot and potato her mother served. Her mother would look at her with a mix of wonder and suspicion, and her father would chuckle as if it were a joke and her sister's expression would get caught, as it did more and more often these days, somewhere between amusement and annoyance.

"I think I am done with those Bulgarians," she said into Lorena. They were headed into the wind and Sandy's progress was slow and their world was loud in a way that was violent and beautiful.

But Lorena heard her.

"But what will take their place in your life? In other words, how will you fill your afternoon hours?"

Elise did not share with Lorena every detail of her life.

"In the barn we could stage a play."

"And freeze to death by suppertime," said Lorena.

"It would be best if staged in the barn because it involves a dramatic death from a great height. I could fall from the hayloft onto a carefully placed pile of hay."

"*Into*, not *onto*," said Lorena. Then she fell silent. She breathed bossily.

"Or *you* could." Elise thought "onto" the better choice, and she wanted to be the faller, but she would do what it took to get Lorena away from their mother's vanity and have something to do with her hands besides clutching mother-of-pearl.

"And what is this play?"

"It is based on an actual true-life event."

"Pray tell."

"Killing in Hobart," said Elise. "L. C. Ivent shoots Charley Sherman in self-defense."

"Then it would be more accurate to say that it is based *in part* on an actual event, given that L. C. Ivent is hardly a reliable source."

"Ivent, upon being asked what he had to say in regard to the shooting, said, and I quote, 'I was forced to shoot Sherman or he would have used the knife on me, which he held in his hand.'"

"Yes, Elise, I read the same article. I believe I read it *to* you, in fact."

Elise continued to quote from the article, which she had long committed to memory. "'Did you ever have trouble with Sherman before?' Ivent was asked. 'No, but I have had some with Jensen, agent for the Schlitz Brewing Company. Just a few minutes before the shooting occurred I told Sherman I did not want to have any trouble with him, and Jensen, who was standing nearby, said, "Well, you *will* have trouble with him."'"

"Your point?"

"In the words of Ivent," said Elise, "'Sherman made several threats and I started to go out the front door but it was locked, so I tried to get out the back way, but I could not as Sherman was following me too close. He had a large knife opened and I made up my mind to protect myself, so I did and fired one shot at him and he fell. I gave myself up to the jailer as I realized what I had done.'"

"And I quote," said Lorena, proving that she remembered the article well herself: "'Charley Sherman was shot at the Palm Garden saloon by L. C. Ivent. They were both Hobart men and widely known. Ivent having run the saloon at the Choctaw depot for the past two years.'"

"Yes?" said Elise.

"If Ivent ran the saloon," Lorena said, "why were the front doors locked? He would have been the one to lock them if it was his own establishment."

"The Palm Garden saloon is different from the saloon at the Choctaw Depot. It was not *his* saloon where he pulled the trigger that fired the fatal bullet."

"Your extensive experience in the saloons of Hobart is revealing itself," said Lorena. "But I will choose to go with the facts presented to me in the paper. Nowhere in the paper does it say that Ivent was not employed at the Palm Garden."

"To continue with the story in progress: 'A few hours before Sherman died, he was in continuous prayer, asking God to forgive, and only let him live until he could reform and become a Christian before he died.'"

"Yes? And?" said Lorena.

"If Ivent was lying, why did Sherman repent?"

"Because he was a drunkard on his deathbed? Repenting while your life's blood is draining out of you is well known to be common among murderers and saints alike. If you had been paying attention in church instead of dreaming your dreamy dreams, you would know that you must get right with the Lord before ascending into heaven."

Elise was about to say that claiming to have paid closer attention to Pastor Womack was not going to win the day, but she felt a charge go through her sister's body.

"Because he knew his limitations," Lorena said in a lofty register, as if she'd been illuminated by the elements. "It is, after all, the *point* of life."

"Who would you rather play," said Elise to steer her sister away from the point of life, "Ivent or Sherman?"

"Sherman, of course. Ivent is dastardly."

This meant that she would get to fall from the hayloft onto or into the carefully placed blanket of hay. Elise suspected this was the root of her argument.

"What makes you say so?" she asked.

"The business of the saloon. You say that it is a different saloon, but that is not clear from the wording of the article," said Lorena.

"Well, it's perfectly clear to me," said Elise. "But in order to appease you, we will conduct our own research into the matter."

"Who do you plan on asking? Father? Big Idea, perhaps?"

"I have never spoken to Big Idea. I would not know how to. It would be like talking to a Chinaman. I will ask Mr. McQueen."

"Mr. McQueen does not frequent those sorts of establishments, and if he were to, he would not need to go to Hobart. Lone Wolf has its own saloons."

And how are you so sure of his doings and goings? Elise said but did not say into her sister's shoulder, which was warmed by her breath.

"Okay," she said instead. "We will just have to go there and see for ourselves."

"Hobart is ten miles from town. That is fifteen miles from home."

"An easy trip," said Elise. "We will go tomorrow."

"Tomorrow is a school day," Lorena said. "Even if it were a weekend and they were not calling for more snow and record-breaking cold, I should not think Mother would approve of our going to Hobart to conduct research in saloons."

"She might approve if she knew the research was for an artistic production." In college, their mother had played the piano and also the organ. She sent both sisters to Mrs. Robertson's for piano lessons, but Lorena showed no talent for it. Elise continued to take lessons. She had an ear. She was allowed to practice at the church as long as an adult was present. Often her father would take her because he loved music, though he was the source of Lorena's lack of talent, according to their mother. Still, he fancied himself a decent tenor and would sing often in the fields, which (also according to their mother), accounted for the lack of rain if there was a drought and the deluge of rain if the cotton fields flooded. Lightning striking the barn had been blamed on his tenor, which he described as an "Irish" tenor, even though he was no more Irish than Damyan.

Sometimes when Lorena was combing her hair with the pearl-handled brush and pursing her lips into (or at?) the pearl-handled mirror, Elise lay on the bed studying the drawings by their deceased brothers, kept hidden in a drawer in a bureau in her mother's room. The paper was crinkled with age and the pencil was faded, but the clouds the boys drew above the prairie seemed pregnant with rain, soon to burst. Elise wandered about in her deceased brother's stormy depictions of the prairie while lying across her parents' bed on her stomach, attempting to kick her fanny with her legs.

"Since it is an artistic production, in this case a play, more specifically a work of the imagination, you can just make it up," Lorena was saying.

"Make what up?"

"Whether or not the saloon in question was run by Ivent."

"But this is a story based upon facts."

"And yet the story related in the newspaper in the words of Ivent is not certifiably factual."

"Who certifies fact?"

"Why *you*, if you would have your way and travel to Hobart tomorrow."

Elise thought about it. "There is a difference between the way a man tells a story and fact."

"What is the difference?"

"A story is never told the same way twice. But the place of Mr. Ivent's employ is, as you say, certifiable."

Elise did not know what "certifiable" meant. Was not the newspaper a sort of certificate?

"You confuse me sometimes," said Lorena.

"Good."

"Why is that good?"

"It is natural to be confused."

"It is good to know your limitations," Lorena said. "I would think you might seek clarity? Also, speaking of limitations, we are severely limited when it comes to your plans to conduct your research."

"Limited how?"

"Clearly you have not thought this through at all. First of all, there is the weather. If you had read the almanac, you would know the cold and snow are meant to get much worse. There is also the fact that we know nothing of Hobart and are not allowed in its saloons. And there is, neither last nor least, the fact that we would be lying to Mr. McQueen."

"Mr. McQueen would not mind," said Elise.

"You've discussed this with him?"

"Of course not. But Mr. McQueen is clearly a supporter of conducting research for a drama based on fact. If you had been paying attention in class instead of dreaming your dreamy dreams, you would know this."

They were hard upon home. Sandy's hooves kicked up foam that laced the edges of waves. Crabs scurried out of the way of a horse eager to escape the elements. The snow was so thick and blowing that they did not see the barn until they were inside of it. How, then, did their mother know they were there, for they weren't ten seconds in the barn before she arrived to unpin them. Snow was a half inch on the blanket and the blanket was as stiff as lumber. Her mother whipped it about to get the snow off and would take it inside to thaw. She could not have seen them from the window, which even if it were not frosted over with ice, would have revealed only whiteout.

"What did you learn at school?"

"The curious name of Mr. McQueen's horse," said Elise.

"Which is?"

"The Beatitudes."

Her mother said her name in that way she did when she thought Elise was making the world up.

"She's telling the truth," said Lorena.

"I did not figure him for pious," said their mother.

Elise thought it odd that her mother, who rarely left the farm, figured Mr. McQueen at all. She had no idea, however, what her mother went around figuring. She knew it was not ideas.

"Your mother feels things very deeply," her father said to his daughters not long after they lost their brothers to prairie fever. Lorena nodded, so Elise did also, but after he left them alone in their room in the attic, Elise said, Well, what is that supposed to mean, and Lorena said, He means well, and Elise said, Does he mean to say that he himself feels shallowly, and Lorena said, He's trying, and Elise said, Why are you taking up for him? Lorena said, Because I don't want to believe that he poisoned them and could have easily done the same to us.

But just a week later she gave up defending him and could not stop accusing him of spreading prairie fever. It was true Lorena did not challenge Elise when Elise protested that he did not know prairie fever was in the water tank, he wasn't some scientist, he was just a cotton farmer. But Lorena stopped speaking to him. He was not around much to speak to anyway. Elise had no idea where her father spent his time. He would appear and her mother would call him Harold as if he'd just gone out to fetch more wood for the stove, and then the next three days they'd not see him. Lorena would sometimes say to their mother, "Where is old Harold?" and her mother would say Lorena's name in a way that made it clear she should never call her father by his name.

"He is not pious," said Elise. "He is good with memory."

"You mean he has a good memory?" her mother asked.

That was not what Elise meant, not really.

"That's a good quality," said her mother. "I often feel my memory has a head cold."

"Mine has a fever," said Elise. She was rubbing Sandy with blankets. He stood still for her. Lorena had wrapped her scarf around her nose and taken her leave of them. Likely she already had her hand curled around some mother-of-pearl.

Her mother laid the back of her hand on Elise's forehead.

"No, Mother, *I* don't have a fever, it's my memory."

"Does it feel on fire?"

"Exactly."

Her mother rubbed her forehead with the back of her hand and said, "You are a special girl, Elise."

"Don't say that. Mr. McQueen calls Edith Gotswegon special."

"Is she the bright orange one?"

"That's Marvene. She's joined the nuns. Edith's hair looks like tree bark."

"Do you miss trees, love?"

Elise did not know to miss them.

"Mother, how did you know we were home?"

"Sandy," said her mother.

"He told you?"

"He certainly did."

"Sandy knows the way."

"Yes," said her mother. She put the back of her hand to Sandy's forehead as if checking for fever.

"Does he know the way to Hobart?"

"Of course," said her mother.

"And can he get us to Hobart and back in a day?"

"Easily," she said. She kissed his muzzle. "Old Sandy. I depend on you so."

Elise giggled.

"Is he not the most handsome thing?" asked her mother, and then she was gone.

In the night came the constant noise of what Elise called coyote wind, crying out in pain, mourning, or warning. Her mother climbed the stairs with them and put the lantern on the table and tucked them both in Lorena's cot and put quilts atop them. They were far too old to be tucked in, but either her mother forgot or the coyote wind warranted it.

"Lorena," Elise whispered into her sister's sleeping shoulder, and the shoulder replied with a slight shrug.

Why was her sister so tired? Was it exhausting to look at yourself in the mirror for hours? Surely her lips were exhausted from all the pursing. Likely her scalp hurt from the brushing. Elise took care not to touch her hair.

What she had wanted to ask her sister was, Do you think Mother still feels deeply? What she wondered was, Is depth of feeling a life sentence? Is one born with it? She wondered if she'd inherited it from her mother and if Lorena, who despised their father, had not been handed down his love of ideas. Elise had *notions*, which she always took. But Lorena seemed to have more restraint. She did not run off, literally, to see if the Bulgarians could take over her mail route in the prairie dog village when she was busy, and she did not run off at the mouth. Lorena made plans. Plans were made for Elise by her notions, without consultation.

Lorena slept. She radiated warmth and Elise loved her for keeping her warm and safe and for not coming down with the strain of prairie fever that afflicted Elise and her mother, much less the kind that took her brothers. Lorena put one foot in front of the other, but she did not stay put. She was not Edith Gotswegon. Together they lived inside a blanket where the air was thin and cold and they breathed each other's dreamy dreams. Elise said I love you to her sister's shoulder, and her sister twitched. That meant "me too." Once Lorena woke herself up laughing. Sister, you may marry Joseph Womack and become a preacher's wife and wear dresses to your ankles and your hair up under a bonnet and deny yourself worldly pleasures on the off chance of some *after*, and you could condemn me to the everlasting fires of hell for my failings and my sins and I would—I will—remember the night you woke up laughing, woke me up with your laughter, and I will remember how I never asked you what is so funny because I am not Edith Gotswegon. We are not Edith Gotswegon.

At breakfast, Elise ate oatmeal until she was bloated. Even her father noticed.

"Were you sent to bed without any supper last night, Elise?" he asked, and when he got up to get more coffee, Lorena whispered, "Had you been here, Harold, you would know that we dined on roast chicken, field peas, stewed tomatoes, and corn bread."

Elise nodded at the steaming pot of oatmeal on the stove.

"What?" said Lorena.

She nodded again, vigorously. They would need to eat enough to last until supper as whatever their mother packed for lunch would freeze before they reached Hobart. But Lorena shrugged as if she did not understand or as if she was watching her figure again and did not want to swell up of a morning with porridge.

Much snow had fallen through the night. Her father's pants were wet to the thigh from a trip to the woodpile. The coyote wind continued, the house creaking as if it were about to be dismantled board by nail. There was some talk between her parents about whether the girls should stay home, but the girls said they'd made it in far worse conditions, which was untrue, but her father seemed satisfied with the answer, or else he was struck suddenly with an idea.

As soon as their mother pinned the blanket tight and slapped Sandy on the croup, Elise whispered to Lorena, "You did not eat enough and you are going to freeze."

"What are you talking about?"

"By the time we get halfway to Hobart, the soup Mother packed will be cold and there will be no stove to heat it up on. Your toes will be black if they are still attached to your feet."

"We are going to school as always."

"We are going to Hobart to conduct research for my work in progress," said Elise.

"That is not possible."

"Why is it not possible?"

"Sandy doesn't know the way and we could not get there and back by the time school is out, even if we were going to cut school."

"Sandy does know the way and we can get there and back in time."

"I suppose you asked Sandy?"

"I don't have to confer with Sandy on such matters. But I did ask Mother."

"You asked Mother?"

"Yesterday when you fled to her room to be with your implements of beauty, I asked her if Sandy knew the way to Hobart and she said yes and I asked if we could make it there and back in one day and she said yes."

"And did you tell her you were not going to school as well?"

"Of course not."

"Well, it doesn't matter to me if you did as long as you did not say I was not going to school, because I am."

"You would leave me to the elements?" Elise was thinking of both the sky and of the unsavory element rumored to frequent saloons.

"It was not my idea to go to Hobart on a foolish errand in the first place."

"But it was. You are the one who is confused as to which saloon L. C. Ivent is the proprietor of."

"Don't end a sentence with a preposition."

"No one has yet died from it."

"*Of* it. And no, perhaps not, but many lesser marriages have been made because of some women and most men badly ending their sentences."

"The man I marry will not care how I end my sentences," said Elise.

"That is a far more terrifying thing than this treacherous journey you have it in your mind to take."

"For us to take."

"Sandy is a horse, Elise."

"How old do you have to be to say such a thing?"

"What I mean is, Sandy is *only* a horse. He cannot do the things you would have him do."

"Such as?"

"For starters, he has never seen the sea."

"How do you know?"

"We were present at his birth. Unfortunately," she added. "There are details I wish I did not remember."

"He does not inform us of every trip he takes."

"Never mind. If you want to believe that Sandy visits the seashore, I cannot stop you. But he does not know the way to Hobart."

"Of course he does. Mother said so."

"Mother indulges you. It's easier for everyone."

Possibly this was the meanest thing her sister had ever said to her. Was it true? Or was her sister just trying to get her to mind? It was not true. Her mother felt too deeply to indulge Elise, which would have been insincere. Her mother was many things, but insincerity called for an effort too concerted for her mind, which skittered about in the manner of a fly unsatisfied with any surface.

Elise wanted suddenly out of the blanket, no matter the severity of the blizzard. But it was hard enough for Sandy to negotiate the snow, which would have come to Elise's waist.

"Elise," said Lorena. But Elise did not answer her. She said nothing at all to her sister for the rest of the journey, nor when they arrived at school and were met by Mr. McQueen for the unpinning and Lorena waited for her to go inside, which she never did anymore. Lately, the moment Mr. McQueen helped her down off the horse, Lorena took off to stand over the potbelly stove in the center of the classroom and talk to Edith Gotswegon. But today she waited for her sister. Elise engaged Mr. McQueen in idle talk of horses, using terms like *withers* and *gaskin* and *pastern*, which impressed Mr. McQueen so much that he asked Elise if she wanted to become a veterinarian. Elise said she would probably become a concert pianist in Asia Minor, and when she grew weary of constant travel, she would start her own newspaper. Mr. McQueen, excited by both these notions, quizzed her on the particulars. Out of the corner of her eye, Elise saw her sister mummify herself with her scarf and disappear into the white wind.

Twenty minutes into the school day, during spelling, which was her favorite subject, Elise raised her hand and asked to go to the outhouse. Mr. McQueen always seemed embarrassed when girls asked to go to the outhouse. Characteristically, he said yes without looking up. But Lorena said, "It's brutal out there, I will go with her."

"Do you *need* to go?" said Elise.

Lorena's face scrunched up with embarrassment and rage. Mr. McQueen had looked up from the dictionary from which he had been selecting words for them to spell. He appeared flustered by whatever was going on between the Stewart sisters.

He said to Elise, "Do you need your sister to accompany you?"

"Of course not. It's right outside."

"I *do* need to go," said Lorena, rather desperately.

But it was too late. Mr. McQueen said, "I think it best to take turns in these situations," which made the boys laugh and made Lorena look like she might have suffered a stroke and gave Elise enough cover to slip into the coatroom and grab her lunch before she made her way to the stable, where Sandy looked up, as if to say, What took you so long?

2

GUS MCQUEEN

Hibriten, North Carolina, 1910–16

The road in winter was red with mud. On his way to school Gus tried to walk on the shoulder to protect his boots, but there were places where it dropped off to steep bank. Either muddy road or the risk of tumbling into briar patch or standing water: these were his choices.

Sometimes he was made late cleaning his shoes by knocking them against the front steps of the schoolhouse.

He was slight for his age, with a fair complexion that suffered under the sun. Because his younger brother, Leslie, had died of measles, his own freckles terrified him. His reddish-blond hair was the source of his nickname, Sandy, although his real name was Augustus McCallister McQueen. Big name for a slip of a boy, his aunt Mattie said. She called him Gussie, which of course he hated.

He often felt he had such a slip of a life that he did not need a name. No one talked to him much, at least not in a way he found interesting. So go along and look beyond. He did not feel sorry for himself.

His mother had died of tuberculosis when he was three, a year after Leslie was born. Five years later, when Leslie got sick, his father took him over the mountain to a place called All Healing Springs. Leslie died two days later. What was the point, Gus wondered at the time, of a spring called All Healing when it did not heal all? Some Healing Springs, it should have been called, though in time Gus began to doubt that fresh water filling the bottom of a bathhouse was good medicine for anything but washing the mud off your feet.

So it was Gus and his father alone in the house that his father had built for his young bride. At first his father farmed, but after two years of drought, his father took work in town. He built barrels by day and worked on the house nights and weekends. He added rooms. Built a new privy. It took Gus over a year to understand that the house, its various improvements (the pond his father dug down by the creek, the arched bridge he built to cross it, the bench he erected that only Gus, Latin homework in hand, ever graced) was a shrine to his mother. Only in the construction of something his father could *see* did his grief recede.

Nights he watched his father work until, an hour's light left in the sky, Gus crossed the cornfield to the river to mute the sound of his father's industry. Yet it carried: saw teeth chewing a felled pine, the chunk of adze shaping log into floorboard, ceaseless hammering.

Gus attempted nightly to cross the river. But something kept him stranded. Either the river was high and fast from snowmelt flowing down from the Blue Ridge or the boulders he could have rock-hopped across appeared striped with sunning serpents.

His desire to cross over—to move beyond earshot of his father's grief, to escape his own—was also what marooned him on the bank. It was the first he knew of the deliciousness of denial.

In his twelfth summer, Gus got work in town at the millinery. The store closed at six in the evening. He stayed to mop, then walked the three miles home. One night in early October, the last light turned the sky pink above the trees. He was two miles from home when he smelled the smoke. He arrived to find cinders in the air, the roof giving way, then the walls, until only the grand chimney remained. He watched from the road, loud with the whinnying of horses pulling the water wagons and with dogs amok with excitement. He heard the sweet swish a fire makes and decided it was a secret whispered into his ear only: rivers never burn.

They moved in with his father's sister, Mattie, a widow who lived a half mile down Hudson Bend Road. Her land also bordered the river.

One night in the spring, his father said, "There's work down in Charlotte." Gus watched his aunt's back, broad and stooped, and knew from the way that she did not turn from the stove that she had been told already that Gus was now hers to raise.

"When will you be back?" Gus knew the answer. He said it to spite.

"Soon as they let me go long enough to make the visit worth the time it takes to make the trip."

It was more words than he'd heard his father utter since the fire.

"And who is 'they'?"

"Whoever it is runs things."

"So you have a job already?"

His father studied Gus. Those days he ate little and without pleasure. He looked at his son as if Gus too were a mealtime that needed to be gotten through.

"There's work down there," he said.

Aunt Mattie put plates in front of them. Gus's father picked up his knife and sawed away at a slice of ham.

"I'm old enough to work," said Gus. "I got on at the millinery."

Gus stopped short of saying he could come along to Charlotte, that if there was work to be found, they—whoever *they* were—could hire him too.

"You're to stay here and finish your schooling," said Aunt Mattie.

His father nodded so slightly that Gus thought maybe he imagined it. He watched his father push his chair back and take his coffee on the back porch.

The next morning Gus came down to breakfast an hour earlier than usual. At the sink he pumped water to wet a comb and dragged it through his hair.

"Mind you don't use too much," said Aunt Mattie. She had just gotten the pump installed and was used to the precious water Gus hauled up the hill from the creek.

They sat down to eat. He would not ask. He wouldn't. Halfway through his bowl of oatmeal, the only meal he would get until dinnertime because his aunt either did not know or chose to ignore the fact that she was to provide him with lunch for school, she answered his question anyway.

"It's a day's ride down to Charlotte. He said to tell you he did not want to wake you."

Gus spooned oatmeal into his mouth. He was no longer thinking of his father or making sure, as he usually did at breakfast, that he ate enough to patch him through to dinner. He was thinking, as he often did, of the river. The dark woods beyond it. There weren't really serpents sunning on the rocks. Only sticks washed down from upriver. Things the river swept away from shore. Once he had come upon a grossly swollen sheep. Large parts of its fur had been scraped to the hide by rocks and trees. He could close his eyes and see it, shorn by the river, then cast aside.

"He said for me to tell you he'd see you soon."

Gus paused, his spoon halfway to his mouth, wondering what "soon" meant to his father.

At school the sound of the river often drowned out Dr. Hall's voice. There might have passed in the night a storm of such force that the banks were littered with wrack. He would be poking through it when Dr. Hall would call on him.

"Say again, sir?"

"I will not say again what you should have been paying attention to the first time."

Even the youngest children laughed.

But in time he redeemed himself. Dr. Hall had assigned them the task of memorizing all the one hundred counties of North Carolina. They were given three days. Gus learned them all in an afternoon.

Alamance, Allegheny, Alexander, Anson. On his way to school he timed his footsteps to the list. At the millinery after school he swept to its rhythm: Pasquotank, Perquimans, Person.

He was the fourth person called upon. No one had yet gotten past Halifax. He stood. Names of counties flowed from his mouth like song. His classmates studied him, a mix of doubt and respect. Elaine Johnson, the smartest in the school, flummoxed, left out Davidson, went straight to Davie. Dr. Hall ordered her to sit but she stood, defiant, unwilling to abdicate her place to a freckly boy too poor to bring a lunch to school.

School grew easier. Gus memorized complicated algebraic

equations. Longfellow's "Hiawatha," the Gettysburg Address. How he came to suddenly possess such talent was a mystery he did not care to ponder.

When Gus was sixteen, he and Aunt Mattie went to visit his father. As Gus suspected, his father had never made it to Charlotte. He had gotten as far as Statesville. It took two hours for Gus and his aunt to get there on the bus that stopped now at the new Sinclair station in Lenoir.

His father had married a widow with two small children and was a foreman in a furniture factory. Gus had not seen his father in four years. His new stepmother hardly looked at him. She was not young, but she was bony, which struck Gus as odd because both her boy and girl were plump. The children swirled around anyone or anything in their way as they chased each other through rooms and around tables and out the door.

"Say, Gus," said his father as they sat for a meal. "Any young ladies in the picture?"

What picture? The picture in which only a burned-to-the-ground, only-thing-left-standing-was-the-chimney farmhouse remained of his father's former life? Did his picture include Leslie? Gus thought to ask. Did it include him?

On the bus home, Aunt Mattie said, "My land." Then she was quiet for ten miles. Barns and silos flanked the roadside farmhouses. The fields were bordered by forest. On the far side of those trees, Gus needed there to be a river.

In the back of the bus a colored woman sang a hymn he had never heard. It was unlike the hymns he knew from Mount Sinai Presbyterian Church. The melody seemed to come from the singer and not from some worn book in a rack affixed to the back of a pew.

She sang the words as if every one were new to her. And yet the song sounded as old as the river.

Outside, it was late autumn. Gus cracked the window an inch. Men tended to barrels of burning leaves in their side yards. This was the farthest he'd ever been from home.

"You needn't visit again unless you want," said Aunt Mattie when they got home.

"I don't want," said Gus.

A few months after his graduation, in the fall of 1916, Gus came home from the millinery to find Dr. Hall in the parlor, sitting stiffly on the scratchy love seat that even Aunt Mattie admitted was uncomfortable. He held a cup of tea.

"Sit for a minute, Augustus," she said. "Dr. Hall's come by with something to tell you."

Gus thought it must be bad if she needed to use his too-big name.

"I should think you would have something to say about it as well," said Dr. Hall.

"We are in agreement," said Aunt Mattie in a way that revealed to Gus her ambivalence.

Dr. Hall knew him as the boy who announced his late arrival by beating his boots against the top step of the schoolhouse. So why was he here drinking tea, a saucer balanced on his knee?

"Augustus, son, I wonder what plans you have now that you have graduated."

"I work over at Caison's Millinery shop. For now," he added, conscious that this was not a suitable answer.

Dr. Hall nodded at the "for now" and told Gus he would come to his point.

It is just like Dr. Hall to tell you he would come to his point instead of coming to it, he thought he might say later to Aunt Mattie, when Dr. Hall had made his point and Gus had politely declined to be a part of anything he had to offer. But then he remembered that Aunt Mattie had already declared herself in agreement with the man.

"I have an old friend who has asked me to put forth someone willing to become a teacher in his community," said Dr. Hall. "You have, I think, some talent for it." Then, as was his nature, he qualified his already qualified compliment by saying that his talent was slow to reveal itself and that there was much about his intellect that remained undisciplined and that teaching, above all, called for expert organizational skills and was therefore many jobs in one. He began to list them: moral counselor, physical education instructor, secretary, in some cases janitor, in others carpenter. The list continued. Gus wondered if Dr. Hall's goal was to discourage him.

Aunt Mattie was staring at Gus as if he'd gotten a girl pregnant. This she might have had an easier time believing.

"The school in question is in Oklahoma."

"You said nothing to me about Oklahoma," said Aunt Mattie.

"My apologies if I failed to mention it," said Dr. Hall. "I thought I'd gauge the boy's interest first."

"Is it so bad off in Oklahoma that they have to come this far back east to find someone to teach their children?" Aunt Mattie asked.

Dr. Hall's smile was familiar to Gus in a way that made him angry. It was the smile he gave Eustace Lackey when Eustace announced he was dropping out of school with only three weeks left.

"As I understand it, the community is made up of mostly cotton farmers and some Kiowa Indians. The climate is not hospitable. There are dust storms and tornadoes. And the winters are quite cold. I have this on authority of my friend, C. H. Griffith. He is a banker. Quite successful. He has been open with me about the limitations and hardships of the place."

"Perhaps this is a position for someone more seasoned," said Aunt Mattie.

Gus tried to catch his aunt's eye, but she was studying Dr. Hall with something between a beam and a glare.

Dr. Hall was talking about the war in Europe now. He was saying that there was talk of exemptions for clergy and perhaps they would see fit to add teachers to the category since, to his mind, teachers were as much responsible for the building of character as the ministry. Gus had given no thought to the war.

Dr. Hall had stopped talking. He was looking at Gus.

"Does this town have a name?" asked Gus. He did not care if his tone was impertinent. He understood that the moment Dr. Hall explained the purpose of his visit he was to become a teacher now, regardless of what he wanted. He had never given a moment's thought to the notion. The type of learning recognized by Dr. Hall as successful came late to him, as Dr. Hall himself had said. His sudden shining was due only to his ability to memorize, which in Dr. Hall's classroom, so driven by the rote, equaled erudition. But Gus knew that memorization had nothing to do with imagination—knew, in fact, that it might well be imagination's enemy.

"Lone Wolf," said Dr. Hall. "Named, I understand, for a leader among the Kiowa Indians."

"Lone Wolf," said Aunt Mattie. She shook her head.

Dr. Hall said, "Do you have any questions, Augustus?"

"Only," Gus said, "when do they need me to start?"

Even though he told her not to, Aunt Mattie rose at four the morning he left. She had fried bacon, boiled coffee. She'd made lunch: a hunk of bread, some side meat, a piece of pound cake, a bruised peach. The sight of a packed lunch waiting for him on his last day with her might have made him angry—all those years of midday hunger—but Gus could hold nothing against her. She married at sixteen and moved with her husband to this farm where she wrung the necks of chickens chased down in a yard she swept with branches. Always in her apron, yet she kept china and a thinly stuffed horsehair love seat for company that rarely came.

"Shall I write to your father?"

Gus sat at the table, blowing into his mug. He sipped, sifting the grounds from his lips with his tongue.

"I suppose so. If it's not too much trouble."

"I will write to him," she said, spreading blackberry jam on a biscuit.

Gus, watching her work, understood that he would probably never see her again. For some reason he was embarrassed by the thought.

"I best be going," he said. "If I eat any more, they might not let me on the train."

"Gus?" she said. She turned around and took off her apron. "You never once asked about your mother."

As he stood, he'd been thinking about the river. There would be other rivers but none like the first that had beckoned as it repelled.

Gus sat.

"Where to start?" she said, but she started right in, saying how smart she was, Gus's mother, how much she loved Gus.

"I knew her since she was eight. I quit school after grade six, but she went all the way through. She made your father wait to marry until she finished. But loving was her real talent. There aren't many people in this world who are brave enough to give themselves over to it. You've heard the word 'headlong'?"

Gus nodded. Aunt Mattie sat. Why was she telling him this now? She must have felt too that they would never see each other again. And so she packed his lunch. And so she sat with him and said,

"Your mother met my brother, and my Lord, it was like a war waged inside of her. You could just about see the sides of her, the one that wanted so much *more* than this"—it would take years for Gus to figure out what his aunt meant by "this"—"and the headlong way she felt for the first time, fighting each other. It was in her eyes and it was in the way she walked down the street with him. I used to follow them. Something in her made her just up and stop, right in the middle of the sidewalk. People had to go around her. She'd just stand there."

Aunt Mattie stopped talking. She looked almost sheepish.

"You might wonder why I followed them?"

She looked down at her coffee. She held up her mug.

"Do you want to take these along?"

They were tin. His teeth clinked against them. He hated the way they made everything, even her strong coffee, taste metallic. He didn't want them, but he nodded yes, please. He studied her eyes, her lips. Gus didn't care why Aunt Mattie followed his mother; he only wanted to know why his mother stopped in the middle of the sidewalk. What was she looking at? What was she looking *for*?

Thirty seconds of silence. He heard the creak of the house settling farther into the earth and decided something of his mother was waiting for him in Lone Wolf, Oklahoma. He could hear it, idling now on the tracks, steaming, whistling, impatient.

"I'd love the cups," he said, knowing she would hop right up, as she did, and wrap them carefully in cloth for his journey.

3

LORENA STEWART

Lone Wolf, Oklahoma, January 1917

"And where is your sister?" said Edith Gotswegon when Elise did not return to the classroom in ten minutes' time.

"She might fallen in," said Andrey the Bulgarian. His grammar irritated me and I was already in a panic over Elise's disappearance, so I asked him why did he not pay attention and learn English.

It was during spelling. Mr. McQueen had called out the word *catastrophe*. Joseph Womack had put an *s* before the first *t*. Castastrophe. Perhaps Joseph had coined a word to fit the matter at hand, for what was soon to come was beyond catastrophic.

Elise was at the very least saddling Sandy by then.

Mr. McQueen put down his dictionary.

I have always thought it might be far more instructive and informative to teach both reading and spelling (as well as current events) by studying the *Kiowa County News.* I myself have learned a great deal from it, obviously, as Elise and I spent many a day and night poring over its articles and committing some to memory, and it would do my classmates well, especially the Bulgarians, to be more knowledgeable about the goings-on in this town. I thought to broach the subject with Mr. McQueen, but then I remembered announcing that I was in need of the outhouse. How Elise had shamed me, asking me if I *needed to go* in front the entire class, but I would come to believe I deserved it, as I never should have said what I said about Mother indulging her. It was mean and not true, since Mother, stricken stiff by grief, was not really capable of *indulging* anyone. She had suffered, it was true, and grief does not let go easily, and yet who had not lost children or kin, and did she not bear equal responsibility to those still with her? I could go on about my struggles to understand, sympathize, and forgive her, but I will leave that for later, the story at hand—my sister's having ridden off into the blizzard of the century—being far more pressing, not to mention dramatic in nature.

I will say first, however, that it was, oddly enough, this very moment—wondering over what to do about Elise, and annoyed at the ignorance of my classmates, and somewhat impatient with the methodology of Mr. McQueen, who it turned out had no more training as a teacher than I have as a blacksmith, aside from having memorized the one hundred counties of South or North Carolina—that I decided to become an educator myself.

But at present I was in quite the cast-astrophe. Edith Gotswegon and her ilk would not forget that I had declared myself in need of the facilities, and with every passing second, it became more obvious that Elise had made good on her intention to travel to Hobart. I saw no way out without embarrassment. I could not very well stand up and say to Mr. McQueen, "Excuse me, but Elise has taken Sandy and ridden into the blizzard on her way to Hobart to visit various saloons."

But what other way was there to save my sister from her stubborn plan? I did not ask to be the oldest child, but (unlike my mother) I was not going to abandon my responsibility to Elise despite the short-term suffering it would cause me.

And yet I waited. Precious minutes passed. The snow thickened as the wind was of the stripe Elise called coyote. Why were we even allowed to come to school that day? Aside from the Bulgarians, who were from Bulgaria, only those within a short walking distance were present: the Gotswegon girls, Edith and Ethel; the Miller boys; Edna and Willy Constantine—city folk, we called them, though Lone Wolf is hardly a metropolis. And yet to Elise and me, town was exotic. Sidewalks, alleyways, saloons, drugstore and millinery, post office and courthouse—Lone Wolf might as well have been Oklahoma City or Chicago.

"Mellifluous," called out Mr. McQueen. I thought of Elise playing "Für Elise." Not a technically difficult song to master, but Elise turned the sparkly highest notes into sleet on a windowpane, and her timing made me, listening in Mrs. Robertson's parlor, feel as if I were levitating. Such great heights she reached, with such a simple melody. It likely helped that she told Mrs. Robertson that Beethoven wrote the piece for her. Mrs. Robertson was tolerant of Elise's imagination but not my lack of talent. Mrs. Robertson was ancient, and her house smelled of cooked cabbage, and the doilies covering her stiff chairs were greasy. She was obviously well past the age where she should have been giving anyone instructions, yet I overheard her tell Mother that I played as if I were wearing oven mitts. Then, if that were not insult enough, she said that were the mitts removed, you'd still be left with a child with absolutely no ear. "Elise, however, on the other hand . . . ," she went on, but I walked out on the porch because I did not want to hear that Elise played like an angel. I had heard it before. There was nothing angelic about Elise, but there was something spectral about her being. She felt her way along, her eyes closed just for spite, her hands tied behind her back. I cannot say her mind was ever given to disciplined thought or sound reason. I know this sounds bold, but I believe she is as intelligent as she is because she had someone there to challenge her. I am not talking about Mr. McQueen, or Professor Smythe before him, whose opinion was that Elise was in some way "off." I am not talking about Mother and I am certainly not talking about Father.

But into my ear, while covered from the cold winds of the prairie under the dark blanket, she whispered things that made my bones go away. She said things, things that might seem silly to others, that made me rise from the burden that was and is still my body. It was as if she herself never bothered with her body—never bothered to think about it, never bothered to compare it to others, to note its inadequacies. To her, it was like a skiff, bringing her from one shore to the other.

Others made fun of her. Edith Gotswegon told me that very morning while I stood by the stove warming myself that her youngest brother was a breached birth and some oxygen was cut off in the process, affecting his mind, and was it possible that Elise . . .

I walked quickly to the coatroom so as not to have to give her the pleasure of not answering her question, and that marked the end of my brief period of friendship with Edith Gotswegon.

I could not see through the windowpanes. When Elise first left they were frosted in the corners, but now the declining temperature had rendered them opaque. By the minute it grew colder, darker. The door to the stove was open as much to provide light as warmth.

Mr. McQueen asked Ella Holman, who was seven, how to spell *facilitate*. I had been having conflicting and somewhat strange-to-me feelings about Mr. McQueen, who I had come to learn was only two years my senior, but at that moment my feelings about him were neither conflicted nor strange.

It was the Bulgarian Elise favored, the moody one with the thick eyebrows, the one who the other boys coarsely referred to as "Damn," who finally brought Elise's disappearance to the attention of oblivious Mr. McQueen.

"Elise has never come from the outhouse yet."

His grammar rankled, but my face burned for having let the Bulgarian do what I should have done myself, ten minutes earlier.

"He is right. She is still out there."

I did not have to affect outrage, as I truly felt it—but at myself. Life presents many situations in which you might manipulate the emotions you feel about your own behavior in order to admonish others.

"In the blizzard," I added, as if anyone could forget the storm. "I asked to accompany her and was denied."

Mr. McQueen appeared unusually confused. At that moment I marked him as a model of what *not to do* if a similar situation were to rise in my educational career.

"I thought you were using the outhouse."

"Clearly I am right here."

"But didn't you say . . ."

"No matter what I said, sir." (I had never referred to him as "sir.") "My sister is out there and we need to find her."

"I don't think it's exactly a disaster," he said. "She's likely just waiting out the worst of the storm in the shelter."

"That is preposterous. We rode four miles here in this weather and she had no need of shelter save for a blanket." I acted offended, as if my sister were far too refined to seek shelter from a blizzard in an outhouse.

"Well, go and fetch her," he said.

"I would require you to go with me."

"Why?"

"In case she has lost her way. Visibility, as you can and cannot see if you look out the window, is close to zero."

The class began to whisper. Chief among the susurrous current, I recognized the breathy voice of Edith Gotswegon.

"Very well," said Mr. McQueen. He closed his dictionary and looked around the room. "Edith, why don't you read aloud from Mr. Franklin's autobiography."

"My mother said he was not at all a gentleman."

"Your mother is not here," said Mr. McQueen, which shocked Edith into obeying.

In the coatroom I could not find my scarf. I took Edith Gotswegon's, which was unattractive, but I was not preparing to walk the runway in a Paris fashion house.

I debated telling Mr. McQueen everything then, but it seemed better to play along with the outhouse lie, at least until, after knocking and calling my sister's name, he wrenched the door open against the several inches of snow blocking it and saw that it was empty.

"Let's check the stable," I said, for I was not going to stand in the freezing cold describing the murder of Charley Sherman by L. C. Ivent and why it was of interest to Elise.

Seeing Sandy's empty stall, Mr. McQueen asked where my sister might have gone. It was not his fault that everything out of his mouth struck me as dumb and obvious, since I had foreknowledge that it was now time to share.

Which I did, though leaving out some details, such as my cruel words to her that morning and the dispute we had over the facts of the case of Ivent versus Sherman.

"So she's on her way to Hobart," he said.

"Yes."

"Surely she's turned back? In this weather you cannot see your horse beneath you. She would be frozen through by now."

"You don't know my sister."

He looked at me oddly then, as if he thought that perhaps he did know her. I had noticed that he was generous in entertaining her inappropriate comments, but Elise had a way of taking strangers by surprise, and to be frank, I had indulged myself in a version of Mr. McQueen that suited my own needs. I had not paid much attention to the things he did or said to others, even my own little sister.

"I don't, it's true."

"She'll not turn around."

"But the horse will."

"The horse, well . . . Elise feels that she can communicate with the horse."

"Many riders feel that way about their mounts."

"This is different."

"I do remember her telling me something about the horse coming from the seashore."

"That's the half of it."

"What is the other half?"

"She is convinced the horse knows the way."

"The way to where?"

"Wherever she wants to go."

"And is this true?"

His question struck me as ridiculous. "It is true that the horse knows the way from home to school," I said.

Then something occurred to me, and it was time for me to look at *him* curiously. "How is it that you are always standing in the barn waiting for us when we arrive?"

"Beg pardon?"

"You are either standing in the schoolyard or you are waiting in the barn. Every morning."

"It's an interesting question, Lorena," he said. "I'm afraid I have no idea what the answer is."

"Just luck, I suppose."

"I don't believe in luck."

"I hope you believe in search parties," I said.

"Of course I do. But first I ought to try to find her on my own. She can't have gotten far in this mess."

"And who will teach the children?"

"I will leave you in charge."

I was flattered, but I was not going to stay there while he searched for Elise.

"I am coming with you," I said. "You can leave Edith Gotswegon in charge."

"Edith Gotswegon." He tried to say the name flatly, without judgment, but there was a slightly interrogative lilt in the penultimate syllable.

"She is at this very minute, at your command, reading to little Ella Holman from the papers of a reprobate."

"I suppose she'll do. I will get The Beatitudes ready. You run in and tell them we will be gone and to break for lunch and, after lunch, to work on their mathematics and, after that, Latin."

"Edith Gotswegon's Latin is mediocre at best."

"That's true," he said, and then quickly covered himself. "She's proficient enough, she just needs to work on her verbs."

"She seems to excel at anatomy."

"She does seem to know her way around a skeleton."

"I will deliver your instructions and hurry back and we will leave."

"Ought we to inform your parents?"

"My parents?"

"Yes, Lorena. Your mother and father."

"A minute ago you seemed confident that you could find her yourself."

"I suppose we don't want to alarm everyone."

Inside, I did not bother to knock the snow from my shoes or take off my wrap.

"Mr. McQueen says for you to continue reading from Mr. Franklin's autobiography until lunch," I said to Edith, who held the volume from which she read one-handed, her other hand pointing dramatically at the ceiling. "After that, mathematics and, after that, anatomy."

"But today is Latin," said Edith.

"Your Latin is subpar."

"Far above the level of your piano playing," said Edith, who inconveniently lived next door to Mrs. Robertson.

"I have decided to switch to the violin," I lied.

"Where is our teacher?" asked Ella Holman. "Where has Elise gone to?"

She has gone behind the preposition, I might have said to anyone else but little Ella Holman, sweet thing. She and Elise collected daisies for chains during recess and Elise taught her dumb half jokes that lacked punch lines. Elise would ask little Ella what the elephant said to the post office and the both of them would laugh until Ella developed hiccups.

"Elise is *about*," I said, making brilliant use of the vagueness of certain vernacular phrases. "Don't worry, she will be *along*."

"How is it that you get to go out looking for her?" said one of the boys.

"I am her sister."

"I feel like this is a man's job," said another of the boys. Why bother with names, they were all alike except for the Bulgarians.

"Your feelings mean so much to me," I said, "but the only man present is on the job already."

"You think you're better than everyone else," said Edith.

"Not everyone," I said.

Throughout all this, the Bulgarian, the one Elise favored, appeared worried and drifty at once, while the other two slept with their mouths open. On my way out, I heard Edith Gotswegon accuse me of stealing her scarf.

"Whatever took so long?" said Mr. McQueen.

"We Oklahomans are an inquisitive lot."

"That has not been my experience," he said. "Though your sister displays ample curiosity."

"She is curious, it's true." He helped me up onto his oddly named horse. He climbed up and he urged the horse through the knee-deep snow of the schoolyard. The road was only slightly visible and there were drifts in the fields as high as my shoulder. The coyote wind made talk difficult, but my voice, in certain high registers, carries sufficiently.

"I admire the nostalgic instinct behind your choice to purchase this horse, who reminds you of your sufferings. True feeling is hard to come by and should be celebrated."

"And yet?" said Mr. McQueen.

"Sir?"

"You needn't call me sir. You seem about to make another point entirely."

"I am just wondering about his ability to navigate the snow."

"Whose ability?"

"The Beatitudes." So far the horse appeared as cumbersome as his name.

"He is a local."

"Unlike yourself."

"It snows where I come from."

"Surely not like this."

"No," he said. "I have never seen anything even close to this."

"This is a record snowfall, according to the *Kiowa County News*. The worst of the century, though a friend of my father's, who has lived in Lone Wolf his entire life, says this is the coldest it has been in over fifty years. This is abnormal. But they say the prairie is a punishing country."

"Who says that?"

"I read it in the newspaper."

"I would think the newspaper would want to emphasize the region's more positive qualities."

"I would think the ultimate goal of the newspaper would be to represent the world as it is."

To this he said only, "Hmmm," as if to remind me he was my teacher, for this is the sound teachers make when they want you to know you have said something ignorant but have not the courage or energy to tell you so.

He was quiet for a time. We were passing through town and it was also quiet. The drugstore was lit, as was the dry goods' store, but the millinery and the tailor and the lawyer's and the doctor's offices were dark. The jail stood at the end of town, an ugly three-story brown stucco building, its barred windows, usually open to the elements, sealed by boards. Mr. McQueen slowed in front of it, as if he were thinking of enlisting the help of the sheriff.

"Do you know the way to Hobart?" I asked.

"I do. We take this road all the way."

"How far is it?"

"Have you never been?"

"Of course. But I did not measure the distance."

"I would put it at ten miles."

"How long ought it to take?"

"On a day like today, a good while. How far a head start would you say she had?"

I considered it. The question rankled, since I could have shortened her head start considerably had I spoken up.

"Between eighteen and nineteen minutes."

"That's very exact."

"You were looking for a guess?"

"You are a very precise person."

Though he meant it as a compliment, this upset me. I wanted to tell him that I would in fact be perfectly happy to have a mind like my mother's and my sister's, fickle, dreamy, romantic, frighteningly lush and fragile. Or like my father's, filled with half thoughts he called ideas. I wanted to say that I did not choose my personality, if that was what he was referring to.

"What do you think is the point of life?" I asked.

"Good heavens, Lorena."

"The question does not interest you?"

"It's minus six degrees out. I have no experience in this sort of weather, but it must be far colder than that, given that we are driving headlong into a wind. Your sister has been out here for an hour and is clearly in danger. The only thing that interests me at the moment is finding her, making sure she's safe."

"You are trying to make me feel bad."

"No."

"You mean to suggest I am in some way responsible?"

He fell quiet. I found his silences insufferable, even in the force of such wind, which could suck words out of your mouth before they passed through your lips and could quite possibly suck thoughts from your head or feelings from your heart. The lacerating wind brought tears to my eyes and they froze. The only warm part of me was my arms, laced about his body. He was slightly built. I could feel his rib cage even through several layers of clothes. He was taller than me by several inches and blocked the wind only to a point. We did not have long to find my sister, but I did not want to consider what might have happened to her.

"It does seem you had an inkling that this might happen," he said after one of his silences.

"If I were to take seriously every crazy thing Elise has threatened to do, I would never let her out of my sight."

"What other things has she threatened to do?"

I told him about the time she asked if I might deliver the mail to the prairie dog village for her, as Sandy had to be shoed and she wanted to be there to comfort him.

"And do they get much mail, the prairie dogs?"

"I don't think *you* are taking this very seriously."

"Of course I am. I've left a class full of schoolchildren alone during a blizzard. I am as cold as I have ever been or hope to be in my life. It is a luxury to think of the mail received by prairie dogs."

A shadow loomed on the road ahead, and a rider emerged from the whiteness. A large man on a stout, low horse. Mr. McQueen held up his hand for the rider to halt.

"Excuse me, sir," said Mr. McQueen. "Have you seen a young lady pass by here on a horse?"

"Why, it's Big Idea," I said, recognizing his overlarge features despite the hat pulled low and tight over his eyes and his coat of some sort of animal fur—bear, perhaps—buttoned up to his throat and the kerchief tied about his mouth.

Big Idea, of course, did not know that he was thus called, and he looked at me oddly as I struggled to remember his given name.

Once you are accustomed to calling someone Big Idea, their real name could be Rumination Honeysuckle and it would be hardly memorable.

"Who do you say?" said Big Idea.

"Why it's me, Lorena Stewart. Harold Stewart's older daughter."

He nodded politely and smiled. He had pulled down his thin kerchief to speak and his beard glinted with ice crystals, but he did not seem the least bit cold. He had ample padding. It was a good day to be ample.

Big Idea asked after my father. I said he was fine so far as I knew. About my father I knew nothing, so as long as I added "as far as I know" to every statement I made about him, I was continuing in the vein of precision.

"Have you seen my sister, Elise? She is headed to Hobart alone."

"I seen a figure pass by on a horse, but in this mess I could not make any determination as to its sex. But now that I think over it, the horse cantered to the left like your nag tends."

I was glad Elise was not there to hear Big Idea call Sandy a nag.

"How long ago, sir?" said Mr. McQueen.

"Oh, I'm bad at time-telling. Especially when you can't see the sun. It's not been too long, though. Is she being followed?"

"Well, yes," said Mr. McQueen. "We are following her."

"Has she escaped? Committed a crime?"

Mr. McQueen whispered over his shoulder to me. "This man is drunk." Big Idea made no sign that he heard. He grinned largely, showing his lack of teeth.

"No, she's done nothing wrong except light out in this weather," I said.

"That's not a crime, but it's not shrewd. I say that having made the same decision and regretted it."

"You have been to Hobart?"

"To see a man about a wagon," he said.

Mr. McQueen scoffed. I had never heard him scoff. He was not generally a scoffer.

"Did you happen by a saloon while in Hobart?" I asked him.

Big Idea brightened. Here was a question he could answer with certainty. "As a matter of fact, I did," he said.

"Did you happen by the saloon run by L. C. Ivent?"

"L. C. Ivent is imprisoned for the crime of shooting Charley Sherman dead some three weeks ago."

"You know him?"

"Everybody knows L.C."

Mr. McQueen said, "We must be on our way," just when I was on the verge of finding out vital facts about the case.

"Ought I to alert the authorities that the young lass is struck out in the storm alone on a lame horse?"

"No thank you, and the horse is not lame," I said, but my words were lost, for Mr. McQueen had urged his lumbering horse forward.

"What was all that about?" said Mr. McQueen.

"It was pertinent to our search."

"In what way?"

"If Elise has reached Hobart, we will find her on the trail of L. C. Ivent."

"Who that fellow claimed was imprisoned for murder?"

"Yes, presently, but it is his previous position that Elise is interested in."

"For her play."

"Yes."

"She is certainly willing to suffer for her art."

I saw no reason to encourage such thinking, since Elise's action seemed to me less sacrificial than selfish.

"Has she written many plays?"

"All her plays feature Sandy. The brunt are musicals. Most include at least one nun."

"Is Sandy a fair tenor?"

"I wouldn't know. Elise sings his parts and mine too."

"Impressive," said Mr. McQueen. The entire line of inquiry struck me as irresponsible. There was something aloof and untethered about Mr. McQueen. To be sure, he lacked rigor. Though he was kind and knowledgeable in certain areas (his Latin was fluent as far as I could tell, Latin not being offered to the girls by Professor Smythe, who said it was not something that would "get us ahead in the world"), there must be a reason why all the boys disliked him. He was not up to the task of pondering the point of life.

There came a break in the storm. Our vista increased tenfold. We were still on the road, surrounded by snowy fields. The tips of fence posts peaked from the drifts. I could make out a smudge that suggested horizon. For three days sky and earth had merged, smeared together by snow. The wind died down as well.

"Finally," said Mr. McQueen. "Here comes a buggy." He attempted to halt it, but its driver paid him no heed.

"I suppose they are making hay while the sun shines," said Mr. McQueen. He seemed unperturbed. The sun had not shown, so I did not know what he was talking about—there was no sign of any hay.

Oddly enough, I was colder now that it had stopped snowing. Later I would realize it was too cold to snow. I began to shiver. Mr. McQueen felt it.

"We should turn back," he said, "and find some shelter for you."

"I am fine."

"I can hear your teeth, Lorena."

I held my tongue between my teeth to stop the chattering.

We made slow progress in eerie silence. Presently a farmhouse appeared. Smoke slightly lighter than the sky curled from its chimney.

"We shall stop there," he said.

"What for?"

"You need to get warm."

I tried to say, again, that I was fine, but my words, wavy with vibrato, betrayed me. It was true that I was freezing. With Elise against me, in the blanket, I grew cold, but it was tolerable always. Mr. McQueen's body, I decided, was not producing enough heat. And if we were, together, this incapacitated, what about Elise, out there alone?

Elise could die out here. She could have already died.

It wasn't only that I would be losing another sibling and that my family would be reduced to Mother, Father, and me. It wasn't what it would do to Mother, which was more than likely turn her mind just far enough so that she would be lost to us forever. It wasn't that it might have killed my mother outright. It was that Elise, for all her annoying habits, brought me such joy. *Oh he did did*, she would say, and I would relax into the swirl that was being with Elise. I rolled down hills with her and swung from vines and branches, all the while sitting atop Sandy or in the hayloft or lying in bed together on a cold night. I dove into rivers, beneath the waves of the sea. Elise took me along.

The sobs that wracked me Mr. McQueen took for a fit of tremors brought on by exposure. He pulled up on the reins and stopped his silly-named horse in the road. He lifted me down and wrapped me tightly in his arms. I had never any more than shaken a man's hand. I buried my face in his scarf, which smelled of wood smoke, sweat, and wet wool. I closed my eyes. I don't know how long we held our embrace, but it seemed several minutes passed before I felt him jerk his head up as if he'd been called. "Good heavens," he said.

I lifted my head just as he rather roughly let go of me and launched himself into the field. I had been holding on to him so hard that I fell backward onto the road. I was too cold to be angry, and I lay staring at the white nothing sky for a few seconds before I pushed myself up and spotted Mr. McQueen in the pasture. He ran splay-legged, his legs snapping like a cloth-bound pair of scissors. Every fourth step he fell. He got up again. He called my sister's name. In the far distance I saw Sandy. He was standing at the edge of the field, which seemed the edge of the earth itself. He was partly in the sky.

On his back I saw only a lump. I took off running. Mr. McQueen was calling out my sister's name, but I knew she could not hear him so I called out to Sandy, who did not speak English or Island, as Elise insisted. He recognized the voices of his loved ones, did Sandy. His name bounced off the snow banks and he lifted his head wearily. He pushed through the snow toward us. We made our way to him, he made his way to us. Mr. McQueen had Elise in his arms when I got to them and he was speaking to her softly. I collapsed against Mr. McQueen, my body taken over again by shudders and sobs. It was indeed my fault, all my fault, and I had no one, not Edith Gotswegon, not Mr. McQueen, least not Elise, upon whom to reflect my self-hatred.

"Just tell me does she breathe," I said to Mr. McQueen. I could not look up. I had my eyes closed and my arms around myself, and I hugged myself as hard as he had hugged me. I could hear him speaking to her, but it was as if through a wild coyote wind. They seemed to be miles away. Of earth and above it. With all the energy I had left, I sent my voice above the roaring.

"Does she live," I asked. In the whistling wind there came a voice, thin, broken, Elise: "After a fashion," it said. "After a fashion, she lives."

4

GUS MCQUEEN

Lone Wolf, Oklahoma, March 1917

Nights in the teacherage, in those weeks following Elise's accident, Gus watched the pages of the *Kiowa County News* lining the walls ripple from the wind Lorena told him her sister called "coyote." He tried to write letters to his aunt. *Dear Aunt Mattie, Please forgive my long silence. I think of you often and with love. Thank you for the postcards.*

Every sentence he wrote, he crossed out. Every page he managed to finish, he crumpled and tossed into the fire.

Pulling his chair close to the stove, wearing gloves and a coat over his pajamas against the chill, he felt the weight of all he wanted his aunt to know, which was not everything. He would never tell her how he used to think he had only two choices, bad and worse. Mud or briar scratch. Sweeping up ribbon snippets at the millinery or Lone Wolf, Oklahoma. She'd not cotton to such a bleak view. Work through it, he imagined she'd say. Put your head down, boy, and push.

But nor could he tell her—or anyone, ever—how, at some point after Elise wandered off into the storm, his choices seemed the opposite: wondrous and excellent. He could not tell anyone this because there was only one choice and it was excellent and it was Lorena.

He could say it was Lorena's sudden shivering that led him to stop The Beatitudes at exactly the place where Sandy was struggling to free himself from the fence, leading them to find Elise (after a fashion) alive. He could say Elise was alive because of Lorena.

He could also say that it was his little brother who showed him where to look.

Gus had only a couple of memories of his little brother. Once, they were down by the river, and Gus had to keep pulling pebbles out of his brother's mouth. Another time, Leslie and Gus were playing in the yard, and Leslie fell and hit his head on the side of a low wall, and their father, who was smoking his pipe and reading the paper on the porch, came running over, scooped him up, and did a curious thing: he ran in circles, round the house. Both he and Leslie were crying, Leslie screaming, and Gus's father in that terrible guttural way that some men cry, as if the emotion driving their sobs is coming from their intestines. Round and round they went, until Gus went inside, got a rag, wet it, stood in a place in the yard where his father was in danger of wearing a path in the grass, and on the next loop passed his father the rag.

In Hibriten, oddly—for that is where all memories of his brother were contained—Gus began to forget him. Perhaps his death was colored by how little attention their father paid to it. There was barely a funeral. Gus remembered only standing in the cemetery—it was fall and the wind whirlpooled leaves into drifts alongside the cemetery walls—and looking at the simple marker his father had ordered (instead of making it himself, of which he was more than capable) and thinking, Is that all he gets? Their mother got new rooms, a pond, a bridge, benches. She got a fireplace built from river rocks Gus's father spent months collecting. After the fire, the chimney still stood. Leslie got his name and some numbers carved into a slab that appeared to be more petrified wood than marble.

But since Gus had been in Lone Wolf, he thought of Leslie almost daily. Was it the bond between the Stewart girls that made him miss his brother so keenly? Sometimes he felt Leslie alongside him, usually fleeting, a sudden gust on a windless day. But one day he came to Gus and lingered, and it was the day Gus needed him most, the day Elise Stewart got lost in the storm.

Elise was intelligent and made good marks, though her sister was far more the scholar. Lorena was the smartest in the school, smarter, Gus worried, than he was, whereas Elise would answer a question about, say, geography, by quoting from a newspaper article that had nothing to do with geography. Gus found it disorienting and not a little annoying at first, as it seemed to him that Elise was, in her roundabout way, making fun of him. And maybe, also, of geography.

But Gus quickly came to relish her departures. Teaching was a chore. Even though Mr. Hall was a sound model (though Gus did not see it at the time), Gus had not been to college, and no one ever taught him the first thing about how to teach. From the start, he was behind. He had fallen into the habit, on nights when he was kept awake by anxiety over the next day's lesson plan, of rising in the middle of the night, starting a fire in the classroom, and filling the board with numbers and figures—dates to memorize, division problems to solve—until it was time for him to shave, dress, and ring the bell. He would have to move out of the teacherage when the term was over. It was not good to work and sleep in the same drafty quarters. Nor was it possible to hold the attention of twelve children between the ages of seven and seventeen for six hours on no sleep.

Because he'd paid so little attention to Dr. Hall when he was in school, it had not occurred to Gus that teaching required one to talk all day long. If it weren't for arithmetic and handwriting and reading, which the students performed silently at their desks, he would have likely had to have his tonsils out before Christmas. This was another reason that Elise Stewart's impromptu departures were a wonderful diversion. Her questions, so wildly off topic and sometimes personal (What is the name of your horse? she asked him once during arithmetic) saved him from being bored by the words out of his mouth. Flustered by Elise's odd questions, he found himself responding to her as Gus McQueen rather than his idea of who a teacher might be. It shocked him, and when the shock wore off, he realized it pleased him.

The day Elise disappeared, it was said to be six below. Just walking from the barn to the schoolhouse, the wind, laced with tiny biting ice crystals, penetrated every layer he wore. When Lorena confessed that Elise had taken her horse and headed out into the storm, he had no choice but to search for her. He'd no time to consider the story behind her departure, and it never was explained to him by either girl. All he knew was that it involved research for a play Elise was writing based on a local murder. That was as much as he understood and none of it made much sense.

Lorena insisted she accompany him on the search. She could be quite bossy in a manner, which, that day, seemed to help. She kept up her banter in the most difficult conditions. She'd even asked Gus what, in his opinion, was the point of life. They spoke of Elise delivering mail to prairie dog villages. Nothing made sense and yet in the frigid wind, her body pressed against his, words, no matter their meaning, seemed vital. Conversation kept them breathing and it gave them hope. But within the hour, Lorena commenced to shivering so badly, Gus saw no choice but to stop and wrap her in his arms. He had it in mind to save them both, for it seemed they were to die there, having failed to find her sister.

The snow had lightened up to the point where they could see a farmhouse in the distance, but it was windy still and somehow even colder.

Gus had never kissed a girl, or touched one. Lorena's entire body bucked. One shivers to regulate body temperature—Gus had read so in a book—but this seemed more like a seizure. He wound his arms around her and pulled her toward him. Through the many layers he felt her breasts flatten against his chest, and with guilt did Gus feel things he had only felt in dreams erotic and not always nocturnal. He reminded himself that they were in danger. Embracing the most intelligent and also the most attractive girl in school was, he knew, wrong. But he had to save himself to save Elise. He needed Lorena's warmth and she needed his. He realized he could claim, ever after, to their children (he was shocked that he thought of children at a time like this, but he felt also relieved, as he'd never considered it before and had already, at nearly nineteen, consigned himself to the lone wolf category; also, it occurred to him later that this is where people's minds naturally drift in the face of death—the children they will have if they survive) that the first time they embraced, they held on to each other for life. He might even say "dear life" even though he knew it to be an overly familiar phrase.

And then he felt Leslie's presence. And heard his voice. It was both high and hoarse, an aftereffect of his ceaseless coughing in the days before he died, and Gus recognized it immediately.

Look up, Leslie said, and Gus did.

Now to the left.

Gus swiveled his head stiffly.

See there?

Good heavens, Gus said, for there at the edge of the visible world stood Sandy.

Fortunately the horse was coal black and not the color of sand, as Elise, in one of her figments, had claimed. He'd strayed, disoriented, from the road and encountered some barbed wire hidden by the drifts. It turned out he'd ripped his flank open, likely in an attempt to free himself from the fence. Later that day, Sandy had to be put down.

As for Elise, she was slumped against the horse's crest, barely conscious. "Just tell me is she alive," Lorena said into Gus's shoulder, but Elise heard her and said, "After a fashion," her wit suggesting she was far more alive than not.

But the exposure took its toll. Elise lost four of her toes on one foot, one on the other, and the very tip of her nose to frostbite. Also a finger.

They got her quickly to a farmhouse and a boy was sent for the doctor, who turned out to be a veterinarian. He lived nearby and was apparently often called upon to tend to the medical needs of families in the vicinity. Gus and Lorena could be of no help because they were themselves suffering from exposure. They were fairly standing in the hearth, covered head to toe in quilts, drinking tea spiced with spirits. Gus retained all his digits, as did Lorena. They had each other or they would have suffered similarly. And Gus had Leslie, whose presence that day felt so real that he came close to telling Lorena that it was *his* little brother who saved the life of *her* little sister. But he did not tell her. Instead, much later, he told her sister.

Soon after the event, there was a write-up of the incident in the local paper. Lorena told Gus that Elise, who was given to quoting the local paper at will and often at odd and inappropriate times, had not read the article and had no plans to.

"The goal of life is never to appear in the local paper. Please wake me up when my name appears in the pages of the *New York Herald*," Elise told her sister after the article appeared.

LOCAL GIRL LOST IN STORM

Dramatic Rescue by Schoolteacher and Sibling. Mystery Lies at the Heart of Her Disappearance from School. Horse Wounded and Put Down by Local Veterinarian. Father, Having Lost Two Children to Prairie Fever, Puts Incident in Perspective.

A Lone Wolf girl was found semiconscious on the back of her horse during last Thursday's record-setting blizzard. Elise Stewart, 15, was discovered in a pasture alongside the Hobart Road, approximately four miles north of Lone Wolf. Her sister, Lorena Stewart, and Augustus McQueen, headmaster of Lone Wolf School and a fairly recent arrival from the Carolinas, are credited with locating the girl just moments before Precious Life would have surely left her.

Efforts to determine why the girl left school and where she was going are as of yet unsuccessful. Neither her sister nor her schoolmaster would consent to an interview with the *News*, which leaves her reasons for setting off in a storm characterized by howling wind and heavy snow that rendered visibility to mere inches, a befuddling mystery to all.

"She just disappeared," said Edith Gotswegon, 17, of Lone Wolf, who is due to graduate in May and plans to continue her studies at the university in Norman. "She asked to be excused, but apparently, instead of proceeding to the facilities, she went and got on that horse and rode away."

O. E. Stout, local veterinarian, who was fortunately at home with his family on Thursday, responded to a call from young Leo Manzarack, son of Paul and Alma Manzarack, who live a quarter mile north of where the girl was found. Young Leo, truly a hero in this tragic tale, was sent by horseback into the storm to fetch the doctor.

"Poor thing was on the door of death itself," said Mrs. Manzarack. "We sent Leo off after the doctor, who lives but a mile from us. Although he is an animal doctor, I trust him to see to any of my children."

Dr. Stout allowed that he is occasionally asked to treat humans but, as he is not licensed to do so by the state of Oklahoma, confines his practice to animals, mostly cattle and horses.

"I've not seen a worse case of frostbite," said Dr. Stout. "In most cases it is prudent to wait a few weeks to see if the tissue repairs itself. But the young girl was not wearing shoes, and as a result, the frostbite was severe in several of her toes and one finger as well. I hesitate to offer more of my professional opinion, but I will say that it did not look good for this young girl."

"As for the horse, it appeared to have gotten caught up in some barbed wire. In disentangling itself from the fence, it sustained such injuries that I was forced to put him down."

Dr. Stout himself delivered the girl to the hospital in Hobart. There she recuperates, in the care of the fine staff and in the presence of her sister and parents, Dorothy and Harold Stewart of Gotebo Road, Lone Wolf.

Though Mrs. Stewart declined to comment, Mr. Stewart, caught by a reporter from the *News* while taking a pipe in front of the hospital Saturday said, "She is of hearty stock and will rise and thrive, as she is a Stewart. It is a misfortune, but we have suffered far worse."

Later Elise would point out that it was her ring finger she'd lost to the elements. She would shrug and declare she had no use for it anymore. Who would marry a woman with five toes and a divot on her nose? Elise would ask Lorena, who grew embarrassed at any mention of Elise's "condition," partly, Gus suspected, out of guilt for letting her leave the classroom.

Lorena was not the only one who felt guilty. There was a moment, early on in his tenure, when Gus was lecturing the class on the

Natchez Trace. He looked up to find Elise staring at him so intently, it was obvious she had a question for him, and an important one. Rather than tend to the matter after class, he called on her to speak to the origins of the Natchez Trace. She didn't care about the Natchez Trace and neither did Gus. This was the moment when he began to fail Elise and also the moment he realized that he was bound to fail them all, and himself, daily.

He had come to Lone Wolf because it had seemed the lesser of two bad choices. He could have said no to Dr. Hall. Aunt Mattie would not have minded had he stayed. But he came, and despite the difficulties he faced in the classroom, he was not ready to leave.

In the hospital Elise felt hemmed in, Gus was sure, and he took Lorena to visit her three times a week and on Sundays. It was appropriate, for he was the schoolteacher. His profession afforded him a measure of respect in the community he did not feel he had earned. A mere working man, transplanted to the area from anywhere farther than Lawton, would have to labor for years to attain the same level of trust from the citizens of Lone Wolf. Yet here goes young Master McQueen, riding off down the middle of Main Street, taking a right on the Hobart Road with the prettiest of his students (he could think that, it was okay to do so, because he was imagining what the people on the sidewalk thought), and of course it was all proper, her arms wrapped around his stomach just above his waist and often, on the return trip, late afternoons when The Beatitudes grew weary and his pace sluggish, her head asleep on the shoulder, her body rubbing against his own, a friction in rhyme with their travel.

Gus did not think that being a teacher made him an upstanding citizen and it certainly did not make him unassailable. But why, leaving town with Lorena clinging to him, did he feel guilty? Lorena's mother was staying with friends in Hobart until Elise recuperated from her surgeries and was discharged, and it wasn't as if her father was going to give up his horse to let Lorena go see her sister.

The weather had warmed up. The snowbanks in the fields were broken with patches of brown—first knee-high dried-up cornstalks and later splotches of mud on the furrows in the roadside pastures. Starlings gathered on the bare branches of the trees, backlit by a sun that turned the remaining snow into white gold.

On the way home, when the sun descended toward the edge of the prairie, the temperature dropped, and sometimes they shivered, but they were not in danger. So why did Gus so often feel as if they were being followed?

"What are you always looking at?" Lorena said one afternoon. They'd just left town and Gus kept switching his head around to see Lone Wolf shrinking in the distance.

"You are so quiet, I thought you had fallen off."

"I just this minute spoke."

"After which came some silence."

"I was waiting for *you* to speak. There is a name for this: conversation. You ought to teach it to some of my classmates. It would be new to them and far more helpful than the Magna Carta."

"Magna Carta means 'great big cart.' It is helpful to know that when you go to the wainwright for a new cart."

"Never order the Magna Carta?"

"Unless you have the means."

"Not likely, for us at least. Father says our land is cursed. He claims he was gypped."

"Did he not win the land in a lottery?"

"He did, but it doesn't matter. It would not matter if the land were as fertile as Mrs. Gotswegon, mother of Edith and eight others not unlike her. Father is no farmer."

"Nor was my father. He gave up after two years and went to work in a factory."

"What was made by your father in this factory in North or South Carolina?"

"It is North and you know that. You just keep mixing them up to rile me. He made barrels and casks."

"Barrels and casks are in high demand. My father is incapable of steady work. He wastes hours discussing something he refers to as ideas with men similarly disinclined toward labor. He is unable to provide for us. If my mother did not have a little money of her own to keep us afloat, Elise and I would be in the poorhouse."

"You would have each other," said Gus. As soon as he said it, he realized it was an insensitive thing to say. You will have each other to share a bowl of gruel and wear each other's ragged clothing. And yet it was hard for Gus not to think of Elise and Lorena as "the Stewart girls," though they did not really favor except in the nose. Elise's hair was auburn and curly. Rarely did it seem to have come upside a brush. She wore what were obviously handmade clothes.

Lorena's hair was darker and straighter and she kept it perfectly coiffed. Her dresses too were homemade—there was not a store-bought article of clothing in the schoolhouse—but Lorena managed always to accessorize her outfit with, say, a scarf. Gus had never noticed scarves before. He wasn't sure what their purpose was save to keep one's neck warm, but Lorena wore them inside, when the woodstove was working so efficiently that the students had moved their desks to the corners of the classroom to avoid sweating. If Lorena sweated, he did not notice. Her eyes were darker than her sister's, brown instead of green.

But Lorena did not appear to be listening. She said into his neck (he felt her warm breath), "I want to go to college."

"Of course you do. And you should."

"There's no money. Why did you not go?'

Gus had considered it, especially after he displayed a flair for memorization and his grades began to improve. But with his father gone, he could not imagine telling his aunt he was leaving her to go off to college. Plus there was no money.

"No money," he said. "But you are smarter than I am."

He paused and turned to look at her, looking also over her head at the empty road behind them.

"Don't ever tell anyone I said that or I will flunk you. But they have scholarships available for people like you."

"I have written to the state university in Stillwater for information about scholarships," said Lorena. "I plan on becoming a teacher."

Gus thought to ask if she liked to talk all day long. He thought to say, Do you care a fig about the French Indian War? But he said (after looking behind them once, quickly, and disguising his glance as an attempt to flick the hair out of his eyes), "You would make an excellent teacher. Far better than I."

"You have your moments."

"You are being generous," said Gus.

"I am not known for my generosity."

They were coming into Hobart. The road to the hospital was lined with saloons. Which one was L. C. Ivent's? Gus often wondered but he would never ask.

"Did you hear back from the university at Still Waters?"

"Stillwater," she said. "One word. Which leads me to believe there is no river there. Perhaps a pond."

Or a birdbath, Gus imagined Elise chiming in. He sometimes imagined her comments, which he missed. It was family only allowed still at the hospital, so he sat in the lobby and read, sometimes listening to strangers describe their ailments in a manner common to hospital waiting rooms the country over, Gus suspected.

"The news was discouraging," said Lorena. "I don't think it is enough for me. I would have to work for a year and save much of what I made."

Waiting for Lorena in the lobby, Gus remembered running into C. H. Griffith in the barbershop. Mr. C. H. Griffith had asked Gus if he had any promising students. He ran the First National Bank of Lone Wolf and was chairman of the school board. He was jowly, prominent, and civic-minded. Perhaps he would be willing to invest in the future of a local youth. Lorena would be thrilled and she could get her degree and come back and take over Gus's post, and Gus could go back to sweeping up ribbon, which he preferred to explaining the Magna Carta and the Natchez Trace, neither of which, at the end of the day, he gave a fig about.

Gus would always appreciate Dr. Hall's faith in him, for it had gotten him out of Hibriten. He loved the learning part of teaching, even when he learned things he did not give a fig about, but he knew he had no real talent for imparting the things he learned. The hollow gazes of the Bulgarian boys terrorized him, but so did the alertness of Edith Gotswegon and even Lorena. He was either boring them or failing to properly edify them. Every day, standing in front of the chalkboard, he felt as if he were on the stage of the local theater. He was playing the lead and he had forgotten his lines. Flustered, he often fell silent in the middle of making some point about Asia Minor. Teaching kept him up all night. Either he was worried about something he had said poorly or not said at all in class, or he was wondering what he was going to say the next day.

But teaching had led him to Lorena, with whom he was spending many hours. She slumped against him, exhausted, on the slow return from the hospital in Hobart. He felt her body heating his and told himself if it weren't for her (and Leslie), he might be dead. Surely Elise would be dead. Leslie had saved Elise, which meant he and Lorena had saved each other. He would not dare kiss her until she graduated, but somehow it had happened that they were unofficially courting. Most of their time together was spent traveling to the hospital in Hobart and back, but there was much pleasure in the going.

"When Elise gets home and is able, and it comes spring, I will borrow a wagon and we will all go to the river," he told Lorena one day on the way home. Lorena only smiled. The river was for courting. Every week back in late summer when Gus arrived in Lone Wolf, the *Kiowa County News* had listed the couples spotted frolicking on its banks. Frolicking meant picnicking, almost always with chaperones. But going to the river was for lovers.

Not at all like the river back home, about which he had not told Lorena. It did not strike Gus as something she would find of interest. He was slightly sickened at the thought of the hours and hours he spent there, not crossing over. Foolish, lonesome, teenage longing, dragged out alongside an element passing always through. It was and was not a river. There were no snakes sunning themselves on boulders; there were only limbs and branches left lying across rocks by storm-swollen waters. There was once a washed-up sheep, but this was not the sort of detail that might intrigue Lorena. Lorena was too mature to be interested in washed-up sheep.

Because her mother was so long lost in her grief, Lorena had little tolerance for sadness. A river-shorn sheep carcass was nothing but sadness swollen by weeks in the water.

Gus decided to move out of the teacherage and rent a bungalow behind the Lutheran church. But he needed money. The teacherage had been free. He mentioned his plan to Lorena, who said he should come work for her father.

Weren't the Stewarts a plague of grasshoppers away from the poorhouse? He did not know how to politely say that he needed reliable and adequate income in order to afford his bungalow. So he said nothing.

"You are wondering if Father can pay."

"Well, I . . ."

"Mother will pay you."

"But I would not . . ."

"You are wondering why Mother stays with a man so financially irresponsible if she has money of her own."

Gus did not attempt another sentence. She would only interrupt him to tell him what he was wondering, though he'd been wondering exactly those things she told him he had been wondering.

"She loves him, I guess. Old Harold must have done something amazing to impress her once. She left college without a degree in order to marry him. She could have finished and gone on to have a career."

Gus said that she could still have a career of some kind.

Lorena ignored his preposterous comment and said, "You are wondering why I don't ask Mother to pay for my college. There is not so much money to both keep us afloat and pay for my higher education. Plus, Elise's surgery has cost us considerably. But it is worth Mother's paying you to do the things Father will not. At least tasks will be accomplished. Your father was obviously good with his hands. Did you inherit his handiness?"

"He taught me how to make things."

"You would be mostly mending and repairing and replacing."

"Even better," said Gus, who liked the notion of upkeep and maintenance, since his father had only been interested in building new things. Had the lightning his father claimed descended that day from a cloudless sky not incinerated all his attempts to circumvent grief, the many things he erected in his wife's honor would have soon fallen apart. When Gus left, the benches were already tilting in soft soil and the bridge was missing several boards. Only the river-rock fireplace remained intact.

"I will talk to him," said Lorena. "First I will talk to Mother, but of course we must allow Father to think it his idea."

Gus, in turn, paid a call to Mr. C. H. Griffith, who received him in his office on the second floor of the bank building. It was well appointed in a manly way, with deep leather chairs smelling of pipe smoke, a fireplace, and an oil painting of Abraham Lincoln looking at once severe and confused.

"Don't tell me you're in want of a raise already," said Mr. Griffith. "Did you not just get off the train last week?"

"The school year is nearly over," said Gus. "I have survived my first Oklahoma winter."

"It was a doozy," said Mr. Griffith. "Not representative, but good that your first was so rough. Your next thirty-odd will be easy."

"If I stay thirty-odd years in Lone Wolf, I will be expecting more than one raise."

Mr. Griffith laughed. His laugh was at odds with his body. It seemed to escape him rather than be cast boisterously in Gus's general direction, which was what Gus expected from this portly and jowly banker. Maybe he was the rare man who could express the contradictions within him. Gus had never met a man like that, but he'd read about them in books.

"If it's not money, what could you possibly want from me?"

"I am moving to a small bungalow on Fourth Street. Behind the church. I thought you should know."

"I see," said Mr. Griffith. "Well, you're not the first teacher to seek separate lodging. I would not care to sleep in the bank vault myself. Perhaps we can use the space to allow students from out in the country to stay over during bad weather. I heard about the Stewart girl. Tragic."

Gus thought to say that Elise was not attempting to get home from school, but he remembered that it was better for people to think that she was. Especially Mr. C. H. Griffith.

"You were the one who found her?"

"Her sister was with me. Lorena."

"I know the father. Harold Stewart is in the habit of dropping by. He fancies himself an inventor. Is the young girl getting along all right?"

"She is due to be released from the hospital next week. Her sister goes to see her regularly. And her mother has taken rooms in Hobart to be with her while she recuperates. They say that Elise is adjusting well."

Gus thought this not exactly the right thing to say about Elise, for in no way could she be called well adjusted, though he realized he wasn't sure what the phrase meant. To what was one supposed to so well adjust? Everything, more than likely.

Mr. Griffith was talking about Elise. As cold as it was, he was saying, she was lucky to have lost only some toes.

"Was there also a finger?" he said.

"There was."

"Hmmm," said Mr. Griffith, as if he were contemplating Elise's lost finger.

"It was her sister, Lorena, who found her, actually," said Gus, betraying his little brother. Leslie had not come around since telling Gus where to look that day. What did it mean? Gus looked up at Abraham Lincoln in solidarity, for Gus was also confused and not at all well adjusted.

"It's the sister I wanted to speak to you about, sir," Gus said. Mr.

Griffith came close to smiling, but only close. His almost smile made Gus wonder if, like Lorena, he could see what Gus was wondering.

"Last time I saw you, in the barbershop, you asked me if I had any good students. I have several."

"Philip Gotswegon's girls are said to be top notch."

By Philip Gotswegon, Gus thought but did not say.

"Yes, especially Edith, who knows exactly what she wants out of life, which is, as you know, a rare quality in an adolescent. But Lorena Stewart, I would say, is the more talented. She has the highest marks."

"Takes after her mother, I assume, though I have never met the woman. She must be the very picture of long suffering."

Gus thought it best to ignore this, for a variety of reasons.

"Lorena would like to go to college, but there is no money."

"I don't doubt that. Harold was in here the other day offering his entire spread as collateral for a loan to build an automatic goat-milking machine. Do you realize that if an Alberta clipper came through and held steady for a week, all the topsoil in this county would end up in the Gulf of Mexico?"

"Certainly not much between here and there to stop it, as I understand." Gus tried to recall the map of Texas. Were there mountains he did not know about? Had he just exposed his ignorance of geography?

"You want me to contribute to this girl's college fund."

"She wants to be a teacher. She would make a terrific one. She is patient and organized and she has a nimble mind. I had this idea, sir, that if you helped out with her schooling and drew up a contract specifying that she return to Lone Wolf and work for a period of time at a reduced salary in order to pay off—"

"Why would she agree to work for a reduced salary?" said Mr. Griffith. His interruption was proof that Gus's idea, though noble, was not going to be treated any differently than a plea to fund a goat-milking machine.

"It does not take much to live in Lone Wolf if you lodge in the teacherage."

"And how will you afford *not* to live in it, if you don't mind me asking?"

Gus did mind, but he said, "I plan to find work over the summer on a local farm," careful to leave out whose farm.

"I see."

Mr. Griffith opened a drawer and pulled out a pocketknife. He opened the blade and then flicked it closed. To Gus, this seemed to be a gesture better suited to a cowpoke. Gus imagined telling both Stewart sisters about it while miming the gesture with his hand.

"Well, your finances are your own business. So long as you show up to school and teach the Bulgarians how to speak proper English, I don't care where you live."

Gus started to say that the Bulgarians came to school only to sleep and to escape working in the fields, except for Damyan, who was deeply engaged. But it was clear that Mr. Griffith was not a fan of the Bulgarian people.

"As to Miss Stewart: I have to say there is one thing I don't understand about your proposal and that is, are you not in effect putting yourself out of a job?"

"I hear there is talk of a countywide system."

Mr. Garrison flicked his pocketknife closed. "Did you read about it in that rag?"

"Rag?"

"The goddamn *Kiowa County News*."

Actually, Gus heard about it from Edith Gotswegon, who heard it from her father, who heard it from the barber, who was likely told it by Mr. Griffith. He did not think the *Kiowa County News* was a goddamn rag, but he did not want to admit his fondness for it any more than he wanted to defend the nation of Bulgaria.

"I don't recall reading it. I dimly recall overhearing it."

"The plans for consolidation are just beginning. It is a good ways off."

"More than four years?"

"I would have to bring this up with the school board. Say it got out. What's to stop every high school graduate in town from coming to me asking for the same deal?"

"Maybe you ought not to take it before the board."

"You mean work out a loan with Harold Stewart's daughter."

"I believe in her."

"What if she fails out or decides she doesn't care for college life?"

"Neither is imaginable in this case, but I can understand your position. I will sign the note."

"You will sign the note," said Mr. Griffith. His repeating it made it sound far more real—and reckless—than it had sounded out of Gus's mouth.

"Yes."

"And you will assume the loan if she decides to run off to Chicago to model dresses for Marshall Field's catalog?"

"She is more of a Sears and Roebuck girl."

"You must have the utmost faith in this child."

"She's no child."

Mr. Griffith looked at Gus for far too long. Then he said, "I'll have the papers drawn up. But it is crucial that you impress upon her the terms."

"Of course."

"I expect I'll be seeing her father in here every other day now that I have agreed to fund his daughter's education."

"Lorena doesn't talk to her father."

"You know a lot about her," C. H. Griffith said, flicking his blade.

"I have been taking her to the hospital to see her sister. Her father is unable to take her because he is busy on the farm."

"I'm sure he is." Gus looked at Abraham Lincoln, who looked severely down at them as if he disapproved of them both.

A week later, when the family-only restriction was lifted, Gus went to see Elise. She was sitting up in the hospital bed, wearing a dress and her new special shoes, which were large, boxy, and very black. She told Gus that laudanum was great for passing the endless hours lying in a steel bed in an overheated room, but that it had unpleasant side effects, such as turning the music of the radiator into Beethoven's Sixth Symphony.

"That doesn't sound unpleasant."

"You know it?" Elise said, and he had to admit he did not. "Just as well," she said, and pronounced it "busy."

"I told the nurse to turn it down so I might nap," said Elise. "Anyway, it's hardly practical, laudanum. Tell me all the schoolhouse gossip."

"Edith Gotswegon has been accepted at the state university in Norman."

"Lone Wolf will weep lonely tears as the blinking lights of the train stealing her away from us grow tiny on the track."

He thought of telling her of his arrangement with C. H. Griffith if only to mimic the flicking open of the knife blade (she alone would appreciate it), but it was Lorena's place to share this news, and besides, he had a pressing question. He had always wanted to ask Elise about the incident that occurred when he was discussing the origins of the Natchez Trace. He had written a letter to his aunt, which he stuck in a drawer, and in this letter he had described that moment when he looked up from his notes to see Elise staring at him imploringly. In his unsent letter, he cited this as a pivotal moment in his understanding of his lack of efficacy in the classroom.

Failures aside, he had long wanted to know what she was thinking at that moment. But Elise, in the manner of her sister, went on about the point of life. Unlike her sister, she had no real interest in the point of life and was easily dissuaded from discussing it.

Gus reminded her of the day he lectured on the Natchez Trace.

"I happened to look up at you. You had a look on your face. It seemed you had something important to say to me. Something urgent."

Elise told him that he had treated the suffering of his drunken seatmate, Charlie Carter, in a manner cruel and dismissive. He had failed to hear—these were Elise's words—the man's "true cry."

The phrase took Gus back to the day of the storm. He stood with his arms around Lorena, who was now, for all intents and purposes (though they'd yet to exchange a kiss), his Beulah girl. He remembered hearing his little brother's voice, telling him where to look to find Elise. But Gus had a horrible thought: It wasn't Leslie he heard. It wasn't Leslie's presence he felt. Leslie was dead. Gus barely remembered him, and he did not remember his mother at all.

The nurse came in and interrupted their discussion, which was fine with Gus. Elise had just said that she had yet to unleash her true cry upon the wilderness and Gus had begged to differ. He was about to say something he ought not, but here came the nurse to save him. Shoo, the nurse said to him, as if he were a rooster on her front porch. He loved this nurse.

He found Lorena in the lobby talking to her mother. Her father was there also, for they were to take Elise home later that day. Gus had started working on weekends for Mr. Stewart, who was as described. The first day on the job he had put it to Gus that he was an idea man. Other idea men dropped by and they gathered in the mouth of the barn talking about who knew what.

"How is she?" Elise's mother asked.

"I would say she is ready to be sprung," said Gus.

Mr. Stewart said he was past ready to stop being charged an arm and a leg to keep her there, which Gus found in questionable taste, given his daughter's dwindled number of appendages.

Lorena was looking at him curiously. She said she would walk him out.

"Is everything okay?" she asked him once they were outdoors.

"I dislike hospitals," he said.

"You've spent much of the last month visiting one."

"The lobby is nothing like those sterile white rooms with their steel beds and streaky windows."

"How did Elise seem?"

"She said laudanum was not practical."

"In other words, she's back to normal."

"You've not told her about Stillwater," Gus said, though she very well could have. He and Elise did not discuss Lorena.

"No. I've told only my parents. All I said was that you helped me procure scholarships. I said nothing about you signing the loan."

"Okay," said Gus.

"Oh, Gus, may I say again how grateful I am? You have saved me. You have given me hope."

She was standing too close to him. Were they on The Beatitudes, making their slow way home, she could rub up against him and he would not mind for no one was looking but the starlings on the bare wintry trees and the occasional bored cow. But she was his student still.

Lorena did not seem to care. She touched his forearm in a way that made him realize, for the first time, that the paper he'd signed in C. H. Griffith's manly office might as well have been a marriage license. First he had started courting Lorena without even asking her to go steady and now it seemed he was bound to her without having formerly proposed.

It did not make him sad or fearful. He had choices and one was wondrous and the other excellent, though he could not tell anyone this because there was only one choice and it was excellent and it was Lorena.

5

ELISE STEWART

Lone Wolf, Oklahoma, Summer–Fall 1917

Then she became Local Girl Lost in Storm. She had five toes, nine fingers, and 89 percent of her nose.

Mr. McQueen is not much.

Sandy is on the run. He has made it to the Mississippi River, where the boys stand around in mud-stained knickers and for a dime will wade into the water and stick their hands into holes in the bank and pull out long-whiskered catfish. Sandy has boarded a steamer bound for New Orleans. His accommodations are first class. He dines nightly with the captain, the first mate, and a lawyer from St. Louis who has it in his mind to purchase him, not knowing that he belongs to no one, never has, especially not Elise.

"I still have not had an idea," Elise told the nurse in the Hobart Hospital.

"What's that, dear?"

"You'd think that I'd have one now, if ever."

"You just need rest."

"Maybe on my deathbed one will come to me."

"Hush," said the nurse, and gave her more laudanum.

Elise remembered hearing Lorena say to Mr. McQueen, "Does she live?" Elise remembered thinking, Who is *she*? and then realizing that *she* was she.

In that moment, Mr. McQueen was her interpreter. Mr. McQueen was not much. Elise said (about the person her sister referred to as *she*), "After a fashion. After a fashion, she lives."

Elise remembered parts of the day Local Girl Got Lost in Storm. For years, the day would come to her from faraway, like watching a storm approaching across the prairie: streaks of lightning followed by wild thunder followed by nothing. It was the nothingness that held her, not the sonic booms or the dramatic forks of lightning. The nothing parts when you are waiting for the next lightning bolt are the point of life, Elise said to Lorena in the hospital. Lorena shrugged and nodded at once, a gestural "maybe so" or perhaps an outright dismissal softened by the notion that her sister, now technically a cripple, must be indulged.

What do you remember of that day? they asked her. Who is "they?" Everyone but her mother, Lorena, and Mr. McQueen. And Damyan, who looked upon her with sadness, offering with his moony eyes his sincere condolences as well as Bulgarian devotion, which was by nature both tenuous and total.

She remembered her sister saying to Mr. McQueen, "Does she live?" But it did not even sound like a question. Why did she say *Does she live?* instead of *Is she alive?*

She remembered hearing in the whistling wind the singing of someone passing close by—they had strayed from the road, which was not visible, so thick was the snow, and Sandy had got stuck in the barbed wire, about which Damyan had proved prophetic—and thinking the singing resembled the voice of Big Idea. She remembered calling out to Big Idea, but the winds described in the local paper (of course she read it, she only pretended not to, she had committed it to memory, awful Edith Gotswegon referring to Sandy as "that horse," how did Edith Gotswegon worm herself into the article, who asked her opinion?) as "howling" took away her Big Idea, swallowed it up.

She remembered being laid out on the farm table. The wife was calm; the husband, jittery. She saw three children peering down from a sleeping loft above the kitchen. The wife fed her sips of whiskey. Elise liked the way it warmed her stomach immediately, but that was all she liked about it.

Meanwhile Lorena warmed herself by the fire, as did Mr. McQueen. Elise did not hold it against them, leaving her alone on the table, as they were also suffering. They had come to fetch her. They too could have easily died. It wasn't too shrewd, her lighting out for Hobart in the storm, though her body often did not obey her mind. The two sometimes behaved as if they'd not yet met. She wanted, needed to find out what some might consider a relatively minor detail about who operated a certain Hobart saloon, so that she might proceed with composing her play. Yet neither Lorena nor Mr. McQueen told anyone why she was trying to get to Hobart (both even refused an interview with the *Kiowa County News*), and when she realized it had become a great mystery, she wasn't about to spoil it.

Laid out on the table, she watched Lorena and Mr. McQueen drink from steaming mugs. They were sharing a quilt as they stood by the fire. They were left behind as the farmer loaded her up in his shay and, with the horse doctor attending to her, took her to the Hobart Hospital.

After she recovered from hypothermia, the doctor came and determined that five of her toes and one of her fingers must take their leave of her, as well as the tip of her nose. She had not seen her toes or her finger because they were thickly bandaged, though she heard the hardened nurses gasp as the digits were uncovered, the tissue obviously blackened. She heard the word *gangrene* from the doctor and her mother held her hand, crying. Then there was ether and pain and days lying in the hospital bed, trying to forget the smell in the room when her useless toes were unwrapped.

Her mother stayed with her, sleeping slumped over in a chair. They gave Elise laudanum and then paregoric round the clock. She missed the laudanum. Her mother cried.

"I know, Mother," she said. "But Sandy is on his way home."

Her mother looked up.

"He is bound for New Orleans and from there he will make his way to the coast of Mexico on another ship."

"Oh, Elise," said her mother. "I thought we lost you."

"But you did," she said. "I was lost in the storm."

Her father was there, at least according to the local paper. He took his pipe down to the lobby and reportedly said to the reporters, "We have suffered far worse." He spoke to the sturdiness of the Stewart clan. One thing he did not do was share any of his ideas with the reporters, and for this Elise was grateful.

Of course she read the article. The nurses had brought it to her straightaway. She only said she didn't read it to illustrate to Lorena that one should quit making pronouncements about the point of life. The point of life had nothing to do with the *Kiowa County News* or the *New York Herald*. Wake me up when my name appears in the *New York Herald* indeed. She had said such to humor Lorena, who claimed Elise was the one who ought to be humored.

Mr. McQueen came to see her in the hospital. He pulled his

chair close. She looked at the perfect part in his hair. It stayed put, annoying her no end.

There'd been a thaw, the snow had melted, the sun was out, and Mr. McQueen had gained freckles riding and strolling about. Mostly he traveled back and forth to the hospital, though often he brought Lorena and stayed in the waiting room because it was family only allowed. This time he was allowed, and alone, which must mean they were letting her go home. He smelled of fresh air and of The Beatitudes.

"I need to ask you something," said Mr. McQueen after a brief but vaguely satisfying update of schoolhouse gossip. Edith Gotswegon was going to university in Norman. Joseph Womack had been called to preach the word, which Elise knew for a fact he could do in his sleep.

"Yes?"

"Once, not long after I arrived here, I was lecturing on the origins of the Natchez Trace. I was, of course, reading from my notes." (Before you started making up history altogether, Elise thought but did not say). "And I looked up and you were staring at me."

"Was I? Of course I was. You were standing in front of me and you were the teacher."

"Would that this required you all to look at me instead of out the window or at your desks. Anyway, you had a look on your face . . . I have not forgotten it. I tried to describe it in a letter to my aunt." (He writes letters to his aunt in which he describes the looks on the faces of his students? This surprised Elise in the very best way.) "It seemed you had something important to say to me. Something urgent."

"Yes."

"Do you remember what it was?"

"Of course. I remember everything that ever happened."

And lots that did not, Lorena would assert were she present.

"What was it you needed to ask me?"

Charlie Carter wakes and cries out for his Beulah girl. She has thrown him over for another and he drinks enough to sleep through three states, and why could we not talk about that instead of how the Natchez Trace was blazed by prehistoric animals before man arrived, as if *man* counts for anything?

"I wanted to know what is the point of life."

"Elise," said Mr. McQueen.

"Yes?"

"No you did not."

"Charlie Carter," said Elise. She wasn't ashamed. She was crippled. Now she could say anything and who cared? Before they thought her odd and listened and laughed. Now that she was maimed, they would pay no attention to her. She could stand naked in front of the First National Bank of Lone Wolf and recite the articles of the constitution in hog Latin, and if they even noticed, they would say, "That young lady lost her digits."

Mr. McQueen looked puzzled. If only the part in his hair were irregular, his confusion would be charming.

"What about him?"

"His Beulah girl!" Her voice was hoarse when raised and it shocked her.

"Yes?"

"It wasn't a joke. He suffered, did Charlie Carter."

"I did not tell it as a joke."

"You told it as a humorous anecdote."

"It was not amusing to you?"

"Not in the least. The man suffered terribly. He cried out, but no one heard his true cry."

Mr. McQueen said, "And do you think it generally true that no one hears our true cry?"

"On that I have an opinion, but I choose to withhold it, since I have yet to let mine loose on the world."

Mr. McQueen sat back in his chair. He appeared to go somewhere else in his mind. She wasn't sure where it was, but it wasn't this hospital room with its white-tile walls that were always inexplicably wet.

"Oh, but you have."

"When?"

"The day you got lost in the storm."

"How was that my cry of truth?"

"Well, it wasn't about research for a play based on a murder in Hobart, for starters."

"It wasn't?"

"No," said Mr. McQueen.

"Well, do tell."

But the nurse came in. She told Mr. McQueen that visiting hours were over. This particular nurse was her favorite, but at this moment she hated her. She wished she had never been born.

Mr. McQueen said his goodbye. He left her there with five toes and nine fingers. The nose was of no real consequence to Elise.

The next time she saw Mr. McQueen was at her house. It was summer and school was out. (She had not returned, but she had gotten credit for the year, because Lorena had brought home lesson plans that Mr. McQueen had specially designed for her, which included amusing questions, like list your favorite stripe on the US flag and say why it is your favorite without employing adjectives, etc.) He was wearing dungarees and a dirty shirt. His boots were dusty. Lorena brought him into the parlor, where Elise was playing "Für Elise" on the piano her mother had waiting for her when she came home from the hospital.

"Elise," said Lorena.

She kept playing. She was almost to her favorite part, where Ludwig van Beethoven, who had written the song for her, lingers adagio on two notes, slowing down so much you worry it's over and your heart yearns for the solace of music over the preternatural silence of the prairie.

Elise thought herself even more capable of evoking this yearning now that she was shy a finger. A weaker pianist would have given up after going under the saw. Maybe Mr. McQueen could appreciate her transcendence. He might be the only one. Lorena seemed fascinated by it, in the way she was fascinated by the Siamese Twins the carnival brought to town, but she was also slightly embarrassed, especially when Elise played in front of others, others being, in this case, Mr. McQueen.

"Elise," Lorena fairly hollered.

Elise turned around. There stood Mr. McQueen, dressed up like a farmhand.

"Hello, Mr. McQueen."

"Elise, you play beautifully."

"It helps that the song is named for her," said Lorena.

"Actually, written for me," said Elise.

"Even though it was written almost a hundred years before your birth," said Lorena.

"So? What great artist thinks only of the living?"

Despite herself, Lorena giggled. Mr. McQueen was beaming.

"I never knew," he said.

"Knew what?"

"That you possessed such musical talent." He turned to Lorena. "And do you play as well?"

"By 'as well,' do you mean *also*? Or do you mean as well as I?" said Elise. Lorena was no longer giggling. Mr. McQueen looked as if he had fallen into a hole in a pasture.

"Why are you dressed like a scarecrow?" Elise asked him.

"Why, I've been hired on as one."

"You can stand still for that long? Even if I weren't crippled, I could never."

"Please stop using that word," said Lorena.

"It's a fortunate thing for those who suffer a similar fate that I have made a significant medical discovery. It is quite possible to walk with only one toe on your foot."

Lorena looked embarrassed for herself, not so much for her sister. Don't be embarrassed, Lorena. It's not your fault. And no one else knows what happened. Only the three of us in this room know the truth.

"Only the three of us in this room know the truth," said Elise.

"About what?"

"About why I went to Hobart."

"I've not really hired myself out to stand in a field scaring away crows," said Mr. McQueen. He had to change the subject, he *had* to. But why? Later she would ask him why. But at the moment she only smiled and said, "I take it you are working for Father?"

"Yes."

"Have the two of you exchanged ideas?"

"Beg pardon?"

"Father is an idea man."

"Oh yes," said Mr. McQueen. "I've heard him say so. We don't talk much."

"That's good. Someone needs to tend to things. What has he got you doing?"

"Right now I'm repairing fence. I'm sort of a handyman."

"And are you handy like that?"

"My father taught me some things. He could build anything. He built houses, barns, bridges, fences, gates. He dug ponds. He built fireplaces out of river rock."

"Your father has passed?" said Lorena.

"Yes," said Mr. McQueen.

"And your mother?"

"Many years ago."

"And have you any brothers and sisters back east?" asked Elise.

"No," he said. "It's only me." Then, after the pause that comes when someone declares that they are all alone in the world, he said, "I had a younger brother, but he died. And my aunt, who raised me, is still alive."

This would be the aunt to whom you attempt to describe in letters the facial expressions of your students, Elise thought to say but did not, for Lorena's sake as much as for Mr. McQueen's.

It was as if because he was standing in his dirty work clothes, in their parlor, they could ask him anything. Though Elise did not feel like anything they had asked him was something she would not have raised her hand and put to him during, say, botany.

"Well, I suppose we shall be seeing a lot of you," said Elise, looking at Lorena.

Mr. McQueen said, "Your father keeps me pretty busy."

"I suppose he does," she said, looking out the window to see her father in the mouth of the barn, holding forth to a group of fellow ideologues.

"You might talk to him about digging the well deeper," said Elise. "The water tastes of granite. Also, the windmill is rusty and in need of repair. Its creaking keeps me awake nights."

Lorena said that she felt sure Mr. McQueen had his hands quite full without Elise adding to the list.

"And are you called Mr. McQueen when you are dressed in those clothes?" said Elise.

Lorena, who was leaving at the end of the summer for university in Stillwater to become a teacher herself said, "You can't very well call him one thing out of class and another when school starts back, Elise."

"And what do *you* call him?"

"I better be getting back to work," said Mr. McQueen.

"Goodbye, Mr. McQueen," said Elise. "Thank you for stopping in. We get few visitors."

Lorena walked out with Mr. McQueen. Presently Elise heard the kitchen door slam, then her sister's ten-toed steps on the stairs, then the door to their bedroom close.

She put her head down on the top of the piano and attempted to find, in a trill of high flats and sharps, the music of her true cry.

That night in bed, Lorena said into the dark, "I have graduated."

"I know. I attended the ceremony, such as it was."

"There's nothing wrong with my seeing him now."

"By seeing him, what do you mean exactly?"

"You know what I mean."

Lorena had never had a boyfriend. Now she had Mr. McQueen. It wasn't that it did not seem fair. It was more that it did not seem plausible. It was as if she had skipped over all the middle rungs on the ladder. Not that Mr. McQueen was the top rung. His part stayed put in a way that made him seem like a photograph, and even Lorena herself had expressed dismay at his teaching methods, especially when he did things like ask little Ella to spell the word *miraculous*.

"No, I don't know what you mean."

"Yes you do."

"Okay, fine. Are you going to marry him?"

"I am going to college."

"Is he going to go with you to Still Waters?"

"No, why would he? He has a job already."

"Does Mother know?"

"Only in the way she knows the things she knows."

"That means you didn't tell her."

"That means, why should I?"

"Okay," said Elise.

"Okay what?"

"Okay, can I go with you two to the river on Sunday?"

"How did you know we are going to the river on Sunday?"

"I read the paper, Elise. That is where courting couples go of a Sunday afternoon." And then Elise listed the couples seen frolicking by the riverside near Lugert. The list was long and Lorena drifted asleep to it, the rhythms of the *Kiowa County News* being both sing-song and soporific. But the words they had spoken remained in the space between their beds. Are you going to marry him? Okay. Okay what? He has a job already.

Sometimes Sandy came for her in the night. Elise could hear him snorting outside, announcing his arrival. Elise would rise and put on her customized shoes the doctor had made for her, and she would steal downstairs past her parents' open bedroom door (it was hard to walk quietly in the cumbersome shoes) and climb atop her waiting Sandy. Moonlight lit the prairie. They took off across it, paying no heed to Father's cotton, jumping the fences Mr. McQueen had been hired to mend. As soon as she was in the saddle, Elise had her toes back. Her once-missing finger sported a ring, which glowed golden in the moonlight. The day she got lost in the storm she had seen the snow turn red. She lost her shoes early on (she remembered taking them off, but she did not remember why) and her socks were wet. Her knickers were wet, her dress was soaked, the hats and scarves and gloves she wore were frozen stiff. She took to shivering so much she could not hold on to the reins. She clung to Sandy's neck. She sang to him. But Sandy stopped moving and the snow turned red. Elise looked down and saw a fence post. She looked back and forth, searching for another, but it was snowing too hard, and besides, of course there was more than one fence post. There is never only one fence post.

Sandy, stay put, she said, but Sandy wanted to get them to shelter. Elise saw the fence post moving and she saw the snow bleed as Sandy broke free. They moved off into the drifts. The road was gone. They had passed to the other side of this life. If hell is supposed to be fiery, heaven, reason would suggest, is but snow and ice and bitter cold. Why is *that* not in the Bible? But Sandy left a trail of red. Elise looked back over her shoulder at the red trail and this is when she got scared.

They say her skin was blue as the veins beneath her skin. They say her lips were blue, her forehead yellow, her fingers and toes and nose finally white. My hair turned blue and Sandy turned the snow red. I lived, but Sandy was sent away. It's okay, though, as Sandy is an ocean horse. In Mexico, he dives from cliffs into the sea. Tourists pay to see him plunge into the surf. The surf licks the rocks far below the cliffs, but Sandy knows just where to aim so that he sinks down among the fish, who welcome his presence. They call him World's Largest Sea Horse. This tickles Sandy every time.

A sadness fell over the days of the summer after Elise was lost in the storm. She had to learn to walk again. The Bulgarians were at work in the fields and she was done with them anyway, even Damyan. She was not self-conscious about her nose, even though children and some adults stared at it. For years, everyone had stared at Lorena, who was prettier and took care to dress appropriately and combed her hair with mother-of-pearl. After she graduated, she took to wearing lipstick. Now Elise drew stares. She preferred invisibility. So she stayed home, played the piano (which she learned had been donated by the Women of the Church, who thought Elise would now be housebound or confined to a wheelchair; she wondered if, when they saw her out and about in her heavy customized shoes, they would regret their generosity), and read books with horses in them.

Mr. McQueen, who Lorena now called Gus, came after church one Sunday to take them to the river. He borrowed a buggy from Mr. C. H. Griffith, who ran the First National Bank of Lone Wolf and had hired him to teach school. Mr. McQueen helped Lorena into the buggy, but Elise refused his aid with a smile. She hoisted herself up and nudged her sister closer to Mr. McQueen with her hip.

The Beatitudes seemed befuddled by the contraption to which he was harnessed and the task he was being asked to perform. Mr. McQueen had to recite The Beatitudes to get him started and even then it was slow going down the Lugert Road to the river.

"Has he never pulled a buggy before?"

"It's been a while," said Mr. McQueen.

"It's like falling off a horse," Elise called out to The Beatitudes, which made Lorena giggle.

At the river Lorena and Elise changed into their bathing suits in the woods, which made Elise feel frisky. The trees, their thick exotic cover, hugged the riverbank, leafy and embracing. But the thrill of being nearly naked in public did not diminish the difficult time she had balancing on her good foot as she stepped out of her knickers. She had to steady herself on a tree. Through the branches she spotted two young boys, spying. She wrapped her arm around the tree trunk, grabbed her all but toeless leg, and hoisted it up for them to see. She heard gasps and the rustle of boys fleeing.

"What are you doing over there?" asked her sister, who was dressing behind another tree.

"Exercising," said Elise.

"Do you need help getting dressed?"

"No," she said, but she had to sit to put on her shoes. She felt silly wearing her bathing suit and her monstrous black shoes. She hardly ever felt silly, so why did she insist on accompanying them? Surely Lorena would prefer she stay home.

The riverbank was crowded with young couples, families, and packs of filthy-minded boys. These boys saw her coming. They watched from the bank as she took off her shoes under the tree where Mr. McQueen had spread a blanket.

Mr. McQueen was slicing a watermelon with his pocketknife, clearly for the first time. It was difficult to watch. He resembled The Beatitudes harnessed to a buggy.

She wanted to fling herself into the river, but that required passing by the filthy-minded boys, who were already loudly discussing her foot. However, she did not come here to watch Mr. McQueen make a mess out of a watermelon, and she knew Lorena would appreciate having some time alone with this Gus fellow.

Slowly she made her way along the bank. The boys were not quiet, being young and filthy-minded.

"She walks like Frankenstein himself,' said one of the boys.

"You will too when I cut off your toes," said Elise.

But this only incited them. They got up and followed her, mimicking her walk. She felt them behind her and for the first time she was ashamed of her condition. She walked a few steps farther when she heard one of the boys cry out, followed by a splash.

Mr. McQueen had taken the last boy in line and tossed him over the bank. He had another in his arms and the boy was squirming.

"Stop it," said Elise. "What if the boy can't swim?"

Mr. McQueen nodded toward the boy he'd just tossed in, who was sculling a few feet off the bank, a smile on his face, enjoying the show.

"River rats," he said.

"Carry on, then," she said, but the other boys were long gone by then. Mr. McQueen held the fidgety boy, whispering something in his ear, which made him shake his head wildly and, when freed, scamper off into the woods.

"That will teach them, teacher," said Elise in lieu of thanks. She did not want him to come her aid, but nor did she mind it.

Mr. McQueen said he fancied a dip.

"What about Lorena?"

"She says she's not ready to get her hair wet."

"Not something I ever need to work myself up to do."

"Nor I," said Mr. McQueen. But she noticed that in the river, even after he'd dunked beneath the surface, his part remained perfect.

They floated on their backs. Normally, only her nose and breasts and knees and fingers and toes would break the surface. Now it was chin, breasts, knees.

Things had changed. She could have died.

"I thought we'd died," she said.

"Just now?"

"Not *us*," she said. "Me and Sandy, in the snow."

"Well," he said. He became sincere and tentative, as were they all when the subject came up.

"I was thinking, when we were dying, that if you burn in hell, you must freeze in heaven."

"That makes sense to me and I am not lost in a storm."

"Everything makes sense in the water," she said.

"I had a river in my backyard growing up," he said. "I went there almost every night."

"What did you do there?"

"Once I saw a washed-up sheep."

"Say more on this subject."

Mr. McQueen said about the river shearing the sheep's fur. He said it was a peaceful river that could turn treacherous. Snakes sunned themselves on rocks.

"What sort of snakes?"

"They might have been branches," he said.

"But the sheep was real? Because surely you know by now that it doesn't matter to me if it wasn't."

"I know," he said, "but it was real."

"Why did you go there?"

"To get away from my father."

"Was he an idea man?"

"The opposite. He was a man whose hands were never idle, lest he feel something." He told Elise about the house, the built-on rooms, the grand chimney, the ponds dug and the bridges built across them. He told her about the bench that only he sat on. He told her about the fire, how he was walking home and saw it before he smelled it and mistook it for the most amazing sunset.

Mr. McQueen's first name was being called, shrilly, from shore.

"It appears Lorena is ready to wet her hair," said Elise.

They had drifted a good ways down the river. Lorena had followed on a path beaten clean by the feet of a thousand lovers. It wound around trees, their naked roots snaking down to the water, the dirt beneath them washed away by the current. They looked to Elise like cages or traps.

Elise said she would swim back.

"Against the current?" he asked, but just as quickly he begged her forgiveness. He saw the look on her face and said he must have forgotten whom he was talking to.

Sometimes Elise went to the river with them on Sundays. Always they asked. But she got the feeling it was mostly Mr. McQueen behind the asking, and out of politeness. Was he polite? She had gotten him to talk about Edith Gotswegon once. All he said about her was that she "made very good sense and that seemed to be her goal in life," which was not on the surface a criticism, but Elise knew Mr. McQueen just well enough to know that it was. It was not polite to talk about your former students, even Edith Gotswegon. But it meant he was alive, despite the perfect part in his hair, which not even a river could disturb.

There wasn't anything much to do on the Sundays Elise declined to go to the river. The Bulgarians drove their wagon thirty miles to attend an Orthodox church with other Bulgarians. When she was not with Mr. McQueen, Lorena was busy preparing to leave for Stillwater. It would not seem to Elise that one needed to prepare much at all to move to a place called Stillwater. When Elise said the name made the town sound terribly exciting, Lorena said it was better than Lone Wolf, though Elise knew she was sad about leaving Lone Wolf because it meant leaving behind Mr. McQueen, whom she now called Gus.

Mr. McQueen could be seen around the property dressed as a field hand. Sometimes on blustery days he wore a kerchief over his mouth and nose as if he had just robbed a bank. Elise saw him in the yard and told him that since she had survived prairie fever, she could breathe all the dust she wanted with immunity. She said by the time she was forty years old, her lungs would have enough dirt in them to grow a tomato plant.

Mr. McQueen said that sounded painful.

"Oh, it doesn't hurt at all if you're used to it. It's only those who did not grow up breathing dust who go around like bank robbers."

Mr. McQueen said he was referring to tomatoes growing in her lungs.

"Not painful in the least," she said. "Tickles a bit, though."

She often thought of floating down the river with him that afternoon when Lorena was waiting until she was ready to get her hair wet. She remembered his tales of washed-up sheep and snakes stretched across rocks in the sun. It seemed he was trying to tell her something else. But Elise liked to believe that everyone was always trying to tell you something else. Even her mother when she said to her father, "Harold, would you please pass the salt?" And Lorena, when she was trying to corral Elise's thoughts during the night with her bossy sleep-breath. Thank goodness everyone was trying to tell you something else entirely, for if the world were made up only of what actually came out of people's mouths, Elise would prefer the frozen eternity of heaven.

In late August, Elise spent several days helping Lorena pack for Stillwater. A steamer trunk appeared in their room. It had a lid curved like a treasure chest and another flat lid inside, also hinged, lined with fabric and fitted with small compartments, a couple of which also had lids.

"Where has this been all my life?" asked Elise.

"Mother used it when she went off to college."

"And she hid it all these years?"

"She knew if she didn't, you would lock yourself up in it and asphyxiate."

"I'm smart enough to poke holes in the sides with an ice pick."

"Even more reason to hide it from your sight."

Elise asked if Mr. McQueen was going to borrow C. H. Griffin's buggy and drive her to Stillwater.

"Stillwater is nearly two hundred miles from here. Do you know how long it would take The Beatitudes to travel two hundred miles?"

"You're saying no, he's not."

"He'll take me to the train."

"Where will we say goodbye?"

"You can come to the station also."

"Are you scared to leave home?"

"Scared?" she said. She looked at Elise in a way that reminded her of times long past, when blanket was sky and nothing could hurt them because they were just a bag of old giggly bones.

"I am ready to get on with my life," she said finally.

Which Elise interpreted to mean: I am and I am not terrified.

Elise lay on the cot watching her sister refold all her clothes. She thought about getting on with her own life. She seemed, often, to be lost still in a storm. How was she to get to school without Sandy? In good weather she could walk, but it would take much longer than usual, for she could not run anymore, or skip, or even walk very fast. Her father's horse was named Buck, because, for heaven's sake, he once bucked someone. Would you name a horse Kick if he kicked someone? Buck could not find his way out of the barnyard. What about when winter came to Lone Wolf? How would she get to school?

Ancient Mrs. Robertson had finally retired. The future musical prodigies of Lone Wolf would require immediate instruction, as well as those as tone-deaf as Lorena. Therefore she might just stop all this school business. Hardly anyone in Lone Wolf continued past the eighth grade anyway. The Bulgarians were on a fourth-grade level (except for Damyan, who was smarter but moonier, so he was a year behind) and only came to school in the winter to escape being put to work in the cold by their father who came from the mountains of Bulgaria bordering Romania and told his sons of winters so cold blood froze in the veins of sheep.

Elise thought it possible to teach piano and travel wildly in one's mind. If Joseph Womack could preach in his sleep, she could teach seven-year-olds to play "Auld Lang Syne" while cliff diving with Sandy in Mexico.

She had a piano, praise be the Women of the Church. It would make them feel vindicated if she put it to constant use. Maybe the *Kiowa County News* would do a feature on the nine-fingered piano teacher of Lone Wolf and the Women of the Church would be given full credit for saving her from a life of idling by the window, staring out at the prairie, dressed in a style popular when she'd suffered her tragic accident. She could throw in a few hymns to keep them happy. She had some feeling in her heart for "Amazing Grace." Also "Jesus Christ Is Risen Today," though she was confused by the verb tense. Most of Mrs. Robertson's pupils had ended up playing in some country church or the other, so it stood to reason that she should include hymns.

The question was, Would parents want to haul their children so far out into the country for lessons? Mrs. Robertson lived two blocks from the schoolhouse. Most of her pupils took lessons after school, when they were in town already. Also, there was the problem of her father and his crew of idea men loitering around the barn. Though there was nothing unsavory about them (with the possible exception of Big Idea, who was rumored to have taken to drink), it did not look proper, a group of grown men standing around idle of a perfectly clement afternoon.

Mr. McQueen had quit the teacherage and rented a house on Fourth Street. She had not been in it, but she had seen it from the outside and it appeared commodious for one person. Maybe he would let her one of the rooms—surely there was a parlor—in which to teach piano. She thought to ask Lorena, but Lorena had much preparation to do in order to relocate to the town of Stillwater. She might as well run it by Mr. McQueen first, rather than distracting Lorena just before her departure from Lone Wolf.

In early September, Mr. McQueen came to fetch Lorena to take her to meet her train. He had borrowed C. H. Griffith's buggy, for which The Beatitudes now showed some begrudging familiarity. Mr. McQueen hoisted the steamer trunk into the back with new muscles gained by working as a field hand rippling beneath his sweat-darkened shirt. Her father hitched Buck to their saggy wagon and they formed a slow caravan to the station. Elise was invited to ride with Mr. McQueen by Mr. McQueen, but Lorena's eyebrows suggested that she politely decline.

Here came the train, steamy and whistling. Lorena hugged her father awkwardly. Her mother shed tears all over the shawl Lorena had "tossed" over her shoulders to distinguish herself on the trip and looked woefully at the steamer trunk she herself had taken so many years ago to college as it was loaded onto the train. Later, when they were back home and the house felt as if half the furniture had been removed in their brief absence (not that her sister was akin to a love seat or pie safe, just that her absence was present in every corner of every room in the house), Elise would accuse her mother of wanting to curl up in that steamer trunk and run away to Stillwater, leaving Elise, her last child, alone.

"Oh, Elise," her mother would say, which is what she so often said.

Then it was time for Elise to say goodbye to her sister. All week she had been thinking of what to whisper in her ear to bring back all the times they had slumped together beneath the blanket, singing songs the words of which were lost in the sideways snow and coyote wind of the prairie. And here was Lorena's ear and Elise's mouth poised to whisper, but all the words got sucked out of her by some unfamiliar and terrifying mix of desire, envy, and shame.

"Stillwater runs deep," she said lamely as Lorena pulled away and fell into a surprisingly affectionate embrace with Mr. McQueen, now just Gus.

For days, Elise wondered why she had said such an impudent thing, not to mention a wasted one, for Mr. McQueen was helping Lorena up the steps of the train car, as if she were the crippled one, and Elise's words were swallowed by the updraft of the steam from the idling train, its deafening hiss.

They stood frozen in the train's wake. Elise smelled the creosote of the ties on the tracks. Thereafter she could smell a telephone pole and recall all the times words failed her, chief among them the day Lorena left home for Stillwater.

All the way home, Elise's mother's nose ran, as was its custom when she cried. It made Elise aware of her own nose, the missing tip of it, and reflexively she wiped it with the back of her hand.

Elise did not cry until she accused her mother of wanting to curl up in the steamer trunk and her mother said "Oh, Elise." The house fell quiet and Elise moved through the melancholy rooms, furious at the shafts of sunlight painting portions of things—a sideboard, Lorena's bed—for their quivering violent beauty.

But Elise preferred home to school, which was soon to start.

"I'm not going back," Elise told Damyan. She met him one hot afternoon in the abandoned sod house, even though she was done with him. But the abandoned sod house was the only cool spot around save the river, and its darkness was mysterious and appealing and maybe she wasn't done with him after all. He was the only one around she could talk to besides Mr. McQueen, and he didn't count.

"What will you work?"

"Do you mean where will I work? Or what will I do?"

Damyan nodded rather than risk the wrong words.

She told him of her plan to take over for Mrs. Robertson. She said she may well need him and his brawny brothers to come pick up the piano and haul it into town to Mr. McQueen's house.

"You have inquired him?"

"No," she said. "I'm going to town tomorrow to inquire him." Then she added, because it seemed somehow necessary, "I have some errands to run."

Damyan asked her if she wanted to get steady. She said that was all she wanted in life and all that she had ever wanted, but didn't he mean "*go* steady?" And if he did, which surely he did, it was sweet of him to ask, but she needed time to think it over.

"Why?" said Damyan. She was shocked by his directness. It was not characteristic.

"Because I am about to embark on a career, which might prove to be all-consuming." As if pupils would be lined up around the block waiting to pay money to mangle Mozart.

She left Damyan in the shadowy sod house, where he said he planned to hide out from his father and sleep through the brutal noon heat. She was tempted to stay with him and nap, but that would mean Getting Steady with him. She knew one thing and one thing only about boys and that was that you can be terribly mean to them, but if you so much as let them touch the inside of your wrist, they presumed you were theirs forever, future mother of their children, and a possession over which they would fight to their death, not unlike their sidearm or horse.

A few days later at the breakfast table, she asked to take Buck into town. She needed school supplies, she said. Her father agreed with reluctance, as if he were going to do anything but talk to Buck if none of his buddies came round to discuss the war in Europe or Woodrow Wilson or whether the government would outlaw liquor or the brilliant inventions they had submitted for patents that would change the world and make them rich. Her father was a talker and Buck appeared to be deaf—Sandy had told her so, at least—so they made a good pair.

Mounting a horse was difficult when you were lame. In this way Buck proved himself worthy, for stillness was required of him, and in stillness Buck excelled.

She went first to the schoolhouse. She was glad, because for some unknown reason she did not feel right going to his house and ringing his doorbell. He was on his hands and knees, scrubbing the wide buckled floorboards with a brush and a bucket of soapy water.

"I have just swept up enough dirt to equal the lungs of forty Oklahomans," he said.

"Actually, I am Kansan by birth."

"Is that terribly different?"

"Is there a terrible difference between South Carolina and North?"

"Terrible does no justice to the gap. As snowy heaven is to fiery hell."

Elise smiled, too embarrassed to ask him again which one he came from. Whichever one it was, she gleaned it was heavenly to him, which seemed at odds with the little he said about it, the dead sheep shorn by the river rock notwithstanding.

"What brings you to town?"

"I have a business proposition to discuss with you."

"Then I should get up off my knees. You strike me as the hard-bargain type. If there is haggling involved, I will not want to be kneeling at your feet."

Mr. McQueen led her outside. They sat on the schoolhouse steps. He wiped sweat from his brow with a handkerchief he had likely tied around his mouth earlier in the manner of a bank robber. She wished they had sat at the desks or that he had invited her into the teacherage, for across the schoolyard was the outhouse where she was once thought to be waiting out the worst of the storm, thus explaining her absence, and just beyond it was the stable, where Sandy had spent his last hours before he had to leave her for Mexico. She wished she had suggested a walk, for everything about the schoolhouse reminded her of what she had come to think of as her great mistake. All the same, she realized that she could not return to school even if she did not take over Mrs. Robertson's practice. She was as done with school as she was with the Bulgarians, except perhaps Damyan, whose offer to Get Steady was still on the table.

They talked of a letter he had gotten from Lorena describing her dorm room and her roommate from Oklahoma City and the food in the cafeteria (which she realized, as he described it, was nearly identical to the one she sent home, which both reassured her and made her a little sad), and then Mr. McQueen said, "We might as well start with what it's going to cost me, this business proposition of yours."

"Only time," she said, and she explained her notion, careful not to label it an idea. The cost, for him, would be that for a few hours in the afternoons and most Saturday mornings (barring holidays or parades or other celebrations, which were common in Lone Wolf, as Lone Wolf loved a parade) he would have to tolerate the sound of children learning to play the piano. This meant mostly scales. To get the worst out of the way, she made it fairly clear that scales, played by those who have no timing and no feel for the space between notes, which is how Mrs. Robertson told her Debussy defined music, are nearly impossible to get out of your head. What she stopped short of saying is that they could quite possibly drive you mad. Lorena was particularly sensitive to Elise practicing her scales. "Enough with the doodling, please play a real and actual tune," she would shout from two or three rooms away.

"Do you mean like 'do re mi fa so la ti do'?"

"The solfa, it's called. You have musical training?"

"No, but I love music. Perhaps you could teach me to play a little."

This was unexpected. She had figured on a percentage of her profits, but perhaps her profits could be larger.

"In exchange for my tutoring you. Because you're not coming back to school this year, are you?"

She had thought this might be the hardest part of all: telling him she was done with school. But he seemed to intuit it from the way she looked at the outhouse and the stable that last held Sandy. Maybe he was remembering those awful boys down at the river with their filthy minds and gills instead of lungs, and he sensed her reluctance to return, given that she had only five toes and a missing finger, and there was her nose, which was most visible. People's eyes went to it.

Then there was the Befuddling Mystery, as it was referred to in the *Kiowa County News*. Her mother had never asked where she was going, so happy she was to have her back, but her classmates would never let it go. And it wasn't as if she could tell them the truth and be done with it, especially since Mr. McQueen, during his visit to the hospital just before they let her out, had made her question the truth, as he was wont to do.

"No," she said. "I can't come back."

"And your parents?"

You know my father, she wanted to say, and she might have were it not that Lorena, who even though she was away in Stillwater, was Getting Steady with Mr. McQueen. He was too polite to say anything critical of either of her parents.

"I wanted to talk to you first," she said. "See if you were amenable."

Mr. McQueen said that he had a spare bedroom.

"And I do mean spare. As of this morning there were some coat hangers in the closet. Other than that, it is empty and will remain so, until your pupils fill it with these scales you suggest I might find irritating."

"If at any time the arrangement becomes a burden . . ." she started.

"I am not so polite as to suffer greatly in order to refrain from telling the truth to someone who demands only the truth."

Elise thought that this was not the most wonderful thing Mr. McQueen had ever said—that would be still, and she felt always, when he told Edith Gotswegon that sometimes different subjects bleed into each other—but it was the nicest thing that anyone ever said to her. She wondered if it were true.

At supper that night, she told her parents of Mrs. Robertson's retirement and of the need created in town for a teacher of piano.

"Why, you have that piano the church ladies bought for you," her father said.

This was her plan: to make her father think it was his idea. If it came from him, he would see it through no matter her mother's objections.

"I think I could do it," she said. "Mrs. Robertson was so encouraging. But I believe we're a bit too far out in the country. It would be a hardship, especially for those in school all day, to come all the way out here. Mrs. Robertson lives smack in the middle of town. We just walked over after school was out. Everyone did."

"Are you saying you want to move to town?"

"No, Mother. I'm not quite ready to build my mansion, and if and when I do, I am not sure it will be in Lone Wolf."

Her mother looked relieved.

"What I need is someone in town to let me a room, where I could put the piano and conduct lessons."

"Why, Gus has moved out of the teacherage," her father said. "He's leased a place over on Fourth Street, just behind the church there."

"What a wonderful idea," said Elise. "I'll ask him tomorrow."

"And what about your schooling?" asked her mother. "Do you plan on going to college?"

"Maybe I could work out a trade with Mr. McQueen."

"He could tutor you after school," said her father. It was easy to lead this horse to water and easier still to make him drink. But her mother saw through everything. In that way, she was terrifying.

"And what would you offer *him*?"

"Perhaps he would like to learn to play the piano," she said.

"That's a mighty big perhaps," her mother said. "A grown man as busy as Gus."

Elise realized that soon, very soon, she too could refer to Mr. McQueen by his first name.

"Gus loves music," said her father. "I have heard him humming on many occasions."

Her mother looked at Elise in a way that suggested that humming and loving music are not the same thing, nor are humming and wanting to take piano lessons when you are a grown man and already doing what most men thought of as women's work. Her mother could communicate a lot in a glance, if you knew how to interpret her glances.

"I suppose I could ask him," said Elise. She made herself sound skeptical if not reluctant.

"I can run into town and work out the details with old Gus," said her father.

Since it was your idea, Father? Elise thought of asking, but instead she said she needed to go to town to speak to Mrs. Robertson about the practicalities, scheduling and charging.

"In other words, to put it plainly, the nuts and bolts of the thing," said her father.

"Exactly. I'll stop by and see Mr. McQueen. Thank you, Father. You've been so helpful."

"Anything for my girl," he said.

"She's no longer a girl," her mother said, blowing into her cup of tea and watching the steam shift in the air of the kitchen, before giving Elise a sideways glance that suggested that after so many years adrift, her mother had willed herself present and accounted for.

Toward the end of September Damyan's father agreed to let his sons off work for an afternoon to move the piano, and he would provide the wagon but only if Elise would agree to play for him as he drove them into town. The piano was roped to the sides of the wagon, as it shifted and rattled on the corduroyed road. Elise bounced on the bench, the legs of which were tied as well. The Bulgarians lay about in the wagon half-asleep except for Damyan who insisted on sitting alongside her to turn the page at her nod.

"What sort of music does your father like?" she asked him.

"He is fond of march."

March? Elise knew only Chopin's funeral march, which was far too lugubrious for the occasion.

"Do you know the march of John Phyllis Susan?"

"Good heavens," she said. "Your father has certainly taken to America."

"I like also 'Grand Old Flag,'" said Damyan.

They were certainly doing her a good turn, and if they wanted a parade, she'd have to oblige. She herself could never get steady with an admirer of the likes of Sousa, but on the other hand, it was not her job to convert him to the Goldberg Variations.

She played "Semper Fidelis," "The Stars and Stripes Forever," and, for Damyan, "You're a Grand Old Flag." As they came into town she switched to the slightly less pompous Stephen Foster: first "Camptown Races" (the Bulgarian boys woke to sing, Oh the doo dah day) and then "Oh! Susanna." Their accents added a desirably melancholic element to the fellow coming from Louisiana with a banjo on his knee. The harshness of their consonants turned even the silliest song plaintive.

People came out of their houses as they passed. Dusty children and bored dogs followed the wagon, and her father, on Buck, pranced alongside, beaming. Elise was surprisingly not mortified. Why? How far was she willing to stoop to free herself from life on the Lorena-less farm? She banged out "Battle Hymn of the Republic" as they pulled up in front of Mr. McQueen's bungalow. He came out onto the porch, looking both bewildered and amused. Elise decided that his amusement came from a false notion that she was being ironic, when actually (and this worried her) she was roused by all this sentimental rubbish.

Mr. McQueen had hung a couple of pictures on the walls of her piano room—a Turner reproduction, which she quite liked for its muted orange light, and a painting of a river with a gaggle of small boys gathered on its banks, fishing poles flung over their shoulder, barefooted, their towheads covered by straw hats. Was this supposed to remind her of the time he flung the nasty-minded boys in the river? If Lorena were here, she would tell Elise not to assign meaning to everything, but Lorena was off in college, learning to assign meaning to everything.

In one corner was a table and, placed atop it, a vase of well-intentioned wildflowers. The room lacked a rug, but she could bring one from home.

Mr. McQueen conversed with the Bulgarian's father in the few words he had picked up from the boys. Elise's father supervised the unloading and placement of the piano, for he had a bad back himself.

Mr. McQueen gave Damyan and his brothers nickels and sent them off to the picture show, then invited the Bulgarian and her father to stroll down the street for a beer.

"We won't be long," he told Elise, and she nodded and smiled and nearly bowed trying to get them out of there. The words "Should auld acquaintance be forgot" were stuck in her head and she set down to play a Bach prelude to try to dislodge them. She was alone in Mr. McQueen's house. She quit playing when her head was clear, got up, and walked around, feeling like a ghost come back to search for still-living kin—in this case, her sister. For she felt Lorena's presence everywhere —in the parlor, in the kitchen, even in Mr. McQueen's spartan bedroom. She opened his narrow closet and flipped through his hanging clothes, searching for one of her dresses. Lorena was there even though she left no physical trace. What was a physical trace worth anyway?

The men came home from the saloon and sat talking on the porch as she serenaded them through the open window. Then the boys arrived, oddly jolly—even Damyan—from having seen *The Virginian*. Elise's father said he would ride home with the Bulgarians and left Buck tied to a tree in the yard. Elise sat down with Mr. McQueen on his front porch, waving at the cheery Bulgarians, her father talking wildly with his hands to his new friend.

"This is the most exciting thing to happen on Fourth Street since I don't know when," said Mr. McQueen.

"Likely since the young schoolteacher moved in. What news of my brilliant sister?"

"She has been advised that she must take chemistry."

"Oh dear," said Elise, though she knew this already from Lorena's most recent letter. "We may well be reading about a ghastly explosion in the no-longer-so-still town of Stillwater."

"As I understand it, it's not chemistry if something does not ignite. As I understand it," he repeated, "not having gone to college myself."

"Did you always want to be a teacher?"

"It never crossed my mind. I was working in a millinery shop, sweeping up ribbon and thread, when you could say I was drafted." He told the story of Dr. Hall coming to his house. Of his mediocre performance in school until, late in his studies, he revealed his talent for memorization.

"Your good memory bodes well for your piano playing."

"More is required than memorization, though, I'm sure. I would wager that the inexplicable ingredient is what makes your playing so graceful and precise."

"The what?"

"Your true cry, Elise."

"Oh, that," she said, as if he were referring to her nine-fingered technique rather than the essence of her very being. "I don't think I'll ever be a serious person."

Mr. McQueen laughed. "Your great appeal is what sometimes makes you hard to understand, Elise. But back to your point: I don't think I will either."

"It's your part," she said.

"My part? My part to play in life, you mean?"

"No," she said, and reached over and touched the place where his comb so carefully separated his hair. "It's too perfect," she said.

"Ought I to alter it in some way?"

"Never. It's the perfect part that makes you imperfect and therefore disqualifies you from serious personhood."

Mr. McQueen said something vaguely profound-sounding about how Persian rug makers always left some irregularity in their stitching to show their belief that no human design could be without blemish. Only God can create perfection, etcetera. But Elise could tell that, halfway through his spiel, he recognized how pedantic he sounded, so she stepped in to save him from himself.

"Lorena is a serious person," said Elise.

Mr. McQueen was silent.

"It's all she's ever wanted in life."

Mr. McQueen's silence grew louder.

"I think it has to do with our raising," said Elise. "My father is anything but serious, given as he is to the endless discussion of ideas."

"Ideas are not serious?"

"Ideas are indeed serious. It's going around thinking you have one and proceeding to tell everyone all about it that distinguishes you as not serious."

"And your mother? Is she a serious person?"

"My mother has lately exhibited signs of rejoining the party."

Mr. McQueen waited for more, but Elise changed the subject.

"We've yet to discuss the particulars of our arrangement. Every time I bring it up you put me off. Why is that?"

"I've no head for business," said Mr. McQueen.

"But I do, and I do not feel comfortable embarking on our joint venture until some terms have been agreed upon."

"You've worn me down," said Mr. McQueen. "State your terms."

"Go fetch paper and pencil," she said. "Nothing in the business world is valid until recorded and endorsed by signature."

In time, they came up with an agreement that Elise felt was too much in her favor. She argued with him, but he put an end to it by saying she was family.

This made her feel not treasured, as he had no doubt intended, but placed in a category that did not feel, well, *right*. She wondered if he and Lorena were secretly engaged. Could Lorena keep something like that from her?

No, she would know if they were engaged, just like she knew when they Got Steady. Lorena went around with her for weeks and said nothing, but Elise knew all the same. Elise was not of the mind that secrets were the same as lies (they were more like second cousins). Hadn't Lorena and Mr. McQueen kept secret the reason for her wandering off into the storm?

The storm made Elise think of Big Idea. She had never spoken to him, but she had heard his voice in the storm. It seemed to Elise like someone else might be speaking to her through that icy wind, when she was convinced that she and Sandy had ridden right into heaven, which was much like the North Pole, apparently. She was turning blue, yellow, and white, and the snow was turning red. The voice of God should come at such moments, but she heard Big Idea. "Big Idea," she called out, and somewhere miles away on the prairie a stranger, fetching her mail or feeding his cows, heard in the wind the true cry of a frozen girl.

"Elise," said Mr. McQueen. She looked over at him. Other people were out on their porches of an evening backlit in pink dusk. Instead of swarms of bugs, the golden light identified each insect. She saw the stingers of mosquitoes and flies rubbing their hands greedily. What a strange thing it was to look right and see other people and then left and see more of the same. She had discovered civilization. Mr. McQueen allowed as how he too had come up in the country without neighbors within sight, and life on Fourth Street in tiny Lone Wolf was a marvel to him. The sidewalks, the gaslights, the church bells chiming on the hour. At night he heard through his open windows the noises of cutlery scraping plates, of babies splashing in bathtubs. He heard singing, from mediocre to atrocious.

"Sometimes I can hear the doors of an icebox suck shut," he said. "I have heard the clothes-less hangers clang together in someone's closet. Think about it."

She thought about it. She thought maybe he only *thought* he heard it, but it was the same thing.

"Do you fear loneliness?"

"I do," he said. "I have. It was why I went at night to the river. But I could have crossed the river to escape my loneliness and I did not do it. I liked the power that came from not letting myself. So you might say I fear it as I court it."

She nodded. "I only wanted to write that stupid play to get Lorena to come with me to the barn. Every afternoon when we got home she went straight to Mother's bedroom and combed her hair. I missed her. So I decided I would write the story of the murder of Sherman by Ivent so that it involved a dramatic fall from the hayloft onto a carefully placed blanket of hay. This is not what happened, as you know. Ivent was shot in a saloon, but I think you will agree that such facts do not matter to the playwright. Anyway, I had to offer Lorena the part of Sherman, who falls after being shot by Ivent, but she was not swayed. We disagreed about some minor details. What she called fact. We had never argued over facts before. It was disturbing, at least to me, for it seemed somehow that our lives changed the moment she held fast to her facts.

"Anyway, the reason I left school and went blindly and with foolish disregard into a blizzard, endangering not only my life but yours and Lorena's, was because I did not want to be alone."

She turned to Mr. McQueen.

"I am sorry," she said. Then she remembered: he knew this already. He knew even more than she did about the real reason she went blindly into the storm. He came to the hospital to tell her. He had pulled his chair close to speak of her true cry.

But he only nodded and reached out and rubbed her shoulder. It was an innocuous gesture meant to say, Please do not give it a minute's thought. But when his fingers touched her collarbone, she felt the presence of her missing toes and the finger upon which some man might have decided to slip a ring in front of a preacher, and also the tip of her nose, which she had forgotten was even missing. She felt her shame blossom into pleasure.

She said, "I need to get going, although, my goodness, but is it not pleasant here at this hour." Porch-sitters out on both sides of the street, old women cooling themselves with cardboard church fans, children hiding behind shrubs, and dogs chasing the children around, everyone as happy as pigs. She wanted to stay until the dark blinked with lightning bugs. She would have liked to wake to the sound of the *Kiowa County News* tossed sidearm but accurately by a boy on a bicycle onto the dew-wet grass. She would have liked to run outside in her nightgown barefoot to retrieve it and read aloud to Mr. McQueen while he sipped his coffee all the doings and goings-on and, if they were lucky, a murder involving an agent of the Schlitz Brewing Company.

"I better be going," she said again.

"I'll be seeing a lot of you."

"Your terms are too favorable toward me."

"As I understand it, a contract, once signed, is immediately binding."

"You don't know the first thing about a contract."

"It's true," he said, smiling. "I don't."

"I can always tell."

"How's that?"

"You were my teacher," she said. "I gave you the benefit of my doubt. I assumed you knew everything there is to know. And you know a lot. But sometimes you know things because you have read them in a book the night before and you remember the facts in the proper order. Like all that business about prehistoric animals blazing the Natchez Trace."

"But that is not a lie."

"You must," she said, getting up, "tell me more about the dead sheep that washed up on the shore of the river. You must say more about the river. More about why you went there. More about whether or not it helped to go there. I want to know what you learned. I dare-say that will be more helpful for me in my pursuits than the origins of the Natchez Trace."

Mrs. Robertson had left a dozen pupils in need of instruction and she was kind enough to write to them recommending Elise. Elise's mother could no longer afford to keep Mr. McQueen on, so he took a job proofreading the *Kiowa County News*. He went to their offices directly after school. Some days she did not see him. On Saturday she came into town to teach an older woman, Miss Pruett. She was nearly thirty, rich, haughty, and without talent. Elise could hear Mr. McQueen moving around the house as she reminded Miss Pruett to curl her fingers at the knuckles. For some reason she pictured Mr. McQueen shaving, though she knew this to be a morning ritual and it was getting on toward lunchtime. Did he wear an undershirt or stand shirtless before the mirror? Miss Pruett finished her scales, and Elise said "Again" in the stern manner of Mrs. Robertson. Miss Pruett disliked taking lessons from a sixteen-year-old girl, Elise could tell, but her only other choice was to travel to Hobart, and she was too busy being rich and idle for that.

Mr. McQueen appeared in the doorway after Miss Pruett left. Elise was packing up to leave.

"I feel it is probably advantageous to start piano lessons when you are still young," he said, referring to the abysmal playing of Miss Pruett and, by extension, to his own upcoming instruction.

"You are not very scientific."

"Pardon?"

"Basing your hypothesis on only one test case. Besides, she is hoping to find a husband, one with money and taste. So she is attempting to round herself out, culturally I mean. She's plenty round otherwise. The sad thing is she is getting a little long in the tooth."

"That woman who just left? She appears to be about thirty."

"An ancient crone in these parts. She might as well settle for a Kiowa. Perhaps one with a couple of wives already."

"The Kiowa are not bigamists."

Mr. McQueen had a special interest in the Kiowa. He once told Lorena and Elise that after he first arrived he asked Mr. C. H. Griffith if he would have to learn their language to teach them and was shocked to discover that they had their own school.

"Your point seems to be that it is too late for you to learn to play the piano. Frankly I am disheartened by such a sentiment. When is it ever too late to learn?"

"I have been set straight," said Mr. McQueen, feigning resignation.

"You will submit to lessons per our agreement. Otherwise we will have to renegotiate our terms."

"'Submit' is an unappealing verb."

"You will enrich your life with piano lessons as agreed upon, etcetera."

"I prefer 'submit,'" he said.

"'Submit,' as you pointed out, almost suggests punishment. But you will love taking lessons."

"And so the student becomes the teacher."

"Does that make you nervous?"

"Not in the least. You have been teaching me since I arrived here."

"So has Edith Gotswegon, in her way."

"You and your sister are obsessed with Edith Gotswegon."

"It is what she stands for. She herself does not exist, or rather, if she exists at all, it is in the music of her name, which is fun to say and so aptly captures what she stands for."

"She makes good sense and that appears to be her goal in life."

"You are distracting me. When would you like to experience the distinct joy of a piano lesson?"

"Some night this week will have to do. I am going to Stillwater for the weekend."

Elise nodded. Mr. McQueen looked at his feet.

The day before, while he was still at his proofreading job at the *Kiowa County News* and she was done with her lessons, she had searched his house for Lorena's letters, which she had found in his sock drawer, of course. But how had she known that men hid everything in their sock drawer? Was she born with this knowledge? Are all women born knowing such?

She read them. Later, when she asked after Lorena (pretending that Lorena did not write home, which he likely knew was not true), the facts he shared were the same Lorena reported: she hated chemistry; her roommate was Oklahoma City society and had so many dresses Lorena barely had room in the closet; the weather; food; football team; etcetera. But the letters went beyond reportage. Elise expected her sister to be mushy, but this was a shock. *Oh, how I long for you to hold me. I miss your lips. I'd give everything I own* (What, wondered Elise, was she referring to? The pearl-handled brush-and-mirror set Mother had lent her? Her mother's beloved steamer trunk?) *to be lying beside you, Gus, running my hand through your hair.*

Elise put the letters back in the sock drawer. So little guilt did she feel for reading them that she worried about herself. This was new and a curiosity: feeling bad about *not* feeling bad.

In her head, leading the stubborn Buck home that evening, Elise imagined the letter she might write to him, were she Lorena. At night, lying awake in the attic, moonlight striping the empty cot of her mushy-letter-writing sister, she sat up beneath a lamp turned low and wrote out a draft.

Dearest Gus—

"Wherefore art thou" does not mean "where are you," sweet man. It means "what are you doing right now, pray tell, I would dearly like to know." I feel like I might die if you don't tell me what you are doing right this minute. I will be found in the morning, stiff as a frozen board, having died from lack of the thing I need to know, which is what you are doing.

I like to imagine you going about your day, having arrived early to school on The Beatitudes, that lumbering sweet-natured beast who behaved so bravely in the storm that tragically disfigured my little sister on that fateful day in our history. ~~The day that sealed our fate.~~

Perhaps you are stoking the stove so that the schoolhouse is warm for those children arriving pinned in blankets from far out in the country, except there aren't any, not after Elise and me. You will never encounter two girls or even one girl or, for heaven's sake, a boy who knows to construct a sky of blanket above them, their own universe with its rules and systems and strange characters (e.g., Big Idea and, of course, Edith Gotswegon). Never will you encounter another horse like Sandy, who knows the way to every destination in all the far corners of the earth and who even knew the way in that storm, actually. The only reason he strayed from the road was owing to human error. Were it up to him, had his advice been heeded, nothing bad would have ever happened and I would have made it to Hobart in one piece instead of missing several key pieces. Did I tell you I heard from Sandy? I had a lovely letter from him. He has joined a circus. He grew tired of cliff diving, as one does. He penned his expansive and news-packed missive in the town of Mexia, Texas. His rider in the circus is a Mexican who goes by Julio but whose real name is Juan. He is a dwarf. He rides Sandy while standing. Under the supposed guidance of Julio, Sandy gallops around a circle while Julio does back flips through rings of fire held by locals plucked from the audience. Sandy let Juan believe he had trained him for this venture because that it is his way, but of course Sandy was born knowing how to please a crowd, his timing being impeccable.

In his missive he said an interesting thing. I have now traveled widely, he wrote. I have lived by the sea and spent time in Mexico City with its overcrowded thoroughfares and drunken men hanging off streetcars in the gloaming. I have been to Houston, a buggy and malarial blight built entirely on swampland, filled with men made ruthless by the promise of fortune and horses equally ruthless in their dream of finer tack and fresh and bountiful hay. I have crossed mountains in the territory they call New Mexico and on stony hillsides I have come across the ruins of ancient peoples. But it is the prairie of which I dream. At night I close my eyes and hear the singing grass. I miss the grasshoppers hopping at the last millisecond out of my way. I even miss the wind. I know it to be relentless and punishing, but in memory it appears as movement, a reminder of the grand contradiction of the prairie. The plains stretch away to the sky and you sense it as it came into being, unchanged and therefore fixed, but in fact the wind keeps it from stasis. Sooner or later every grain of dirt is picked up and set down elsewhere. Horses succumb to its movement, finding new pastures to feast on, and in time people do also, but often not traveling far. Sometimes they erect new houses within sight of the old home place.

It was time for me to move on, wrote Sandy in his missive postmarked Mexia, Texas. But I know my way home.

Back to you, Gus. I see you going about the business of preparing for the school day. From a book held open, you copy pithy aphorisms on the board for the children to learn. You sit at your desk and go over your lesson plans. The children begin to trickle in. You hear them before you see them, for they are raucous in the schoolyard, knowing their day will be spent in silence. You are a gifted teacher, Gus. You know how to ask the question, even if you don't always, my dear, know the right questions to ask. At least you know enough not to presume to know the answer, for who but Edith Gotswegon expects that from you, or even cares about it?

Oh, Gus, I miss you so. But I must now share a vision I had that involves, well, *sharing*. The other night I was coming home from a study session, and my route back to the dorm took me right past the music building. The windows of the basement practice rooms were open and from each came the sounds of musicians honing their skills. (Some, I should add, were not yet in possession of what I would call skills, but still, they were, as my father would say, "hard at it.") I lingered awhile beneath a tree—a weeping willow, in fact, which is as you know my favorite tree—and listened, and it was then that I had my idea. You love music. You told me once you wanted to learn to play an instrument. Why not get Elise to teach you the piano? Elise is, as we know, an impetuous girl, but she is a gifted musician and an assiduous teacher. I even thought it might prove both convenient and mutually beneficial—and pardon me for being presumptuous—if Elise moved her piano into your spare room. She could give lessons to others there, which would be a good thing for her, as I highly doubt anyone would want to travel from town out to the farm for instruction. You might gussy (pun intended!) up the place, for it is a bit bleak in there. Perhaps you might hang the Turner reproduction on one wall, as it gives off a solemn but transcendent aura, much like the music of Chopin.

Of course this is for you and Elise to decide, but perhaps you could work out some remuneration that involves the cost of lessons for you? Oh, tell me, Gus, what do you think of my idea? Write to me this minute. I want to hear your thoughts. If only I were there to discuss this with you in person. But for now this flimsy paper will have to suffice.

With all my deepest love,
Lorena

Reading over her letter the next morning, Elise realized how bad she was at pretending to be anyone other than who she was. The first half of the letter, with its lengthy update on Sandy, was pure *her.* Why would Sandy ever contact Lorena? He loved her deeply and protected her equally from the elements, but Lorena, who claimed always to be the "rider" to Elise's "passenger," did not share with Sandy the special bond. Lorena often described Sandy as "a very fine horse." Once she even said to Elise, "Sandy is a horse." This showed just how much she knew. All she did not know about Sandy, about the world beyond the world in which Sandy and Elise moved, would never be taught to her at college in Stillwater.

Only toward the late middle of the letter did Elise remember to speak from her sister's voice. She proved a feeble parrot. Lorena's voice was both proper and wry. Certainly she was capable of a sharpness of tone. Plus the letters found in Gus's sock drawer were all of a type. If Elise had to classify them, she would put them in the mushy category. Lorena had no example of Elise speaking to Gus of matters that were serious.

Then she understood the reason she'd written it: someone had to tell Lorena what was going on. It would not do for her to find out that Elise had taken up partial residence in Mr. McQueen's house. It would certainly not do for Lorena to find out from someone else that Elise was, in effect, running a business out of Mr. McQueen's house. Therefore the solution was to rewrite the letter but address it to Lorena. She must broach the *idea* (pretending, of course, that the enterprise of which she spoke was not already well established, that contracts had not been drawn up, that she was adding students, etc.) and do so with such persuasive skill that Lorena, in the manner of their father, with whom she had more in common that she cared to admit, would think the idea hers alone.

It had not occurred to her to think about Lorena in her dealings with Mr. McQueen. But she knew that Lorena would not be exactly happy to hear that she was doing what she was doing. Yet why should she concern herself with what her sister would think, since Mr. McQueen never mentioned it? Elise spent many hours debating whose responsibility it was to inform Lorena of the arrangement. On the one hand, she had known Lorena longest. On the other hand, she had read enough novels to know that when one falls in love with the stranger-come-to-town, one always forsakes family.

In Lorena's case, there was not much to forsake. She hated their father and she treated their mother as if she were a child, except when her mother was presenting her with the ceremonial college steamer trunk, which she accepted with alacrity.

Sandy was away, traveling.

That left only Elise to leave behind. They were but a single bag of giggly bones beneath the blanket that was the sky. Was that not forever? Had the two of them taken off for Hobart together that day—had Lorena not remained in the classroom—Elise would walk, and even run, like a normal person.

Elise understood then: that was the moment when she had been forsaken. Lorena had chosen Gus over her sister, with whom she had shared a skin and a sky.

6

GUS MCQUEEN

Lone Wolf, Oklahoma, Fall 1917

With both Lorena and Elise gone, Gus found even less pleasure in teaching. He even felt the loss of Edith Gotswegon, who could be counted upon for an antagonistic friction that kept everyone half-awake.

Gus put his energy into teaching the Bulgarians to properly employ articles, but they came to school only for the first week and then disappeared. He did not see them again until they brought Elise's piano to his house a few weeks later. Their father drove the wagon while Elise played his favorite patriotic songs.

Climbing down off the wagon, watching the Bulgarians unload her piano, Elise looked both embarrassed and enthused. Gus supposed she was enthusiastic about setting up her piano studio in his spare room. He had little furniture, but the house was solidly built (crucial in the windy spring and frigid winter) and the fireplace drew so well he barely needed kindling. There was indoor plumbing, a luxury he had never experienced. Two rectangular bedrooms with closets opened onto a hallway that led to the tiled bathroom. A back porch had been converted into a kitchen (a summer kitchen stood still in the backyard, as well as a good-size barn for The Beatitudes), and the floor sloped, but the cookstove was new. Gus was twenty years old and he had a house and a sweetheart. His fireplace drew. He had a job. He needed another now that he had to pay for his lodging and was no longer working for Mr. Stewart, who had let him go after the cotton harvest.

After school one day Gus went down to the *Kiowa County News* and asked if they needed a part-time reporter. He had met the editor, a Mr. Jeremiah Starling, and made it clear, lest it get back to C. H. Griffith, that he would be keeping his teaching post but could work nights and on the weekends when he did not travel to Stillwater.

Mr. Starling said there was no such thing as a part-time reporter, nor was it customary when seeking employment to reserve the right to take weekends off to visit your sweetheart up at the university. However, he said, he could use someone to proof the columns written by community correspondents.

"Mrs. Eleanor Singleton, who covers Gotebo, cannot spell Gotebo."

"That's a tricky one," Gus said to appear agreeable.

"No, it's not. It is spelled exactly like it sounds. I have to sit down with her column and translate every word into standard English. Not only her, but almost all the others. There is one man, a lawyer from out at Retrop, who might know a sentence if it crawled into bed with him, but the others are hopeless. It is time-consuming and it takes me away from my principle task, which is to afflict the comfortable."

"When do I start?"

"I can't pay much. People around here believe the paper ought to be free. They think it is a public service. Advertisers are slow to pay their bills, and folks who consider themselves upstanding will steal their neighbor's paper without the slightest bit of Christian remorse."

"I am a huge fan of your newspaper, Mr. Starling," said Gus. He thought but did not say that it did a lousy job of keeping the wind out of the teacherage and that it had indirectly caused a girl to nearly die of frostbite, both good things to leave out of the interview, but he had been introduced to the paper by Elise quoting from it, and he was— he remained— a devoted reader.

"The job is yours if you will answer one question for me."

Gus figured the question would involve grammar. His grasp of grammar was mostly instinctive, though thanks to Dr. Hall, he could diagram a sentence.

"Fire away," said Gus, preparing to be shot down.

"You were mentioned in an article I wrote about the Stewart girl who got lost in the blizzard."

"Yes?"

"You declined to be interviewed. Why?"

This was his question? Gus was flustered by it.

"I declined at the request of the mother, who did not feel the publicity would be good for the girl," he said. This was not exactly a lie, since should Mrs. Stewart have been capable of expressing her desires, surely she would have felt this way.

"Now that the girl has recuperated and has been given a piano by the Women of the Church as reported in the paper, and has, I hear, recently taken over Miss Mary Margaret Burke Kerr Robertson's piano practice, I wonder if you might answer the question I would have asked had you consented to the interview."

Gus would not betray either sister for a job correcting the grammar of the writer of News from the Gotebo Community. But he realized that he did not have to betray anyone. He could say, honestly, I don't know. He knew what Lorena had told him, and she was not a liar, but when he visited Elise in the hospital the day she was discharged, and she had talked about hearing one's true cry, he realized that her trip was only ostensibly about research. He had said as much to her. She had asked him to elaborate. Then the lovely nurse had come, saving him as he and Lorena had saved Elise, and also themselves.

Gus said, "I don't know why she left school that day or where she was going."

Mr. Starling looked at him in a manner that reminded Gus of the expression of Abraham Lincoln in the office of C. H. Griffith, but when he walked out the door, he was employed by the *Kiowa County News*. When Elise had come to the schoolhouse, asking if she could teach piano lessons from his spare room, Gus had said yes without thinking about it. He liked the idea of his house filled with students of Beethoven and Bach. He thought to inform C. H. Griffith, in case the neighbors gossiped about the goings-on at the schoolteacher's house, but it was easy to talk himself out of a trip to C. H. Griffith's office.

He meant to tell Lorena in each letter he wrote, but for some reason he did not. He was planning on it. If he were a list maker, telling Lorena that Elise was operating a business out of his spare bedroom would top his things to do.

But it was easy enough to believe that Lorena would be thrilled. She was away in Stillwater and he was alone here, and it would not hurt for him to have someone to talk to. Who else but Elise? The scale-practicing Elise predicted would drive him crazy was beautiful to him. Do re mi fa so la ti do, climbing up and down the keyboard, in and out of tune, wrong notes and right ones, he could hear it from the street walking up the sidewalk, and it was as lovely as birdsong.

If Elise were with a pupil when Gus got home, he would set up at the kitchen table and work on his proofreading, which Mr. Starling allowed him to take home because he paid by the page. Mr. Starling was prone to sneaking in, between the community reports, reminders to readers to settle their bills:

> Is there an X in front of your name on this paper? Look and see, and if there is, it means your subscription has expired and you are gently reminded that the editor needs the money as much as you do.

Gus wondered why Mr. Starling, instead of gently reminding his readers in arrears, did not simply stop delivery. He decided Mr. Starling took great delight in being slighted. His gentle reminders gave him obvious pleasure. Gus shared them with Elise, who loved them, especially the one about the farmer and his wife, which he read to her several times the day it appeared in the paper.

TOLD IN A DREAM

A FARMER HAD a dream. He dreamed that he had raised a thousand bushels of wheat and he was happy over the fact. Then he dreamed that he had sold his wheat for a dollar a bushel and his happiness was great. But now he dreamed that he had sold it to a thousand different people, a bushel to each person, and that nobody had paid him and he was sad. When he awoke it was broad daylight and leaping out of bed he exclaimed to his wife, "Rebecca, I have had a solemn warning and I know the meaning of it. I am going right off to town and pay the editor the dollar I owe him for the paper.

"He is lucky, that farmer," said Elise. "I have had many solemn warnings and I haven't known the meaning of any of them."

"What I would like to know is Rebecca's reply to the farmer," said Gus.

"You be the farmer and I will be Rebecca," she said. She studied him, still in his school clothes. "Go and tie your handkerchief around your neck at the very least. You look too much like a schoolmaster to play the part convincingly."

Gus got up and went into his bedroom. He rooted around in his sock drawer, searching for his bandanna. Lorena's letters were hidden there or, rather, stored there—he had no reason to hide them, at least until that moment, when he realized that they were on the opposite side of the drawer from they'd been that morning. (Gus was strongly right-sided and would *never* have hidden the letters on the left side of the drawer.) He doubted Elise allowed her students to wander about his house, but he knew that her lessons sometimes went over, as he had come home to find pupils sitting in his parlor, impatiently waiting their turn. It could have been one of them. He remembered going through his father's drawers and finding, beneath his socks, a photograph of his mother and a purple felt box containing a wedding band with a tiny diamond. His mother's, obviously. There was also a photograph of his father and Aunt Mattie atop a donkey, the river in the background. When his father left to find work in Charlotte, he took most of his socks but not the wedding ring or the photographs. Gus had brought them along with him to Lone Wolf. The only reason they were not hidden in his sock drawer (they were just below, in his underwear drawer) was because he took great pains not to be like his father.

Perhaps it wasn't a good idea, storing Lorena's letters in his sock drawer. It seemed an obvious hiding place, though he would not have put it beyond Elise to rummage through his underwear drawer. He could have left Lorena's letters on the table, tied with the snippet of ribbon he'd found in a pants pocket, a reminder of his life in

Hibriten, his past securing his future, but it did not seem in good taste, given the tone of the letters. They were impassioned. Lying in bed nights, he reread them and he could feel the blood start to flow through veins that became a vast network of tracks conveying trains to a central location. And then the convergence in his groin, and minutes later he would catch his breath with his pants around his shins and his stomach coated with semen. This is the only way he knew to truly answer her letters. He did not know how to write the sort of sentences that brought to life, in the push and pull of their very music, he and Lorena, lying beneath a weeping willow by the river, twisting around on a scratchy Kiowa blanket, kissing until their lips were chapped, for that was as far as they had taken it, as far as they would take it until they were properly married.

How, he wondered, did Lorena know to write such sentences? She knew because there was nothing between her words and her feelings. Even the paper she wrote on—even the envelope that transported the letter to Lone Wolf, even the stamp—seemed extraneous. She loved him, did Lorena. And he loved her, though what came between his feelings and his words?

"Your wife awaits you," Elise called from the dining room.

Gus found his kerchief and tied it around his neck. He did not have a thing to hide from Elise and yet the thought of her reading Lorena's letters made him queasy in the way he used to feel when Aunt Mattie failed to pack his lunch and he grew so hungry his stomach ached. Why should Gus feel empty instead of spied upon? He pictured Elise standing right where he was standing, her hands in his sock drawer. Her eyes would be closed. She would be pretending that the drawer was filled with salt water and the balls of socks were sand dollars or shark's teeth. Or maybe she would yank open every drawer in the house, contents spilling out of them, as if the place had been ransacked. She would find the letters and read them aloud sitting on the edge of the bed, her sister's impassioned sentences climbing up and down the keyboard, mostly wrong notes to Elise's trained ear, annoying as a crow's caw.

Gus pulled his kerchief up over his mouth as if prepared for a windstorm.

"Tell me your dream," Elise said when he came into the room.

"Rebecca," said Gus. "I have had a solemn warning and I know the meaning of it."

"Lucky you," said Elise.

"Don't interrupt," Gus said, speaking as Gus. "And stay in character."

Elise sighed. She recomposed herself and sat up straight in the guise of Rebecca.

"I have had a solemn warning and I know the meaning of it," said Gus as the farmer. He said it again, slower and louder. He pulled his kerchief off, unable to continue.

"What is it?" said Elise.

"I really should get back to work," said Gus.

She nodded and got up quickly. He could tell she was upset by the way she walked. When something was bothering her, she took care to walk lightly, in such a way that her specially built shoe made no more noise on the floorboards than a slipper.

Gus wanted to say he was sorry, but he had had a solemn warning, and it was not Elise to whom he should have been apologizing.

But the next day Elise was still there when he got home and she helped him proofread by reading aloud (with great delight) the copy while he double-checked the spelling and grammar. He forgot all about the letters. A few nights later, they sat late on the porch as up and down the street his neighbors visited in front yards or strolled up and down the sidewalk, calling out one another's names. Gentlemen tipped their hats. Everyone was smiling and no one was tipsy. He and Elise spoke of how refreshing it was to observe such street life, growing up as they both did in the country, with forests and a river for neighbors in his case, grassland and pasture and a stubby range of hills in hers. He told Elise of sounds he heard in the night: cutlery scraping plates, babies splashing in tubs, an icebox sucking shut.

"I have heard clothes hangers banging together in someone's closet."

"Do you fear loneliness?" she asked.

He thought about it and decided that the image of empty hangers clanging together was a rather lonely one. Only the unfeeling, like his father, did not fear loneliness.

Elise told him about the reason she rode blindly into the storm atop Sandy. At first Gus thought to shush her, lest he feel duty bound to report back to Mr. Starling, but her reasons—that she wanted Lorena to play with her because she was lonely, that Lorena's insistence on a single "fact" was the beginning of what Elise called "the shift" in their lives—did not warrant a report.

He had a house and two jobs and a fireplace that drew like a magnet. He had indoor plumbing and the cookstove was new. He had a wedding ring that was not doing anyone any good, hiding out in his underwear drawer.

When they were engaged, Lorena would not mind at all if Elise taught piano lessons in the spare room. If he told her of the arrangement after he presented her with his mother's ring and asked her to marry him, she would be thrilled, for she still felt guilty about what happened to Elise, and it seemed the meaning of the solemn warning was for Elise to come and live with them in the bungalow.

After Elise left each night, he often went into the spare room and sat at the piano. He ran his fingers over the keyboard without pressing the ivory. Any sound he could get out of the instrument would not be music and would, he knew, make him feel things he did not want to feel. Elise had offered to teach him, but for some reason they never got around to it. She had offered again a couple of nights before he was to leave for Stillwater.

When he told her he was going to Stillwater, he had looked at his feet.

The next night he stayed late at the schoolhouse, finishing up the proofs for Mr. Starling, who did not care for the fact that Gus was going to see his sweetheart in Stillwater, until Gus let slip that he was going there to propose. Mr. Starling said, "Well, then, that changes the landscape considerably." Gus had already turned in his edits when Mr. Starling added, along with another notice to readers who were in arrears, the following lines on the second page of the paper, which Gus did not read because (a) he had turned in his edits and (b) he was on a train to Stillwater when it came out.

> Gus McQueen, schoolmaster in Lone Wolf, left on the 8:37 for Stillwater, where he will visit with his fiancée, Lorena Stewart, of Gotebo Road, now enrolled at the university.

When Gus got home that night, on the kitchen table was a note from Elise in which she admitted to stealing mint from a neighbor to make tea and suggested he speak to Lorena of their "business arrangement."

On the train the next morning, Gus took out Elise's note from the inside pocket of his suit jacket and reread it. Lorena's letters were in his bag, beneath his socks and underwear, but it was Elise's short note that he reread. *"Wherefore art thou" does not mean "where," but I do mean "where," even though it is hardly any of my business.* The rest of the note—*I waited for you because I thought we ought to discuss informing Lorena of our business arrangement. I have not written to her about it, as I thought I should speak first with you, and since you are going to Stillwater on the train, perhaps it would be better coming from you?*—struck Gus as uncharacteristically rational. Everything about it sounded false. She was forcing herself to say something she felt she ought to say and her ambivalence was as obvious in the writing as Lorena's love was in the music of her letters.

Had they done something underhanded? Was it his fault? He was the one who was supposed to inform Lorena. And he would do so, after he gave her the ring that bulged in its purple felt box in the pocket of his trousers.

Few women attended the university, and the platform in Stillwater was packed with college men waiting on their sweethearts. Gus had not even noticed all the young women in his car. The men, his age or younger, frowned at him as he exited his car, and he felt both lost and conspicuous until he heard his name and spotted Lorena farther up the track.

After dropping his bag off at a rooming house near campus, they spent the afternoon kissing on a bench on campus. There were no trees to hide behind, and even though he knew no one in Stillwater except for Lorena, he felt exposed and a little embarrassed and was glad when it began to get dark out and he could claim to want supper. Lorena chose a restaurant staffed by Italians who sang and joked with one another as if the room were not filled with diners. Gus loved listening to the Italians far more than he liked being around the students, who made him feel self-conscious.

"Aren't you glad to see me?" said Lorena.

"Of course."

"You appear reticent."

If he was going to marry her, he should share with her his innermost feelings. But when he told her that the students made him feel unworthy, Lorena said, "That's ridiculous, Gus. Half of them are in the School of Education. You already hold the job that if they're lucky they'll get when they graduate. If anything, you should feel superior."

Gus smiled and nodded, as if he were being ridiculous, as Lorena had suggested, but he didn't care to be told how he ought to be feeling. Hearing that he appeared reticent made him feel worse, so he searched his pockets for Mr. Starling's fable about the farmer, which he had brought along to show her, thinking she'd love it as much as Elise did. Instead, he pulled out Elise's note. Seeing what it was, he refolded it and stuffed it back in his pocket.

"What was that?" Lorena asked.

"I have something I want to show you from the paper if I can find it."

"It looked like Elise's handwriting," said Lorena.

"Oh, it was. I mean, it is. I saw her the other day on the street and asked her if I might take piano lessons. I've always wanted to learn. She said she'd have to check her schedule and the next day she left me a note at the teacherage. I guess she wasn't aware that I'd moved."

"How could she not know that? I would think, in Lone Wolf, it would have made the newspaper."

"Speaking of the newspaper," said Gus, and he read aloud Mr. Starling's fable, which he had finally located in the flap pocket of his jacket and which failed to distract her from her previous line of questioning.

"What is Elise doing with her time if she's not reading the paper?"

"Who says she's not reading the paper? She is most definitely reading the paper. We discussed this very article."

"So you've seen her?"

"Yes. I told you I ran into her on the street."

"This is when you asked her about taking lessons?"

"Why are we discussing this?" asked Gus. He felt awful for lying, but Lorena was scaring him. Gus had always known she was prideful, but it occurred to him, in the Italian restaurant with the waiters yelling and laughing at one another and the students ignoring everything but their plates of spaghetti and talk of the upcoming football game, that her pride would turn, in time, to righteousness. As she aged, she would be beset with rectitude.

Gus thought of Aunt Mattie telling him that his mother had more to lose than anyone she'd ever met. He had never understood this as a good thing until now. Lorena had far less to lose than most, and considerably less than her sister.

Lorena was talking and he leaned into hear her, but he heard only someone singing an aria.

"Let's get out of here," he said. "It's too noisy."

"We have to pay the bill."

Gus put down a five.

"That's too much," said Lorena. It was three times too much but worth it to Gus.

He stood up and offered her his hand. They walked in silence down the streets, which were filled with male students. They were boisterous, clean, and tedious. Alongside them he felt reticent, dirty, and interesting.

But he did not feel superior. He felt stuffed—with spaghetti, with the weight of his choice. The ring box bulged in his pocket and he took care to walk to Lorena's left, lest she spot and ask about it.

"You must be exhausted from your trip," she said, sparing him from making excuses to return to his rooms. He wanted to be alone and she felt it. Could she feel other things? In front of the boardinghouse he kissed her goodnight, a chaste peck on her vaguely offered cheek.

There were four bunks in his room and he was the first to bed. He lay awake listening to the men come in and loudly undress, their belt buckles banging against the floor as they lurched out of their pants.

Soon they were snoring and belching, and the room smelled of sour beer breath. He had lied to Lorena about Elise and saw no way out of it without more lies. He did not think of himself as a liar, as he'd never had anyone to lie to except, of course, himself.

In the morning, Lorena arrived for him properly at nine. He was waiting in the lobby and greeted her effusively. They had coffee and rolls in a cafe, then went on a tour of campus, teeming with excitement for the ball game. Lorena could care less about football, though Gus could tell that the experience of college required of her a certain investment in its rituals, and as a result, there was some giddiness mixed in with her obvious anxiety. She'd not forgotten the incident at the restaurant and he understood from all she did not say that it wasn't the letter that upset her but his unwillingness to discuss it.

She pointed out the science building, home economics. They were on their way to see the School of Education when it happened.

But what happened? Gus was walking alongside Lorena, listening to her, asking questions, and then he was not walking. Something made him stop and stare.

"What are you looking at?" she said.

Gus suspected his father used to ask his mother the same thing when she stopped on the sidewalks to stare not into the storefronts but beyond them, beyond her life. Just like his mother, Gus could not answer. He could not say what he was looking at. A bush? The edge of a building? The shoes of passersby? He saw everything and nothing. He saw his choice and it was already made for him. Later, he would realize the choice was made the morning his aunt sat him down and told him all about his mother, for had she not, he would be married to Lorena.

"I lied to you," he said.

"About Elise."

"Yes."

"Her letter?"

"Yes. Well, not just that."

"You love her."

"Yes."

Lorena's lips quivered, and then she smiled and nodded.

"But nothing has happened. Between us, I mean. We have never even spoken intimately."

"But you love her."

"Yes."

"And she is the one you want to give that ring you're carrying in your pants pocket, even though she has no finger for it?"

Gus wanted to tell her what he'd been looking at: everything and nothing. He wanted to say he saw his choice and it was made for him. He wanted to tell Lorena about his aunt Mattie, sitting him down on his last day with her and telling him about his mother. But he said nothing.

There were no tears and there was only one more question: Do you know your way back to the boardinghouse? She didn't wait for the answer. She was walking away and then she was trotting and then running. He watched her until he was gone. Then he walked the other way, not knowing if it was the right way. He hadn't been paying attention to where they were going. Gus hardly ever knew the way.

PART TWO

7

ELISE STEWART

Lone Wolf, Oklahoma, Fall 1917

The night before Mr. McQueen was to leave for Stillwater to visit Lorena, he was late getting home from the newspaper. Elise got it in her head that he did not want her to be there when he arrived. So she stayed.

She even made iced tea. She crushed up some mint stolen from the neighbor's side yard and stirred it into the pitcher. Why did he not want to see her? Perhaps he had bought Lorena a gift that wanted wrapping and he did not want her to see him attempt to wrap it, since it was well known that men could not wrap presents. They might as well put a gift in a gunnysack and toss it in your general direction.

Finding Lorena's unwrapped gift would require going through

Mr. McQueen's drawers and closets. Since she did this so routinely, she had high doubts that a search would turn up anything.

She was getting hungry. In his icebox she found milk, butter, eggs. She could scramble them up a plate of eggs. But perhaps he had stopped off at Parson's, the lone restaurant in Lone Wolf, for supper. Judging from the contents of his kitchen, Elise suspected he did this often. She doubted his knives could cut butter. She recalled his hacking away at a watermelon with his pocketknife the first time they all went to the river.

Anyway, there was no apron. She couldn't very well cook without an apron.

Outside the shadows grew longer, the light softer. She decided to write him a note. She had planned to speak to him in person on a particular subject, the same subject she (pretending to be Lorena) had written him a letter about already. But she could not speak for Lorena. Time was, she felt the current of Lorena's thoughts. They tumbled down out of her ears at night, filled the space between the cots.

She could not speak for Lorena. Not anymore.

> Dear Mr. McQueen—
>
> "Wherefore art thou" does not mean "where," but I do mean "where," even though it is hardly any of my business. I made iced tea with purloined mint. All the tastier. I waited for you because I thought we ought to discuss informing Lorena of our business arrangement. I have not written to her about it, as I thought I should speak first with you, and since you are going to Stillwater on the train, perhaps it would be better coming from you?

Elise read this line over and thought to cross it out. But it was true and it made her cry.

She wrote but did not write: After all, Lorena forsook me the moment she let me leave your classroom.

Plus (she wrote but did not write), Were *I* the messenger, I would surely return even more maimed.

There was the question of a valediction. *Sincerely* was out of the question of course, unless she sought to make him disregard the contents of the entire letter. Surely he would not take her seriously if she closed with *Sincerely.* Yet there was nothing *in*sincere about the note. It was only the word that was wrong, not what it meant.

Finally she settled on a dash, followed by the first letter of her first name. It felt familiar but casual. The dash suggested the note had been dashed off, rather than labored over for forty-five minutes, every second of which she listened for the sound of his feet on the porch boards.

When she arrived the next morning at Mr. McQueen's house for her Saturday morning lessons, she saw that the note was not on the table where she left it. This meant one of several things, which she listed in her head while Miss Pruett was banging out her scales in a way that made Elise feel guilty for not suggesting she join the nuns.

He took it along with him to read on the train. He would read the lines and also in between them.

He threw it away! The notion threw her into such a panic she had to check all the wastebaskets immediately. She excused herself and told Miss Pruett to continue with her scales, then went from room to room, calling out vague encouragement. The baskets were free of waste entirely, which led Elise, somewhat settled, back to the piano stool and Miss Pruett.

He hid it in his sock drawer. This idea came to her with ten minutes left of Miss Pruett's lesson. She thought of the stack of Lorena's letters, which she'd discovered there, and imagined hers on top. But she did not want her words to mingle with Lorena's. It was a matter of some concern, and Miss Pruett noticed, for she stopped playing.

"Are you all right?"

"Of course. Why?"

"You seem jittery."

Jittery she was and would be until Miss Pruett was out the door and she was running her hands through balls of black and blue mostly ribbed socks.

"I'm afraid I had too much tea this morning," said Elise. Then she cut the session short with a shamefully exaggerated appraisal of Miss Pruett's progress.

"What do you know of the gentleman who lives here, this Mr. McQueen?" said Miss Pruett, lingering in the parlor.

"Why?" said Elise.

"Why?" Miss Pruett repeated, her tone suggesting Elise was the impertinent one.

"Yes, *why*."

"I'm just wondering. I have heard him about when I've been here before, but I've not seen him and I have not heard him about at all today."

"He's away."

"What is he like?"

"Beastly, actually."

"Oh?"

"Yes, and unkempt. I have to arrive an hour early to make the place presentable."

"That is disturbing."

"My father is also unkempt. Many men are." She said this as if it were something, like glissando, that Miss Pruett was unlikely to ever learn on her own.

"Not that part. The beastly part."

"We have only a business arrangement," said Elise.

"But he goes with your sister, correct? Are they not engaged?"

"They are not."

"I understand that they are."

"Take away the wind and the gossip and the wolf in Lone Wolf and you'd have only the lonely word 'lone.'"

"So you plan on leaving?" said Miss Pruett, looking down at Elise's special shoes.

"I *am* leaving," she said. And as she said it, it became true.

"Not before I master Chopin, I hope."

"I'd prefer to leave while I still have a tooth in my head and a halfway decent figure," said Elise.

"I beg your pardon?"

"My sister is not engaged."

"I am repeating what I read in today's paper."

"That's the most ridiculous thing I've ever heard anyone say," said Elise. She had not read today's paper, but she did not need to. She had pegged Miss Pruett as a snob and a fool but not a liar.

"You should stay away from tea altogether," said Miss Pruett.

"I have another student," said Elise.

Miss Pruett looked out the open screen door at the empty porch, the empty sidewalk beyond. The street was empty as well.

"Due any minute," said Elise. "I have to prepare for him."

Myra Lundquist strode into the yard, her pigtails swinging with purpose. She held her blue Number 2 piano primer (Miss Pruett was still on Number 1, which was bright red) against her chest like a shield.

"I mean *her*," said Elise. "Saturdays are so busy, I get them mixed up."

"It is true what they say about you," said Miss Pruett.

"There comes a time, Miss Pruett, when in order to live with yourself you must submit to ruthless honesty."

"You speak as if you know things, and yet you are a sixteen-year-old farm girl who I am told brought much grief to her family."

"And what else am I?"

"Exceedingly rude?"

"You're forgetting something."

"Your skin is remarkably clear for a girl of your disposition."

"Wrong, and wrong. I am *owed*, by *you*, for today's lesson."

"I feel as though I paid in advance for the month."

"That was five weeks ago," said Elise, though it was three.

"But surely it wasn't."

"We farm girls have nothing to do at night but cross the days off calendars given to us for free at the Feed and Seed store, which we frequent for the burlap to fashion our sack dresses."

"Have I in some way upset you, Elise?" said Miss Pruett.

"Just put the money in an envelope and send it in the mail to me. I live on Gotebo Road. The postmaster knows me."

"I can just bring it by and give it to Mr. McQueen."

"Mr. McQueen is not my clerk."

"But he is your sister's fiancé? And the person who saved your life, as I understand it."

"Goodbye now, Miss Pruett," said Elise, opening the screen door. She yanked Myra's hand free from her chest, pulling her inside while nudging Miss Pruett onto the porch. She took Myra to the piano and put her to work practicing her scales. In Mr. McQueen's room, she closed the door. She put her head against it, shaky from her encounter with Miss Pruett. Engaged? She would know. *He* would have told her. She could no longer count on her sister, who was lost in the storm of Stillwater. She had been buried beneath chemistry, football, roommates, and cafeteria food. Elise and Mr. McQueen had ventured out into the storm to find her (on Sandy, of course, The Beatitudes being good for nothing but standing around waiting to inherit the earth.) Elise was the rider, Mr. McQueen the passenger.

Myra banged away proficiently on the scales. Excellent, Elise called through the closed door, with sincerity this time.

She plunged her hands into the sock drawer, her eyes shut. Balls of socks, wood beneath: no letters at all. What did it mean? He was the rider and she was the passenger. He had gone to rescue Lorena from the storm that was Stillwater. Elise would prefer to be buried in snow than football, roommates, food served on trays.

The next day Elise was hiding out in the hayloft, moving her eyes across the pages of *Black Beauty*, when Damyan rode up on his father's plow horse.

Damyan wanted her to go to the river. She thought it over for two seconds and decided that any sort of distraction was welcome.

"You will have to ask my father."

"To also go?"

"You will need to ask him if I can go. Specifically you will need to ask him if I can go with *you*." Elise felt bad when she realized she was shouting.

Elise's father was fond of all the Bulgarians, who often helped him get in his crop when he was behind or shorthanded, which was frequent. Of course he agreed to Damyan's accompanying his saturnine daughter to the river. He probably paid the boy to take her away, so distant and cross had she been since her encounter with Miss Pruett the day before.

Once on the dusty road, Damyan noticed her demeanor.

"What is wrong with you?"

"I'm not exactly sure," she said. "Part of me has gone away. And yet I feel it returning."

She hated the way she sounded—like Edith Gotswegon in the school play.

"Sometimes I understand the words of you but more when you are quiet," said Damyan.

Well, why did you ask, she thought to say, but she was moved by Damyan's claim to know her deeply, all the words, whether she said them or not. He knew about barbed wire. She had never asked him how he knew because she feared he would tell her.

In the distance, waving to them in the prairie wind, appeared the dusty trees lining the river.

"Do you miss trees? I assume there are trees in Bulgaria and that they are more or less similar to the ones that do not grow around here."

"Yes, many trees. We lived on the forest. We ate the nuts from all the big trees and pulled berries from the ones that leave at the waist."

"Bushes!" said Elise, as if she were taking a quiz.

"Mostly," said Damyan.

"Did you come here to seek your fortune?"

"I come because my father put me screaming in the boat."

"Yes, me too. Not a boat, a wagon. We were in Kansas for the railroad and apparently we went to Nebraska for corn, I don't remember that, I was very young, and then we went back to Kansas and then we came here for the land, which father says is not as advertised. He thinks he was gypped. He has ideas about moving. Texas and silver mining, or Mississippi and chickens."

"Is this the journey you said about earlier?"

"That's another one," said Elise.

They found a weeping willow free from couples and filthy-minded boys. Weeping willows were Lorena's favorites. She drew them over and over when she was a child, until her mother made her start drawing teepees. Her mother was sad to begin with and all the weeping trees made her sadder.

Damyan spread a blanket and produced some sausages, bread, cheese, and wine. Elise declined the spirits. It did not run in her family as it did in Damyan's.

"How is Blaguna?" Elise asked, but Damyan had gone off to change clothes. He had said he was going and she had heard him and yet she did not notice when he left. What is wrong with you, he had asked, and Elise realized this was the first grammatically correct sentence in his adopted English that she had ever heard out of his mouth.

"Are you also swimming?"

She looked up to see him, well proportioned in his suit. His part was imperfect, his lips full, his eyes, as always, damp with old-world want.

Elise remembered Mr. McQueen plucking the filthy-minded boy mimicking her walk and tossing him into the river. Would Damyan do this for her? He might club the boy in the head with his wine bottle. Damyan knew things Mr. McQueen did not. Mr. McQueen knew nothing of barbed wire and likely next to nothing about sausages.

"In a bit," she said. "Maybe. Sit back down."

Damyan leaned back on the blanket, which was of Kiowa origin and dirtier than the ground it covered. She recognized it from the abandoned sod house where she had spent many hours among the potatoes, carrots, and rotting hay, reading aloud from the newspaper. She thought of Mr. McQueen's silly claim about the imperfections in Persian carpets. Were not magic carpets driven by Persians? Who cared if the pattern didn't match? Similarly, who cared if the Kiowa blanket that covered the dirt was dirty?

Elise wanted to know what was in Damyan's head, for she was weary of what was in hers, which was the perhaps not-so-secret engagement of Lorena and Mr. McQueen.

"When we were in school together," she said, "and you looked out the window all the time?"

"Yes?"

"What were you primarily thinking about?"

Damyan took his time answering, which told her he was going to tell the truth. Thoughts required gathering. They were, if they were alive and breathing, like cattle spread across the plain. They needed herding up and bringing together.

"Mr. McQueen, when we would do the numbers, said of how they did not ever stop."

"Infinity?"

"Yes. I used to think of the numbers as ladder into the sky. I could climb away."

"Excellent. That's what I thought you were thinking."

"Sometimes of lunch."

"Well, naturally."

"And of going away in the train."

On the train, not *in* it, Lorena would have said, though technically one got inside the train unless one was a hobo, which Damyan was probably not.

"Where were you thinking of going? To Chicago? There's plenty work there. What sort of work would you like to do, Damyan?"

Damyan thought about it. He said he liked hats, and dogs. Equal, he added, by which she assumed he meant he liked them both the same.

"Do you think of yourself as an explorer?"

He looked confused.

"Never mind. Listen. I would like to go swimming, but I have to take off my shoes. I am just telling you because of my toes."

"You do very well with the number of your toes in the world."

Elise would have said, You do very well in the world with your number of toes, but she liked his way better, as it put her toes out there in the world. She was grateful.

"Thank you, Damyan. I believe that you believe so."

"Why would I say if I did not believe it?"

He confirmed what Lorena had said and she did not want to believe about the Bulgarians—that they were, on the whole, terribly literal-minded.

"Well, sometimes it is enjoyable to say one thing and mean another."

"Give the example."

Elise thought of praising Miss Pruett's wretched running of the scales the day before in order to buy time to rifle through Mr. McQueen's wastebaskets. But that was not a good example because it wasn't enjoyable. She couldn't think of one.

"It's complicated," she said, grabbing the toe of her black shoe. "Off is coming the shoe now," she said.

"Off with it, off!" said Damyan, which made her giggle for the first time in days.

The filthy-minded boys left her alone, Damyan being well proportioned in his suit. He swam vigorously with his head out of the water, like a dog wearing a hat. The river churned so much in his wake she was worried it might drain entirely. When he swam back to her, she suggested they float down the river and walk back up the path. Like most men, Damyan was a sinker, so he kept up by dog-paddling. Sandy could teach him not only various strokes but also proper technique of each, swimming being, in Sandy's own words to her once, a technique-driven endeavor.

So were the negotiations she was called upon to do in life. For instance, fending off Damyan when they returned to the dirty blanket beneath the weeping willow. Elise liked Damyan's combination of moony and brawny. She liked that, to look at him, you would have not a clue that in his head he was climbing a ladder of numbers. The technical aspect of fending him off called for what she dubbed Door Slightly Ajar. In other words, and to be blunt, she closed her eyes and kissed his full lips, which tasted of wine and sausage and, faintly, nuts gathered from the ancient forests of the Old Country.

But in her mind? A timetable, approximate of course, for the Rock Island Line. Mr. McQueen would be arriving home on the 7:20. The hour was approaching. She eased shut the door to Damyan.

"I must be home for supper."

"It is only four of the o'clock."

She needed to get into town to see Mr. McQueen. She would know with a glance whether or not Miss Pruett's lies were true.

"There is to be held a dance. The grange is to be holding it next Saturday," said Damyan, dropping her off home.

She pointed to her foot.

"I believe you dance as you swim."

It was a sweet thing to say even if its meaning was vague. It was not true. She was a terrible dancer even before her fateful journey.

"Would you like to soon come visit me in the old sod house where we used to?" he said.

It felt nice to be desired. But Elise thought she was too old to kiss among onions and potatoes and hay. She said yes because Door Slightly Ajar.

An hour later she had Buck saddled. She had a special makeup lesson, she told her parents. She was giving her father two dollars a week, ostensibly for the use of Buck, but in fact she was paying him to stay out of her business. Her father had never involved himself in her business until she secured a paying job, at which point he was full of ideas stemming from his stellar business acumen.

Miss Pruett was lying about the newspaper. If there were an announcement, would her parents not know? Her father, so mindful of getting ahead in life, would have something to say about Lorena marrying a schoolteacher. Also, Gus—Mr. McQueen—would have told her, since she had lately been helping him proofread the paper at nights.

Down the tracks, a mile east of town, she heard the whistle of the 7:20, though it was going on 7:37. What would he think when he saw her, waiting? His eyes would determine the truth for her. Words were a hindrance, bandages swaddling the perfectly healthy. Elise had known for years how words were blowing snow.

He stepped down off the train carrying a beat-up satchel and, slung over his shoulder, a canvas bag that reminded her of a mailman. She imagined the satchel was full of Lorena's letters. In the canvas bag, among balls and balls of blue and black socks, was her note.

Mr. McQueen did not seem surprised to see her standing there.

Miss Pruett was a liar. Her lack of talent made her petty. A pity not even the nuns would take her. The man who got off the train was not engaged. Clearly he was disengaged.

He made his way slowly to her and said, "I made a terrible mistake."

"Let's walk," she said. It is what you say when someone has made a terrible mistake. You want to ask questions—she had a dozen at the ready—but you hold off. Elise knew to hold off. This was the only thing she knew at the moment.

"I heard your true cry," he said. "In the storm. But I thought it was my dead brother. I wrote to my aunt and I told her my dead little brother, Leslie, had led me to you. And because my little brother had saved the life of Lorena's little sister, I thought it was Lorena with whom—"

"What did you tell Lorena?" said Elise. She had stopped walking. The train was steamy and whistling.

"I *told* her."

"She's always known," Elise said, surprised that she said it aloud, to Gus. "She knew in the way my mother knows."

"There are different kinds of knowing, though."

"Persians of old left mistakes in their flying carpets because only Allah or God is perfect," said Elise.

"Are you trying to make me feel better?"

She was trying to get him to stop telling her things she already knew.

"I had a terrible row with Miss Pruett in your parlor."

"Who is Miss Pruett?"

"She is no one, who claims you and Lorena are engaged."

They were walking alongside the train, filled with impatient passengers eager to put Lone Wolf behind them.

"I told you I made a terrible mistake."

Elise stopped walking. She looked away from him, at the station. Its windows were streaked with coal dust and grime. Someone had tried to smear open a vista, but the effort to clean it up had further obscured it.

"Well, at least she has a ring finger," she said.

Gus had pulled a box from his pocket. It was small, purple, felt. He said, "I made a terrible mistake and I am asking you to forgive me."

Elise was studying the grimy windows of the station. If she concentrated on cleaning them, perhaps she would not cry.

"For what?" she said. "She is lovely, smart, shrewd, and she has what is abstractly referred to as a future, which actually means something quite specific."

"She said I ruined her life."

"She's been sitting around waiting for her life to be ruined for some time." But in fact, it was a fact that ruined Lorena: the particular saloon of which L. C. Ivent was proprietor. Had Lorena not challenged Elise on this insignificant point, everything would be different. They would have staged their play and Elise would have generously allowed her to fall from the hayloft onto a carefully placed pile of hay in a writhing death scene. Elise would not have embarked on her fateful journey, Sandy would not have been forced to leave (though he might have anyway, as he was an explorer), and Mr. McQueen would not have heard her true cry.

"We will have to go away."

"I see that you are packed already. And of course she has at her disposal a splendid steamer trunk, though not the clothes to fill it."

"No, I mean us. You and me. We can't stay in Lone Wolf."

Elise looked at the ring box. He held it in his palm, an offering.

"What are you saying? It was in the paper."

"What was in the paper?"

"News of your engagement."

"That is the craziest thing I have ever heard in my life."

That is what she had said. "Miss Pruett is mean and uppity, but is she a liar?"

"Who is Miss Pruett, and yes, she is a liar if she said news of my engagement was in the paper. Did you not read the paper?"

"For once in my life, no, I did not."

She couldn't very well tell him that after Miss Pruett's visit she could barely make it out of the hayloft until Damyan came along and distracted her with a trip to the river.

"Well, then, we will go get one and I will prove to you that this Miss Pruett is as you described."

Elise was looking at the box he held in his hand: small, purple, felt, and obviously not brand new.

"It was my mother's," he said finally.

"And you were going to give it to my sister."

"Does that mean you don't want it?"

"It?" she said. "Do you mean the ring I have no finger for?"

"It doesn't matter which finger, Elise. That's just a custom. You don't care about such things. And the ring is only a symbol."

"I don't care about symbols any more than I care about customs."

"So, no?"

"Why are we discussing 'it'? Are you not offering me more than a symbol customarily worn on some arbitrarily chosen appendage?"

"I am offering you myself."

"Then get to it," she said.

Gus got down on one knee. A porter pushing along a cart loaded with boxes tipped his hat and smiled.

"I know the circumstances have been difficult to say the least," he said in a grave voice. "I realize that my prospects are not—"

"Oh, for heaven's sake," said Elise. "I'm not Edith Gotswegon. I don't care about prospects and I'd prefer you to look me in the eye."

Gus hoisted himself up slowly. He straightened himself out with the creakiness of a man who has disembarked from a train more disengaged than engaged.

"I find myself confused," he said.

"Well, I can't imagine why. You have been so clear of late."

"You are going to make me pay."

"Do you think you deserve to pay? Just a little?"

Gus said, "I have been looking over my shoulder for weeks. Since you went into the hospital. I thought someone was following me. I have been seeing and hearing things."

Elise, despite herself, was engaged.

"What things?"

"My brother. I heard his voice. Or I thought I did. It was you, actually."

So she sounded like his dead brother? Was that what he was saying?

"What else?"

"My mother. I thought she was behind my stopping and staring. But I stopped not because of her but because of you."

Now Elise was confused. Still, she wasn't uninterested.

"Everywhere I went with Lorena, I thought we were being trailed. I am sure I drove her mad."

"Not the kind of mad you're referring to. But yes, I'm sure."

"It was you," he said. "Your shadow."

The train pulled away, revealing Oklahoma. It was endless and muted, but if you knew not *where* to look, as much as how, you could see, in the distance—as Elise did at that moment—the villages of prairie dogs, hidden in the wind-ruffled grasslands. There were windmills, stock tanks, even awnings over porches.

"We have to go away?" said Elise.

"Yes. We can't stay here now."

"Can we go to Texas? Father has decided to become a miner of silver and I want to be close to Mother."

"Of course. Wherever you want. And we can take the piano and wherever we end up, you can teach lessons."

"No, we can't. It doesn't belong to us."

She liked saying "us," even if it meant losing her piano, which she planned on taking, despite what she said. The Women of the Church did not need it. She imagined loading the wagon after nightfall, sneaking out of town, the strings of the piano singing out as the wagon bumped over dry creek beds on a night lit by a high prairie moon.

But there was her sister to think about. Now and for the rest of her life.

"I suppose Lorena hates me now."

"No. I told her we had never even spoken intimately."

"That would be a lie."

"No, it's not."

"You have forgotten your visit to the hospital that day?"

"I said nothing that would qualify as intimate."

"Your business about the Natchez Trace would qualify as intimate."

"In what way?"

"Prehistory," she said.

"If I follow you, which I do not always, and it is for some reason fine that I don't, you are saying that I was talking about something else?"

"Poor Charlie Carter! His Beulah girl left him high and dry. He slept his drunken slumber through three whole states! You felt his suffering. I saw it in your eyes when you looked at me. It embarrassed you not to acknowledge it. You got down on your knees and you begged my mercy."

Mr. McQueen laughed, but his laughter, though not soft, seemed in danger of dead-ending in hiccups, then tears. "Telling her was the hardest thing," he said. "And yet I know it was right."

He took her arm then. Not here, not right out in public, some part of her tried to protest, but it was outdated and easily outvoted.

8

GUS MCQUEEN

Lone Wolf, Oklahoma, Spring–Summer 1918

Three weeks before school let out for the summer, Gus went to the office of Mr. C. H. Griffith to resign his job. Elise's parents were about to leave for Texas. Mr. Stewart was to make his fortune mining silver in a place called Shafter, but Gus and Elise were planning on settling in a town some sixty miles north called Fort Davis. A drummer passing through Lone Wolf had praised its beauty and left a copy of the local paper, which both Gus and Elise read cover to cover, searching for the news between the lines of fading ink. They liked the pictures of the chiseled hills and the high stretching desert beyond. They liked its proximity to Mexico. Both had dreamed of visiting other countries, and a grand tour of Europe seemed out of the question, given that they'd married at the office of the justice of the peace with only Elise's parents in attendance.

Lorena was invited to the wedding but wrote to her mother to say she was too busy with her schoolwork. Elise had suggested waiting until summer so that Gus's aunt Mattie could come, but Gus thought it best, given the circumstances, to go ahead with the ceremony.

'We can go see Aunt Mattie later," he said.

"On our honeymoon?" Elise said.

"Of course. We'll take the train. You would love Aunt Mattie. When she is fed up she says, 'My land!' I've never not seen her in her apron. Also, when I think about her corn pudding, my knees buckle."

A reception was held at the home of the bride. In attendance were two out of the three brothers Bulgarian. Damyan was absent, and Elise, when Gus asked her about it, was cagey. He resolved to follow up, but in fact it mattered not at all to him that only two out of three of the Bulgarians seemed to have come for the refreshments and that the bulk of the attendees were Mr. Stewart's idea men. He was stuck talking to, or rather listening to, the idea men for most of the reception. Elise talked to the Bulgarians, who stuffed squares of chocolate Texas sheet cake into their mouths and, when they left, into the pockets of their jackets. Maybe they were taking it home for Damyan, who Gus decided was ill. Then he gave no further thought to Damyan, eager as he was to take Elise home to the bungalow and proceed with marital relations.

"I have heard that people find pleasure from having their toes licked," said Elise when they were home in the bungalow. They had stripped without reservation, shame, modesty, embarrassment, haste, or zeal. They had just gone home and put down their things and walked into the bedroom and taken off their clothes as if they were hanging up their wraps in a mudroom in winter.

Now they were naked and hugging each other by the bureau. Gus's excitement was obvious and barely containable. He remembered all those nights, staring across the river at the other side, all those nights of not crossing, savoring the deliciousness of denial. Was that a good thing? Was he a good person? He couldn't believe he was thinking these things while in a naked embrace with his wife of five hours.

"Who told you that about the toe licking?"

"One hears things." She seemed embarrassed to have learned about or even talked about sex, but she did not seem the least embarrassed about the fact that she was about to commit it.

"I have heard things too and I would like to try them all," said Gus.

"I won't ask where you heard them because I am not Edith Gotswegon and also because this is why," she said, and she kissed him. They knew how to kiss. They had kissed plenty and in many ways, which had come to them naturally. It had felt different than with Lorena. With Lorena it sometimes went on a bit and with Elise it never ended. That is how he knew it was right. If you grow tired of kissing and want supper at an Italian restaurant among the raucous college students and waiters singing off-key arias, you know that you have made a mistake.

One thing Gus could never quite believe about that first time was how long he managed to last. When he finally came, he was atop Elise, and her head was hanging off the side of the bed and her arms were splayed out against the walls. Palms against the plaster, elbows locked, she was braced, but barely. It was not the look on her face, combined with the odd angle, which he would never forget. It was not the way she had gone rigid, then slack. When he finished, he cradled the crown of her dangling head and it was the cradling he would always remember. He spread out his fingers. With his hand he made a basket. Her head in the basket of fingers, he lifted it up to his lips.

"Stop smiling," he said, for it was time to kiss. But she didn't stop smiling, so he kissed her smile until he was smiling. They took a bath. The day slipped away in slanted light, which quivered on the claw feet of the tub and on all five of Elise's toes, propped up by the spigot. Soon it was dark. Neighbors called their children and their dogs in for the night. Elise noted the similarity of the names of pets and children in Lone Wolf, Oklahoma. Gus thought to say that it was general all over but did not, for everything that was happening in the world was happening only in that bathtub.

A month later, down at the First National Bank of Lone Wolf, Mr. C. H. Griffith received Gus as if he vaguely remembered him, but the look on his face—as close to a smirk as a gentleman banker can display—suggested he knew everything that had happened to Gus since he'd last seen him. Gus decided to see if Mr. Griffith was such a liar as to feign surprise, but after telling him he was now with Lorena's sister, Elise (he left out the fact that they'd married, as it was in the newspaper), Mr. Griffith said, "Lone Wolf is a small town, Mr. McQueen."

He was looking at Gus in that way older men often looked at him, as if he'd incorrectly knotted his tie or were wearing socks that clashed with his trousers.

"So you went with the one who was maimed?"

"She was injured," Gus said, bristling at the word "maimed," though Elise herself often used it. "She lost some toes to frostbite."

"And a finger?"

"Yes."

"The older sister is certainly stout."

He seemed to be speaking about livestock. Knowing nothing of livestock, Gus saw no reason to respond.

"Dr. Hall told me your aunt was your guardian," he said.

Was she his guardian? Had she been declared so by a court of law? If so, no one had bothered to tell him, though he didn't see what difference it would make.

"She was far more than my guardian."

"And your father?"

"He moved away to find work after my mother and brother died. He has another family now."

"I gather, then, that Dr. Hall served as a sort of father figure to you in your formative years."

"Perhaps he feels so," Gus said, horrified by the thought.

"No doubt he did try."

"Yes," he said, because he was not raised to run a man down in front of his friend.

"You're grown and obviously free to marry whomever you want. But perhaps I might fill in here for Dr. Hall, who so graciously filled in for your father. It is my opinion, Mr. McQueen, that your first choice was the better."

"And why is that? Because she is stout?"

"By stout, I meant she possesses vigor. I wasn't referring to her waistline. Though she has a fine figure, as far as I can recall. She has beauty and intelligence and drive. She got herself out of Lone Wolf to attend college. For women, that is rare. But that is not all."

"Oh?"

"The younger girl. Why is it that she wandered off on her horse during the worst blizzard we've had in years?"

Gus figured Mr. Griffith knew the answer to this, or some ridiculous lie told by the likes of Edith Gotswegon or another student, far more damning than researching a fact for a play.

"I think the point we all ought to remember is that her life was spared."

"Yes, the good Lord intervened. She could easily have frozen to death. I am sure that you established a special bond with both girls during that experience. But I have heard that it left the younger girl . . . well, I don't know how to say this, Mr. McQueen, but to say it. I hear she is a bit touched."

"Touched?"

"I have been told that she believes her horse, the one that had to be put down after her rescue, to be alive and performing tricks in a Mexican circus."

Gus couldn't help himself. He laughed, mostly over the fact that such a statement would make its way around Lone Wolf, dead-ending at the First National Bank.

"This may be entertaining now, but over the long haul? I just urge you to consider that her condition, which perhaps you think is only temporary, because of the trauma she suffered, will grow worse. I have heard that the mother herself suffers similarly."

"Her mother lost two boys to typhoid."

"Yes. Many children were lost. You could call it an epidemic."

"Everyone grieves differently," Gus said. "There is no handbook, let alone blueprint."

"Ah, but there are both," he said. "I lost a son myself. I read the Bible nightly, attended church regularly, and adhered to a regimen here at work, which is not unlike a blueprint."

"I am sorry for your loss but glad to hear you got over it so swimmingly."

Mr. Griffith was too busy speechifying to notice Gus's tone.

"People love to claim you never get over such things. And, on the one hand, it is true. There remains always a place in your heart for those you've lost. But at a certain point you must honor God and the living. You get over your loss to the extent that you can carry on with your life, that is, if you follow the proper guidelines."

"Which would be the ones you mentioned."

"They've worked for thousands. Millions, I daresay." Mr. Griffith leaned forward. His chair creaked under his weight. "I am only trying to say that the older one seems a much better match. She is exemplary, both mentally and physically, and she can be counted upon to stay the course."

His metaphors had moved from the barnyard to the high seas. It appeared he wanted to marry Lorena himself. He seemed not to know that Gus and Elise were already married, or perhaps he expected Gus to divorce his wife of four weeks and three days and marry her sister as per his suggestion. Gus, his duty discharged, left without shaking the man's hand, and wished never to lay eyes on him again.

But a month later Mr. C. H. Griffith came to his house. They were leaving for Texas the next day, and Gus was loading up the wagon, with the help of some schoolboys. Elise, thank goodness, was out.

Gus received him on the porch. "I'd ask you in, but as you can see—"

"Never mind that, this won't take long. I've come to tell you that I was wrong."

Gus was fairly stunned. He'd almost believe a postcard from his father turning up sooner than C. H. Griffith come to his house to admit wrongdoing.

"I've had a note from your Miss Stewart. Or, rather, the Miss Stewart you threw over. It seems I misjudged her character. She writes to say that she has chosen not to return to college."

Gus nodded.

"You realize what that means."

"I'm to pay back the money she borrowed."

"You are to pay back the money *you* borrowed."

"I'm good for it," said Gus.

"Where are you moving to, if I might ask."

"Texas."

"Good God," said C. H. Griffith. "That means I'll never see a dime. Every scoundrel who crosses that line becomes twice the scoundrel. The boundary between Oklahoma and Texas is not only geographical."

Gus said (again, but softer, if only to annoy the man) that he was good for it, though he had no idea how he was going to come up with it, since he was due only one month's pay and that was already spent on a wagon and team for their move to Texas.

"I will say this, speaking about character," Mr. Griffith was saying. "You've heard the phrase 'the apple does not fall far from the tree'?"

"Why, no," said Gus. "Did you come up with it yourself?"

"I did not. It's a common saying, out here at least. Perhaps it has not yet reached the South."

"We're simple people, it's true. We're more apt to put it literally: 'Like father, like son,' is how we say it. But you are speaking of a father and his daughters?"

"I am speaking also of the mother. I don't know the woman, but from what I've heard—"

"I'd like you to leave," Gus said. Plenty of people spoke ill of Harold Stewart, and it wasn't as if what Mr. Griffith were saying about him was untrue, but Gus could not allow him to say a word against Elise's mother. She had been nothing but sweet to him in her intermittently present way.

"I have written already to Dr. Hall."

"I'm sure you have."

"I feel as though he'll pay a visit to your aunt."

"I feel as though he likely will. And here's what is likely to happen if he repeats your vile and ignorant judgment of people you have never met: my aunt will tell him to get off her property. I *asked* you to get off my property. Need I now tell you?"

"I want the money in full now."

"That is not in the terms of the agreement."

"I would say that your leaving the state for that republic of reprobates south as well as west of us is grounds for me to change the terms."

"Even I know you can't just change the terms."

"I believe any Lone Wolf lawyer would side with me." Mr. C. H. Griffith paused. He shifted his gaze to the window of the bungalow. He stepped up to the glass and peered in.

"I assume you are planning on taking that piano."

"I don't understand your question."

"It wasn't a question."

"But of course it was. You can't come up on my porch and tell me you are taking my wife's piano."

"Indeed I can if you owe me five hundred dollars."

"That piano was a gift to my wife. It is how she makes her livelihood."

"I feel sure they sell pianos somewhere in Texas. Though come to think of it, probably not. You might have to come back to Oklahoma to purchase anything other than a steer or a firearm."

"You are certainly one to lecture a man about character."

"I am a banker, Mr. McQueen. It is my job to protect my money. I invested in your former fiancée's future, and she has decided not to have a future—she informs me that she is moving to Wyoming, which is almost as bad as Texas, perhaps worse for a single woman of her age and looks—so therefore I must do everything in my power to insure that I don't lose money."

"I can't let you take that piano."

"What else do you have equal to its value?"

"You can have all the furniture."

Mr. Griffith walked over to the cart. The schoolboys he'd hired were watching from the shade of a front-yard maple. Gus went over and paid them a dollar each and told them to come back that evening. Then he went back to the porch and watched C. H. Griffith study the sideboard, the crude pine table, the pie safe with its bent and rusty tin, the paint-flaky iron bedstead. He rifled through a box of kitchen implements, extracting a rolling pin still caked in flour. He shook his head, disgusted.

"I will send my man over later this afternoon to pick up the piano."

"You should send more than one."

"I don't expect you to help load it."

"I wasn't thinking of helping you load it."

"Ought I to send the sheriff?"

"If you see fit."

The sheriff saw fit to send a deputy, along with two Kiowa to load the piano while he kept the peace. Gus was not at peace as he watched from the porch, especially when Elise came home as they were carrying her piano across the yard.

Gus took her inside and explained about the loan.

"So my piano is paying for her year of college?"

"Yes."

"You might have told me about the loan."

"I saw no need," said Gus. "Never would I have figured your sister for a dropout."

"She is trying to punish me," said Elise.

Gus thought to say that it wasn't Lorena who took her piano away. It shamed him to remember the day the piano arrived at his bungalow, Elise playing Stephen Foster in the back of the Bulgarian's wagon, her father prancing alongside on Buck, dusty dogs and skinny children in tow.

"Maybe she did not care for Stillwater," he said, which shamed him even more, for he ought to be apologizing instead of making excuses for Lorena's defection. Why would she not go to Wyoming? Likely she wanted to get as far away from him—and Elise—as possible without having to learn a foreign tongue.

But Elise was smart enough to see through his excuse. "Whether she liked her college is not the point. You signed that loan and you ought to have told me about it."

Gus said, "You're right," in a way that sounded penitent and final, but it seemed that Elise did not consider his statement either.

"So she left college after a year because she got a job. Was that why she was going to college in the first place? To live in some drafty teacherage and deal with the Edith Gotswegons of Wyoming?"

"She wanted to be a teacher," said Gus. "She didn't have the money, so I went to C. H. Griffith on her behalf."

"On her behalf."

"Yes."

"Which behalf? The behalf you thought you loved? Or the one you thought it more sensible and respectable to marry?"

"She deserves to go to college."

"I don't dispute that. And I find it noble of you to go to the overfed banker on one of her behalves. But it doesn't seem fair that you two cooked up some financial scheme, and the poor crippled girl to whom the Women of the Church gave a piano is now listening to her piano being loaded carelessly onto a wagon."

It was true. From the foyer, they could hear the strings inside the piano, off-key, plaintive, and in obvious protest.

"You're right," said Gus. He wondered if she knew what Lorena had told him—that their mother had some money, a considerable amount of which was used to settle Elise's medical bills. He remembered Lorena telling him about her brothers dying of prairie fever and Elise not understanding that it was typhoid, and he wondered to what extent the family had, as Lorena put it, "indulged" Elise's character, or at least parts of it. He did not care to keep secrets from his wife, but he felt sure she was keeping secrets from him. She breathed oxygen. If she were to cut herself on a piece of stationery, she would bleed. She needed food and water. Therefore there were things she did not share with anyone else.

And there were things between the sisters that predated him, things he would never know about, that he had nothing to do with. Sometimes Gus understood that after leaving Lorena for Elise, he was in some way responsible for everything that ever happened, even events that occurred when he was back in Hibriten. He had become a date, by which all other things in their lives were timed. He remembered Dr. Hall defining a noun as a person, place, or thing. He ought to have also added: a date.

Gus knew this and many other things that, had he let himself fully *feel,* he'd have likely sought out a riverbank alongside which he might squander many an abject hour. Sometimes he could not help but think of Lorena, but it wasn't so fully formed as to be called a thought. More like a quickening in his limbs, a twitch to ward off, lest he allow himself to feel the brunt of his guilt. Lorena *and* Elise, for he knew he'd yanked off the blanket that once kept them together, knew he'd exposed them to an element worse than icy wind, which was the jealous hurt of the heartsick. But he had found a way to combat feeling wretched. He employed it now, easing shut the front door with his toe, leaning back against the wall, and pulling Elise into him.

"The bed is in the wagon already," she said.

He grabbed her around the waist and flipped her so that she was against the wall. He pulled off his belt. He kicked off his shoes. He lifted her dress.

"This is how we say goodbye to Lone Wolf," he said into her ear.

Elise said with her body that she could not think of a way that suited her better, though Gus could tell that a part of her—not so much the missing parts of her, but the part of her that had got lost in the storm—was not coming with him.

9

ELISE STEWART

April 20, 1918
Sandy
c/o Lorena Stewart
113 Morton Dormitory
Oklahoma State University
Stillwater, Okla.

Dear Sandy,

Last I heard from you, you were visiting our nation's capital. I enjoyed hearing of the abundant statuary and of the cherry trees beautiful in their flowering. I have always wanted to visit there even though government is not something about which I am deadly curious.

I was unaware that it is a low city compared to New York and Chicago. I trust you in such matters, as you have traveled widely yet still prefer the haunting and eerily beautiful symphony of the prairie.

I first heard the grass sing while riding atop you, Sandy. I first saw the grasshoppers spring out of the way of your hooves and knew that the earth was teeming with life, that dirt was alive, and the prairie lived even in winter when buried beneath snow. But it was spring when we rode across the prairie to the swish of its singing grasses. Were we off to deliver mail to the prairie dogs? Perhaps we were stopping in on the Bulgarians, in their sod house filled with hay.

But why am I telling you what you already know? Because I am mailing this letter to you in care of an unstated party. Oh I am, am I?

You know everything that happens in my life, but writing to you makes it newly true. There is old true (truth you were born with, color-of-your-eyes truth) and there is new true. There is also the unstated party who might not want to hear news from me, but how could she ever refuse word from you, Sandy?

Some random items from the *Kiowa County News*:

"J. M. Williams is having a front porch added to his house on Slocum Avenue."

"Mr. Gus McQueen's wedding reception will be held next Saturday week at the home of Mr. and Mrs. Harold Stewart of Gotebo Road, Lone Wolf. All who read this notice are invited to attend." (This is not from the *Kiowa County News*; it is a "special" to this letter.) Perhaps, Sandy, you could arrange to pick up the unstated party at the train station? While I can understand why she might not care to attend, it is my sincerest hope that she be able to distinguish between old and new true and call upon that born-with truth that was and will forever be a blanket protecting us both from the elements, a universe of two, plus you, Sandy.

That is my hope and it is sincere.

Love,

Elise

May 1, 1918
Sandy
c/o Lorena Stewart
113 Morton Dormitory
Oklahoma State University
Stillwater, Okla.

My dearest Sandy—

You and I know that words are wind. The sky uses wind to say "This is what I want," expressing its innermost desires, while people use words to order a pound of butter or state their "ideas" while standing about in the mouths of barns.

Wind leaves you chapped, but not for long, unless accompanied by snow, ice, and single-digit or below-zero temperatures. Wind can maim. Single-digit or below-zero wind can subtract digits, resulting in floppy gloves and socks three-quarters filled.

Can words maim?

From yesterday's *Kiowa County News*: "M. E. Wade was badly burned last night caused by an explosion of the gasoline lamp at his home. His face was badly burned but is said not to be serious."

Who says it is not serious, Sandy? Who gets to say what is and is not serious?

Words written are said to mean more than words spoken. That is why I am writing to you, Sandy. That is why I persist and will continue to persist in writing to the unstated audience, whether she writes back or not. She might like to know some things. She might like to know that we are moving to Texas. I will bring along my piano and continue to teach young and old alike how to bend their fingers at the knuckle. The instinct of most is to slap at the keyboard as if they are playing patty-cake. Sometimes instincts are to be ignored. I speak here no longer of proper keyboard technique. Yet sometimes instincts must be honored if you are to be a living thing like the prairie, even in the part of the winter referred to erroneously as "dead."

Love,
Elise

July 16, 1918
Sandy
c/o Lorena Stewart
c/o Edna O'Connelly
326 Coffeen Ave.
Sheridan, Wyo.

Dearest, loveliest Sandy—

When I was little, I had multiple names for everyone I knew. One of my names for you, Sandy, was Everybody's Sunshine Crocodile. I called my mother Mother of Pearl, even though she did not have a child named Pearl. (Mother of Pearl, as you are well aware, is not fake pearl; it is my mother's nickname.)

I had no other name for myself. I would rather not have a name at all. Then no one will come to the edge of the prairie and say a word that means supper is ready. No one will yell out the window into the yard some word that means now.

When I was upset with my sister (which was rare, Sandy) I called her Edith Gotswegon. I might have called her other names, but they were childish and slipped from my tongue in the heat of anger, and why can we not forget all such times, as if we were to tally right now, it would not be the bad times that would emerge in the victory column.

From outside Hobart, some sad but also somewhat exciting news to share:

BARN BURNED

A BARN CONTAINING 300 bushels of corn belonging to C. W. Erwin was burned Tuesday morning just before day. It was the work of an incendiary, the tracks of the horse he rode being found near the house. When this was learned, Johnson and Duckett of Altus were phoned to come over with their bloodhounds. They hurried and as soon as hitting the ground the dogs took up the trail and chased it right to the home of a bad character and enemy to C. W. Erwin, about two miles away. They think they have the fugitive located; an arrest will probably be made today.

In other news not recorded in the *Kiowa County News*, we left Lone Wolf for Fort Davis two weeks ago, for good. Father and Mother left before us, Father having sold the farm for what he deemed peanuts but what Mother told me was more than a fair price considering its state. They are already settled in tiny Shafter, in southwest Texas near the border, where Father has taken up the mining of silver. We stayed behind while Gus finished out the school year and I packed up the bungalow. It was well appointed, as you know, Sandy, and the fireplace drew like a dream. I will miss it and many things in Lone Wolf, most of all the prairie, of course, and its glorious symphony I'd not have heard had it not been for you. Also I will miss my piano, which was taken from me to settle some complicated financial arrangement with C. H. Griffith. It involved a loan Gus McQueen cosigned for, which was defected upon, if that is the proper terminology—I confess, Sandy, I did not understand the specifics and I especially did not understand why my piano was taken. One day I arrived home from visiting Mother to find it being loaded in a wagon by two Kiowa. A deputy sheriff oversaw the piano loading from the back of his horse while cradling his shotgun. They sent along an armed man as if we were no more than barn-burning incendiaries, set upon by bloodhounds. I miss my piano. What of the songs inside me? How are they to find their way out into the world now?

By the way, Sandy, and I include this only because I know you were always fond of Damyan: he did not attend the wedding reception. He was not traveling, like you, Sandy. He was holed up in the old sod house with the hay and potatoes and, according to his brothers, a bottle of plum wine. He had long wanted to Get Steady with me, as he called it. His brothers came to the reception and said I hurt his heart. They said I took the color from his skin. As they said all this, they were stuffing their mouths with cakes. Crumbs were falling from their mouths. I did not feel bad because the person I most wanted to be there was not there, and besides, people are not supposed to eat with their mouths full and it is difficult to tell the difference between a word and a tiny crumb of cake.

We were over a week on the road. Mother loaned us the money to purchase another horse because the wagon was overloaded, and, well, you know The Beatitudes. Perhaps he should inherit the earth as he has proven himself not adept at moving across it.

We were not long getting to Texas from Lone Wolf, but once you get to Texas everything is long. The Texans do not think so, though. They think nothing of traveling for days, to Amarillo or El Paso, for a new bridle or a spool of red thread.

The Texas panhandle is no different than our corner of southwestern Oklahoma, though Mr. C. H. Griffith told Gus McQueen that the border between them is not only physical. Like all native Oklahomans, he looks down on Texas, as Kansans look down upon Oklahomans, does Mr. C. H. Griffith, who took my piano to settle a debt I had no part in and more than likely sold it for far less than it is worth. Whatever he got for it is less than its value to me, Sandy, for I miss it so much I requested Gus McQueen to cut a board the exact length of the keyboard upon which I have painted all the keys in black and white. While we traveled from Lone Wolf to our new home in Texas, sharing those bumpy lanes with herds of cattle, shady characters, Women of the Church in bonnets, tinkers, drummers, Mexicans, soldiers, and the ostentatious automobiles, which thankfully one can hear coming from far away, allowing one to make ample room as they think they own the roads, these motorists, having forgotten in a day how people traveled (by *horse,* Sandy, and I shall never not travel by horse) for centuries, I played the songs I have committed to memory, chiefly and repeatedly "Für Elise," which carries well in the high flat plains of the panhandle.

On the other hand, speaking of horses and automobiles, holding on to the past is not in some cases healthy, for what is done is not to be undone by poring over its doing.

Love,

Elise

August 1, 1918
Sandy
c/o Lorena Stewart
c/o Mrs. Edna O'Connelly
326 Coffeen Ave.
Sheridan, Wyo.

Dear Sandy,

I neglected to mention that on the way here, we came across the most beautiful spring! Gus got in and floated on his back. Men are not natural floaters, but Gus is the exception. While we were enjoying ourselves in the spring, a man came by and ordered Gus out of there (I was sitting on the bank, my piano across my knees, regaling Gus with hymns as it seemed he was being baptized). The man had come down to fill his water jugs. He claimed that the spring was the source of his drinking water and not a swimming hole for Oklahomans to befoul (he had asked first thing where we were coming from). As he filled his jugs, Gus engaged the man in conversation, which would not have been my inclination. The man said many unkind things about Mexicans, leading us to believe he was a native Texan. That is one way you can tell. Gus said to this man, after listening to his unflattering remarks about Mexicans, "Mexico was outright stolen, if you think about it," and the man said he did not have to think about it, how it came to be was how it came to be. Apparently this is another way to tell a Texan. They don't need to think about how it came to be.

Love,
Elise

September 2, 1918
Sandy
c/o Lorena Stewart
c/o Mrs. Edna O'Connelly
326 Coffeen Ave.
Sheridan, Wyo.

Dear Sandy—

Fort Davis is a half-day's drive to Shafter, where Mother and Father live. We chose this town based on a newspaper given us by a traveling salesman Gus McQueen met in Lone Wolf, and we are happy with our choice. Our cabin is in a grove of cottonwoods along Limpia Creek, two miles from town. Right upside our property (which we rent but would like to someday purchase) are bluffs that change color all the day long. In the morning they are muddy brown; in the full noon sun they are dirty blond. Then the afternoon clouds roll in and they turn boot black. In last light they are bright purple. That is just to describe them on one randomly chosen Tuesday.

Sometimes, when the sun is about to drop behind the bluffs, I see a wolf. Silhouetted in the last light, he looks out over the canyon. He has come from the prairie to watch over us all, our lone wolf.

Love,
Elise

December 4, 1918
Sandy
c/o Lorena Stewart
c/o Mrs. Edna O'Connelly
326 Coffeen Ave.
Sheridan, Wyo.

Dear Sandy,

It is not as if I have no curiosity about Wyoming. Curiosity abounds. I wonder if the town is filled with cowboys, bandits, speculators, lawyers, painted ladies, and incendiaries. I wonder about the sky above and the earth beneath your feet. Is the sky as huge as it is in Lone Wolf and is the earth teeming with life? Does the wind blow? (It does here.) Do people use their words to communicate or is it a land of grunt and shrug? I have it in my mind that people point quite a bit. I have an image of a young and strikingly beautiful transplant from the Oklahoma prairie detraining at Sheridan Station and asking directions of a tilted, whiskery man, who points in a direction unhelpfully general.

I wonder what you hear in the night. Coyote wind or just coyotes? I have many questions, Sandy, about life there in Wyoming. I wonder—for instance and finally, for a sadness has taken over me, and making marks on a page takes all the effort of chopping the tree that produced the pencil I wield—what in the world is a Coffeen? Do they mean to say Coffee Avenue? Or is it how you spell *coffin* in Wyoming?

Love,
Elise

P.S.: Have you any prairie dogs there?
P.P.S.: How does one (say, for instance, the unstated audience) stay warm on her way to school in cold that can subtract digits?

Dear Sandy,

Our cabin in the cottonwoods is just about perfect. This being a penny postcard, I have not the space to draw you a picture, but next time, I promise. We don't yet have curtains, but I am going to make some soon only so I can see them aflutter in the wind of your arrival.

Love,
Elise

December 21, 1918
Sandy
c/o Lorena Stewart
c/o Mrs. Edna O'Connelly
326 Coffeen Ave.
Sheridan, Wyo.

January 14, 1919
Sandy
c/o Lorena Stewart
c/o Mrs. Edna O'Connelly
326 Coffeen Ave.
Sheridan, Wyo.

Dear Sandy,

I write with some real "news." Gus McQueen has gained employment at the local newspaper.

One Joe Dudley out of Odessa is the publisher. Joe Dudley, who is an atrocious speller, handles layout and circulation and operates both the linotype machine and printing press. Gus is the editor and sole reporter, as well as the photographer, though he knows nothing of photography. He writes all the articles save the columns written by correspondents from the smaller hamlets in the region—Kent, Balmorhea, Toyahvale, Valentine, Marathon, Marfa. The nearest paper is in Alpine, which covers some of the same territory, including many areas populated by Mexicans. Mr. Arturo Gonzalez translates some articles into Spanish at Gus's insistence, Joe Dudley out of Odessa being of the opinion that they can start their own paper. However, the Mexicans are loyal customers and the subscriptions have increased since Mr. Gonzalez started writing his column, though some Texans dropped the paper in protest, to be expected.

The correspondents send in weekly accountings of the doings, comings, and goings of their neighbors—who is down with la grippe, who had their horse stolen, who is taking the train Saturday to El Paso. Oh, but why am I explaining this to either of you, who grew up reading these very columns in the *Kiowa County News*? As you know, these columns are the heart of a small-town newspaper, and Gus McQueen is ever mindful of it. He knows his readers want just a little of what the crooks are up to in Austin and Washington, and some of the European situation, though the more important feature is wheat and cattle prices.

I have asked Gus twice if he might allow me my own column, which I would like to call News from Limpia Creek, but he told me I ought to wait until more people live on the creek, which is his way of saying no.

Gus McQueen does not appear to miss teaching at all. I do not think I am alone (I believe the unstated audience might be in agreement with me on this) when I say that although he had his shining moments in the classroom, he had not the patience for it. As I have pointed out to him since we have been in Texas, he sometimes went on about things of questionable significance (the Natchez Trace, his "theory" that a noun is more than simply a person, place, or thing, which he never thoroughly explained), and sometimes he flat out made stuff up and passed it off as fact.

Love,

Elise

P.S.: Gus has hired some Mexican men to help him dig a well and he is trying to get them to teach him Spanish. Even though I have a million chores to take care of, I bring the men water every half hour because I too want to learn Spanish. I was told by one of the well diggers that my Spanish is *muy bueno*, which I attribute to my being more musically inclined than Gus. Spanish is a musical language, as you well know, Sandy, from your time cliff diving in Acapulco.

P.P.S.: Gus McQueen sees me writing letters. Sometimes he

says, “Who are you writing to, Elise?” and I say, “Sandy, of course,” but he knows who I am really writing to because I give him the letters to post. The first time I gave him a letter addressed to you, Sandy, on Coffeen [*sic*] Avenue in Sheridan, Wyoming, what he did, and all he did, was nod.

January 17, 1919
Sandy
c/o Lorena Stewart
c/o Mrs. Edna O’Connelly
326 Coffeen Ave.
Sheridan, Wyo.

Dear Sandy,

The baby is due the first full moon of June. The baby is due the first full moon of June. Writing it down makes it true. The first full moon of June. The baby is due. First moon June.

Love,
Elise

February 6, 1919
Sandy
c/o Lorena Stewart
c/o Mrs. Edna O’Connelly
326 Coffeen Ave.
Sheridan, Wyo.

Dear Sandy—

I just realized, writing the above, how many you have to care for you there in Sheridan, Wyoming.

That is as it should be, Sandy. Everywhere you go, you leave that place all the wiser. You spread yourself thick. When people see you, gasps are sucked from their lungs. At night the ocean weeps for lack of your hoofprints sucking the wet sand from its shoreline. With each wave it sends millions of shells to entice you to return. The shells tinkle like frozen letters of words falling from the unpinned blankets of yore. And this is your finest moment, Sandy. You bore us gallantly and selflessly through winds icy and coyote. You kept intact, always and overhead, the blanket of sky. Not everyone—certainly not I—can say they always know the way.

Love,
Elise

July 7, 1919
Sandy
c/o Lorena Stewart
c/o Mrs. Edna O'Connelly
326 Coffeen Ave.
Sheridan, Wyo.

Dear Sandy and also dear Unstated Audience,

About a month ago, Mother came up from Shafter where Father has a stake in a silver mine. I did not have to ask if they had struck it rich for she was a bag of ungiggly bones and wearing the same pale plaid dress she'd worn when I was playing in the old sod house with the Bulgarians. She might have worn it in Nebraska, or in Axtell, Kansas, where I was born. Perhaps it was packed in the steamer trunk when she went off to Knox College in Illinois. The day she arrived, she went with me to the garden to pick some butter beans. I looked up to see her lift her arm to wipe sweat from her forehead and saw sunlight streaming through the fabric.

Mother stayed with us until the baby was born. That was three weeks ago. I was outside practicing Spanish with Rodrigo and his wife, Juana, who live just across the creek from us, when my water broke. The two of them helped me into the house, where Mother was resting in the bed. Mother started crying. Juana ordered Rodrigo to stay on the porch. Mother cried because she had not brought along some special soap to wash the baby's head. When she heard this, Juana went outside and spoke to Rodrigo. The window was open and I understood her. "La madre no ayuda." The mother is no help. "Ve a buscar a María." Go and get María. While he was gone, Juana moved about the room like a draft. Shadows grew long in Texas. *Contraction* is an ugly word, and yet even in its ugliness, it does not do justice to the pain it is meant to describe. Gus came home. For an hour he wandered in and out until Juana ordered him to stay on the porch with Rodrigo. María García, who lives in town and has brought seventy-three babies into the world and not a single white one, spoke so softly and rapidly to Juana that I could not understand her. Mother cried in the corner and sometimes she put a cloth on my forehead and other times she sang songs. Mostly lullabies. In the long night there came a train. I heard the whistle and had my boy. And so my boy came on the train.

Love,

Elise

August 15, 1919
Sandy
c/o Lorena Stewart
c/o Mrs. Edna O'Connelly
326 Coffeen Ave.
Sheridan, Wyo.

Dear Sandy and dear Lorena,

On that day so long ago, in our Lone Wolf parlor, when Gus, then called Mr. McQueen, appeared, dressed as a scarecrow, the day he claimed his father was dead, he also changed the subject. I said, "Only the three of us know the truth," referring to the day the wind took my finger and toes, and he changed the subject.

Last night after I put Leslie to bed, I asked Gus why he changed the subject.

"Do you remember everything?" he said.

You used to say, Lorena, that I remembered things that did not happen. But I remember every last ride I took with you, Sandy. I remember those nights you would come stand outside the window after I lost five of my toes, a finger, a sliver of nose (actually I forget about this, because I am not much on mirrors, or noses), and I remember buckling on the special shoes I had to wear then, before I learned to walk by placing the weight on my midsole in the manner of stealthy Indian warriors. I remember sneaking past my parents' open bedroom door and climbing bareback atop you for moonlight rides across the prairie, the grasshoppers hopping, the rabbits scampering, the snakes slithering out of our way, look out, prairie, here we come, all the way some nights to the Red River and maybe beyond. Maybe we crossed, some of those nights, into Texas and didn't even need to think about it.

"Yes," I said to Gus McQueen. "I do remember everything."

"Do you remember the day of the blizzard?"

"Yes," I lied. Because, sometimes, Sandy? I have moments of I suppose you could call them panic, when I worry that the only reason Gus is with me is because I am maimed and he feels sorry for me. I do not remember that day in the way I remember my rides with you and the coyote-wind mornings you ferried Lorena and me to school. I remember the in-between, the nothing. If you remember pure nothing, you remember everything. No one realizes this. Elise turned blue, the snow was red. In the wind I heard the whistle of Big Idea, but it went past me to the ears of someone far away, maybe Rodrigo out rounding up cattle in the pasture beneath the bluffs. Maybe Rodrigo had himself a big idea. Hell is fire and heaven is the North Pole. So far as I know, this is not in the Bible. I saw the fence post move and then the snow bleeding. I lost both of my shoes, I have no idea how, where, when.

"I haven't really hired myself out to stand in a field and scare away crows." That is what Gus said when I told him, "Only the three of us know the truth."

"You had just accused me of looking like a scarecrow."

"That was *well before* I said anything about the three of us and the truth."

Gus turned over heavily in bed.

"I suppose you *do* remember everything," he said.

I turned over heavily in bed. I put my chin on his rib cage. I let him know I was not going to change the subject. I had Gus in my sights and I kept him there.

"Why did you change the subject?"

"Because," he said. "I don't know why."

But I know why. The three of us were one too many. It's not right or wrong. It may involve numbers, but it is not arithmetic.

Love,

Elise

December 5, 1919
Lorena Stewart
c/o Mrs. Edna O'Connelly
326 Coffeen Ave.
Sheridan, Wyo.

Dear Lorena,

Today we woke to snow. It is December and it has been cold out, at least for Texas. People here are unaccustomed to the cold. Last week it snowed two inches and they sent the children home from school, the sheriff retired to the saloon, the Catholic priest announced he would not take confession. When I say they are unaccustomed to cold, I am comparing them to us (and Sandy, of course) who used to venture out in weather that here would shut down the saloons, which are rumored to have stayed open twenty-four hours a day since the first beer was drawn.

The locals are scared of snow, which is only words falling like pieces of wedding cake from the mouth of the sky.

Today the snow fell all morning and was thick on the ground. After lunch I bundled up Leslie, who was half-asleep and in that contemplative state infants often lapse into, wherein they appear to study intently the winking sunlight as it flashes across the patterns of the blankets we bought from the Kiowa. I took Leslie with me out to the barn and put him down in a pile of carefully placed hay. He sat there watching me, looking very serious, as I saddled The Beatitudes. I strapped Leslie to my chest papoose-style and wrapped the Kiowa blanket about us. I had brought pins. I attempted to pin the blanket on the mother and child. Leslie watched, fascinated. He made his little noises that are actually words. I can understand him.

"Why, is that the sky?" he said, looking up at the blanket pinned badly above us.

I had done a wretched job of pinning. The only *worse* pin job I have witnessed was by Gus, back when he was Mr. McQueen. But it was okay because it wasn't needed, really—it was not that cold out to me and it would not have been to you, Lorena, for I hear Wyoming makes Oklahoma seem like Florida.

It was not needed, but it was wanted. I wanted Leslie to know the feeling of moving through the cold with a sky of blanket. I wanted to sing into his ears and hear him sing back to me, even if the words were lost to wind and blowing snow. I wanted to lift the blanket off when we arrived at our destination and hear his words break into slivers of ice, letters tinkling like chimes as they fall to the ground.

But it was all wrong. The blanket would not stay put. Almost immediately, the baby began to wail. And that horse, of course, did not know the way.

Love,

Elise

March 28, 1920
Lorena Stewart
c/o Mrs. Edna O'Connelly
326 Coffeen Ave.
Sheridan, Wyo.

Dear Lorena,

In this letter I shall repeat faithfully everything I saw or heard on our visit. Not that I have not, in previous unanswered correspondence, been a faithful reporter, but this case calls for verbatim reportage of conversations.

Last weekend we went to see Mother. While there, we saw a bit of Father.

Mother, who is supposed to have indulged me—by which I think the person who made this claim meant that Mother tolerated, rather than sought to curtail, what others have called my "fanciful nature"—is much taken with Leslie. She was thrilled to hear that I am again with child.

"Will it be another boy?"

"I'm only four months along." Many women claim to know the sex of their child immediately and instinctively, but I am not one of them.

"I hope so," she said. Father had taken Gus on a tour of his mining operation. They live in a two-room adobe structure perched on the side of a hill overlooking the mine. In a square mile there must be seven mesquite trees. Most would call them bushes. The soil is not soil but sand and rock, hospitable only to mesquite and ocotillo cacti.

"Why do you hope so?" I asked Mother.

"I would have my boys back."

By which she meant our brothers, lost to us so long ago.

To reach Shafter from Fort Davis, you head south through the high grasslands between Fort Davis and the tiny town of Marfa. Eventually the earth begins to drop. The distant mountains are purple in the shadows and a breeze running through the grass can take you right back to Lone Wolf. But as you near Shafter, the road worsens as it twists and switches through deep arroyos. Were you to travel past Shafter and follow the road until it bottoms out, you would hit the Rio Grande and Mexico, which is dusty and smoky year-round with outdoor fires.

It was then that I asked Mother if she would like to come live with us.

"With you and Lorena?"

"With me and Gus."

"That would be lovely," she said. "I could sew you some curtains."

It occurred to me that I ought to have checked with my husband first, but just as quickly, it occurred to me that our mother would never leave our father.

"You might name the next one Elton," she said. I recalled the day our father won the lottery, affording him 160 acres of land in Lone Wolf. When they called his number, he threw his hat in the air, and our little brother Elton whooped and clapped.

"You always miss them, don't you?" I said.

"Every day."

She had given Leslie a biscuit and was much amused by the fervent way he clutched it.

"I miss Lorena," she said. "Have you heard from her?"

"No," I said. "I have not heard from Lorena."

"She likes it in Wyoming. Winter does not slow her down

a bit. She wears many layers and has had a new fur coat made to fit. Do you write to her?"

"I wish you would come home with us today," I said. "We could start packing your things now."

"That would be lovely," she said, "but I would need curtains."

Propped-open shutters covered the crude windows of their adobe shack. The roof was sheets of rusted tin, the floor unsecured planks laid atop the sand. Hourly she opened the front door and swept out the wolf spiders and the scorpions. Often a rattlesnake sunned itself in the yard, coiling and retreating as she swept dirt and venomous bugs its way.

"Do you miss trees, Mother?"

"Lorena loved to draw weeping willows. I made her stop."

"You made her switch to teepees."

She laughed. She was rocking Leslie in a chair by the fireplace. The hearth was six inches deep in ash and the house was filled with flies. A slab of butter covered by a piece of wax paper sat out on the table. Flies swarmed the wax paper. I have lost the war with the dust, she declared when we arrived. She held up her hands in surrender. Her palms were black. I am a casualty, she told us, reaching out for Leslie with her black hands.

"Elise?" she said. "Should it be a girl, you will name her Lorena May."

Leslie was nearly asleep, but something in Mother's voice made him stir. Something in her voice stirred *me*.

Oh, Lorena, I am sorry. I know you will never forgive me but still: I knew the whole time what prairie fever was. I just don't believe some things have to be real and that makes them not real. Words are wind, and numbers are not arithmetic. I hurt you and I am sorry. I could go on, but what is the point? Do you need me to go over every moment, starting with the day he unpinned us from Sandy, the day he asked Sandy's name and I saw the look on his face and heard the murmur of his heart when we told him that he and our horse shared a name?

It has been two years since I have heard from you. I know the number of days and this number is not arithmetic, it is absence, and I'm sorry and I am worried about Mother. She wants to see you so. As do I.

It is a girl, I know it. She will be called Lorena, but you and I, Lorena, have often discussed our mutual dislike of the middle name May. So just plain Lorena. Lorena May is the name of a cow and our Lorena will be beautiful.

Once we lived in our world, you and I. A blanket was our sky and we were a giggly bag of bones.

"Elise?" Mother was saying to me.

"Yes," I said. I told her yes, Lorena, I said yes. So when you come, there will be another Lorena, not named after a cow, and as beautiful as you are.

Please write back.

Love,

Your sister,

Elise

10

Lorena Stewart
326 Coffeen Ave.
Sheridan, Wyo.

May 6, 1921
Edith Gotswegon
c/o Elise "McQueen"
Limpia (sp?) Creek
Fort Davis, Tex.

Dear Edith Gotswegon:

I write from Wyoming, as you might have deduced from the postmark, if you are the type to read postmarks. But of course you are not, which is why I am writing to you in the first place.

I got your address from your mother, who filled me in on all your doings, including the dashing young engineer you met and married. As I read the description of your wedding, I thought of you hiding behind a tree in the quad up at Norman and flicking your long tongue around the engineer, and in this way you have made him yours.

Actually, I made up an address for you: 3 Winthrop Manor, Oklahoma City, Oklahoma. (Does it not *sound* made up?) I am going to mail this letter, however. Just not to its stated audience. Which is you, Edith Gotswegon. You who is never only Edith, always Edith Gotswegon.

It's me, Lorena. Lorena Stewart, from Lone Wolf! Though we have known each other since my father hauled my family to that godforsaken place in a wagon pulled by his mulish horse, Buck, and his big ideas (which took up most of the wagon) and a mess of tools I never once saw him use and my mother's chest hidden beneath quilts, away from the eyes and grubby hands of my younger sister, we were friends, you and I, for nearly half a week during my last year at Lone Wolf School. Yes, that's correct, I borrowed your hideous scarf that day you read aloud dramatically from the sordid memoirs of Mr. Franklin, of whom your mother did not approve. But your mother, as our teacher at the time pointed out, was not there! What a stellar argument to uphold the standards by which you were raised. I think that I will not emulate it.

For I am a teacher myself now. I came west from Stillwater, nearly three years ago. It is a curious story, which I will share with you, not because it is any of your concern how I ended up in Wyoming and why I have stayed, but because (unlike some others, Edith, who write cryptic letters to deceased livestock) I am not hiding from anyone or anything.

As I was finishing up my first year at Stillwater, just before final examinations, a recruiter showed up on campus one afternoon. I happened to pass within yelling distance of him (roughly the length of your tongue) and he enticed me over to the table he'd set up beneath an elm outside the gymnatorium (a ridiculous word, I bet you employ it every chance you get) with a series of penny postcards bearing images of snowcapped peaks. These here are called the Bighorns, he said, and these—he held up another—are the Tetons. The mountains were craggy and imposing. They brought to mind a host of words ending in *-ic*: prehistoric, volcanic, iconic. I wanted to wake up and look out my window at them. I wanted to walk out onto a porch with my coffee and have them rising above me of a misty early morn. I took the postcard and studied it and paid little attention to the recruiter who was telling me about the quality of the air. He compared it to the water of a mountain stream, which confused me. Did he mean it was frigid year-round? Or clean? I gazed above his head at the air of Stillwater, which was clear enough but for the black smoke of coal fires streaming from chimneys. I am not overly concerned with air and told him so.

I quizzed him on latitude, then longitude. On both, he failed me.

"What is produced there?"

"Beg pardon?" he said. He was tall and wore a tight striped suit and a western hat. His boots were muddy. I studied his

Adam's apple, which was sizable. His hands were mottled with age spots, though he seemed to be in his forties if I had to guess.

"How do the Wyomingans, or Wyomans, earn their keep?"

"Various trades," he said. He did not seem to have much past some postcards to sell a soul on settling in an area still considered by many the frontier.

"For example?"

"Most are ranchers."

"Well, here we go," I said. "A breeze has blown up, and the kindling is caught! Continue."

He smiled, encouraged.

"There's mining!"

"Of what material?"

"Coal. Ore. Copper. Silver."

My father was in the process of reinventing himself as a miner of silver, according to my most recent correspondence with my mother. Actually, she said he had bought a stake in a silver mine in Texas and was going to "mine silver," but "miner of silver" sounds more passive and therefore accurate.

"I do not want to teach anywhere near a silver mine," I said.

"Are you okay with sheep and cattle?"

"I know nothing of sheep but that they are said to lack independence. I am fond of cows. And horses too."

"We got more of them than we do people."

"And what of culture?"

"I hear there is a movement afoot to change the state motto."

"Progressive," I said. "But I am afraid I am wasting your good time. I'm just finishing my first year in the School of Education."

He looked at me blankly.

"I've three more years yet to go."

"You mean in order to acquire your degree?"

"Yes."

"Not something we can't work around. Can you produce a letter of recommendation describing your progress thus far? Normally I would ask also for some testimony as to your fine character, but already our short interview suggests this is not necessary."

"Was it the longitude or the latitude?"

"It was the one about the culture."

I thought, Edith Gotswegon, that the educational standards in Wyoming must not be terribly high given their representative. I thought also about the letter he was requesting. Of course the first person who came to mind to ask (the person who knew my mind best) was not who I ended up asking. I would never ask him for anything. If I were driven mad by starvation, and a biblical or secular plague had wiped out all the food on earth except for a crust of rat-nibbled-upon bread, which he held out to me, I would subsist ere longer on my inner strength, which is formidable. Also, Edith Gotswegon, what would *he* know of my character? Obviously nothing, as he seriously misjudged it.

One might expect a woman who, partway through her first year in college, was thrown over by her fiancé for her younger sister, to suffer academically as a result. But my grades improved. I had not a foolish boy masquerading as a man to distract me. I had rid my hair of lice. My living quarters were free of vermin, as if *the act of* his throwing me over for my little sister was but a cat that now lived only to trap repellent rodents.

It is a complicated metaphor and I did not expect you to follow it. I should have begun this missive, Edith Gotswegon, by advising you to skip past anything that is over your head. Also and in addition, if you do not get the joke, there is no need to laugh.

"I can produce said letter within a few days' time," I told the recruiter.

"My train leaves for Laramie at nine in the morning," he said.

"I will go now to the office of my professor and have his testimony to you within the hour."

In fifty-eight minutes I returned with the document, and for the second time in my life, a man called me "precise," though this time I did not mind at all.

Two weeks later an official offer arrived in the post. I was to teach in Sheridan, which by Wyoming standards is a metropolis. It is in the northern part of the state, not far from the Montana border. There is a railroad terminal there as well as a stockyard. I was offered the quite unbelievable sum of fifty dollars a month. Room and board is not included in the deal. I was instructed to look for housing in the home of a local family. This struck me as an odd provision to include in an official offer, but I suppose there had been issues with teachers living above saloons or in tent cities. The letter writer, a Mr. Gordon, superintendent of Sheridan County schools, said that the schools ran through the summer because of the severity of the winters, which would make travel to and from school difficult even for town children apparently. You yourself are more or less a town child, Edith Gotswegon, and if you ever missed school due to weather, I don't recall it. I remember you as always being there, as if you were glued to your seat in the front row, answering questions with what might charitably be called alacrity.

I was needed there just a few weeks after the semester ended. That left me no time to visit my family and say goodbye, so I wrote posthaste to my mother to inform her of my plans. She begged me to stay in school and attain my degree, but frankly (may I be frank, E. G.?) I did not see the point of it, since I had been offered a job with only a year of university. Of course in some backwater areas of the country they will hire teachers who have not attended university at all and have no training—I think you know where and to whom I am referring—but the education I received in Stillwater in one year undid the damage done me—and *you*—by our former teacher, whose methods were questionable and shockingly imprecise.

Because I was busy with my schoolwork, I was not able to attend the "wedding" of my sister to Gus McQueen, which took place at the courthouse, presided over by a justice of the peace. According to a letter I received addressed to a horse (it is a long story, Edith Gotswegon, and because of my respect for you, you will be spared it), her "reception" was attended only by two of the three Bulgarian boys who lived close by and who apparently came only for the cake.

If the description of this event was meant to make me feel guilty, it failed; it made me feel pity, which calls for far less emotional investment than guilt.

It has been so long, Edith Gotswegon, since we've talked. How wonderful to be back in touch. In the letter I received from your mother, I reveled in your good fortune. A daring young engineer husband. A mock Tudor house at 3 Winthrop Manor. (Every house should have the wit to mock some style of architecture!) I imagine that your in-laws reside at 1 Winthtrop Manor and that you have married into an old and established family there in Oklahoma City. I am sure there are options open to anyone lucky enough to have money to burn in the stove to warm your kitchen on a brisk fall morning, when you have nothing at all to do but read the society column in the *Oklahoman*. I imagine you are a regular reader now that you have entered society, though you never showed any interest in the *Kiowa County News*, bless that veritable fount of knowledge from which I learned not only how to spell but some part of what I know of human nature.

It is nature itself with which I have been acquainting myself here in Wyoming. I am not *un*acquainted with nature, having grown up—well, you know where I grew up—but this is nature of a completely different order. I am five feet seven inches tall and have never felt less until I stepped off the train in Sheridan. In the distance loomed the Bighorns, as advertised by the learned recruiter, but they were far more imposing than the postcard. This is as it should be, I realize, though my father once showed me a photo of the Fountain of Youth in Florida that made it seem magical, and he claimed to have gone there once and found nothing but a weed-choked dip in the ground covered by a rusted grate. Photographs, my point being, can lie. But so can my father, and others.

The mountains seemed very close—right atop the city, as if I could reach up and touch them—though the kindly porter who helped me with my bags told me they were a hard two-hour ride away, depending on your mount. Between the city and the mountains, as clouds pass over the sun, huge shadows patchwork the vast valley. They move slowly, the clouds, darkening splotches of pasture and grassland. I could watch them out the window all the day long.

Though I have gone on record as being largely unconcerned with air, I must say that I now understand the recruiter's metaphor. There *is* something of a mountain stream in the taste of the air (or what I imagine a mountain stream must taste of, having never seen a mountain higher than those of the Wichita range, which are anthills compared) once you get away from the smoke of the steam engine and into town proper.

Before I provide a thumbnail description of the town proper, I should pause and say that I have often imagined leaving Lone Wolf and, indeed, have long fantasized myself in exotic locales. A western outpost filled with ranch hands spilling out of saloons to spit into gutters was not among these locales. Like many a progressive-minded midwestern girl, I saw myself in Chicago. Now is perhaps the time to confess to having asked the recruiter another question, the answer of which sealed my fate.

"How far is Wyoming from here?"

"From Oklahoma?"

"From where we stand."

"Well, I came through Chicago. So it's hard to hard to gauge the distance as the crow flies."

"I am not a crow and I won't be flying. All trains go to Chicago. If you were going to see the Pyramids in ancient Egypt, it is said that you would first have to change trains in Chicago."

"Is that a fact?" he said. "Ancient Egypt?"

"How long did it take, no matter your route, for you to travel from Wyoming to Stillwater?"

He thought about it while working a toothpick between his teeth, which is something I have seen other men do when considering the distance between places, a curious and unseemly habit.

"Two and a half days," he said. "But they were hard ones."

It was then that I agreed to go. Had there been someone there recruiting for schools in Maine, and had the recruiter worked his toothpick and come up with an answer exceeding two and a half days in duration, I would be getting reacquainted with you from Maine.

But here I am. I have taken rooms with a Mrs. O'Connelly. She is Irish, Edith Gotswegon, which means she is a both a pious Catholic and partial to spirits. She speaks to me harshly of her six boys, who are more or less grown and live in the area, and indeed one of them told me she was in the regular habit of boxing his ears for every impertinence when he was younger, but when they all show up for Sunday supper she puts on such a spread and is so indulgent and tolerant of their crude table manners and incessant interrupting of endless stories involving the high jinks of their youth that I find it hard to believe her ever a strict disciplinarian. I like it when "the boys" come, because otherwise it is just the two of us and a Mr. Richard, who quarters in a basement room by the boiler. He is a desk clerk at a local hotel and he has a persistent cough that I have heard described in books as "hacking." I can hear it even two floors above, though he is rarely there—he seems to take his meals at the hotel. He does not attend Sunday suppers with "the boys." Once I asked Mrs. O'Connelly what Mr. Richard did of a weekend and she rolled her eyes and laughed her raunchy Irish laugh. When something amuses her, her cheeks turn pink as does her laugh. I like her, though she often reeks of sherry.

I am not so sure you would like her, Edith Gotswegon. She is a far cry from 3 Winthrop Manor. The only way she might appear in those hallowed halls is in service, uniformed and aproned and cooking up her specialty, a stew of lamb and potatoes. That brings me to a point. I do have one; this letter is not just to describe the hacking cough of Mr. Richard. The manner in which I chose to move two-and-a-half hard days' train travel from Oklahoma may seem impetuous. Perhaps it may even seem petty to some. I have admitted that I based my decision on distance, and that not much forethought was applied. But I am here now and I have made a choice to live my life among the sort of plainspoken, honest, heartfelt people around whom I was raised (people not unlike yourself, Edith Gotswegon). My dreams of Chicago mostly took me over in the afternoons, after school, when I wasted much time combing my hair with my mother's comb-and-mirror set. I imagined myself working for a newspaper, writing my very own column, which thousands would read while sipping their morning coffee. I would be known across the city and beyond. But then something happened that convinced me that these sorts of dreams, of glamour and city lights, of lipstick and fame, are but a manifestation of a certain kind of pride. I have nothing against pride, if it is used as motivation to better your circumstances and stand up for yourself. But my mother, weakened though she was by the loss of our brothers to typhoid, is an example of a debilitating meekness, and my father an example of the dangers of pride, since he used it as an excuse not to soil and callous his hands with hard work (or, actually, any kind of work). When I went away to Stillwater, my mother presented me with her steamer trunk, which she had kept hidden from us all these years. Inside one of its various compartments was the aforementioned mother-of-pearl comb-and-mirror set. Laid atop it was a train letter in which my mother, in a rare show of support, expressed how proud she was of me and how good I had always been to my younger sister. I saved her life, Edith Gotswegon. Everyone knows that I saved her life. Once, during the half week when you and I were friends, you mentioned that your brother, who is commonly thought of as slow, was breached at birth, and you inquired of me if the same circumstances had not befallen my sister. My sister is not slow. Her mind is forever alight. She is the opposite of slow. She is scheming, always.

I saved her life, so that she might ruin mine.

After a certain schoolteacher threw me over for my sister, I sent the trunk home. It was meant to be a wedding present to my sister. I included the comb-and-mirror set with a note to my sister, which was brief, and if by any chance the intended party of this letter, which is not you, Edith Gotswegon, did not receive the steamer trunk and its contents, which were only the brief letter and the comb-and-mirror set, I repeat the letter here, in its entirety: "Mother-of-pearl is not pearl."

My sister is not slow. She is the opposite of slow. I have no doubt she understood my meaning.

It occurs to me that now that you are married, you have changed your name? No matter, for I will always know you as you were when I last saw you, and never will I ever think of you as anyone other than Edith Gotswegon.

I sincerely hope all is well there with you—and with *yours*!

For you flicked your tongue, and you made him yours.

Oh yes you did did.

Sincerely,

Lorena Stewart

PART THREE

11

GUS MCQUEEN

Fort Davis, Texas, 1935

Only at night, after the children were in bed (they had four now: Leslie was sixteen, Lorena was fifteen, Henry was seven, and Mattie had just turned three), did Gus have time to talk to his wife. They had been married seventeen years and he still wanted to talk to Elise or, better yet, listen to her, but there was so much work to be done, both at the newspaper and at home, that they scarcely had the chance during the day.

When the children were asleep, or at least in their beds, Gus and Elise closed the door to their bedroom. Even little Mattie, who was prone to nightmares, knew not to knock. Elise liked to lie with her head on Gus's stomach, her feet on the wall next to the bed. "Count my toes," she would say, and Gus would say, always, that he couldn't count that high. Sometimes Elise would read aloud to Gus her favorite parts of the paper. They would say what happened that day and then they would, too quietly for both their tastes (for the house was not that big and sound carried), begin stripping off each other's clothes and kissing their way up and down each other's body before one ended up atop the other. Soon they would trade off, as they were in every way democratic.

But first, they would talk.

Gus rarely spoke of his life before he came to Lone Wolf, for by that point he had spent more time in Oklahoma and Texas than he had back east. But one night, when they were lamenting how little time they had to be together in the way they craved (alone, slowly stripping and kissing), he told Elise about how when he was living with his aunt—and even before, when he was with his father still—he was terrified of time.

"Terrified how and terrified why?" said Elise.

"It just seemed so vast."

He had school to go to when it was in session, he said, and there was the long walk to and from school, almost an hour each way. He had his chores both before and after school and, from the age of twelve, his job at the millinery. And still, he said, there were all these hours. He remembered them, looming, a blankness stretching away like desert or prairie to an eye unaccustomed to the bounty of both.

"Time was the enemy," he said. "I wanted to run and hide from it."

"In the hayloft?"

"Every night I went to the river that ran behind both my father's house and my aunt's. I've told you about the river before."

"Where you saw the sheep," said Elise.

"Yes."

"You told me first when we were floating in the Red River."

"Yes."

"Say more about the river. I much prefer it to the Natchez Trace."

"One of these days I am going to throw you in the back of the truck and drive you to the Natchez Trace and leave you there."

"Return me to the river, please," said Elise.

But he couldn't tell her how it had been for him, though he remembered it perfectly. Every night he planned to cross over. The other side seemed the answer to his problems—or maybe to the question he did not know how to ask. Over there, the trees fluttered in a breeze that never reached him. No-see-ums would swarm him and he would swat at the air like a blind man. The sun would go down as he sat there, looking west, toward Lone Wolf. Every leaf and twig on the other side would turn golden. If only we had settled over there, he would think. If only I had the courage to cross.

"I wanted to cross it."

"What kept you from it?"

"More than one thing," said Gus, confident and grateful that Elise would not ask him to list all the things, as anyone else might have done.

Elise was silent for a long while and then said, "I felt the same, darling."

"In the hayloft?"

"Atop Sandy. I would ride him across the prairie all night long, while listening to Lorena's sleep-breath trying to boss me around in our attic room with the two saggy cots."

There came a hard knocking on the front door.

Gus let in a rider, a young man name Mills, who had something to do with the silver mine. He had ridden up from Shafter to inform them of Mr. Stewart's passing.

"How did he expire?" asked Elise.

This Mills looked into Elise's eyes and then away. He appeared to decide something.

"He said he would like it to be known that he met his end in a mining accident."

"Which means he did not."

"No ma'am," said Mills.

"I am grateful to you for not lying," she said. "How did he actually expire?"

"He took sick."

"What variety of sickness?"

"That I don't know, ma'am."

"No doctor was called?"

"That's the strange part," said Mills.

Gus watched Elise carefully. Her expression shifted as she appeared to understand what had happened in the adobe shack.

"Why is it strange?" she said. "Doctors in these parts are known to be addicted to that patent medicine they peddle."

"Yes ma'am," said Mills. He seemed relieved by this response rather than challenged by it. "That one comes up from Presidio is a known drunkard."

"Precisely. It is an occupational hazard and one that can be forgiven until their services are gravely needed, at which point . . ." She seemed to grow bored with this notion and asked if her father lingered.

"He did."

"How long?"

"A week or more, as I heard it."

"And my mother?"

"She stayed by his side."

"Is anyone with her now?"

"An old Mexican woman by the name of Pilar. She is said to be a healer. It is my understanding that Pilar covered your father in poultices made from agave pulp and ground sage and some other ingredients, but it must have been too late."

"When was Pilar called for and by whom?"

"By your mother and toward the end."

Elise nodded. "You'll stay the night. I will ride down with you in the morning." She led Mills upstairs and cleared a bed for him by picking up a sleeping child and dropping it into a bunk alongside two other sleeping children. There were noises that were not words, a rustle of readjustment and then quiet.

Alone in their bedroom, Elise said, "Juana will care for the children while you are at work."

"Ought I not come along?"

"What for?"

"It just seems proper."

"At last he has struck it rich," said Elise. "He is turning blue in the snowy heavens."

Gus put his arms around her.

"Or not," she said. "You'll telegram Lorena in the morning?"

"Of course," said Gus. "Shall I tell her you will wait for her arrival to commence with the burial?"

"It is two-and-a-half hard days' train travel from wherever she was in Wyoming to Stillwater, according to the letter she wrote to me via Edith Gotswegon some fifteen years ago now."

"Perhaps she has moved."

"She has. Mother hears from her and has given me her new address."

"Have you written to her?"

"I have not. Have you?"

They rarely talked about Lorena. At first they did—it would have seemed all the more the betrayal had they not—but it had all happened so long ago. But Gus knew that Elise missed her. He knew she thought about her. He thought of her sometimes himself, with more than a little guilt but never regret.

"Of course I have not written to her," said Gus.

Elise was silent, so Gus said, "What do you think your mother would want?"

"Mother of Pearl," said Elise. They stood together by the bed, Gus's arms around her, but she was moving, she was adrift.

"What about *your* father?" she said upon her sudden and unsettling return.

"My father?" Gus said.

"Do you want to know if he lives still?"

Gus thought about the last time he saw his father. He and his aunt had taken the bus to Statesville, and his father asked him if there was a girl in the picture, and Gus remembered how affronted he was by his father's use of the word *picture* as the two plump kids ran in circles and his father's bony wife would not look Gus in the eye. He remembered on the bus ride home his aunt said only, "My land." He remembered seeing farmers burning leaves in barrels in the side yards and the brilliant foliage of fall in the foothills of the Blue Ridge.

He thought about how he wanted to see his aunt again.

"Yes," he said, but he was speaking of his aunt. He was worried she would leave without his having the chance to say goodbye.

"He needs to be put in the ground," she said, about her own father, Gus assumed. She was adrift again. "If Mother has not done it already."

"She can come live with us now."

"Yes."

"Rodrigo and I can build her a casita back by the creek."

"She will require curtains."

"That can be done."

"And she'll need some new dresses."

"We will see to it. Are you sure you don't want me to come along?" said Gus.

"You've a newspaper to put out."

"Joe Dudley can manage without me for a few days."

"Joe Dudley cannot spell properly."

This was true. Like many a smooth talker, and successful salesman, he was barely literate.

In two days' time, Elise returned with her mother. If there was any sort of funeral, Gus never heard of it. He never learned where his father-in-law was buried. The only thing he ever heard Mrs. Stewart say was that it was a shame Lorena was too busy to come.

The morning Elise left with the fellow Mills, she had handed Gus a telegram to send to Lorena.

> father killed in mining accident stop mother has come to live with us stop she would love to see you again stop as would sister stop oh she would would she yes she would would

At the Western Union office, the telegraph officer read it and opened his mouth, but before words came out Gus said, "Type exactly as written, please." It was beyond him to explain what he could not understand. He did not need to understand it. He did and did not understand what his aunt meant when on the bus back from Statesville she said "My land" and then nothing for miles and miles while he looked out the window at the men leaning on shovels, keeping watch over piles of burning leaves.

There was much that Gus half-understood, and much that he did not understand at all.

Once, at work at the newspaper office, scrambling to get the paper out on deadline, he felt nauseated. He wondered if it weren't something he'd eaten, then realized he'd not eaten all day. To think food was the culprit, instead of the lack of it—it took him back to Hibriten, where he was so often hungry and where he often blamed his loneliness on the actions or reactions of others, not knowing his pain came from waiting for things to begin.

Parts of him, left behind, scattered about. He liked to remember waiting out lunch hour in the woods, pulling back pine bark to study the hieroglyphics of burrowing bugs. He liked remembering the nights he was so anxious about the next day's classes that he rose from the cot in the teacherage, built a fire in the classroom, and stayed up filling the board with figures and facts until the children began to trickle in.

Parts of him scattered about and other parts just a puzzle. Maybe everyone was like this? Elise certainly was a puzzle. Often she said things that more than puzzled Gus.

Just before Leslie left home to work on the 360 ranch down near Marathon, as a kind of going-away party, they'd loaded up the wagon with picnic baskets and blankets and traveled over Wild Rose Pass to the San Solomon Springs.

Spread out on the banks on a couple of old Kiowa blankets they'd brought from Lone Wolf, eating pecan pie for dessert, Elise, clutching the edge of the blanket, said to the children, "Your father was my schoolteacher. He rescued me from the elements. It was his little brother, whispering in his ear over the coyote wind, who told him where to find us."

"Us," said Lorena. "You mean you and your sister?"

"Me and Sandy."

"Where was your sister?" said Lorena.

"She was with your father."

"And Daddy's brother was there also?" asked Leslie.

"In spirit," said Elise.

"This is when you got frostbite?" said Leslie.

"Why was Aunt Lorena with daddy?" Lorena said.

Henry said, "Who is Aunt Lorena?"

Mattie, who was only three, said, "What does frost bite?"

"Your father was engaged to my sister before he was engaged to me," said Elise.

Gus said his wife's name. He looked into the faces of his children, which were worried with questions, none of which they knew how to ask. Or maybe they knew how to ask them but did not know whether they ought to. Gus knew the only way out of this was to start talking so that Elise would not. He could tell the truth. But what was the truth? Ought he to tell his children how he had fooled himself into thinking he loved one sister only to ditch her and marry another? He did not want them to know they could fool themselves into doing such drastic things, although he knew he could not prevent them from finding out on their own.

"I was not engaged to her, not officially. I had the ring in my pocket. I had traveled by train to Stillwater with the idea of proposing."

"Stillwater," said Leslie, who liked the names of places, and of things.

"And why didn't you?" said Lorena.

Gus was not raised to have conversations of this sort, and especially not with his children. The closest he had ever come to a personal conversation with his father was when his father had asked him, in front of that bony woman his father had married, in front of Aunt Mattie, if there was a girl in the picture. The most intimate conversation he'd ever had with a member of his family (pre-Elise) was with Aunt Mattie, during the last hour he spent with her.

"Your mother put a spell on me," said Gus. "She is a sorceress."

The younger boys looked at their mother with the appropriate mix of fear and awe. Lorena looked disappointed, as if she were being patronized. Only Leslie, in the spirit of his namesake, who Gus remembered being able to always and easily move to laughter, smiled.

But Gus was not smiling when he called Elise a sorceress, and he did not smile the rest of the way home or when they went to bed that night. Elise was distant, he supposed because of Leslie's leaving, as he felt sure it had not occurred to her that telling the children about his involvement with their aunt might be something about which he would want to be consulted.

They did not speak of it until the next morning, after they saw Leslie off and the children were gone to school.

Gus said, "You know what, Elise?"

"No, what?"

"Sometimes I envy you."

"Why?

"Because you know exactly what you've lost."

Elise said, "Are you referring to my severed digits and compromised nose?"

"Yes."

"You envy me these?"

"For knowing the parts of you that are lost," he repeated.

"You think because I walk funny and wear my wedding ring on the wrong finger that I am lucky?"

"I don't believe in luck."

"Enviable? Is that the word? You think that I am enviable?"

Words, their meanings, were so often where their arguments led. The actions got lost in the words they chose to defend, explain, or apologize. It wore Gus down. He wanted it to be over. So the children knew about Lorena. Chances seemed high that none of them would ever lay eyes on her, so what difference did it make. He thought to say, Let's just forget it, but Elise was not one to abandon a good skirmish.

"It's not the worst thing anyone ever said to me," she said, in a way that suggested it was in the running.

Gus wanted to ask about the competition but knew it would be unseemly. He knew, many years ago, Elise had received a letter from Lorena. He imagined Lorena's letter was not kind. Perhaps it contained the worst thing anyone had ever said to Elise?

When he told Elise that he envied her, he'd been thinking, mostly, of himself, of the things that were missing, the scattered parts of him. He'd aimed low. He knew that the parts of him scattered about or altogether absent were not comparable to the toes a doctor had sawed off in the Hobart Hospital. Elise's accident, her losses, just made her more desirable to him, he realized some years after he married her, when she was showing her lone left toe to two-year-old Leslie and teaching him to say *Wee, wee, wee, all the way home.*

But an hour after this fight, one of their worst, they were down by the creek. Vultures circled high in the cloudless blue sky. Shaded by the only cover for miles, a thicket of cottonwood hugging the creek, their clothes came off an item at a time and were tossed between rocks, upon branches. One of Gus's boots landed in a puddle. Elise leaned back against a live oak. The rhythm of their friction echoed off the cliffs above the creek. It made them laugh, the echo.

They lay sunning their winter-whitened flesh in a patch of sand on the creek bank. In the canyon, quiet save the steady swish of creek, Gus felt a little melancholy. The near-intolerable pressure of his passion was gone and what followed was not catharsis but a mildly anxious lassitude, until Elise, ever intuitive, having forgotten the horrible thing he said to her an hour earlier, said, "Afterward?"

"As in right now?"

"I never feel either completed or depleted. There is always some part of us lost, Gus McQueen. There is always more to lose."

12

LORENA NELSON

Recluse, Wyoming, 1938

Many years ago now, I received in the mail a series of letters addressed to a horse. The writer was obviously of infirm mind, as—aside from the fact that they were addressed to a horse—the letters were hardly coherent. Included were intimate details of the writer's domestic life as well as disjointed ruminations on past events. As to style, I would describe these letters as chaotic. The aftereffects of reading these letters were what I assume a hangover to be like. (I am not and have never been a drinker). I felt dyspeptic and confused.

Then I met the man I would marry. I put the letters away, and they went away.

Isaac had come to town to sell cattle. He owned a ranch a good distance east of Sheridan. In those days he came to Sheridan four times a year: once to sell his cattle, once for supplies, once to see the Christmas lights, and always on the Fourth of July. Isaac was a fan of parades. He was not a fan of fireworks, having served in the trenches during the Great War. "No veteran who did not sit behind a desk stateside could find such commotion entertaining," he told me. He had seen the Fourth of July fireworks once after his return from Europe and could not sleep for a week afterward. This is one of the few times he has admitted to having been emotionally riled by anything. He is much stirred by certain hymns, and he can be effusive about pie, particularly rhubarb, but otherwise his emotional range is as unchanging as the ranch land that has been in his family for three generations.

Isaac is straightforward. He is steadfast and loyal. He uses words as he does dollars, which is to say carefully and without waste. *Deliberate* is a word I would use to describe his character. He is a man of lists and goals. Since returning home from the army, he had had in it his mind to marry a schoolteacher. He himself is not given to reading much past the newspaper, the Bible, and the dime westerns he buys in bulk during his quarter-annual shopping trips to town, but he appreciates education and wanted his children to be raised by a woman of some cultural refinement. Many years into our marriage I was told by one of his cousins that Isaac had a crush on his schoolteacher, an Irish woman who had survived the potato famine and loved the poetry of Robert Burns. This is not the sort of thing I would have ever gotten out of Isaac himself, which suited me fine, as I grew up with a father who felt the need to give voice to everything he had experienced in life, not to mention every idea that came half-formed into his head. There is a lot to be said for the *un*said, especially where men are concerned. It did not bother me to learn, so many years into my marriage, that Isaac's stated reasons for wanting to marry me were not comprehensive. In fact, I suspected such already, for I had often heard him reciting Robert Burns to his collie dog, and when I asked him how he came to be a fan of a poet known for his bawdy verse (for my Isaac is a devout Christian), he told me of this Missus McConigley and I saw something not in his eyes but in the way he averted them.

One afternoon, a couple of years after I arrived in Wyoming, I was sitting at my desk in my classroom after school, working on my lesson plan, when someone knocked on the door. It was open. Isaac was standing in the doorway, dressed in his Sunday best. He held his hat in his hand and he had obviously come straight from the barbershop, for I could see the white skin on his neck and about his ears that his hair had hidden from the sun, exposed now by the barber's blade.

"May I help you?"

He asked if he might borrow a moment of my time. He said he was interviewing schoolteachers.

"Are you a journalist?"

"No ma'am. Why would I be?"

"Journalists conduct interviews."

He nodded, as if this were news to him.

"The only other reason to conduct an interview is if you have a job to offer. Are you a prospective employer?"

"Oh no," he said. "I'd never dare pay for it."

"Pay for what?"

"Why, a wife."

"Well, that bodes well for you. Any man who purchases a wife, or attempts to, should be horsewhipped."

At this time in my life my tongue was sharp. I had been described as insouciant. I had even been accused of being a suffragette. In fact, I had high standards and firm morals, which men of weak intellect often confuse with a militant streak in a woman.

"I agree with you," he said. "No woman should sell herself."

"No man ought to offer to pay."

"Is it not the same thing?"

"Not at all."

He looked confused and intrigued at once.

"Might I take a seat?"

I looked him over. From a distance he appeared to be clean, and he was mannerly enough. He was tall, lean, springy on his feet, blue-eyed. There were signs in the wrinkles about his eyes of a life spent in the elements.

I motioned for him to sit. Of course the seat was too small for him. He could not fit his knees beneath the desk. He spent some time arranging his legs in the aisle. His boots were worn but well polished. His hands were large and rough, but his nails were trimmed.

"So you are interviewing for a wife?"

"Yes."

"And are you going door to door?"

"Oh no," he said. "I am only interviewing schoolteachers."

"A narrow field, especially in Wyoming. Might I ask why you've chosen such limitations?"

"I am a cattle rancher, ma'am. I work hard and my spread is a good ways from any town. Forty miles, in fact. I have given much thought to the type of woman I would like to marry and I have decided that an educated woman best suits my needs."

"Are cattle ranchers better suited to educated women all around?" I asked, though the question that came to mind was, Are educated women suited to cattle ranchers, especially ones that live forty miles from a town? I had explored the country outside of Sheridan and knew that in Wyoming the word *town* often meant a crossroads store, a school, and a church.

"Well, I enjoy learning. I am not a man who knows everything."

"Then you are the exception. I suppose you are educated yourself?"

"I attended school until I was needed on the ranch."

"At what grade did your schooling end?"

"I had six grades behind me when I left. I should add that had it been up to me, I would have continued. But a boy must listen to his father. I have never been accused of shirking."

Six grades was several more than the average in this part of Wyoming. The man was a veritable scholar.

"Of course, when I was seventeen I went into the service."

"You are a veteran."

"Yes."

"You must have seen a lot. Were you wounded?"

"I was fortunate. The good Lord watched over me closely and kept me out of harm's way."

Oh dear. I was not raised in the church, and at that point my life had not been graced by the presence of any power higher than my own desire to overcome early hardship and some emotional suffering.

"You are not a believer," he said.

I was not one to advertise my lack of faith, so I lied and said I was certainly a believer, which was only a lie in the context of his question, for there were many things I believed in strongly.

"That's good. I would have had to take my leave if you weren't."

"What other qualifications aside from schoolteacher and believer are you searching for in your wife?"

He appeared stymied. He crossed and uncrossed his long legs. His lap was hard up against the desktop.

"What about you," he said, rather cannily, I thought. "What do you require of a husband?"

"I don't recall saying I am in search of a husband."

"Are you not, then?"

In fact, I had been engaged once. Well, not officially—I had been serious with a man, a schoolteacher, in fact, who had, on the heels of proposing—the boxed ring visible in his pocket—changed his mind. He is, as far as I know, married still to my younger sister.

"I would never marry another schoolteacher."

"I would never marry another rancher."

"There are female ranchers?"

"Sheep," he said with obvious derision.

"What is wrong with sheep?"

He seemed shocked by the question. It was the first I would learn of the acrimony between sheep and cattle ranchers.

"They are unintelligent."

"Their wool is indispensable."

"You can get far more out of a cow than you can a sheep."

I went quickly from wondering why I was discussing the relative differences between sheep and cattle with this handsome but pious rancher to realizing I was enjoying it. The conversation itself was moving quickly and I did not want it to.

"Do you realize that your method of finding a suitable wife might put off many a good prospect?"

"No doubt it has already," he said. "But they won't the right fit."

"*Weren't*," I said. "Not *won't*."

He beamed, as if he had been waiting years to have his grammar corrected and found it almost intolerably amorous.

"Begging your pardon. They *weren't* the right fit."

"I should beg your pardon for correcting you," I said. "It's only that much of what I do in this room all day is broker agreements between subjects and verbs."

"And here I come adding to your workload. Desecrating the place at that," he added, staring up at the rafters. "Like cursing in the Lord's house."

"Well, it's not really of that order," I said, and for the first time I smiled.

"I would like children," he said.

"Yes?"

"I don't care much for sweet potatoes or turnips."

"Then you should not plant, buy, or cook them."

He laughed. "You've got some spark in you."

"I've no idea what is meant by that."

"I would like permission to ask you to dinner."

"Where did you have in mind to dine?"

"The Sheridan Inn."

"I am not a fan of 'Buffalo' Cody and his western equivalent of a minstrel show," I said.

"I agree that he is a dissolute opportunist, but Cody has not managed the place in over a decade."

"His presence lingers. I'm afraid if that is all you can offer, permission is denied."

"I was thinking it was your father I'd ask."

"You will have to travel to the part of Texas that is mostly Mexico."

I noticed a shift in his appraising eye.

"Ah," he said, "a Texan!"

"Good gracious, no. I was born in Kansas and raised in Oklahoma."

"There's some decent calf ropers out of Oklahoma here lately."

"Decent sorts can be found there."

"You are making fun of me now," he said, banging his body against the desk.

"Actually, I am, in a roundabout way, admitting my ignorance of rodeo."

"I can take it or leave it myself," he said earnestly.

"What else can you leave?"

"Beg pardon?"

"Never mind. What can you *not* leave?"

"My ranch. The church. My horse."

A man who does not love his horse is suspect to me, though I took note that family did not appear in his list. However, I did not judge him for it, as the word means nothing, or rather it is a word that evokes sentiment only in those who have never felt born into the wrong clan. I thought the rancher and I might be, in this way, kindred spirits. Perhaps he too was the only normal product of his bloodline.

"What is your horse called?"

"Newt," he said, staring at the desk like one of my third graders.

"Is he wee in stature?"

"No. He is sixteen hands."

"Then why call him Newt?"

"My middle name is Newton, and when I was a tyke, I was called Newt. But a grown man can't go around being called Newt."

"But a grown horse can?"

"People will name a horse all sorts of things not suitable for a person."

"Yes, it's true," I said, thinking of The Beatitudes, and of Sandy, though I knew a man who was called Sandy in his youth.

"Is Newton a family name?"

"I am called after Isaac in the Bible, for my father was nearly sixty when I was born. Newton seemed to suit as a middle name."

"It certainly has a familiar ring. As well as a certain *gravitas*."

He made no sign that he got the reference. "I feel like you are getting way more out of me than I am out of you," he said.

"We must save something for dinner," I said. "I'm not terribly interesting, and if we don't stop now, we might be sitting in silence, in the manner of couples who have been married for decades, before the soup arrives."

"Maybe such couples know each other so well they don't have to be remarking on the quality of the coffee just to prove to the world that they're happy."

This remark was both terrifying and oddly comforting to me. I decided to put it immediately out of mind, lest I get distracted by its hidden implications.

"Before I agree to dinner—"

"I thought you'd done . . . I'm sorry, I meant to say, I thought you already had agreed."

"There's something I would like to know first and that is, who else is in the running?"

He begged my pardon, as he was then in the habit of doing.

"How many schoolteachers have passed the preliminary interview and are now to the wine-and-dine stage?"

"I'm afraid I never touch spirits."

"That makes two of us."

He looked relieved. "To answer your question and to answer it honestly, there was one other who invited me home to have dinner with her family."

"A local girl! She must know calf roping."

"I now feel it my duty to cancel our engagement."

"And how will you do that?" I said, not-so-secretly pleased to be knocking out the competition.

"How will I cancel? Why, I'll tell her the truth."

"And what is the truth?"

"That I have met you."

"It might be best to be general."

"Beg pardon?"

"Better to say you met 'someone' rather than to use my name," I said. I had endured enough gossip back in Lone Wolf, thanks to my younger sister, and it was one of my objectives, since relocating to Wyoming, to keep from being talked about behind my back.

"I don't even know your name."

"Lorena Stewart," I said.

"Isaac Nelson," he said, rising and bowing comically over the too-small desk.

"Formerly known as Newt."

"You'll not let me forget that."

"I find it charming, actually, that you named your horse after your childhood self."

"Well, he's a lot like me when I was a boy."

"I suppose I will soon see evidence of his boyishness, and of yours."

"I like to hear you talk."

"That is good to know, for I am not sure I agree with you about the contentedness of the couple sitting in silence at the dinner table."

"I only meant people are quick to judge a book by its cover."

"I find it hard to disagree with that, even if it is a cliché."

"I know what a cliché is," he said, raising his hand as if he were in class. It was a rare display of outright humor. I told him to please wait his turn and let others talk.

"I miss learning," he said. He pointed to the pull-down map of the United States, which would never roll up fully and always exposed the Mexican border, the very region where my sister and mother, when last heard from, were living. "I like a map."

"Most men do." I wondered if he worked a toothpick between his teeth while studying one.

"I am not just some *man*." I liked that he said this, even though I suspected, out of instinct, that his declaration was debatable.

There was a dinner, and then another a couple of weeks later. Isaac began to make the trip to Sheridan twice a month. He was good company. His table manners were passable, meaning he did not pour coffee into his saucer to drink or use a crust of bread as a knife. His enthusiasm for his work was attractive to me, having grown up with a man who did not love his work. (To love something, you need to actually *do* something). I did notice straightaway that topics of conversation were few and, impressive as they were, not of a bent I would call stimulating, by which I mean he was not given to talking about the following: art, culture, music, literature, what makes people behave as they do, other people (save for his ranch hands, about whom he had humorous anecdotes, mostly involving mishaps with livestock), the seriousness of other people, politics (except for those that affected his livelihood), and family (his own kin and the concept of family.) But he knew cattle and he knew horses, and I found refreshing a mind trained in the daily existence; there was such *discipline* in his life, such focus and expert management of time, and his skills seemed far more valuable and nobler than a reading knowledge of Latin.

Isaac had sought out an educated woman, and he had said in our first interview that he loved learning, so all the things we did not discuss seemed inevitably forthcoming. I looked upon Isaac at first as a rough gem. And, just as he said of himself, I am not one to shirk away from a challenge.

After four months he announced that the trip to and from his ranch was getting long.

"I intend to make an offer," he said.

"You sound like you are buying a piece of land."

"You ought to know by now I am not so good at this business of courting."

"It would help not to refer to it as a business. But you ought to know by now that I have little to compare you to."

I had not told him about the man who was married to my sister. It would not be until a few weeks later, when we were making our wedding arrangements and he asked who I might want to attend, that I told him the story. He listened and he nodded, as was his way. Either he sensed the subject was still tender or else he did not find it interesting. Or perhaps he formed, from the story, a negative opinion of both my sister and her husband, which his Christian charity prevented him from stating. At any rate, he made no comment, which, as was often the case with Isaac, left me feeling both comforted and slightly judged.

We were married on May 11, 1920, at the Immanuel Lutheran Church in Sheridan. Isaac had wanted to have the ceremony at his "home" church, ten miles from his ranch, since I had no affiliation. But that would have required Mrs. O'Connelly and my two favorites of her sons, Sean and Patrick, and their wives, Molly and Kathleen, who would serve as my attendants, to travel a good distance, and of course there were no accommodations in the area. Isaac said there were dozens of ranchers who would be happy to put up the wedding party and all guests, but when quizzed, he admitted that these ranchers were spread out over a fifty-mile area.

It made more sense to be married in Sheridan. Isaac went along with it because I reminded him it was tradition to marry in the bride's hometown, and he had respect for tradition. Sheridan was—oddly enough—the closest I had to a home. I knew no one in Lone Wolf, and I no longer had family to speak of.

There was the question of who ought to give me away. Mrs. O'Connelly suggested Mr. Richard, he of the hacking cough and the basement room. I was not at first taken with the idea, since I had laid eyes on him fewer than a dozen times in my life and suspected him a man of questionable habits, but the notion of a complete stranger standing in for the complete stranger who would have stood in for me had I invited my parents appealed to me. Isaac was perplexed but did not question me about it. Mrs. O'Connelly saw to it that Mr. Richard was presentably attired; his wool suit smelled, curiously, of pavement after a hard summer rain, and his boots were not evenly polished, but the look on his face was so amicable that I wondered if Mrs. O'Connelly had not remunerated him in some way I did not care to further consider. Midway through our vows he erupted into a fit of coughing best described as hacking, but it came just when I was repeating the preacher's words to Isaac as instructed. *Love* was clear, but *honor* and *obey* were drowned out by Mr. Richard's wet cough. He would die not long after of consumption. I will always remember him, just as I will never forget the words his fit rendered inaudible.

Isaac's brother was his best man, and his two cousins served as groomsmen. They arrived an hour before the wedding and did not stay for the reception. I found this peculiar until Isaac explained that they were tending to his ranch in his absence and could not be away any longer. I knew better than to push, given the situation with Mr. Richard, which I could tell embarrassed Isaac, who was left to explain to his family who this man was to me, as I merely smiled at the question and pretended that their words had been drowned out by the most hacking of coughs.

Thank goodness for the Irish Catholic tendency toward procreation, for the church was packed with Mrs. O'Connelly's sons, their wives, their grandchildren, and I believe perhaps their in-laws. Isaac was paying for it and had slaughtered a pig and several chickens for the feast as the head count grew, but I think it appealed to his vanity to have such a well-attended wedding, and Mrs. O'Connelly won him over with her rhubarb pies, which were served in place of cake, at Isaac's request.

That night we took rooms in the Sheridan Inn, previous odious proprietor notwithstanding. Before he came to bed, Isaac spent such a long time on his knees, praying for God to make our union long and happy, that I fell asleep. Isaac did not think it polite to wake me. To his mind, there would be plenty of time to consummate our union once we arrived at his ranch.

We were over three hours getting there. The wagon was loaded with all I owned, which fit into two trunks and several boxes containing hats I would rarely need. It felt liberating traveling so lightly to a new life. I felt myself capable of anything, really, adaptable and dependable and several other things that ended in *-able*. But midway through the journey, I understood why Isaac had been ready to make his "offer." It was rough going through broken hilly country just east of town before the hills fall away and the plains stretch to the Dakotas and beyond. The road was deeply rutted when it was not washed out completely by snowmelt. There was much mud, and where there is mud, I discovered, there are generally swarms of flies. Isaac paid no attention to them—he seemed as immune to them as the horses—but I spent much of the journey waving a church fan in front of my face, not that I was overheated, just that I did not care for flies.

The house was a quarter mile off the road but visible from much farther, as there were no trees. Why not plant trees? Other settlers had chosen naturally wooded plots or else planted shade trees they kept alive with well water. Not Isaac's family. The house was two-storied, whitewashed, and without the slightest adornment. Mrs. O'Connelly's house in town, with its scrollwork about the porch and the triangular lattice lacing its gables, was like a castle compared. Isaac's farmhouse appeared wind-blasted. It looked, from the driveway, cold in winter and hot in summer. A box in a vast field, surrounded by a barn, a silo, a pen for horses, a chute for branding cattle, a stock tank, a windmill, and several leaning sheds.

Isaac took me inside and led me on a tour. I took in the furniture, functional and unattractive. There was plenty to be done to keep up the house, which had long gone without a thorough cleaning. But the most pressing need was for curtains. I cannot live without curtains and see no reason to. Men apparently do not care who is looking into the windows at night, nor do they have the sense to block the heat of the day with heavy drapes.

There were other challenges. Isaac had been honest from the beginning about how isolated the place was. Having grown up in Lone Wolf, I was not intimidated. We'd not grown up in Lone Wolf proper (as if "proper" in Lone Wolf meant much) but four miles out in the country. Our nearest neighbors, a mile away across the prairie, were a family of Bulgarians. I had only my sister to play with, and she either wanted to play with the Bulgarians or in our barn, which was stifling in summer and freezing in winter and smelled, year-round, of barn.

Play suggests the deep differences between our sensibilities. My sister liked to indulge herself in elaborate games and in made-up scenarios constructed from the articles we read in the local paper. Many involved our horse, which was just a horse, who was given talking parts and, more often than not, special powers. Years later, when I began to attend church with Isaac, I would first hear the following lines from 1 Corinthians 13:11: "When I was a child, I spoke like a child, I thought like a child, I reasoned like a child. But when I grew up, I put away childish things." You could say I grew up earlier than most, and you can say, fairly, that last I heard from her, there was evidence that my sister clung still to childish ways. Especially did she speak, think, and reason like a child.

I preferred to spend my time indoors, helping my mother—who had her own struggles with behaving as a responsible adult—or studying. But my sister was always after me to participate in one of her elaborate scenarios and more often than not, I indulged her, as it was easiest in the end.

Lone Wolf had not actually been all that isolated—the town itself had a half-dozen stores, a train station (the famed Rock Island Line passed through there), two churches, and a couple of saloons. But, having had to give up childish things at an early age, I felt an isolation that transcended geography.

And then I came to Isaac's ranch. When he told me that the nearest town was forty miles away, I expected a town the size of Lone Wolf. The aptly named Recluse, Wyoming, consisted of a general store selling mostly farm implements, a church, a schoolhouse, and several abandoned houses. Isaac's quarterly trip to Sheridan for supplies involved much calculation and planning, for it wasn't as if, should we run out of sugar, we could easily borrow some from a neighbor. The nearest ranch was seven miles away.

When I first arrived at the ranch, I was much taken by its starkness. Mountains are visible on the horizon, but often they are indistinguishable from banks of clouds. The land is flat and the sky wide. The vista is such that a cow grazing several hundred feet away can seem, at first glance, a hillock. There are several ponds on the property and a spring creek fed by snowmelt runs near the house, but it does not produce enough water for trees.

It is a dry country. I was there for several weeks before Isaac admitted that, on a good year, it took twenty acres of land to feed a single cow.

"How many cows do you have?"

"It depends," he said.

"On average."

"Two hundred and eighty-seven." That was a precise number and I admire precision.

"And how many acres?"

"Six thousand five hundred and thirty-one."

"That strikes me as a lot of land."

"Maybe back east," he said. "Out here, not especially sizable."

"I'd like to see it."

"See what?"

"I would like to explore your ranch."

"Nothing much to explore. What you see out the kitchen window's about what you're going to see if you ride for an hour."

The response was typical of Isaac, who was often puzzled by my curiosity. I had married a cattle rancher who owned what he referred to as "a decent spread." I wanted to see the land, and to know it. To Isaac's mind, there was nothing to *know*. Nevertheless I persisted until one Sunday after church he agreed to take me on a tour.

When I met him in the barn, he had tacked only Newt, though there were three other horses, idle in their stalls.

"I'd prefer my own mount."

"Tell you what," he said. "You ride with me and Newt today and after the spring auction I will buy you a gelding."

"I can buy my own horse. It may be a filly or it may be a mare. Perhaps it will be a stallion. I highly doubt it will be a gelding. It will not be bought without my consent, as it must pass my requirements, which for horses are more elaborate than people."

"Horses are necessary and I will mourn Newt when he passes, but they are not on the same order as people."

"Are we not all God's creatures?" I said.

"People are given the ability to reason for a purpose," said Isaac.

"I have known reasonable horses and deeply unreasonable people, and as for the purpose behind the giving, I would like for you to tell me, as we explore your six thousand five hundred and thirty-one acres, what that is. I fear it might take you that long."

"I still like to hear you talk."

"I hope it is still true after we finish our exploration."

"I will love you when we are the old couple we spoke about in our first meeting, sitting in silence at supper."

"My silent supper will be my last supper."

The tour was tersely narrated. We rode through grass that swished against my dress, keeping the Bighorns behind us, for over an hour. In time, the land broke and rolled with low hills, blond with sun-bleached sagebrush and cheatgrass. These were the only plants I recognized. When we came upon a bluish grass, I asked after its name and was told it was called bluestem. I pointed to another plant, tall and spiky, and Isaac said it was a weed.

"Mullein. Good for nothing. Indians smoked it. Said it cured a cough. I believe it might have been the cause of one."

We rode for a half hour in silence, there being no new vegetation to query him about. We came over a hill at the bottom of which cattle stood in the shallow of a pond.

"This is a delightful valley," I said.

"This a draw, not a valley."

"Back east it would be called a valley," I said, though aside from a couple of spots in the Wichita range, we had no valleys in the prairie.

"We have our own terms for things," Isaac said.

"Have you a term for those hills?" I pointed to a ridge, so flat it resembled a mesa.

"Shelf," said Isaac.

"And what differentiates it from a mesa?"

"Whether you're talking to a Mexican or a white man."

I knew many foreign terms that had been adopted by Americans, but I knew better than to point this out, as I was aware of the limits of what interested Isaac. I knew him to have an interest in geology—at least he could talk for more than a minute on the subject or rocks—so I asked him what caused it to be so flat.

"The Lord God might be able to tell you. I imagine it was here when my great-grandfather came from England."

He looked over his shoulder at me. "Where do your people come from?"

I thought to say Bulgaria, just to see his reaction. But I never lied to him. The things I did not tell him were things I did not fully know to say. If a thing is half-formed inside you, not even what my father might call an idea, there is no point in making it known. Half the things my sister said did not bear mention, since they made no sense to anyone aside from herself and the person I was once.

"Ohio and Pennsylvania," I said.

"And before that?"

"Scotland, I believe," I said, though they might well have been Irish. I would later learn that Isaac had a low opinion of the Irish, though he was kind enough not to share this with me at my wedding, attended almost entirely by the O'Connellys.

"And your father, you say he was a farmer?"

He knew so little about me. I could make myself up to him. Was it not why I had come west? It wasn't because of Gus McQueen or my sister. I had envisioned a certain life for myself and it did not happen and I came west on a train and now I was married to Isaac. When I thought of it like that, it seemed as irrefutable as Isaac's beloved Gospels.

"After a fashion," I said.

Isaac nodded.

"Corn?"

"Cotton."

"Ah," he said, which meant either he had a firm opinion about a subject or he did not know the first thing about it and was not interested.

"And your mother's people, were they Scotsmen as well?"

"Some were undoubtedly Scotswomen."

We had dismounted and were down by the pond in the draw. The horse was drinking and nearby, cows swatted flies with their tails. My clothes were dusty and I was standing by my husband. I studied him in the flat afternoon light. I had chosen him, but I knew that you hardly ever make such choices with all of yourself. Parts of you vote by proxy, if at all. What parts of me wanted Isaac?

Isaac's gaze was fixed on his cattle, or beyond—I could not tell because I looked up at the sky. It was not and would never be a blanket. It was a light blue sheet tautly stretched and endless overhead. Everything beneath it belonged to my husband. Did I belong to him?

"I am going to make a choice," I told him.

"Between?"

"Your being a stranger to me and your not being a stranger to me."

He looked at me as if he expected me to say this, as opposed to, say, whether to have stew or steak for dinner. He looked at me like he knew me. Then he said, "You're thirsty?" As if my comment were a symptom that might be easily cured by fetching a flask of water from the saddlebag.

I did not mind. There was a lot to be said for such attentiveness. But it's not exactly right to say there's a lot to be said about it, for if it's right—if it feels right—why say anything at all?

It wasn't long after that day that I borrowed a horse one morning when Isaac and his crew had taken a wagon loaded with posts to some far part of the ranch to mend fence. I paid a visit to the schoolhouse eight miles away, which served the children of ten or twelve ranches.

I have heard it said that a roof is 90 percent of the health of a good structure. By that standard, the schoolhouse was on its last gasp. Many of the shingles had been blown away by the wind. There was a lone outhouse and a pump in the schoolyard. The children had brought their lunches in pails and lined them up beneath their wraps in the coatroom. On pegs hammered into a board hung twelve tin cups, each with a name written on it, though there were only seven children present the day I visited.

The teacher was a young woman who came up from Gillette. She bunked in the teacherage Sunday night through Thursday. She had a gentleman in the mines down in Gillette, and she did not hold school on Friday on account, she said, of his getting paid. She had to be there to take his money lest he spend it all in the saloon before she made it home. I thought to say that he sounded like quite a catch, but I felt for the girl. She appeared overwhelmed. I spent some time with her, questioning her about the curriculum, observing her teach. She was clearly unsuited for the position—I knew good teaching, as I had been subject, in Lone Wolf, to its opposite—and it did not take long to see that she was planning on leaving.

Isaac was in the barn when I returned home. I had gotten a later start than planned, and the sun was low enough to backlight the grass, wind-rippled in the pastures.

"Where've you been?"

I told him about the young teacher. I described her incompetence and said I would be taking over for her when school started back in the fall. He was tinkering with the wagon trace and did not look up.

"If you are going to borrow a man's horse, you'll need to put it up proper."

"I planned on doing just that."

He would not look at me. "He'll need grooming and turning out a bit before you put him back in the stall."

"I grew up on the back of a horse," I said. "I know how to take care of a horse. I need my own horse, so I will not have to borrow one."

He got up and fetched a tool. He was upset, but it wasn't about the horse.

It took two days for him to confront me, which was typical for Isaac. He was not so much a brooder as someone who waited to say what he needed until he had the words to say it. He said it at night, when we had just gone to bed.

"About this teaching."

"You are against it."

"There is plenty to do around here. More than enough for one person. I worry you'll run yourself ragged trying to do both."

But that wasn't the reason and I knew it.

"I imagine there will be times when the weather may necessitate my staying over in the teacherage."

I said this to provoke him and it worked.

"Why are you doing this?"

"Because I am a teacher."

"I thought that was over and done."

"So you were looking to marry a *former* schoolteacher? Or a *retired* one?"

"I can support us. It's my job to provide."

"This is not about twenty dollars a month."

"What, then?"

"I told you. I am a teacher. You knew that when you married me. In fact, I seem to recall that you married me *because* I am a teacher."

"It's true I was looking for an educated woman to spend my life with. But I married you because you are you. And you are the one for me. There's not but one and you're it."

That there is one of me and I am "it" certainly seemed inarguable.

He patted the sheets between us. "I want to wake up every morning with you right here. A little closer'd be even better."

It was perhaps his most tender moment to date. It was enough for me to change my mind. I did not set foot in that schoolhouse until the day I took my firstborn up to enroll him.

My decision to stay on the ranch did not mean I adjusted easily to what I will call its hardships. Isaac kept a shotgun by the door and another in the barn. I noticed it the day I arrived and had in mind to ask why, but the next morning, as I was washing up after breakfast, I heard a blast. I ran to the door, expecting to see cattle rustlers surrounding the house, only to find Isaac nosing the barrel of his gun up under a rattlesnake almost as long as I am tall. He spied me watching and smiled. The snake twitched and he tossed him into the yard and shot him again. He had been on his way to the outhouse, beneath which (he thought to tell me *after* this incident) a "mess" of snakes made their home.

"Sometimes one will make it inside the privy," he said when I came out into the yard to look at the snake. "Doesn't happen often. Still, you should always wear boots, especially at night, and shine your lantern in the corners."

"Have you thought about relocating the outhouse?"

"I've heard it said that if you kill the alpha male, the others will get gone. I might have taken care of the situation," he said, pointing the barrel of his gun toward the snake that lay still now in the weeds.

"That would be an awfully convenient thing to happen on my second day."

"You're bringing us good luck."

But luck had nothing to do with the abundance of snakes on that ranch. I had grown up in rattler country, but in my first month on the ranch I saw more of them than in my prior twenty years. Then there were the stories. The worst I heard, told by a ranch hand named Jed one night at the dinner table, was about an older woman who lived on a nearby ranch, a Mrs. Weatherspoon. One evening she was knitting a sweater for her baby when the baby woke in need of feeding. She laid her yarn down and went to tend to the infant. When she came back to her chair, she reached down to retrieve her yarn and grabbed instead a rattler coiled up alongside it.

"All she seen was a ball, I reckon," said Jed.

"What was her name again?" I asked.

"Weatherspoon."

"The name sounds made up." I said this only because I suspected the hands were trading tall tales to terrorize me, though Jed was my favorite among the hands, as he often said things that surprised me.

"Aren't all names made up? Those that don't come from the Bible, of course," he said, looking at Isaac. "I mean, somebody somewhere had to make them up. God don't just up and assign you a last name, does he, Mr. Nelson?"

Isaac looked at me and smiled.

That Jed had a point, and that it had never occurred to me, made me blush.

"I believe she is suggesting the story itself is made up," Isaac said to Jed, though I could tell by the delight in his eyes whose side he was on.

"Well, should you want to pay the lady a visit, you might ask to shake her right hand. She's missing two fingers on her left."

"My sister lost a finger to frostbite," I said, without thinking.

"And four toes. That was on her right foot. She lost another toe on her left."

"Gracious," said Isaac. "How did this happen?"

"She wandered off in a blizzard. The horse she was riding had to be put down."

"*Where* did this happen?" asked Jed.

"Oklahoma."

"I wasn't aware you could get frostbit that far south."

"It gets quite cold in southwestern Oklahoma. But if you are suggesting that my story is made up," I said, "you can go to a town in the western part of Texas I have forgotten the name of and look up my sister. If it is fair out, she will be going without shoes, because she has always hated wearing shoes, but if she is wearing shoes, you can look to her left hand to see she's missing her ring finger. While you are there, you should also observe the tip of her nose."

"I believe you, ma'am," said Jed, at which point I realized that I might have sounded a bit defensive. I felt bad, because I liked Jed. Isaac was particular about his help. He preferred God-fearing men, but churchgoing cowboys were hard to find. He had a pronounced bias against Indians because, he said, once they take a single draft of alcohol they are ruined for life. I had a hard time believing such a thing being true of an entire race of people, but then the only Irish hand he'd kept around more than a couple of weeks was Jed, whose parents both died young from drink and the general misery and public embarrassment that accompanies it, leaving him to never touch a drop. According to Isaac, all the other Irish hands had lasted less than a month before they showed their true sodden colors.

I was expected to feed the hands except on the weekends, when they ate in their bunkhouse. If at first I longed for female company and tired of talk of cattle and fencing and weather, in time I got used to the men and thought of them as I once had my students. I even considered tutoring them at night and brought it up with Isaac, but he said if his men had enough energy to attend school at night, he had not worked them hard enough. From this I surmised that an educated woman appealed to him but that he had little use for educated men.

A couple of days later, Isaac said, "Does she get along all right without her toes, your sister?"

"Last I heard."

"When was it you heard last from her?"

"Such questions," I said.

"Do you not think it wise to let your family know where you are?"

"I told you the story," I said, referring to my sister marrying my former fiancé.

"You did. But I don't see how your parents are to blame for the actions of your sister and this schoolteacher scoundrel."

"You think I should invite them out for a visit?"

"Lorena," he said. He so rarely spoke my name that I stopped what I was doing—chopping onions, I believe, for I was near to tears—and turned to him.

"I lost both my parents the same year. Within weeks of each other. Don't a day go by—"

"Doesn't," I said. "Or you could say, conversely, 'Not a day goes by.'"

"Don't a day go by," he said, "that I don't miss them."

"Mine were of a different ilk, Isaac."

"Blood kin still."

He was a good man and sometimes I resented the goodness in him.

It took us several years to have children. I will say that it was not for lack of trying, and I will add that in my opinion it is only loose girls who get pregnant on their first trip to town. At some point, Isaac thought the Lord was punishing us. But for what? Isaac did nothing wrong but deprive me of a horse (for a time) and forbid me to teach his ranch hands. In the scheme of sins and faults, that was not enough for even Isaac's vengeful God to deprive us of offspring.

My first child, a boy, was born the sixth winter after my marriage, in 1926. We called him Isaac Newton Nelson Jr.

The term *confinement*, used in the context of pregnancy, was certainly applicable to that first pregnancy. It began to snow in mid-October. By late February, when Isaac Junior was born—assisted by a neighbor lady, Mrs. Pedersen, an inexhaustible if dour woman witness to dozens of births (she claimed to have brought Isaac Senior into the world, though Isaac claims he doesn't remember seeing her in the room)—I had not been out of the house since Christmas.

Mrs. Pedersen was of the bed-rest school. I suppose it made sense. Women often died in childbirth. I was to lose two children before my daughter, Elena May, was born three years later, when I was nearly thirty. And even though neither child did I carry to term, I mourned them as if I'd held, nursed, and loved them for years. I gave them names, which I never shared with Isaac. I did not share everything with Isaac, especially my fears, for I did not care to be told—again—to put my trust in the Lord. I had come to put trust in him with a consistency that surprised me, but my faith, steadfast as it was, did not prevent me from *feeling.*

It is comforting, for some, to put all one's trust in a higher order. I do not care to relinquish *all* control, especially over my emotional life. Therefore I have cobbled together some system of belief in the way a bird makes her nest from whatever is at hand: the obvious and failsafe materials provided by nature (straw, leaves, grass, twigs) and the happened-upon, the found (twine, a strip of shredded rubber from an inner tube, the tip of one finger of a cast-off glove.) Sometimes, when Isaac speaks to me of how I ought to put my trust in the Lord to see me through this, that, or the other, I picture his nest, so expertly woven from only what God delivers—the fruits of nature—and I judge it the weaker for not making use of what scavenged trash might fortify it. Is it that I came late to the Lord and lack the inner strength and habit to trust only in his straw, his grass, his twigs, or am I only making it *my* faith so that, patchwork though my nest may be, it works *for* me?

But, when Elena came along three years after Isaac, I had less and less time to grapple with such questions. I had heard other women say that only when they became mothers themselves did they understand their own mother. My reaction is, When did you find time to contemplate your mother's character? I was kept busy raising my children and keeping house in a place so remote and inhospitable that the longer I stayed there, the more I wondered if it was ever meant to be settled.

Once I made the mistake of saying as much to Isaac, who told me to think of Canada—an entire country above us, and much of its southern regions populated and cultivated. I bit my tongue to keep from telling him that I did not think I was alone in the world in never thinking, when the temperature dropped below zero and what on the Oklahoma prairie we used to call the coyote winds began to howl, of Canada.

As difficult as the winters were, the dry summers were no respite. There was so little rain that a garden was impossible. I found I could grow only a patch of rhubarb along the side of the house, placed so that it might receive the runoff from the roof should a storm materialize, but mostly I nursed it alive with dirty dishwater, saved in a pail.

So many summer days I spent watching the children play through the kitchen window. They were to stay within my sight, for I worried constantly that they would step on a rattler. Isaac, obviously, had not killed the "alpha male." As soon as the snows melted and the sun turned the yard to dust, I would hear the shotgun blasts, sometimes several times a week. The hands were in the habit of severing the rattlers and giving them to Isaac Junior as toys. I took them away from him and put them in a cookie tin, which he was allowed to shake but not open. The skins they stripped and hung on the fence to dry before tanning them. Then they would take them to a cobbler in town and have him cover their boots with the awful patterns. It was a mystery to me why anyone would want to look down and see the skin of that most vile and fearsome of serpents I scoured the ground in order to avoid.

"Perhaps it is good to be reminded of your deepest fears," Isaac said.

Out the kitchen window, on a summer afternoon when the temperature rises above one hundred, a wind kicks up dust. A cyclone of red sand forms in the field alongside the barn. The children spot it and they give chase. I watch them run circles round the dust devil and resist running after or even calling out to them. Be careful, look where you're stepping, watch out: Who hears such commands after a while? I wonder if I felt compelled to say such things because there was no one saying such to me when I was their age.

I had never feared much until I came to live on Isaac's ranch. The weather could change so rapidly. Days of drought and then down from Montana would come storms so violent the house seemed in danger of washing away into one of Isaac's draws. And of course the cold—I knew what it could do, and I knew how quickly it could do it, as even though I had survived that day, even though I had all my appendages, I could have easily died because of my sister's irresponsibility. Then the lesser but still present threat of snakes, and of bobcats, wolves, and the occasional bear, though Isaac thought animals only dangerous when provoked. He thought the same, however, about the elements. Survival was a given if one kept their wits about them. How one keeps one's wits in a flood or blizzard was too obvious to bear explanation.

Slowly I also came to realize that motherhood (if taken seriously) was terror-inducing. But it did not dampen my fearlessness, for I knew that I would do anything for my children, that no sacrifice was too great when it came to their safety. And though he never said it, Isaac would have died for the children. Neither of us had any inclination toward the dramatic. (Compared to Isaac, I sometimes felt histrionic.) If I expressed worry, dismay, if I chided or nagged or complained, I appeared weak—not too much to Isaac (who would not have said) but to myself. What made me so conscious of my failings? The wind did, and the taut sheet of sky. The grasslands stretched forever, in every direction, and next to such expansiveness, what weight had my feelings?

Around this time I received a telegram from my sister informing me of my father's death. Its arrival was somewhat delayed as it had been sent to Sheridan, the last address at which my sister had known me to reside. It was fortunate for me that it was delivered when Isaac was working his cattle on the far northern border of the ranch. After I read it, I carried it around with me in the pocket of my apron for a week, until one morning when Isaac was out milking I climbed up to the attic, took off the apron, folded it, and stowed it, telegram and all, inside Mother's old steamer trunk, which was filled with things I had no use for.

A few years after the children started school, I had made for them, by a tailor in Gillette, three sizes of sheepskin coats, corresponding to the severity of the weather. The longest was ankle length and so thick it made the children appear obese. Isaac, professed hater of sheep, suggested it. He had worn them himself, as had his brothers, though he was quick to point out that it was the outer layer, made, of course, of cowhide, that kept the wool dry and the child warm.

"So cows yet again win the day," I said.

"Hands down."

We were at table, finishing supper. "Who put their hands down?" asked Elena.

"Your father does not believe in sheep," I said to both children.

"Do you not count them when you can't sleep?" said Isaac Junior.

"He needs no help falling asleep," I said.

Isaac seemed to get my meaning—since Elena had been born, he had been consistently tired of an evening—and he gave me his stern not-in-front-of-the-children glance. But by this point he knew me well enough to know that I would not say anything off-color around the children, and he also knew me well enough to know that still, nearly two decades into our marriage, I desired him. Our marital life would never be as exciting (and busy) as when we were first trying to have children. One day, during the first of those six years before Isaac Junior arrived, Isaac said to me, "So I have been cataloging the sorts of weather that make you loving." ("Loving" is his word for lustful, and though it seems a tepid euphemism, it is fitting, as he really does, and has always, loved me.) "Come a squall down from Canada and you come looking for me. Thunderstorms set you off, and so does extreme heat. And snow? Don't matter if it's an inch or twelve. Springtime brings it out, as does the first cold spell of autumn."

I told him if he was trying to suggest that the elements did not matter, since my level of desire remained steady whatever was going on outside the kitchen window, he was dead wrong: all those things "bring it out," I said, careful to quote his words. There were other things as well, such as all waltzes, and the sound of the front door creaking open, and a horse's neigh, and hot water filling a bathtub. But I did not share these things with him because I knew (though we had never discussed it) that Isaac felt the business of initiating "loving" should fall to the man.

"I never understood the practice of counting sheep to fall asleep," he was saying to the children. "First off, they all look alike. How can you even tell them apart to count them?"

"You could try counting the same one over and over," I said. "I believe the effect would be the same."

"Some sheep are just big old lambs," said Elena.

"Cows, I gather, are each distinctive?" I said.

"Each single one," said Isaac.

"Hands down," I said to the children with an exaggerated roll of the eyes. "And in what ways do they distinguish themselves exactly?"

"They aren't all white, for starters."

"I have seen a muddy sheep once," said Isaac Junior.

"Yet if you gave him a bath he would be white again," his father said to him. "I can tell my cows by their voices."

"Isaac Newton Nelson!" I said. The children, so used to such an exaggerated name-calling directed at them when they told a lie or misbehaved, grew giddy and interested. They sensed that this was no longer sheep versus cows. "You can no more tell which cow is out there mooing than you can read Latin."

"I've never seen any Latin nor heard it spoke," said Isaac, "so it remains to be seen whether or not I can read it."

"I've a volume of Virgil on the shelf. Would you like me to bring it to you?"

Isaac leaned forward suddenly. "E pluribus unum!" he shouted, then sat back in his chair as if he'd won a debate.

Aside from church and the ranch hands, we saw very few people. Only when I took the children to town were Isaac and I apart for more than a workday. He did not like to spend more than a night away from his cows. I knew that he considered educationally vital only what his parents had exposed him to, which was not much more than visits to other ranches and church suppers. He thought—and often said—that before he shipped off to Europe, he'd hardly left the ranch, and he'd turned out all right. I told him I suspected it was his time in Europe that led him to want to marry a schoolteacher, but he insisted he had always liked schoolteachers and I remembered the rumor of his crush on the Irish teacher of his youth.

Still, you never know what aspects of your youth will change you. I have often thought of the many men who have passed through here, working for a while on the ranch, who are in hard flight from what they left behind. They never speak of where they came from or whom they left behind, but there is a brittleness to the one, which I've decided is the result of a shedding. You'd think crawling out of one skin and leaving it to wither would make you vulnerable and tender, but in the case of these drifters—and in my own case—the opposite was true. It toughened us. In no other way was I like these men, many of whom were drunkards and otherwise unsavory, but in this way I was their sister.

In the spring of Isaac Junior's tenth year and Elena's seventh, I took them to stay with Mrs. O'Connelly in Sheridan. We were gone an entire week. Isaac had stopped accompanying us unless he had cattle to sell or supplies to fetch. Too much work to be done around here, he said, no matter what season it was.

We spent most of the first day in the library. It was new but well equipped for a town considered by many to be an outpost. I assigned the children subjects to look up in the *Encyclopaedia Britannica*, the famous (or so the librarian said) eleventh edition, donated by a Mr. Kendrick, a cattleman who had built a thirteen-thousand-square-foot mansion in town after (according to the librarian) making his fortune by marrying his boss's daughter. The librarian, who was uncharacteristically chatty for her profession, also told me that the entire third floor of the mansion was taken up by a grand ballroom, and she had been there for a dance and had her picture taken there, though she confessed she did not have the picture on her person. Mr. Kendrick had also installed a central vacuum system in his mansion, though when I pressed her, she was not sure what duty such a system performed.

I enjoyed chatting with the librarian, starved as I was for the sort of idle gossip that I had once shared with other women, so much that I neglected to check on the children for nearly a half hour. Isaac Junior was to look up Tasmania; Elena May, the history of the hot-air balloon. They were to take notes and make a presentation to me, Mrs. Connelly, and one of her boarders, an elderly man who smiled through his whiskers and stomped his cane on the floor in lieu of applause, after which we had peach ice cream.

I took them downtown to the Golden Rule department store. We bought their father a pair of socks so that the children might see the clerk place the money in a pneumatic tube, which shot up to the green-visored cashier on the mezzanine. We visited the local museum, saw a herd of bison a local eccentric kept in his backyard, and had a ham sandwich at a lunch counter, a luxury I myself did not experience until college. The final night, we attended the circus, to whose appearance in town we had timed our visit. It seemed the entire city turned out to watch the circus train roll up the tracks, the giraffes' bobbing heads visible in the middle distance despite the cloud of coal smoke that hung always over that town.

The next day we returned to the ranch. It might have been easier on all of us if the children had been dejected, as their father might then be able to use their low spirits to argue against future trips. But they were ecstatic, still charged by all they had witnessed. They wanted to tell Isaac everything, but their testimonials lasted only until Isaac Junior announced that he no longer wanted to be a cowboy but had his eye on trolley operator when he grew up.

"I would like to be a waitress at the lunch counter," said Elena May.

I looked at my husband, who said nothing. He did not have to. The matter of their future was decided before we had been blessed with children. Isaac Junior was to take over the ranch. Elena would marry a rancher, if we were lucky to find one with a neighboring spread, so that the holdings might one day be consolidated.

But Isaac's attachment to his ranch was impressive to me, given my father's tendency to move hundreds of miles because of something he read in the paper or overheard in the barbershop. Isaac never raised a hand to either child, though as they grew older, he often accused me of pampering them. Once Isaac Junior turned twelve, Isaac insisted he could drive his sister to school on the sleigh, no matter how cold it was. I had been in the habit of accompanying them, and taking Jed along in particularly bad weather, dropping them off and picking them up. The thing I feared most in life was not having my feet covered in the skin of a rattlesnake, but my children getting lost in a blizzard. Isaac, having grown up in this place, having lived here all his life, paid no attention to weather, and only once, when it was forty-five below, did he agree to keep the children home for the day.

"We'll wait until it warms up to forty," he said at the breakfast table.

"Hardly likely until spring."

"I mean below."

"What is the difference between forty and forty-five below zero?"

"And all this time I thought I had married an educated woman."

"I'm serious, Isaac. What difference does five degrees make?"

"In these parts, the difference between school and no school."

"Jed will take them and I will go along."

"Jed's got to help me shoe a horse, and you have your own work to do."

"Have you looked outside?" I said. Isaac was slowly drinking his coffee with three spoonfuls of sugar. I pulled back the curtain to expose a view of nothing. Snow so thick you could see only thick snow.

Isaac did not bother to look up from his coffee. "The horse knows the way," he said.

"What did you say?" I asked him, not because I wanted to hear it again, but because I wanted to make sure I heard it right the first time.

He said it again.

I put down the dish I'd been washing and climbed the stairs to the attic. In a trunk I found the letters addressed to a horse. They were bound by twine. I untied them and pulled out one and opened and read it. "You and I know that words are wind," the writer wrote to her dead horse. I sat down on another trunk and I kept reading. "Wind can maim . . . Can words?"

I read another. The letter writer had bundled up her baby and pinned the two of them (badly) beneath a blanket so that they might venture out into the snow. But the horse could not find its way out of the stall. The horse did not know the way, but Elise was not interested in actually *going* anywhere. She never has been, really. She was trying to find me. Or, more accurately, she was trying to find us as we were before Gus McQueen got off the train in Lone Wolf.

I had closed the door to the attic. I could hear Isaac calling to me from two floors below. In the trunk, in the pocket of an apron I'd been wearing when it was delivered, I found the telegram I had hidden from him: *Father killed in a mining accident . . .*

The attic door opened. Isaac called up to me. His words climbed the stairs slowly.

"Lorena, are you up there?"

"I'm coming," I said.

But he must have heard it in my voice. I did not come, but he did. I heard his boots on the creaking stairs.

The afternoon Mr. McQueen—who I then called Gus—threw me over for Elise, we were walking across the campus. He did something peculiar. He stopped and fixed his eyes on something, and he appeared frozen in place. He was not looking at anything in particular, it seemed—he was looking at *everything* but without moving his head. I knew he had a ring—I could see the box in his pants pocket—and I thought, what an oddly unromantic way to propose. I asked him what he was looking at (as if it mattered) and he told me he had lied to me and I made him say it, even though I had known all along. But I would have gone to my grave rather than admit it to either of them. Why? Well, I'm certainly not the first person on earth to choose love over family. Everyone does, unless they marry their cousin. And yet I knew they were better suited. But I thought, at the moment, that the only reason she got to have him was because she had gone and lost her toes. She had maimed herself while researching her play. That made her "pure." In that moment, and for many years, I hated her.

"What in the world, Lorena?" said Isaac. He was at the top of the stairs and he was looking at me like I must have looked at Mr. McQueen when he stopped in the middle of campus and stared at nothing on that day so long ago.

Why was I so far from civilization? She was always the tomboy. She lived on the back of that horse. She would have slept in the hayloft had Mother let her. She played in the fields with the Bulgarians and came back so dusty we had to dip her in the stock tank. That ring that bulged in the box in his pocket she likely wears on a string around her neck. I bet she lost it years ago.

And it had been years. So many years had passed.

What did she look like now? Were there runnels in her brow from the brutal heat of that desert she favored? Did she still call herself a cripple and pretend she was joking?

I would not know until I watched her walk down the sidewalk. I wouldn't know anything sitting up in that freezing attic, reading old letters. I would not know until I searched for the string around her neck that held his mother's diamond ring whether or not I could stomach it.

I would not even know what it was I could or could not stomach. There was Mother to think about. So I thought about Mother.

"I am taking the children to see their grandmother," I told Isaac.

"Now?"

"As soon as it warms up to forty."

He stared at me as if I were speaking Latin.

"Below," I said, to clarify.

"What has gotten into you?"

"You're the one who suggested it."

"That was years ago."

Everything was years ago.

"What is that in your hand?" he asked.

"This?" I said, holding up the telegram. I folded it and the letter. I put them both in the pocket of my apron, remembering when Gus McQueen did the same thing, hiding from my eyes a letter sent to him by my sister.

Life presents many situations in which you might manipulate the emotions you feel about your own behavior in order to admonish others.

"Where are the children?" I said, shocked by the harshness in my voice. "Who is looking after them? Why are you up here?"

Isaac looked stunned. It was so cold in the attic. I was wearing my housedress and an apron, and I was freezing. I had not been so cold since the day we found Elise in the snow. The attic had no insulation. I was exposed to the elements. Through the boards I saw white sky. Isaac said something, but I only saw his breath. His words were puffs of wind.

13

ELISE MCQUEEN

Fort Davis, Texas, 1940

"I wonder whatever happened to Damyan," Elise said to Gus. It was early afternoon, a weekday in February, warm out and sunny. They were sitting on the front porch after a sprawling and rapturous hour of stolen midday lovemaking. They'd been at the newspaper office when Elise had told Gus she needed his help at home.

"He was rather bright, I always thought," said Gus.

Elise chose not to repeat Damyan's opinion of Gus—that he was not much.

A wind blew up, carrying the smell of west Texas—dust, creosote, and cattle. Elise loved their cottage by the creek, but sometimes she felt hemmed in by the mountains. Only when she was atop, beneath, or alongside her husband, only in the stolen sprawling and rapturous hours, did she feel the endless prairie. She stretched her legs toward it, like a chute toward the sun.

"Another thing I wonder is what Joe Dudley out of Odessa thinks I needed your help with here at home."

"Why don't you ask him?" said Gus.

"Lorena used to always say that. Every time I would ask her a question she did not want to answer. For instance, once I asked her why you never told us the name of your horse and she said, 'Why don't you ask him?'"

"She is direct, your sister."

"Am I direct?"

"You are more abrupt than direct."

Elise understood that abrupt was worse than direct. Did it not mean rude? Did Gus find her rude and Lorena honest? Oh well, she was certainly capable of rudeness.

"I never told you what I said to Miss Pruett in your parlor."

"Who is Miss Pruett again?"

"The rich woman who felt that learning to play the piano would guarantee her a suitable match. She was at your house the weekend you had gone to Stillwater to propose. I had left you a note. She was not gifted and I lied and told her she was playing beautifully and excused myself to go rifle through your sock drawer. I still want to rifle through your sock drawer. It is an impulse, I suppose, like the tendency toward spirits, which I hear never leaves you. You can only stave it off, not make it go away entirely. Speaking of spirits and returning to the subject of Damyan, I hope his use of spirits has not become habitual. I suspect it has. Anyway, Miss Pruett: I was trying to get her to leave so I could go run my hands through your socks. I must have said something uncomplimentary about Lone Wolf because she asked me if I was leaving and at that moment I realized that I was. With or without you, Gus McQueen. Miss Pruett said, Well I hope you don't take your leave before I master Chopin, or some other composer, I can't remember, and I said that I would prefer to make my exit while I still had a tooth in my head and a decent figure."

Gus laughed. He was messily eating a peach. Across the way, Elise's mother was sitting on the front porch of her casita. She suffered from rheumatism and sadness, but she never complained. She did not like to leave her little house, with its calico curtains, so the children took her most meals and Elise and Gus stopped in several times a day.

"What did she have to say to that?" said Gus. He tossed the peach pit into the yard, because he had told her that another tree would grow from it. He thought this also about the watermelon seeds he spit off the porch, despite zero evidence of peach trees or watermelon vines in the yard.

"She said that it was true what they said about me in Lone Wolf."

"Whatever happened to Miss Pruett, I would like to know. Probably the same thing that happened to Edith Gotswegon."

Edith Gotswegon made her think of Lorena. It had been more than twenty years since they had seen her. She thought of her many times during the day. She read aloud to Lorena from the newspaper as she was laying it out. The children, who were there to assist her but mostly played with cast-off letters from the linotype, dipping them in ink provided by Gus, thought she was reading to them. They ignored her in order to ruin their clothes with ink stains. Elise could say anything and they would think it was some boring quote from News from the Toyahvale Community. So she said, aloud, to Lorena: I wonder why you chose to live some place so cold. A place where blizzards far worse than the one that took my toes and my finger, not even to mention my nose, are as routine as a new moon. Elise wasn't sure what, exactly, was behind this question. An accusation? An insinuation that Lorena could handle, every other Tuesday in the worst of the winter months, the sort of weather that maimed her sister? Elise had always scoffed when people said, I don't even know where to begin. You just choose where to begin. You don't begin in the beginning. Begin with, say, the prairie. Just pick a word and say it out loud and you are somewhere else.

But then there was Lorena, whom she had not seen in over two decades. She had so many questions for her, so many things she wondered about. Elise did not know where to start and it made her feel stupid and old.

"Have we gotten old, Gus?"

At forty-one, Gus did not look old, though he was thicker about the stomach. His sandy-blond hair was thinning at the crown, requiring him to don a ridiculous straw hat on the sunniest days to keep his scalp from crisping. Elise was thirty-seven. Her hips had broadened and her breasts felt different. She shared this fact with her daughter Lorena, who was nineteen then and mortified by her mother talking about how her breasts *felt.*

"I would like to take us on a vacation," said Gus. In answer, Elise supposed, to her query about their being old? She did not mean to imply that they were too old to travel.

"To Lone Wolf? To visit the prairie dogs in their tidy villages?"

"I bet they have a post office by now."

"Where would you really like to go, because I know it is not Lone Wolf."

"To see my aunt Mattie. Before she dies."

"I would love to see the place you come from," said Elise. "I have always wanted to. But should we go, I have two questions. The first is, What about Mother?"

"Juana and Rodrigo could see to her needs while we're gone."

"Juana and Rodrigo have five grandchildren and they also have jobs."

"She could come along?" said Gus.

"I'm not sure she could make the trip. But if we did take her, might we visit Knox College in Illinois? It would mean the world to her to go back there."

"I'd have to look at a map, but it's not in the wrong direction. We could head east and then take the kids to see Washington, D.C."

"I would like to see the oversize seated Lincoln."

"I would like to go to the Library of Congress. If going to Knox College would make your mother happy, it is worth the detour. What is your other question?"

"I now have two."

"Understandable," said Gus. "Questions are like rabbits."

"The first is, Who would run the paper in your absence?"

"Joe Dudley out of Odessa, as you insist on calling him. You will say that he cannot spell and it is true, but I have bought him a new dictionary put out by American Heritage. It feels comprehensive when you lift it. I will fine him a nickel for every misspelling."

"You had best charge a penny for every misplaced apostrophe."

"We could pay for the trip and have enough left over to finally buy a truck. The paper is in dire need of a truck. What is your other question?"

What Elise wanted to ask was, How do you know your aunt is alive still? but she decided that was too abrupt. Instead she said, "How old would she be now?"

"I am not exactly sure. I think seventy-three. If she were alive, my mother would be seventy-five."

"How old is your father?"

"My father is dead."

Elise looked at Gus. He was staring at the ground, as if he

expected the peach pit to have sprouted already and was watching a tree slowly grow.

First he had claimed his father was dead and then he said he was not dead and now he was saying he was dead. She was fine with the story changing, but at this point she felt it ought to be verified.

"You've had word of this?"

"I wrote the editor of the paper in Statesville, where my father was living."

"You wanted to know?"

"Not really," he said.

"You could not have just asked your aunt?"

"Elise," said Gus. Which meant: I know that *you* know that every letter I have ever written to her is at the bottom of my sock drawer. And also: I suspect you are familiar with their contents.

In fact, Gus was in the habit of sealing his letters, which made it impossible to snoop without getting caught. Over the years, the strip of glue weakens; the seal, worn out by time itself, gives way. She read snippets of an early one, written in Lone Wolf. She remembered only his description of the prairie, which was both overly composed and so touching (because Elise felt that the true subject of his tribute was not the prairie but their burgeoning love) that she copied it down and committed it to memory:

> The landscape, so different from our own, is appealing in a stark way. The prairie is the physical evocation of a mood I have never experienced. It brings out in me feelings I did not know possible. Some might call it bleak, but bleak is not the opposite of lush. There is bounty here, of a far different stripe than our verdant foliage, the wild green explosion that is spring in the high piedmont of North Carolina. The prairie grass sings in the evening wind. Free from the impediment

of forest or mountain, light lingers long of an evening, and the suns appears to lower itself beneath the lip of earth itself, instead of behind tree line or hill. Even on the shortest, coldest days of winter, the fact that a gaze in any direction affords an open and expansive vista, of field and grass and sky, gives a body a sense of freedom and, curiously, of movement. It's hard to feel hemmed in here.

"Do they help, the letters you write?"

"Did they help, is the question. I've not written one for some time."

"Did they?"

"Yes," he said. "And no, because they made me miss her and all I want her to know is how grateful I am to her, but I can never seem to find the right words to tell her. It makes me feel bad to even think about it, much less talk about it. So, no. I would not say they have helped."

Elise, thinking of the letters she had written Sandy, knew she would have died had she not written them. She was most grateful to Sandy and of course to Gus, both of whom heard her true cry. Also to her mother. She was grateful to Lorena, so grateful, because the blanket was the sky, and words were wind, and when the blanket was unpinned and they were exposed to the elements, their frozen words fell to the ground, tinkling like broken glass.

"What did the editor of the paper in Statesville say?"

"He sent an obituary."

"Oh."

"I was not included among the list of my father's survivors."

Elise reached out for her husband, but he shifted in his seat and she managed to grab only his elbow. "I'm sorry, Gus."

"For what? I am certain the obituary was written by his second wife. That is the custom there, for the next of kin to write the obituary. It certainly makes it more entertaining, though it allows what should be factual to be colored by revenge or exaggeration. But I am not upset by it, because, in fact, I did not *survive* him. I think of him still and with not a little anger. Had I survived him, I would think of him either not at all or with love."

You are putting a lot of emphasis on the word "survived," Elise thought to say but did not. She liked that he refused to take the word literally but understood that he felt about his father the same way Lorena had always felt about their father: abandoned.

The children ran up from the creek. Leslie had left home and was working as a ranch hand near Marathon. Both Gus and Elise had wanted him to attend college, but he had loved horses ever since Elise had tried to pin them in a blanket and take a ride in the snow, and all he wanted was his own cattle ranch.

Lorena stooped to tie Mattie's shoe. She was a good sister and as serious in some ways as her namesake. She had put off college to help Elise take care of the children, but she had been accepted at Sul Ross State Teacher's College down in Alpine for the next year. Elise realized that when she was Lorena's age, she had met Mr. McQueen already. She had the same number of fingers and toes as the rest of the world. Perhaps she even made very good sense back then, but she doubted it, and besides, that was never her goal in life.

She remembered when her sister was always going on about the point of life. It made her smile.

Henry said to Gus: "Daddy, you promised you'd make us peach ice cream."

Gus said to Henry: "Since you have been gone, I have grown too old and feeble to crank the handle or handle the crank."

Henry and Mattie said together that they would crank the handle and handle the crank. In fact, they would fight for the chance to crank the handle for a half hour, until the ice cream was thick.

Inside, Lorena peeled peaches while Elise made the custard.

"On the way back from the creek, we stopped by to see Grandmother and she thought I was my aunt," Lorena said.

"Well, you do share a name, and you favor some."

"No, it was more than that. She got up and hugged me so hard I think it scared Mattie and maybe Henry too. 'You've come finally,' she said. 'Right on time too. How was the trip?'"

"She said that?"

"Yes. It was odd. And she didn't sound . . ."

"What?" Elise worried that Lorena was going to say "crazy," a term Elise detested.

"Like she was remembering something from a long time ago."

Well, it could not be that, for Lorena had never visited them here.

"I will go and ask her if she wants ice cream. Keep an eye on the stove."

Her mother was still on the porch. She wore a housedress, boots she wore everywhere in Shafter to guard against snakebite, and a light smile.

"You will never guess!" she said to Elise as she drew close enough for her mother, whose eyesight was weakest at dusk, to see who she was.

"What?"

"I had this feeling I would see my oldest child and it got stronger and stronger, this feeling, and then she showed up."

"Really? How is she?"

"You never wrote to her, Elise. She told me. She looks just as she did when she went off to Stillwater with my trunk. She brought her children. Two boys. They are handsome, and of course you know they would be well mannered."

It was what she had so long wanted and so long feared. When she was a girl lying in an attic room, Lorena a cot's length away, she'd feared that her big sister would someday walk past her on the street and not even say "boo." That had come to pass, if staying clear for twenty-odd years were the same as snubbing her on the sidewalk.

"I hope she decides to visit me as well," said Elise. "Do you want to come for peach ice cream?"

"Oh, I'm to bed soon, darling. I have had a lot of excitement for one day, as they say. Though I have never understood how you can have too much excitement and why that is a bad thing, as they imply it might be."

"I believe they are using the word in a different way," said Elise, thinking of Gus having survived, or not survived, his father.

"That's the problem with words," said her mother. "I taught you that. Did I not?"

"You did, Mother," said Elise, even though she felt it was perhaps something she had figured out on her own.

A date was set for their trip. Joe Dudley agreed to the terms of a nickel per misspelled word but balked at the apostrophe, telling Gus that he could not even spell apostrophe, how was he meant to use one correctly? He said he'd just as soon not use one at all. Gus told him that if he could put out an issue of the paper without using an apostrophe he was a grammatical genius. Joe Dudley heard only *genius* which, coming out of Odessa as he did, had never been applied to him. He beamed.

The house filled up with road maps. Maps on the kitchen table, maps on the children's walls, a map on the back of a toilet.

"Do they not all show the same routes?" Elise asked her husband.

"Oddly enough, no," Gus said. "Turns out there are dozens of ways to get from west Texas to North Carolina via Knox College and Washington, D.C. What would I know about such, having come west by train?"

Elise thought of Charlie Carter. She wondered where he was now, if he had found his Beulah girl, or if he had continued to fill the hole she left in his life with drink.

"New roads are being built all the time," Gus was saying with an enthusiasm that both amused and slightly unnerved her. "We will be at least twelve days on the road, maybe longer. Some of these maps will be obsolete tomorrow. I will have to buy new ones."

"Well, we will need to hitch a trailer to the car just to haul them if you don't quit."

"That is another thing we need to discuss."

"Which?"

"Luggage."

Elise said she had lived her entire life without discussing luggage and even her deep love for Gus would not allow her to break her streak.

"Fine," said Gus. "We can talk about clothes."

"What I like to talk about is the weather with people who clearly have no interest in the weather," said Elise.

It was night again. Sandy was off someplace interesting. The west Texas sky stretched above them like the curve of the universe, star-studded, blue-black, brilliant. The coyotes were on about something. The children were either asleep or pretending to sleep. Gus was lying across their bed studying a map that covered the mattress. It was creased, torn, massive.

"Is that a bedspread or a map or both?" said Elise. "Does it have Asia Minor on it, because if it does not, it should."

"I remember once asking you what you wanted to do when you graduated and you told me you were going to go on a grand concert tour of Asia Minor."

"Yes? And?"

"And here we are in Texas."

"Do I understand you to be suggesting that I have not fulfilled my hopes and dreams?"

"No. I am saying that I am happy."

"Saying you are in Texas and saying you are happy are not synonymous," she said. She thought for a moment, and added, "Not for everyone at least. Plus, you are happy because when I was not looking you amassed a library of road maps."

"Come over here," he said, but she didn't. She was combing her hair, which had not been combed in days. Several teeth on her comb were sacrificed to the effort, which Elise found funny. She laughed as she pulled out the broken teeth and examined them carefully, as if they were gems sifted from buckets of creek mud.

Gus got up and went to her. She sat at the vanity, where she never sat. He wondered why she was sitting there until he remembered the map he had spread across the bed.

He put his chin on the crown of her head. He lifted her wild hair and smelled it. He said she smelled of prairie and lavender and told her to stop torturing the comb.

"What about luggage?" she said, on to him and his prairie-and-lavender. She knew she smelled of coyote wind and creek mud.

"Lorena cannot be allowed to bring all the clothes she owns."

"She is not the Queen of Sheba. If she packed up all she owned, it would fit in that satchel you used to bring to school."

"We have six people in a Willys Jeep. I am trying to impress upon you, Elise, the need to think about space."

"Never in my life have I had to worry about space." It was true.

She'd grown up with more than her share of the world, prairie stretching away to the horizon, only the Bulgarians within walking distance. Now she could just see the smoke from Rodrigo and Juana's house across the creek on cold days. Otherwise she saw only the high pasture leading to the bluffs of Sleeping Lion Mountain. Sandy had told her about Mexico City, where people were stacked atop one another. He had been in San Francisco just after the earthquake, seen the tall buildings toppled, even helped pull bodies from piles of bricks.

"We could take the train," she said. "I've always wanted to."

"To Illinois, then to Washington D.C., then to North Carolina?"

"It doesn't stop at all those places?"

"We will drive the Willys. Just tell the kids to pack lightly. If they get their clothes dirty we can stop in Fort Worth where a fellow has opened a washeteria. I read all about it in the *Dallas Times Herald*. We can pop in and wash a load of clothes."

"You mean along with the general public?"

"Why not?"

"I don't want to see the underwear of others."

Gus laughed. "I am going to fold up my map now and you are going to leave your hair just as it is and come to bed, where there will be no more talk of the underwear of others."

Two days later, Elise was down at the office, proofreading the paper. It would be the last edition before their departure, and Elise did not trust Joe Dudley, even if he was being paid extra not to misspell a word. She wanted to make sure this week's paper was without blemish.

The front door of the office opened into a room with several desks, but the real work of the paper took place in the back room, where the entire staff was gathered. The bell above the front door rang. Gus, who was laying out an advertisement for Miller's Feed and Seed, said to Elise, "Go up and see who that is, please. If it's Mrs. García saying she did not get last week's paper, give her another, even though she's been in twice this week already and I know she uses it to light fires and line her birdcage. I also know she's getting her paper because she's complained so many times I deliver it myself, and I put it between the screen and the front door, and she watches me do it from her kitchen window, but what I am going to do, call the woman a liar?"

"So you want *me* to call her a liar?"

"Yes, please."

"Done," said Elise.

Elise went to the front room, fully prepared to make Mrs. García feel as if she had been grievously wronged by the *Fort Davis Sentinel*.

A woman stood by the door, along with two children. The children were handsome and sleepy. A girl hung off the woman's left hip. A boy, sporting more hair than was called for and big ears, which perhaps the hair was meant to hide, held his mother's right hand. The woman wore gloves and a wool coat. None of them appeared attuned to the elements. Clearly they were oblivious to the sky and the wind of its desires.

The woman was in the process of pulling off her gloves. Slowly she performed the task, tugging with her right hand the pointer finger of her left. And then a repeat with the right. She had all her fingers. No accident had befallen her in Wyoming since Elise had laid eyes on her.

Elise said her sister's name and her sister said yes. Then her sister said Elise's name and they fell together, a giggly bag of bones pinned immediately beneath a blanket of sky. Their bodies were thicker, but their bones were in the same place. No words but tears, which were words not yet frozen, watery half words. The tears mixed as their cheeks touched, and Elise remembered smiling into her sister's shoulder during long cold nights in their attic room and she remembered the smile entering her sister, causing her to laugh in her sleep.

Sandy was hitched outside and ready. Everybody's Sunshine Crocodile at their service.

Elise was too confused to remember all the times she had imagined this very scene. She was too ecstatic to dwell on the far more frequent times she had imagined Lorena walking right past her on the street, which was what she had done every day for the past however many odd years it had been. For years, Lorena had walked past Elise in whatever hallway of whatever house she inhabited, or in the front yard, on the sidewalk, Lorena's chin high and her eyes focused on the horizon.

"As it turns out, I have not yet had a big idea," said Elise, and her sister said, "As it turns out, guess what?"

This led them both to laugh. It was the laughter of those who knew their limitations.

The sleepy children, perked up by laughter, smiled.

Behind them, the door swung open. Elise heard her husband's breathing and she felt her sister's body tighten (for they were entwined still) and then slacken slightly.

Elise said, "Lorena has come calling," as if Lorena had strolled over from a block away.

Gus said Lorena's name and Lorena said Gus's.

To Elise, it sounded cordial enough. They did not get to embrace, not yet, because Elise would not let go of Lorena.

"Hello," said Gus to the boy with big ears and more than necessary hair. "My name is Gus."

"*Uncle* Gus," said Lorena, still precise.

"Either one will do. I am pleased to meet you." He shook the boy's hand. A smile was blooming on the boy's face. He seemed to

Elise the son of a very serious man. It showed in the slow, cautious spread of his smile.

"My name is Elena May Nelson," said the girl, who took after Lorena, obviously. Exhausted by whatever long trip they had come to the end of, the girl was alert enough to assess everything and everyone. Like her mother, she was present, while the serious boy was just *along*.

Elise said to Lorena, "I guess I ought to let go of you."

Lorena said, "At some point."

Elise said, "At some point you might want to eat."

Lorena said, "Or powder my nose."

Elise said, "Powder mine while you're at it, what's left of it," and Lorena said, "Elise," reminding Elise that Lorena had always hated it when Lorena mentioned her injuries.

Then she let go. Gus stepped forward as if to embrace her, but Lorena did not move.

"Well, how old is everybody?" said Elise.

"You first," Gus said to Elise.

"I am nineteen and three-quarters."

"That's impossible," said the boy. "Mother says you have a son who is about as old as that."

"Okay, fine. I am in my fourth decade on earth, which means I am not in my forties but my thirties. It's needlessly complicated."

"She never paid attention during math," Lorena said, looking at Gus.

"Goodness, y'all take off your coats," said Elise. "You look to have come from Antarctica."

"We live in Recluse, Wyoming," the boy said.

"What a striking name for a town," said Elise. "It reminds me slightly of Lone Wolf."

"We have over six thousand acres," said the boy.

"Sheep or cattle?" asked Gus.

"Cattle!" the children cried in indignant unison.

Gus said to Lorena, "I have heard it said that there is no love lost between the sheep men and the cattlemen."

"You have your facts straight," said Lorena.

"For once," said Elise, and Gus laughed and put his arm around Elise's waist.

Something in Lorena shifted.

"We've come to see Mother, of course."

"Of course," said Gus, taking his arm off her.

"I want to see her, naturally, but I also feel it important for Isaac Junior and Elena to meet their grandmother."

"You have some cousins to meet as well," said Elise, but Lorena was pulling her gloves on and did not seem to have heard her.

"Have we far to travel?"

"Not by Texas standards. A couple of miles," said Gus.

"We live forty miles from town," the boy said.

"Do you have a creek?" said Elise, but Gus interrupted to say he would run everyone out to the house, that he just had to let his coworkers know.

They waited for Gus. Lorena studied the framed awards from the Texas Press Association, which hung on the wall.

"You decided on journalism over concert pianist?"

"Gus is the editor. I only work part-time. Mostly I help with the proofreading. His partner is out of Odessa and can't spell 'dog.'"

"He must be dumb," said Elena, and Lorena said her full name, Elena May Nelson, in a tone that was to let her know she'd said something rude.

Elise knew she was making it worse when she leaned over and whispered, "He *is* dumb," to the girl, but when she rose and saw the look on Lorena's face, she realized that everything was not simply the way it was before Gus, then called Mr. McQueen, showed up in their lives, unpinning the blanket, saying violently beautiful things. Was it Gus's fault? She'd never thought so, but Lorena looked at her in a way that suggested it might be.

On the ride out to the house, Lorena spoke of her husband, Isaac Newton Nelson. "He is a good man" was the first thing she said about him, and Elise thought to say (but didn't, no she did not), You might as well have led with "He provides for me, even dotes on me, but is deaf to my true cry."

As for Isaac Newton Nelson, it seemed *his* true cry was Jesus Christ our Lord and Savior. Elise was not shocked by Lorena marrying a pious rancher and it worried her how *not* surprised she was.

"How did you meet?" said Gus. Elise wanted to say, Gus! as in, Gus, just don't. It was an inappropriate question for him of all people to be asking, since he had met both the woman he had boarded a train *prepared* to propose to and the woman he had *actually* proposed to in his classroom. (There was also the fact that the women were sisters.)

"He came to my classroom in Sheridan," said Lorena, after a pause long enough to let Gus know it was none of his business.

What did she mean, he "came" to her classroom? Why did the rancher go to the classroom? It sounded like a joke.

The seriousness of his namesake son suggested a man too occupied to roll around in a pasture with his children.

"He is a veteran of the Great War," said Lorena.

"I bet he has seen a lot," said Elise, thinking that this might have been what they call a foxhole conversion.

When Lorena did not answer, Elise said, "Do y'all have a lot of horses?"

Elena May said that she owned a pony, but Isaac Newton claimed it was half his.

"Which half?" Elise turned to ask the child. He eyed her blankly.

"What does she mean?" he whispered loudly to his mother.

"Don't whisper," said Lorena.

Elise meant, Don't whisper. She meant, Do you lead or are you the passenger? What she meant was, Would you give your life, lie down in front of a train, for your little shared pony?

"My father's horse is named Newt," said the boy.

"Is he wee in stature?"

Improbably, unexpectedly, Lorena laughed. Seemingly it was against her will, as it was like a burst of thunder on a day cloudless and bright.

"He is sixteen hands," said Elena May.

"Goodness," said Elise. "I would need a stepladder."

"I would need a footstool myself, and I am five feet eleven and three-quarters inches tall," said Gus.

"You put your foot in the stirrup and use the pommel to pull yourself up," said Isaac Junior. He was taking the subject seriously.

"How is Mother?" asked Lorena. It took her long enough. Elise had never minded taking care of their mother because she understood her. They were in tune. Her mother's sadness sometimes made her sad, as you could catch sadness, especially from schoolteachers—Elise had caught it more than once from Mr. McQueen—but you had to be prone to it. It was a bit like her sock drawer habit. She knew it would not go away, but she wasn't always off running her hands through balls of socks. She would stop herself. There were ways to stave off sadness, though at the moment Elise was hard-pressed to remember them.

"It is hard for her to see much at night."

"What is there to see at night?" said Lorena. "Do you mean she cannot see well in the dark? That seems trifling."

"Easy for you to say," said Elise. She did not expect her sister's help taking care of their mother, but just because nothing was expected of her did not mean she could be rude.

Gus, who was shifting gears, let go the shifter to cuff Elise on the kneecap. She could see why Gus would be disposed toward peace in the current situation.

"Actually, it was *very* easy for me to say," said Lorena. "It is easy to say things when they are obvious."

"It is not easy to say anything, really, if you think about it."

"Really, Elise?" said Lorena.

"Yes. Or I mean, No. No, it is not easy to say things. See? I just perfectly illustrated my point."

"You made yourself clear to me," said Lorena, "after a fashion."

"But whether or not you understand me is beside the point."

"It *is* the point."

"No," said Elise. "The point is, Do the words line up with what you are trying to say and the answer is almost always no."

"What does she mean, Mother?" said the boy child, and Lorena said, "She means, Don't whisper. I think. I'm not sure, darling."

"To answer your question," said Gus, "your mother suffers pretty severely from rheumatism."

"Of which joints?" said Lorena, as if she were Florence Nightingale about to offer an expert diagnosis.

"Fingers and knees?" Gus said, tentatively, posing his question in Elise's general direction.

"She keeps her curtains closed," said Elise.

"A local remedy?" asked Lorena.

"They are calico."

"Ah. Calico is the best choice for those who suffer from rheumatism," said Lorena to her confused offspring.

"We have four children," Elise said loudly. "Leslie, our oldest, works on a ranch a couple of hours south of here." She turned to face the backseat and said, "Boys and girls, Leslie is a cowboy!" Then she turned around and continued. "Lorena, my only daughter, is an excellent cook and everything I say embarrasses her. There is Henry next. He is fond of ice cream and dragonflies, and he has found over three dozen arrowheads on Sleeping Lion Mountain."

"What is an arrowhead?" said Elena May.

Elise found it odd that a child from Wyoming did not know what an arrowhead was, but maybe it was against their religion?

"It is a rock of a certain shape that people like to claim is an Indian artifact," said Lorena.

"Finally there is Mattie. He is our youngest. He has a wonderful singing voice and I expect he will be the musician in the family, but he is shy. Still, he will be thrilled to meet you children, as will they all, except for poor Leslie, whom I would so like you to meet. Maybe he can get away for a visit. He has a beautiful if stubborn stallion named Psalms."

"Mattie," said Lorena. "Is that not also the name of the aunt who raised you, Mr. McQueen?"

Earlier she had called him Gus. Now he was Mr. McQueen and they lacked a half mile to home.

"Yes," said Gus.

"You named your son after your aunt?"

"His proper name is Matthew," said Elise. "Mattie is his nickname." And Edith Gotswegon is yours, she thought but did not say.

"What do you hear from Edith Gotswegon, anyway?" Elise asked Lorena.

"And what is your aunt's proper name?" said Lorena to Gus, ignoring Elise.

Gus looked agitated. "You know what?" he said. "I have no idea. I never asked her."

"Might it be Madeline, and you were to call her Maddy, but you got it wrong?"

"Could be," said Gus.

Satisfied, Lorena turned to Elise. "What do you hear from your horse?" she said.

But they had arrived. Elise looked with pride at her house, set back among the cottonwood grove. Even though earlier in the week there had been snow in the Davis Mountains and the creek was gurgling loudly from runoff, it was nearly seventy degrees out, in late February. There were even tufts of grass growing in the sandy yard. The windows were open and curtains fluttered in and out of them, waving at them to come right on in, we have been expecting you.

Elise pointed to the casita at the back of the property. "Mother lives there," she said.

"By herself, at her age?"

"She gets along fine."

"I guess we are about to find out," she said. "Come, children. We're about to meet your grandmother."

When they were out of earshot, Elise said to Gus, who stood beside her in the drive, "Don't whisper."

Gus leaned over and kissed her forehead. He was forever kissing her forehead. Her mother used to kiss Sandy on the muzzle. She called him sweet and confirmed that he knew the way.

"Well, there for a little while at least she called you Gus."

"It doesn't matter," said Gus.

Oh but it did. To Elise it did, suddenly and shockingly.

"We should unload their bags," Gus said.

"A telegram would have been nice," said Elise.

"Think how happy your mother is right now."

"Yesterday, or maybe it wasn't yesterday, but recently, Mother thought our Lorena was *that* Lorena." She felt a little guilty about the "that," did Elise.

"So maybe there was some notice after all?"

"She could not have gotten word to Mother without our knowing it. Mother never leaves the house."

"Well," said Gus.

"She was mean about Mattie and your aunt."

"Well."

"But Gus! Never ever ask a woman where she met her husband."

"Why not?"

"Think about it."

"Okay," said Gus. "I will."

"Never mind. I have a joke."

"You don't know any jokes."

"I know one. Why did the rancher go to the classroom?"

"I don't know. Why?"

"I don't know why either."

"You need a punch line for it to qualify as a joke," Gus said.

"But I don't like that part. I only like the question part."

"In other words, you don't care why the chicken crossed the road."

"I just assume it had good reason, and I have never understood why it is anyone's business other than the chicken's. The answer to the question should be 'none of your business.' But on the subject of crossing the road, what about our trip?" said Elise.

"Postponed."

"Really, Gus?" She had not thought of it until that moment. She had never been on a real trip and she was in her fourth decade.

"Well, we are to leave in two days. Surely she did not come all the way from Montana to stay two days. I imagine it took longer than two days for them to get down here."

"Not Montana, Wyoming. Recluse, Wyoming. It sounds made up."

Gus said, "I believe it is a real place, because based on what I have seen of that boy, he does not make things up."

"She hates me still."

"She laughed at some of the things you said."

"She is unused to humor. So unused to it that she laughs at things that come out of my mouth that are not funny."

Elise's thoughts twirled round in her head. All these years, she'd never stopped thinking about her sister. The first time Elise heard an oscillating fan, she thought she was hearing herself thinking about Lorena. Close in and loud and faint and far away came the noise of the untrained fan, and that was the noise of Elise thinking of her sister in the now and her sister in the past.

"The children will be so upset."

"Yes, well. They have their cousins to get to know."

"I am not going to say a word. I am not even going to whisper."

"Don't." Gus began to unload the bags. He handed one to Elise and she started for the house but stopped after a few steps.

"And Mother! I told her we were going to see Knox College and she got excited about packing up her trunk."

"We hardly have room for it," said Gus.

"It could hold all your maps."

"The maps!" said Gus. "We must hurry and hide them lest your sister know we were about to go away on vacation."

"I don't care to hide things from her *now*," said Elise.

"I don't want to make her feel uncomfortable."

"We are twenty-odd years too late for that."

They put Lorena's bags in their room. They put all the children in the room they'd added upstairs. They would sleep on the floor by the fire. Their children were due home from school any minute. Gus had gathered up all his maps and stowed them away somewhere, and Lorena, *her* Lorena, would know as soon as she walked in the house that they were not going on their trip. She would sulk in the manner of her namesake, whom in this way she favored.

When would they ever have time to go on a trip? Why had Lorena decided to come back here now?

Time was an element that fell like snow from the sky. The sky was stitched together with safety pins, but sometimes the pins worked loose and out came the elements and one of them was time. Mrs. García waited on Wednesdays for her paper, and the editor himself delivered it, his boot steps on her porch setting off the barks of her two Chihuahuas, but the next day she wanted another paper. She would not recognize that it came only once a week. People could not hear time. They could not hear wind and they could not recognize the true cries of others. They talked over it and heard only some great strange gargle. In the distance, like a coyote wind, it murmured, this muted lament of love and of time. Love and time fell from the sky like snow, or floated across it, like clouds, and people washed their socks or nibbled corn on the cob, their chins shiny with butter.

Elise said, not to Gus but to Sandy, "We almost died out there."

Twenty-odd years had passed and Elise still felt the same way she had when she had waited in Gus's house for him to come home from school. She wanted to sit on his porch with him and listen to Lone Wolf. She wanted to hear what he heard (a refrigerator door sucking shut in the night, the hollow clank of naked coat hangers in an empty closet) and to be, only to be, with him. But he wasn't there and she was alone. Now, all these years later, she felt alone.

The children had burst through the door, shedding their books and coats and descending on the refrigerator, its door sucking shut.

"We should go tell them we're going to have to postpone our trip," Elise said to Gus, but Gus was in the kitchen already with the children. She was alone, but why?

Sandy was noticeably absent. She called to him, but nothing.

Lorena was here and she spoke to Elise instead of passing right by her on the sidewalk, but nothing was easy to say, not even hello, see you later, or how old is everybody now?

Elise looked out the window. Here came her sister and her nephew and her niece and her mother across the yard. She looked at her sister and wondered if, should it snow, their mother might pin over them the old Kiowa blanket and slap Sandy on the croup. Off they would go into the world, whispering things with and without words, protected from the cold by the heat of their bodies and the blanket of sky.

She wondered if, had Lorena not forsaken her that day, what it would feel like to go through life with all her toes and fingers and 100 percent of her nose. She was never cold when it was Lorena leading the horse, but then it was Sandy they were riding, not The Beatitudes. Sandy knew the way.

Not a word from Sandy. Elise had never felt so alone, and downstairs, the house had filled with bodies. And in the distance, sweeping across the prairie, the muted lament.

She found them all in the kitchen.

"Mother was telling me about your upcoming trip," said Lorena.

"Have you met your namesake, Lorena?"

"I have met everyone," her sister said.

Elise said to *her* Lorena, "Why don't you take the boys and your cousins and go to the bluffs to search for arrowheads?"

Her Lorena gave her a look only slightly less annoyed than when asked to take her brothers somewhere, because she too liked to be alone with mother-of-pearl implements of beauty and also movie magazines after school. Who could blame her, at her age?

But there were too many people. It was like Mexico City where the drunken men hang off the trolley cars at dusk.

Then it was Gus, Lorena, and her mother at the kitchen table. Elise made iced tea. She opened the refrigerator more than necessary so that she might listen to its sucking shut.

Lorena said, "The telegram I received after Father's death said he died in a mining accident."

Elise said, "We worried that it never reached you," leaving out the reason why, which was obvious, but not easy to say: You never responded.

"Mother told me it wasn't a mining accident after all."

"Did I?" said their mother.

Elise was pouring tea. Gus looked as if he wanted to go back to the office.

Elise said, "Do you need to go back to work, Gus?" and Lorena said, "I think it would nice if he stayed for a bit."

Gus smiled his assent to Lorena, but to Elise his smile said, I believe I might need to stay? His eyebrows were question marks.

"It has been a good while since he died, Lorena," said Elise. "Going on five years."

"Not so long that you've forgotten *how* he died."

"What does it matter to you?" Elise said. "You hated him."

Her mother said Elise's name in that way she used to say Lorena's name when Lorena called their father Harold.

"He was not around enough for me to hate," said Lorena.

Elise looked at her mother. It was easy to think that her mother had trailed off to Knox College and mostly stayed there, but in fact she had long since returned to the party, though it was often her preference to leave early.

Her mother said, "This is what he wanted you to think and at the time I saw no reason not to honor his wishes. In the long run, I did not see that it would make a lot of difference to either of you."

"But why, Mother? For years he dragged you around to the most godforsaken places with his ideas of striking it rich and he did not hit a lick at a snake."

"Hit a lick at a snake" was a phrase her mother used to describe those days, which was often, when she berated herself for not having gotten enough done. At the mention of it she smiled, though she understood that it was *she* who was being criticized. Elise saw that in her smile.

"Well, how *did* he die?"

"The causes were natural," said her mother. Elise could tell Lorena was upsetting her and she knew without ever having discussed it with her mother what had happened, how she had let him linger and finally fetched Pilar the healer to plaster him with useless poultices.

"So you have left your husband?" Elise said to Lorena. It was of no interest to her if Lorena had left the pious rancher, but really she just wanted Lorena to leave their mother alone.

"I have not."

Then Lorena said a curious thing.

"His ranch has been in his family for four generations."

"I bet it is lovely country," said Gus.

"It is vast. It has given me perspective. It has changed me and for the better."

"Your point being that your husband, having inherited six-thousand-some-odd acres from his ancestors, did not drag you all over kingdom come and he has no problem hitting a lick at a snake," said Elise. She resented being forced to supply a translation, but a voice from the past kept repeating, over and again, Why don't you ask her?

Lorena tipped her nose slightly toward the ceiling, which was neither sky nor blanket of sky. It was not even an element and it was certainly nothing to get uppity over.

"My point is that this family has always been given to lies and I have traveled all this way to find it continues. I find this troubling at best and corrosive at worst," she said.

Elise held up her spoon, examining it in the late afternoon light that turned a square of kitchen floor into gold. She said to the spoon, "What is corroded around here I would love to know."

"The values by which one lives?" said Lorena.

"Have you turned to God?" Elise's mother asked her sister, which made Elise laugh.

"I'm not ashamed of it," Lorena said to Elise.

"Nor should you be," said their mother. "I played organ for services at Knox College chapel. I ought to have taken you two to church more often. But I let myself go. My boys died and you girls suffered because of my weakness."

"Prairie fever," said Elise, to cut her mother off. What was the point of making her pay now? Daily Elise saw the curtains of her casita drawn, an attempt to keep the sadness at bay.

"In a letter I received that was addressed to a horse, the writer of the letter admitted that she knew the *real* meaning of prairie fever," said Lorena. "She said also and I quote, 'I just don't believe some things have to be real and that makes them not real.'"

"You received a letter addressed to a horse?" said Elise's mother.

"I once received a letter addressed to Edith Gotswegon," said Elise.

Her mother turned to her. Clearly the excitement was beginning to affect her. She said, "Not the beige one, but the one who joined the nuns?"

"The one who joined the nuns is more orange, and no, not her, the older one, who is prim and has hair like tree bark."

"Well, how is she getting along?" asked Elise's mother.

"It was not *from* her, Mother, it was written *to* her."

Elise's mother said it sounded to her like the post office was in worse shape than she'd heard. She said something about the Pony Express, but no one paid attention except Gus, who was even more passionate about the Pony Express than the Natchez Trace, though he knew better than to change the subject.

"Back to my point," said Lorena. "Certain things cannot be made to be not real by pretending they aren't real."

"Your sister makes a good point," said their mother, rejoining the party.

"Does she?" said Gus.

Until then, he was thought to have trailed off. Elise thought he was down by the river or off somewhere else contemplating the Pony Express. No one realized he was there. But he started talking.

"My mother died when I was very young. I remember nothing about her. My father never spoke of her. He moved away and left me with my aunt. On the night that I was to leave for Lone Wolf, my aunt sat me down and told me what she remembered about my mother. There wasn't much. She loved me and my little brother, Leslie, who died of measles. She was smart. Also she had a habit of stopping in the middle of a walk, say, on the sidewalk of our small town and staring into a store window. Or across the street. She would stop for a long time and she would stare and then without a word she would continue along to wherever it was that she was going.

"What was she looking at? That is what I wanted my aunt to tell me. But I had no idea how to ask her or if it was okay to ask her. But I never stopped wondering. First I wanted to know, and then I needed to know. Finally I realized I would never know, that I could only *pretend* to know.

"Only by wondering what my mother was looking at, and by looking myself and pretending to see—because I will never know, we'll never know—and only by looking where others directed me to look" (here Gus looked at Lorena and her mother, and then he turned to look long at Elise, saying in his silent way that the two of them had everything to lose and were all the better for it) "did I learn to live through my grief and loneliness."

Then he sat back and was quiet.

"That is a lovely story," said Lorena. "But knowing what your mother was looking at and having to pretend because you will never know is not quite the same thing as making something real by pretending it is not."

Gus nodded at Lorena. "You might be right. But here is one thing I know. I came west to be a teacher only to learn that I knew next to nothing. I knew how to memorize things, but I did not know what anything meant. I was raised by a wonderful woman, my aunt Mattie, but we never talked of the sorts of things we are talking about now. For instance, how one ought to go about living one's life. So everything I know? I learned it from all of you. And I am grateful."

Elise was pretending to have the sniffles, even though she did not care to pretend. Why could she not just cry? She would not look at Lorena, not after the way she had dismissed Gus's story—which was more than Elise had ever heard him say about his mother in the twenty years she'd known him—as irrelevant.

"I would have loved to have known your mother, Gus," said Elise's mother, "though I feel that I know her now through you.

I will keep her with me in my house, and I'll pull the curtains tightly to."

She smiled at her daughters and said, "I have had enough excitement for a while. Gus, will you see me across the yard?"

Gus came around and helped her out of her chair, but before she took a step she leaned toward Lorena and kissed her forehead.

"Your father was a flawed man and there is no denying or excusing his laziness. But he did love you. He admired you. He said often, before you left and right up until he took sick and died, 'Lorena has more gumption than anyone I have ever met, man or woman.'"

Lorena said, "I will be over in a while to visit, Mother," and her mother leaned over and kissed her again and said, "Do."

A cloud came along and blocked out the sun. The sky sealed shut, the blanket tightly pinned.

In the dark kitchen, Lorena said, "I don't know what kind of husband he has been to you, or whether or not he has hit a lick at a snake, but he loves you. You two deserve each other."

Usually when people said "You two deserve each other," it was meant to be mean, but Lorena, Elise decided, did not intend it as such. Yet there was a hint of spite in it still. Elise heard it, and she knew there would always be. She could understand why Lorena might find Gus's tribute to his mother's habit of stopping and staring off into the distance not, personally, all that moving. In fact, seeing it from Lorena's point of view, which she was just now able to do, it seemed inconsiderate for Gus to tell that story. Like a lot of things, it was both inconsiderate and honest.

"Thank you,' said Elise. "Also, I'm sorry."

Lorena shrugged, uncharacteristically. She had never been a shrugger.

"He meant what he said about being grateful to you," Elise said.

"I'm sure he did, in his way."

We all have our ways and only our ways is what Elise wanted to say, but instead she said, "Is it best if we never speak of him again? Because that is going to be difficult."

"I don't know what's best."

"You always have."

"No, Elise. I am not who you would have me to be."

Elise thought about the phrase "would have me to be." It was the "have" that bothered her most, likely because it was true. She would *have* people, places, things—non-nouns, her husband liked to call them—be what they were, if only she knew how.

"Who are you, then?" said Elise, unable to ignore the voice that said, Why don't you ask her? "Tell me, so I can know."

Something in Lorena's face shifted, like the way the light falls away from the mountain behind the cottage when the sun goes down. Dusk had come to her and Elise watched it and sang the buried songs to Lorena. Against the icy wind, Sandy struggled, but they were all safe and warm beneath the blanket of sky.

Finally Lorena said, "What a ridiculous question."

What part of it was ridiculous? Who are you? Or the fact that Elise could, after all that happened, after time dropped from the sky, ever *know* her sister again? Maybe the ridiculous part of it all was the notion that knowing, instead of pretending, could change what happened.

All this made Elise's head hurt. She squeezed her eyes shut. The words she sang to Lorena were drowned out by a coyote wind, lost forever in the blowing snow.

"Are you okay?" said Lorena.

Elise opened her eyes. They were sitting in the kitchen of her lovely cabin. The sun had found its favorite square of floorboard. There it basked. Lorena was there. She had come to visit their mother. Certain questions were ridiculous to her. Certain questions are just ridiculous, period.

"I would like to hear more about your husband," said Elise, and this was true, mostly.

"His middle name is Newton."

"Isaac Newton Nelson," said Elise. "Is he very scientific?"

"He is very precise. Sometimes people he has just been introduced to make the mistake of calling him Ike. He is too precise for nicknames, especially when delivered by strangers, so he corrects them by saying 'I was given the name Isaac and for now I choose to keep it that way, but if things change I will let you know.'"

"That makes me like him. I would not like it if someone I did not know called me El."

"Nor would I like it if someone called me Lo."

"Do you have a photograph?"

"In my bag. I can tell you that he is dashing in a chiseled way."

"Has he a prominent jawbone?"

"It appears to have been sculpted by the wind."

"Does the wind blow there?"

"You would not believe it. Also, not a tree in sight."

"You must feel just a little bit at home?"

"I feel like I have no real home. Sometimes I feel like I would like to move with the children to Chicago. Sometimes it seems the logical end point for a simple prairie girl."

"Which you are not. Simple, I mean."

"I wonder if Blaguna is in Chicago," said Lorena. "I have not thought of her in years."

We can ask Sandy, Elise thought but did not say.

"You can stay as long as you like," said Elise.

"It is pleasant here," said Lorena. "I like that it is above zero. Of course I must return to Wyoming with the children. I am no more going to Chicago to look up Blaguna than Edith Gotswegon has married into Oklahoma City society. But we just got here and it is pleasant. The sun makes me want to take off all my clothes and stretch across a boulder by your lovely creek. That sounds like something you would do."

Elise said, "It *is* something I do whenever the weather and my schedule allow for it."

"Maybe you can distract my children while I expose myself to the elements."

"Of course."

"Might I stay while you take your trip?"

"I wish you would come along."

"I don't think we'd all fit in Gus's Jeep," said Lorena.

"Gus wants to see the Library of Congress, but that does not interest me in the least."

"Nor me. I do not see the point in traveling hundreds of miles to see rows of books on shelves. While he is wasting his time there, you and I can take the children to the Smithsonian Institute."

"And to see the oversize seated Lincoln."

"I would like to see the cherry trees," said Lorena.

"I am leery of the trees," said Elise.

"Why?"

"I feel that they might suffocate me."

"It would be a good way to go, though," said Lorena.

"There are far worse," said Elise.

"We have read about them in the *Kiowa County News.*"

"Sherman shot by Ivent."

"Sherman would have cut Ivent with a knife," said Lorena.

"Self-defense," said Elise. "But the both of them were dastardly."

"It's true."

They were quiet. Twenty-odd years of silence hovered in the sun-drenched kitchen, settling in the patch of golden floorboard.

"Texas Woman Suffocated by Violently Beautiful Trees," said Elise.

"On Trip to View Oversize Seated Lincoln."

They might have continued trading headlines of their upcoming trip together had the children not come spilling through the door. The junior Isaac held a rock in his hand.

"The boy has discovered an arrowhead," said Elise.

"Let me see," said Lorena. Her children gathered close to her, watching her as she held it in her hand, weighing it, then pronounced it, after much scrutiny, to be authentic.

ACKNOWLEDGMENTS

Many of the quotes from newspapers in this novel came directly from newspapers of western Oklahoma and west Texas between 1900 and 1920. In some places the details of actual events and incidents referred to have been altered to fit the needs of the story.

My thanks to Joy Harris, Terry Kennedy, Nancy Vacc and family, the University of North Carolina of Greensboro for a research leave during which much of this book was written, the Jentel Arts Foundation for a place to write and run in Wyoming, sweet Adobe Chi for space and quiet and wild west Texas storms. Special thanks to Laura Furman for reading an early draft of this novel and offering sage counsel, and to my editor, Kathy Pories, for once again taking some pages and making them into a book. Extra special thanks to Jude Grant for fixing my arithmetic.

And, hey, Maud Casey? Thank you for everything—then, since, tomorrow.

Prairie Fever

Lone Wolf, Oklahoma
An Essay by Michael Parker

A Conversation with Michael Parker

Questions for Discussion

LONE WOLF, OKLAHOMA

An Essay by Michael Parker

I never knew my maternal grandmother—she died just days after I was born—and because the man she married, a Presbyterian minister whose Calvinist streak and patriarchal ways tended toward overshadow, lived until I was in my mid-teens, I never heard much about her. But the couple of things I did know about her made her seem exotic.

The first: she came from Lone Wolf, Oklahoma. My grandfather the preacher had been born in South Carolina but came to his senses and moved at an early age across the state line to Gastonia, North Carolina. My people on my father's side had been in North Carolina since their arrival in America, as far as anyone can tell—they weren't great record keepers and they had a talent for disappearing. (My great-uncle Charlie stole a train idling on a siding by a sawmill, drove it to the end of the tracks, and was never seen nor heard from again. There is speculation that he was shot dead by a man whose daughter he had gotten in the family way, or that he went to Texas, fates that are always delivered as if they are equal.)

Oklahoma brought to mind, of course, the musical, but once I got over that association—and got the corny song out of my head—I thought of dust storms and sod houses, treeless prairie and wronged

Cherokee. I grew up in Eastern North Carolina on the edge of the Little Coharie swamp. In late spring the piney woods came alarmingly alive with scrub and weed, so lush that shoots and tendrils seemed to creep into the yard while I watched. Land was cleared for tobacco and produce, but beyond the cultivation, the dark mouth of forest loomed. Woods were everywhere and shadowy with secrets and hideouts. An Oklahoma vista seemed lunar.

The second thing my mother told me about her mother was even more evocative. In the harsh winters of the prairie, with nothing but fence posts for thousands of miles to stop the wind, my great-grandmother sent my grandmother and her older sister to school on the back of a horse, pinning heavy blankets around them and slapping the horse, who knew the way to the school. When they got there, the teacher would unpin them, stable the horse, and re-pin them in their cocoon for the trip home, if the weather necessitated it.

I knew a couple of other things about my grandmother—she and her sister had both gone to college, a rarity for women in those days, and they had paid for it by taking turns, one working while the other studied, so that it took them eight years to graduate. My grandmother met my grandfather, who had been sent to Oklahoma after seminary, in church. She played and taught piano. Her sister, my great-aunt, answered an ad for schoolteachers in Wyoming, where she met and married a rancher. She remained in Wyoming for the rest of her life. The one time she came east to visit her sister, who had moved to Lenoir, North Carolina, where my grandfather preached for forty years, she had to leave early because, she said, the trees (those trees! That dense Eastern forest!) gave her claustrophobia.

But it was the horse that stuck with me. I wrote a three-page story about it and published it in a book of similarly short stories, but it was the only story in that collection that I felt needed to be longer. Then a couple of people said to me, "That story about the two girls on the back of the horse needs to be longer." It's easy to ignore such criticism from one reader, but two? That would be critical mass.

I had no clue, however, that I was writing a novel about the relationship between two sisters, even as the anecdote dictated it. I just put the girls back on the horse, and I made it snow. Soon it was a blizzard (both on the page and in the accumulation of pages, for the first draft came quickly; I wrote three hundred pages in five weeks) and both sisters had fallen for the teacher who unpinned them from the horse. The novel began in Oklahoma and ended up (perhaps like my doomed great-uncle) in Texas, stopping off very briefly in North Carolina before a stint in Wyoming.

But it is Lone Wolf, Oklahoma—a place I'd never visited until after I wrote the first draft—that shapes the sensibility of the sisters, and therefore the novel. The shared sensibility of siblings, and the forces that emerge to disrupt it as we age—politics, religion, geography, other people—is something that I've written about before, but not with such focus. The blanket the two girls share becomes a solar system whose stars are ever present above, even though the girls become women and mothers themselves and settle thousands of miles apart. They need only look up to see the same twinkling planets. But looking up—remembering with the vigilance of the childhood imagination a familiarity weakened by time, by choices, by circumstances—is difficult for all of us.

I stopped through Lone Wolf on my way from Texas to Wyoming in the fall of 2017. It was September, high summer still, and dry. In the Panhandle, tractors and combines worked the roadside fields, followed by billowing parachutes of dust. My GPS asked me to take a left not far outside of Lone Wolf. I always do what that crisp voice tells me to, and I ended up on a dirt road in the middle of a cotton field. Town appeared in the distance—a few blocks of low buildings and modest, vinyl-sided houses. I parked my car in front of a diner that had gone out of business with dishes still on the table. Midmorning and crazy hot, there was no one in sight. Finally a car chugged up from the west. I kept window-shopping along the mostly abandoned storefronts, but I heard the car brake. I looked over. A woman about my age was rolling down her window by hand. She was smoking the longest cigarette I've ever seen. When the window was three-quarters open she leaned over and said, "Well, are you here?"

Had I the slightest doubt, still, that this novel should have remained its original three pages, it disappeared in that second.

"My grandmother is from here," I said, after telling her that I was, indeed and blissfully, in Lone Wolf, Oklahoma.

"What's your grandmama's name?"

"She moved away in 1918."

"But what's her name?"

"Hallie Hall."

"Knew her well."

This was beyond impossible. But it made sense in the spirit of the novel I'd written, in which two sisters have a bond so tight—despite an event that leads to their decades-long estrangement—that they believe in things with a fervency that makes those things, if not exactly true, their own inviolable truth.

A CONVERSATION WITH MICHAEL PARKER

author of Prairie Fever, *and editor Kathy Pories—*
about telling a story straight, POV, bodies, and outer space.

KP: *When your agent and I first talked about this novel, Joy described it as a love triangle. And it is, but it is also of course so much more than that, especially because each character's perspective is sympathetic—there really is no character who can't explain why they did what they did, and there is a fair amount of betrayal that goes on here. What is it about a love triangle that led you to want to write about it?*

MP: I'm not sure that there is "no character who can't explain why they did what they did." I agree that the characters are more aware than, well, most human beings (such is the beauty of fiction—you can understand people in ways you never could in real life). But I think Gus is not able to fully articulate why he does what he does when he does it. He acts instinctively and is guided by his emotions and perhaps because he never had an adult in his life who showed any emotional intelligence, or cared to talk to him about his feelings, he's sometimes only dimly aware. (This reminds me of one of my favorite lines from the poet Rodney Jones, who wrote "we live in a dim inkling or a rapt afterness.") I wasn't aware that I was writing about a love triangle until midway through the book. The genesis of the novel was the image of the two girls on horseback, on their way to school in a winter storm, blankets pinned over them—which came from my grandmother, who is actually from Lone Wolf, Oklahoma, and had this very experience with her older sister. At some point, when Gus got to Oklahoma from North Carolina, and began his disastrous stab at teaching, the attraction to both girls just developed. I'm not a planner—I go from scene to scene, line to line, actually—so I went with it, thinking at the time that this would not be a major part of the novel. But I wanted to chart the relationship between the sisters from that blanket until later in life, and I found that Gus, his presence, his role in their lives, was my way in—and out.

Of course, there is the undeniable fact that love triangles—at least to my mind—are almost always interesting. They've been around since classical mythology. I don't think they're going out of style, so long as we live and breathe and do other things with our bodies.

KP: *Over the course of your career, you've often adopted the POV of the female perspective, actually even in your first novel,* Hello Down There. *And then in* Towns without Rivers, If You Want Me to Stay, *and* The Watery Part of the World. *I'm probably forgetting some here, even. And now in* Prairie Fever, *along with Gus's, we also hear the story from each sister's point of view. I know that you grew up in a pretty large family, with both sisters and brothers. Do you gravitate toward one perspective more than the other?*

MP: I'd say point of view in my work is split pretty evenly between genders. I have three books of stories and they tend to be told more from a male perspective (though the story that got the most response of any I've published was written from a female point of view). But I confess I would not do this if I were told I had to stick to writing stories from the point of view of a sixty-year-old retired white college professor. Part of why I write is to be someone other than myself. Yes, it's an inward pursuit, but it's also a way of getting out of yourself, out of your confined experiences.

Of the novels, the first two alternate between a brother and a sister's point of view, the third is about two brothers and their father (I don't think the mother gets a point of view), the fourth is about three brothers but told from one brother's point of view, the fifth is split between two sisters and a man, and the sixth novel is split, almost evenly if I remember correctly, between a man and a woman. And this one is also two sisters and a man. I'm not real good at math, but I'd say I'm squarely bisexual in this regard.

KP: *So much of this novel is about the ways in which we perceive what really happened, and the accounts we are given. There are newspaper articles about a shooting that Elise feels compelled to investigate, there are the stories about what really happened to Elise when she disappears during a blizzard, and much later, there are Elise's explanations about what transpired between her and Gus, and why she never told her sister. What is your obsession with alternative accounts about? Rather than, say, telling a story "straight," as people sometimes say?*

MP: I happen to be writing this a couple of days after the fiftieth anniversary of the moon landing. I was ten when it happened, and my younger sister was nine. She called me up and said, "Where were we when it happened?" My memory of it was different from hers, so we looped in another sibling, who had a different memory. (I think we were too busy memorizing the words to every song on the Who's *Tommy* to pay much attention. Outer space, as they called it then, was never sexy to me, and still isn't.) It is inevitable that our version of the past be colored by our emotions. I wrote one first-person novel and it was really short, as I felt constrained by sticking to a single point of view. (If you remember—you were the editor—I at first wrote it from a retrospective point of view so I could have some wiggle room, some way to contrast the character's version of events, but you quite rightly said it was more convincing without the intrusive older narrator weighing in.)

Even a first-person story that people would describe as "reliable" (how I hate that this term was ever introduced into the lexicon of craft) contains, to my mind, some other story—the story that the narrator is not telling—which is far more interesting, and which contains the real power of the narrative. So, I'm not sure about this whole "telling it straight" business. Back when we believed that history was what was written down in textbooks, and what we copied down in our notebooks off the chalkboard was the truth, we still understood, I maintain, that perspective accounted for mystery, and mystery is what we're after. So, offering conflicting or slightly different accounts of the same event might seem to be about adding complexity, emotional texture, but it's also about accessing mystery.

KP: *These two sisters, Lorena and Elise, are so bound to each other and really can't imagine life without the other, and yet, they are also in many ways polar opposites: Lorena is logical and procedural and doesn't understand why everyone doesn't do things in the right order; Elise is pretty much allergic to logic and rearranges events and chronology as freely as she plays with words and meaning. I guess you could say she has a kind of feverish imagination. And this is exactly what leads to her near-fatal accident. I'm wondering if you'd talk about sister dynamics (or really sibling dynamics): to what extent are these two interdependent, as they've cultivated a lifetime of letting one be the logical one and the other less bound to any sense of order? And more broadly, do you think we are bound by our initial family roles for the rest of our lives?*

MP: Well, yes: I think we are bound by our initial family roles for the rest of our lives to an extent. But the extent is based on how much we allow ourselves to be bound by those roles. We're free to change, to grow out of who we were and present ourselves in a new context (the family we choose, for instance, rather than the one we're born into), but are we able to shake off those initial roles? I don't think so, and I used to think this was a kind of life sentence, but now that I'm older I see it differently, and more generously.

Lorena and Elise are ultimately able to overcome their different ways of seeing the world by focusing on their shared sensibility. This is what saves us with our families, if we're lucky. We have developed, over time, a unique sense of how the world works, tailored by the personalities of our parents, but also the result of our collective idiosyncratic perspectives. These girls' mother, though pretty unlucky in love and stuck with a man who lacks ambition and the ability to make a living, has a capacity for wonder. So does Lorena. It's far less free-ranging and wild than Elise's sense of wonder, but it's there, and in that last scene, what I wanted to show was that it never goes away, that sensibility. I can go months without talking to my siblings, and five minutes on the phone and we're talking straight-up smack. It's what we do. Both my parents were wry, and they were both good listeners. They both died within the past year and a half, so I'm ever aware these days of how lucky I am to have been raised by these amazing, imperfect, sometimes maddeningly inclusive (my mother invited a woman she met at a rest stop on the way to my wedding TO THE WEDDING—is that inclusive or nutty?) people. It was good for my work, sure, but finally, it was good for me in my dealings with the world. I care more about the latter than the former.

KP: *At one point, Elise tells Gus, "I never feel either completed or depleted. There is always some part of us lost, Gus McQueen. There is always more to lose." And yet, Elise is one of the cheerier characters I've ever met in your novels. Explain (!).*

MP: Can't you be cheery and also aware of life's tenuous nature? She would be insufferable if she were *just* cheery. You would have sent me back to my desk had she not had the capacity to appreciate how much of life is about loss. I remember hearing the Janis Joplin version of "Me and Bobby McGee" and thinking, about that line "freedom's just another word for nothing left to lose," that it sounded good, but it was probably baloney. I was probably nine or ten. I wasn't a particularly advanced thinker, but I was well acquainted with exuberance (brought about by music first and literature later, and by the intensely improvisational nature of adolescence, at least in the 1960s and 70s—there was this sense that you could just make yourself up every day) and melancholy (there was also this sense that you would never be able to be anything other than who you were at the moment). That contradiction—between delight and sadness—is what made me want to write. It wasn't sitting on the porch listening to stories, as people assume to be the truth if you have an accent as swampy as mine. It was stimulation from what little good literature I read, in part, but it was more the very thing you point out about Elise: a sense of life's infinite pleasures and of its mysteries and of its hardships, of loneliness, of feeling forever out of place.

KP: *Aside from Elise, Lorena, and Gus, I also had such a soft spot for Sandy the horse. Have you spent a lot of time around horses?*

MP: It is now time to admit that I am terrified of horses. I was thrown from one at an early age and haven't been on one since. But I admire them. I like to watch them, up close and in movies. I find them mysterious and terrifying. Beautiful and brooding. I aim to get back on one. They have them here in Texas. Not so much in Austin, but I wouldn't have to drive far to find one, I don't think.

KP: *You do so many inventive things with language in this novel, more than any other novel of yours, constantly pressing at the given meaning of words, and then turning words around to show us other ways of looking at them (*well-meaning *vs.* meaning well *is one that comes to mind). Why do you focus on that more intently here than in your other work?*

MP: I think that interest came, like everything else here, *out of* the characters and their desires. Elise is fascinated with words, as is Lorena, who is a stickler for the correct pronoun and may appear less inventive than her sister where syntax is concerned, but I tried to show, in her letter to Elise (via Edith Gotswegon), that she's pretty fluent in the music of her emotions. So we're back to that shared sensibility. I think I'm always interested in investigating language as a tool, but here maybe more so, you're right, and not because I sat down to do so, but because it came out of the characters and their concerns.

KP: *Since you've confessed that you haven't really spent much time with horses, have you ever been in a blizzard? (And I'm hoping, in these days of scorching temps, that they aren't confined to historical novels from here on out.)*

MP: I have survived many blizzards, coming from North Carolina (emphasis on North). At least once a year we got blizzards of up to two inches of snow, though in NC a half inch can shut down schools, interstates, power grids, etc. So many times have I gone to the store pre-blizzard only to find a lone bottle of goat's milk to see me through the storm. During blizzards my fellow Tar Heels can be ruthless at the checkout line, though because our schools close down for two weeks after one of these half-inchers, and the parents have to feed and entertain dozens of half-frozen-from-trying-to-sled-down-an-embankment-with-a-dusting-of-snow children, I can't hardly blame them. The worst part of it was driving. If there were flurries, I just would not get in a car. It was just too treacherous. It's the other guy you have to look out for! Plus, we'd usually spent our sand and salt allotment on Fourth of July fireworks. Not that I was in favor of that, as fireworks to me are about as sexy as outer space. Outer space lasts longer, so I guess it's sexier.

QUESTIONS FOR DISCUSSION

1. The prairie is central in the novel, as is the landscape of Wyoming and of West Texas. How do the descriptive passages of landscape reflect on the emotional aspects of the characters, and in what ways does the landscape heighten the overall tensions of the novel?

2. *Prairie Fever* makes much use of newspapers—both the *Kiowa County News*, which the sisters quote from, and the newspaper that Gus and Elise end up running in Texas. Why is the newspaper so important in the lives of these characters? What does it represent?

3. Michael Parker has said in an interview that he wanted the novel to depict the "shared sensibility" of siblings, in particular the ways that you might fall out of touch with your sibling but remain connected by the forces that shaped your youth. Can you relate this to your own experience with family?

4. The middle section of the novel is composed of letters that the sisters write, although not directly to each other. How do these letters function? Why do you think the author chose to present the material in epistolary form rather than a straight narrative?

5. Sandy the horse becomes an important character in the novel, especially to Elise. After the accident, he continues to live on in Elise's mind, with his own share of adventures. Why is their bond so strong, and what is it about Sandy that keeps him so present to her? Were you moved by Elise's stories about Sandy, and if so, why?

6. Gus is obsessed with an anecdote his aunt told him about his mother. What is it about this anecdote that Gus finds so fascinating and how does it suggest his own actions in the novel?

7. Gus moves West to teach, but the students seem to disagree as to whether he is a good one. How do you feel about him as a teacher? What do you think makes for a good teacher: depth of knowledge, or engagement with one's students?

8. The book ends with the sisters together for the first time in twenty years. Do you think their reunion is a successful one? Does it resolve the issues that led them to stop speaking? What do you think their future relationship might be?

9. These sisters have markedly different worldviews. Did you find yourself privileging one sister's perspective over the other's, and if so, why? Is one more valid than the other?

10. *Prairie Fever* focuses mostly on the relationship between two sisters. Do you think the fact that it's written by a man affects how he portrays the sisters? Were you aware of his gender as you read, or not?

TASHA THOMAS

MICHAEL PARKER is the author of six novels and three collections of stories, and has been awarded the Thomas Wolfe Prize for his distinguished body of work. His short fiction and nonfiction have appeared in the *Washington Post*, the *New York Times Magazine*, the *Oxford American*, *Runner's World*, *Men's Journal*, the *O. Henry Prize Stories*, and *The Pushcart Prize*. He lives in Austin, Texas. Visit him at michaelfparker.com.